JULIA

ALSO BY
HEATHER B. MOORE

The Paper Daughters of Chinatown
The Slow March of Light
In the Shadow of a Queen
Under the Java Moon
Lady Flyer

WITH
ALLISON HONG MERRILL

The Paper Daughters of Chinatown Young Reader's Edition

JULIA

A Novel Inspired by
THE EXTRAORDINARY LIFE
OF JULIA CHILD

HEATHER B. MOORE

SHADOW
MOUNTAIN
PUBLISHING

Image credit: p. 339, Lynn Gilbert, via Wikimedia Commons

© 2025 Heather B. Moore

All rights reserved. No part of this book may be reproduced in any form or by any means without permission in writing from the publisher, Shadow Mountain Publishing®, at permissions@shadowmountain.com. The views expressed herein are the responsibility of the author and do not necessarily represent the position of Shadow Mountain Publishing.

Visit us at shadowmountain.com

This is a work of fiction. Characters and events in this book are products of the author's imagination or are represented fictitiously.

Library of Congress Cataloging-in-Publication Data
Names: Moore, Heather B. author
Title: Julia : a novel inspired by the extraordinary life of Julia Child / Heather B. Moore.
Description: [Salt Lake City] : Shadow Mountain Publishing, 2025. | Includes bibliographical references. | Summary: "Julia leaves behind a privileged life in California to join the OSS during World War II, decoding covert messages and aiding the Allied effort. Amid her far-reaching missions, she meets Paul Child, whose love leads her to postwar Paris. There, Julia Child's daring pursuit of French cuisine transforms her into a culinary trailblazer and icon, forever changing the way America cooks"—Provided by publisher.
Identifiers: LCCN 2025003199 (print) | LCCN 2025003200 (ebook) | ISBN 9781639934256 hardback | ISBN 9781649334633 ebook
Subjects: LCSH: Child, Julia—Fiction | LCGFT: Biographical fiction | Novels
Classification: LCC PS3613.05589 J85 2025 (print) | LCC PS3613.05589 (ebook) | DDC 813/.6—dc23/eng/20250219
LC record available at https://lccn.loc.gov/2025003199
LC ebook record available at https://lccn.loc.gov/2025003200

Printed in Canada
PubLitho

10 9 8 7 6 5 4 3 2 1

Dedicated to my readers—
Thanks for joining me on this journey.

FOREWORD

Many great men and women instilled in me a sense of patriotism in my youth, long before I understood what patriotism meant. I grew up in the Cold War, during a time when secrets and intelligence gathering was critical to our national security, and my desire to serve my country led me into a career with the Central Intelligence Agency.

This desire to serve is something many women have shared throughout the years, particularly during World War II. Within these pages, Heather B. Moore does an incredible job portraying the life of Julia Child, who entered the intelligence world when the Office of Strategic Services (the precursor for the CIA) had yet to discover exactly how much of an impact women could have in a space that men had long dominated.

Educated women of a high social standing were highly sought after in the intelligence world, and as the daughter of a real estate mogul and a Smith College graduate, Julia Child had both the pedigree and the education to be a top candidate for the program. She also had the desire to move beyond the little piece of California where she was raised. And so Julia joined the ranks of the OSS.

While many of the other top female recruits were well-traveled, Julia had never been outside the United States, but as opportunities presented themselves, she forged a path that would take her into parts of the world where few women in her generation would go. And it didn't take long for her to become an invaluable asset within the intelligence world. It also gave her great opportunities to expand her love for food, even though cooking had yet to become her strong suit.

Heather B. Moore paints a beautifully detailed picture of Julia Child, taking us from Julia's early adulthood years living in Pasadena, through her entrance into the OSS, and on to her married life and cooking revolution. Moore guides us through the hidden treasures of Julia's life abroad

FOREWORD

during World War II and the moments that led to Julia's love of cooking and how that love translated into an inspired career.

By anyone's standard, Julia Child lived a fascinating life. She was a pioneer in every sense of the word, moving beyond the secretarial roles most women of her era held and becoming a household name. Her wit, spontaneity, and intelligence are well documented in this delightful journey through her world.

You will be blown away by Heather's deep, heartfelt storytelling. This endearing tale is one only she, one of the most skilled historical fiction writers out there, could tell.

—Traci Hunter Abramson,
CIA retiree and best-selling suspense author

GLOSSARY OF ACRONYMS

AVG: First American Volunteer Group
BHV: Le Bazar de l'Hôtel de Ville
CIA: Central Intelligence Agency
COI: Coordinator of Information
ERES: Emergency Rescue Equipment Section
OSS: Office of Strategic Services
SEAC: South East Asia Command
USIS: United States Information Service
WAC: Women's Army Corps
WAVES: Women Accepted for Volunteer Emergency Service

CHARACTERS

HISTORICAL CHARACTERS

Julia McWilliams
Carolyn (Caro) McWilliams
John McWilliams Jr.
John McWilliams III
Dorothy McWilliams
Paul Child
Charlie Child
Fredricka (Freddie) Child
Rachel Child
Erica Child
Jon Child
William J. Donovan
Betty MacDonald McIntyre
Paul Helliwell
Jane Foster
Cora DuBois
Virginia (Peachy) Durand
Rosamond Frame
Eleanor (Ellie) Thiry
Virginia Pryor

Louise Banville
Mary Nelson Lee
Jeanne Taylor
Max Bugnard
Harrison Chandler
Gay Bradley
Mamie Valentine
Betty Washburn
Katie Nevins
Katy Gates
Simone (Simca) Beck Fischbacher
Louisette Bertholle
Avis DeVoto
Bernard DeVoto
Dorothy de Santillana
Judith Jones
Russ Morash
Miffy Goodheart
James Beard

PART ONE

1941–1946

CHAPTER 1

San Malo, California
August 1941

"Have decided I am really only a butterfly. All I want to do is play golf, piano, and simmer, and see people, and summer and live right here.... I shall be interested to see if I am ever a happy success."

—JULIA McWILLIAMS, DIARY

"Marry me, Julia," Harrison Chandler said.

Julia had to turn away from the sunset to look at him now, her heart bottoming out.

The August sun lowering on the horizon framed Harrison's dark hair and earnest gaze against a backdrop of lavender sky quickly fading into a deep blue. They sat in beach chairs near the mellow surf at the base of the cliff in San Malo, where they'd eaten dinner with friends. Their friends had remained above, at the top of the cliff, chatting and laughing together. The salty breeze still held the lingering scent of grilled food.

Julia blinked and turned more fully toward Harrison. She could practically see perspiration beading on his forehead, hear the sharp, rapid draw of his breath as he waited for her answer. He looked as awkward as she felt.

This man was Julia's good friend, had been for the past couple of years, since she'd returned home to Pasadena after her college years at Smith. His father ran the *Los Angeles Times*—the most influential newspaper in California. And Harrison worked as vice president for its affiliate, Times Mirror Printing and Binding House.

Among their mutual friends, there'd been some pesky comments about how they *should* be a couple. They looked good together, after all, with Julia's lithe six-foot-two-inch frame and Harrison's similarly tall build. He was a nice-looking man, always well dressed, with a secure financial future—something her father was over the moon about. They were comfortable around each other, enough to share a few confidences, and they attended all the same social functions because they both enjoyed dancing.

"Marriage, Harrison?" Julia said over the sudden rasp of her throat. "I wasn't expecting you to propose. We've never spoken of a future together."

His nod was quick, his swallow audible. "I know that, Julia, but I thought . . ." Another swallow. "I thought we could maybe discuss it?"

Julia smiled, although it was one of those tight smiles that made her stomach pinch. Harrison had been a friend, but he was like a faithful, stoic dog. Following Julia everywhere, smiling at her humor but not providing any wit of his own. He was steadfast, sure, but he was too quiet, too formal . . . *Stiff* might be the right word for Mr. Harrison Chandler. Julia was the one who instigated all conversation, bringing him out of whatever deep thoughts occupied him.

Yet Harrison had always been attentive—she couldn't complain about that. She supposed she'd let his sweetness get ahead of her since she still smarted from time to time over the colossal rejection she'd received from Tom Johnston. But *marriage* to Harrison? She'd definitely let their friendship become too progressive.

Julia folded her arms and studied Harrison, really studied him. As far as proposals went, this was her first, so there wasn't anything to compare it to. In for a penny, in for a pound. His steady gaze was unwavering, but she noticed the tight grip of his clasped hands. He was nervous, but at least he hadn't tried to kiss her. The ill-timed thought created a bubble of hysteria in her chest. Maybe that was what was wrong. Harrison hadn't ever tried to kiss her. How could she know if there was anything romantic between them?

No . . . that wasn't the issue here. The issue was that he liked her more than she liked him. Maybe he even loved her. And she . . . she viewed him like a brother. A friend, sure, but nothing more.

His imploring gaze tugged at her heart, just a little. "Where do you see yourself settling down?" she asked. "And what about children? You've never seemed to favor them. Whenever we've been around our married friends, you steer clear of the little ones."

Harrison's neck went blotchy, but to his credit, he answered directly, though his words were stilted. "A child with you would be a . . . blessing, of course. Every woman wants children. I'm not immune to that notion."

Julia almost scoffed. "I've always imagined myself with three or four children, you know. A houseful." She was the eldest of three and couldn't imagine growing up without her brother, John, and sister, Dort—even during their epic rivalries.

"Y-yes," Harrison said. "Three sounds nice. I mean, I have a lot of siblings, and although I certainly don't want eight children, like my family . . . I could live with three. Or four."

His father had remarried after his first wife's death, and Harrison had two half sisters and five other siblings.

"That's good, we can agree on at least one thing." Perhaps her words were snarky, but they were true. She certainly couldn't discuss politics with Harrison. He spent inordinate amounts of leisure time at LA's Lincoln Club, the California Club, and Sunset Club, pontificating about his family's practically religious hatred of FDR. Harrison's political viewpoints were extreme right, even more hardened than the *Times* ultraconservative reporting.

Another reason Julia's father, John McWilliams Jr., would completely approve of the match. Julia wasn't one to back down from a political discussion, although with her father, it was easier to let him have his say without her interference. If there was one thing she'd learned growing up in the McWilliams household, it was that her father would never change his right-wing viewpoints.

"Julie," Harrison said, using the name that most of her friends called her, although he'd always kept things more formal. "There's no hurry on this. Think about it. I'm happy to wait. I-I can't see myself with anyone but you."

Still, Julia didn't feel it—the *it* that her girlfriends had gushed over. She'd turned twenty-eight two weeks before, on August 12. Back in New York, she'd thought Tom Johnston had been the man for her. Tom, who was inches taller than her; Tom, who was gregarious, charming, and affectionate and had hung on her every word. But then he'd left New York. Disappeared from her life. Until one day, she received a wedding notice in the mail. A knife to her chest would have hurt less. So what did Julia know about love? Maybe . . . maybe love and a happy future sat right next to her.

"Julie! Aren't you going to have dessert?" Katy Gates called out, coming down the winding path of the cliffside. Katy, one of Julia's childhood friends, was a regular at the weekend parties. "You two have been down here for ages. What are you doing? Counting sand crabs?"

"I'll think about it," Julia told Harrison before unfolding her body and standing to face Katy. "What's for dessert?"

Katy laughed and tossed a glance at Harrison, her face a map of curiosity. "Cherry pie and vanilla ice cream."

"Sounds delicious."

Julia sensed rather than heard Harrison coming along behind them. Maybe once the surprise of the proposal wore off, she'd be able to think clearly. For now, she joined her group of friends inside the brick-walled courtyard that surround her father's beach house. She quickly became caught up in conversation about the war in Europe, how Hitler and his Nazi Germany were blazing their way across the continent, and how the US oil embargo was aimed at Japan. Each day brought more war news, worse than the day before.

Talking about the war always felt disconcerting to Julia while she was living in a virtual paradise, with only the sounds of laughter, waves, and summer breezes to pepper her days and nights. Yet she felt the foreboding, like hearing the sound of rolling thunder, knowing the storm was coming closer and closer even though all she could see was clear skies. She felt so helpless, especially since other countries were establishing women's military sectors, including the Canadian Women's Army Corps and the Australian Women's Army Service. Whereas in the US, *LIFE* magazine had featured a pinup photograph of Rita Hayworth on a beach.

JULIA

Conversation buzzed among Julia's friends Gay Bradley, Mamie Valentine, Betty Washburn, and Katie Nevins—all regulars at her parties—and their spouses or boyfriends.

"Welcome back," Betty teased, her short wavy hair held back with a stylish scarf. "We thought you might spend the night on the beach."

The others exchanged amused glances. Had Harrison told them about his intent to propose?

The discussion soon moved back to war news about the US pledging support to the Soviet Union, including them in the Lend-Lease program, and the Germans moving in on the eastern sectors, such as the naval base at Mykolaiv. And also the fact that British bombers had, in turn, recently raided the railway yards at Hanover.

As the conversation swirled about her, Julia wondered again what she was doing with her life. She'd hardly accomplished a thing. Sure, she was a Smith graduate—her mother's alma mater—but Julia hadn't been able to make it completely on her own. Not yet. She'd either been in school or living with family. Her aim of becoming a respected journalist had already crumpled. She'd graduated in 1934, six years before, and since then, she hadn't held down a job of any importance. She'd majored in history and taken an inordinate number of classes in Italian, French, and music to develop her character. She'd even attended secretarial school at Packard Commercial School in Pittsfield while living with her aunt Theodora in Massachusetts. That had turned out to be a mistake, and Julia had lasted only one month.

She'd thought a break had come when she'd been hired for an entry-level job at W. & J. Sloane—a high-end furnishings company in New York City. She was the "girl Friday" and divided her days between secretarial work, scheduling photo shoots, and writing press releases. At a salary of eighteen dollars a month, she had to tap into her $100 a month allowance from her parents in order to afford living expenses, but she loved rooming with two friends Julie Chapman and Lib Payson in a brownstone on East Fifty-Ninth Street and First Avenue. It was her first taste of true freedom, a real chance to be an adult woman who made her own decisions and schedules. So when she'd run into Tom Johnston at a mixer, she'd decided to get to know him better.

Oh, they'd crossed paths several times before since he was a Princeton guy. His size always commanded attention, as a football player and boxer, and he had a charm and confidence that she couldn't look away from.

Besides, he seemed to like her too.

Or at least, she thought that as they attended dinner parties together, browsed bookstores on Fifth Avenue, talked for hours at a time, laughed until their stomachs hurt . . .

It had all been a ruse. Julia still remembered the day she'd received a letter from Tom: September 6, 1936. He'd left New York City for Detroit—where his real girlfriend had lived. He'd been a two-timer, and to make matters worse, Julia had known the other woman. Izzy McMullen had graduated from Smith a couple of years ahead of Julia. And if there had been anyone who Julia had felt inferior to, it had been beautiful and petite Izzy. Julia was the complete opposite in everything.

And to add insult to major injury, Julia had written to Tom in a desperate attempt to change his mind. Or turn his heart toward her? No matter. It was foolish and rash and did nothing but fill her with mortification as she'd waited and waited for his response. Nothing had come for months, until she'd received his marriage announcement in early 1937. He'd been married on New Year's Day.

It was over.

One would think that four years would be enough time to heal a heart. One would think that she could look at Harrison Chandler with clear, unaffected eyes . . . but the image of the larger-than-life Tom Johnston still haunted her most quiet moments. She couldn't trust her own heart. So, yes, Harrison was right in one thing: there was no rush. They could take their time—she planned on taking her time. Her parents had known each other for years before her mother, Caro, had agreed to marry. And that was only because her invalid sister had become engaged, freeing up Caro from caretaking.

JULIA

Julia helped herself to the cherry pie. She felt Harrison's gaze on her—it seemed to always be on her. But it was only now making her aware that his thoughts had leap-frogged far above a casual friendship. Julia wanted more though; she wanted to be in love. Would she hold out for it? Or would she settle for the easy way, the easy answer? The one who would make her father happy?

After a handful of goodbyes and a long questioning look from Katy, Julia headed into the dormered house, which the family affectionately referred to as Ye-Old-English house. Katy would probably check on her later, but for now, Julia was going to enjoy the quiet.

She settled onto her designated bed, slid between the cool cotton sheets, and pulled out her faithful diary that contained all her grievances. She flipped through several entries and paused at the ones surrounding the death of her mother three years before, in 1937. Her mother had had what the family called the "Weston curse" and had suffered from uremia, which had eventually shut down her kidneys.

Regrets stacked themselves in Julia's heart. She could have spent more time with her mother, been more attentive, kinder, more loving. Julia took after her mother in many ways: her height, her strawberry-red hair, her swooping voice that spanned two octaves.

Was there a right way to say goodbye to your own mother? Tears pricking her eyes, Julia wondered what Mother would have thought of Julia's recent aimlessness—working at the start-up magazine *Coast*, being fired from the Beverly Hills branch of Sloane's for not making advertising copy corrections mandated by the higher ups—and now holding a lackluster marriage option.

Julia puffed out a breath and turned to a blank page to write the date at the top, then detailed the proposal from Harrison Chandler, finishing with the statement, "I have an idea I may succumb."

CHAPTER 2

Pasadena, California
September–December 1941

"Of course, no one ever studied, so we got 100 percent. Julia was the center of attention and activity; when we were all together she was always the focus, always the funny one, always the clown (of course, she had her serious side); when she was little she was always the first one throwing butter at the ceiling, the ringleader.... Always the kind of person people follow because she had great magnetism."

—GAY BRADLEY

"Do you still have that list of marriage requirements?" Dort asked.

Julia chortled a laugh at her younger sister's question as they lounged on the back porch of their father's Pasadena home. The porch was screened in but let in the warm, fragrant breeze coming off the patio gardens. They'd slept on this porch as children since their parents firmly believed in J. C. Elliott's philosophy of children sleeping outdoors to cut back on disease.

"You're talking about the list I made after Tom Johnston jilted me?"

Dort's smile widened, making her freckles dance. The sisters were nearly five years apart, but they both had strawberry-red hair, hazel eyes, and their fair share of freckles. "Yes, that's the one."

"It's buried deep in my diary somewhere." Julia stubbed out her cigarette. Then she took a sip of the cold lemonade that she'd poured after returning from a golf outing at the Midwick Country Club with her father about an hour ago. He'd stayed at the club with his cohorts, discussing politics and smoking cigars.

If there was one thing to be said about John McWilliams Jr., it was that he loved conversation—as long as the person agreed with him. And plenty of his old-time friends did just that. But secretly, Julia knew that he was also chatting with the ladies. A wealthy, ultra-right-winged widower was quite the catch in Pasadena.

Julia had mixed feelings about her father possibly remarrying someday. It would certainly let her off the hook of watching over him. Although now her sister, Dorothy, had graduated from Bennington College and returned home. She'd spent a year before that working at the Cambridge School in Waltham, Massachusetts, and stage managing for operas in New York City. Julia's little sister had grown up, and they'd finally become close friends.

"I'm sure that Harrison Chandler meets at least a few of your requirements," Dort teased, stretching her long legs in front of her.

Dort was taller than Julia by a few inches. At six five, Dort had gone through more than one identity crisis that Julia had talked her down from. Julia probably hadn't helped much with her sister's self-confidence since Julia had been a merciless tease as a child, going as far as to give away Dort's favorite doll to a neighbor.

"Well, I'm not going to dig up my diary right now, but I do remember putting 'fun' on the list as well as 'complete mutual understanding and respect.'"

"Hmm." Dort grimaced. "*Fun* doesn't describe Harrison at all. Although I'm sure he respects you, there's not much mutual understanding between your viewpoints."

"True." Julia heaved a sigh.

"And John agrees." Dort held up a letter from their brother, waving it.

"What? You told him about the proposal?"

Dort laughed. "How could I not? It was too delicious to hold back. Besides, John is the only married one out of us, and I hoped for some sound advice."

"Oh, hand it over." Julia swiped for the letter, and Dort released it with another laugh.

Julia opened the single page and scanned through her brother's words. John McWilliams III lived in Pittsfield, Massachusetts, with his wife, Josephine. They'd married last June, and he worked for the Weston Paper

Company, a legacy from their mother's side of the family. He was also the financial manager over her and Dort's inheritance from their mother.

"Well, it appears that John is perfectly happy if I wait to marry," she said. "I don't need to settle for Harrison, even though he does come with a long pedigree and financial security." Julia felt grateful for the support from her brother. Maybe it was because of her father's continual comments about what a fine young man Harrison was.

Julia folded the letter and handed it back to Dort. "I know that not everyone has the instant falling in love that John had with Jo, but it sure would be nice." She moved to her feet, then released a soft groan.

"Your knee?" Dort said, turning her head, concern in her eyes.

"I might have overdone it today on the golf course." Julia rotated her leg, then rubbed at her knee. She'd had painful knee surgery that March, and although most days she was fine, the odd pain crept back in once in a while. "Well, I'm off to call Harrison and cancel on him for tonight's dinner party."

Dort joined her at the back door. "What? Are you turning him down once and for all?"

Julia had explained to Dort that although she hadn't given Harrison a yes or no answer yet, they'd agreed to keep spending time together.

"Only for tonight," Julia said. "I'm going to a volunteer meeting for the American Red Cross of Pasadena. They have some openings in the organization, and I'm tired of lazing about."

Dort walked into the house with her. "You're the most busy and active person I know. If you're not golfing, playing tennis, or organizing a social outing, you're volunteering for something. Sounds like the Red Cross is just another step."

Julia paused and turned to her sister, her tone growing serious. "I want to do something that truly matters. There's a war going on in the rest of the world, and there's a major refugee crisis on top of that. All I've done the past few years is act the part of the proverbial social butterfly. What's the point of that? Cheering up a few people, keeping friendships alive, following Pop around? I mean, I know Mother's motto was Personality

JULIA

Is Everything, but she also told us to do more things, and don't be a nobody."

Dort set her hands on her hips. "Maybe I'll come tonight too."

In spite of her sister's enthusiasm, Julia ended up attending the Red Cross meeting alone because Dort's friends pulled her away to attend a theatrical performance sponsored by the Junior League at the civic auditorium.

Julia walked away from the Red Cross meeting with a firm resolve to help in the war effort where possible. She'd become the newest appointed head of the Department of Stenographic Services, typing and mimeographing.

Over the next weeks, Julia devoted most of her days to working in the Red Cross office, doing the grunt work of typing, filing, and copying. She sent out information to collect supplies for emergency kits to send overseas, then typed up more fundraising letters.

The weeks turned into months, and Harrison had come over for family Thanksgiving dinner. It had been a swell day, but Julia hadn't felt any significant pull toward him. Pop had sure enjoyed the visit though.

Julia continued to focus on the Red Cross work, recruiting a few of her friends along the way. She'd return home each evening, feeling exhausted but exhilarated. On some nights, she'd go out with friends, but mostly she stayed in, scrounging around in the kitchen for something extra to eat that Pop's cook had left after hours or listening to the radio or enduring her father's opinions on the incoming news, which consisted of criticizing anything on the Democratic agenda. Her father also employed a gardener, a laundress, a butler, and a part-time seamstress, so there wasn't much opportunity for Julia to busy herself with homemaking tasks.

And she had never been a cook, by any means, likely due to the fact that her mother hadn't cooked—save for three items—baking powder biscuits, codfish balls, and Welsh rabbit. Those were the menu items when their cook had the day off. Grandmother McWilliams's cooking had been excellent—her donuts had been divine and her broiled chicken perfection. Mother had told Julia it was because Grandmother had grown up on a farm in Illinois, and at one point, the family had had a French cook. Not that Julia ever had much to do with French food. Her father found anything French—or foreign, for that matter, which included "East Coast liberals"—abhorrent. And it was better to avoid entertaining one of his rants and never even suggest that they eat at a French restaurant.

On one such quiet evening, after the news radio programs had switched over to music and a light rain battled against the windows, Julia dug out the recipe book *Joy of Cooking*. She'd used it a few times in New York but hadn't touched it since returning to Pasadena. As she leafed through it, she admired the approach author Irma Rombauer took with cooking meals, but Julia couldn't get her mother's recipes out of her mind. She knew them by heart—they were easy to remember.

So when Dort returned from an evening out, Julia was wrist deep in all-purpose flour.

"What in the world has gotten into you?" Dort asked.

Julia glanced up with a start. She'd been so focused on cutting the shortening into small pieces, with the radio music featuring Jimmy Dorsey and his orchestra as background noise. "I'm making Mom's biscuits."

"Oh." Dort's brows lifted. She set down her black leather handbag on the far side of the counter. "Can I help?"

"Apron's over there." Julia nodded toward the pantry door.

In moments, Dort joined her at the counter, and after Julia blended the dry ingredients with the wet ingredients, she turned out the dough onto a floured board, and Dort set to kneading. Then, after patting her portion into a half-inch layer, Julia used a glass to cut out the rounds.

"How did you remember the ingredients?" Dort asked.

"Had them in my head." Julia shrugged. Things like recipes were easy to remember.

"You have a gift, you know," Dort said.

Julia looked up. "What? Making a mess?"

"No." Dort laughed. "Remembering things. I wish I were half as smart as you are."

Julia had to scoff at this. "Your college grades outshone mine."

JULIA

"That's not as hard to do in theater subjects," Dort said. "You just have to be sincere and creative. Dig deep."

"Still, I was a B student in the best of times," Julia said. "Smith College was a great time but not as academically inspiring as I'm sure Mother wanted it to be for me."

Dort paused as she set the dough rounds on a cooking sheet. "Is that why you're baking tonight? You miss her?"

Julia couldn't deny it. "Yes, I miss her. I mostly regret not appreciating her as much as I should have. I mean, I was kind of a terrible kid. My pranks went too far—stealing cigars, sneaking into vacant houses, and throwing mud pies at passing cars." She frowned and shook her head at her own stupidity.

Dort slipped an arm about Julia's shoulders. "Mom knew we cared about her and loved her. She was the loveliest woman. She loved life—her dogs, her children, her tennis. Maybe in that order?"

Julia smiled through her brimming tears.

"You remind me of her, you know," Dort said.

This surprised Julia. "What? How?"

Dort leaned against the counter, folding her arms. "Your spontaneity. How you can make friends with everyone you meet within minutes. You're funny and full of life. Mom was always playful, keeping us from being too stuffy and serious—especially Pop. She spoke her mind and her opinions without hesitation."

"That's definitely true," Julia mused. "I suppose I do that, too, for better or for worse."

Dort winked. "Remember when Mother would tell us to open the windows in the middle of dinnertime? She'd say, 'Oh, hot flash, hot flash, open the window,' and Pop's face would turn red."

"I do remember that." Julia laughed, or maybe it was a small cry too. She dragged in a deep breath. "It's only fitting we eat these biscuits tonight, then sort out the Christmas decorations. Christmas will be here in a few weeks, and we need to start decorating soon." It was Mother's favorite holiday after all.

"It's a deal." Dort continued loading the cooking sheet, and Julia popped the first tray of biscuits into the oven.

Soon, she pulled out the lightly browned biscuits and drenched them with butter that promptly melted down the sides.

Julia and Dort stayed up way too late sorting through boxes of Christmas decorations, but at least the next day was Sunday, and Julia planned to sleep in a little.

But the morning came too early anyway, and for some reason, Pop had the radio on screeching loud. Julia climbed out of bed, bleary-eyed, and reached for a robe. Gone were the days when Mother would prepare a Sunday brunch for the family, and then they'd haul off to church. Walking into the kitchen, Julia was about to reach for the radio knob to turn the thing down when she stopped dead.

Pop was sitting at the kitchen table, the phone receiver gripped in his hand. He wasn't speaking to anyone, just staring into nothingness. At sixty, he was still a handsome man, well-spoken and decisive. But right now, he looked as if he'd aged ten years. His skin was gray, and his eyes seemed to have sunken into his face. Julia hadn't seen him look this deflated since Mother's funeral.

Her mind raced with terrible possibilities—had something happened to her brother, John? Or another relative? Why was the radio volume so loud? Then her mind shifted to the words coming from the newscaster. Words like: *Pearl Harbor. Oahu. Bombed by Japanese war planes. Harbor in flames. Ships and planes destroyed. Hundreds dead, maybe thousands.*

Julia sank to the chair opposite her father as she tried to piece together what the news report was saying.

"We have a live report from KGU in Honolulu, Hawaii," the newscaster broke in.

Hello, NBC. Hello, NBC. This is KGU in Honolulu, Hawaii. I am speaking from the roof of the Advertiser Publishing Company building. We have witnessed this morning the distant view of a brief full battle of Pearl Harbor and the severe bombing of Pearl Harbor by enemy planes, undoubtedly Japanese. The city of Honolulu has been attacked and considerable damage done.

JULIA

Dort appeared in the kitchen and sat next to Julia before taking Julia's hand. It was then that Julia realized she had tears streaming down her face.

This battle has been going on for nearly three hours. One of the bombs dropped within fifty feet of KGU tower. It is no joke. This is a real war. The, uh . . . public of Honolulu has been advised to keep in their homes and away from the army and navy. There has been serious fighting going on in the air and on the sea. The heavy shooting seems to be . . . One, two, three, four . . . Just a moment, a little interruption. We cannot estimate how much damage has been done, but it has been a very severe attack. The navy and army appear now to have the air and the sea under control.

Julia had never been to Hawaii, but she imagined it as beautiful as California, and to think of bombs being dropped along the beautiful coast, destroying people and ships and buildings, made her shudder.

The news continued to blare, making her feel as though a firehose had been pointed directly at their house. One devastating report after another.

"Pop, what's going to happen to us?" Dort eventually asked.

Their father looked at both of them, the lines about his face dragging his mouth downward. "We're going to war, that's what. Even a Democratic president won't let this slide."

Despite Pop's ongoing criticisms of FDR because he considered the man too intellectual, Julia saw and heard pride and stoicism in her father's voice that morning. Republican or Democrat, America was uniting in a single cause.

The phone rang, jolting them all from a numb daze. Julia wasn't even sure what time it was now. Had any of them eaten? Pop answered, and it was clear that it was John calling.

"I understand, son," Pop said. "If I were younger, I'd be enlisting too."

When he hung up, he folded his veined hands atop the table. "John is enlisting in the army tomorrow."

Julia wasn't surprised, but her brother going to war meant that this was now personal. Very personal. Her throat ached with a burning heat, and she could barely catch her breath. She thought of all the men she knew—young men—some married, some still in school, but that wouldn't stop any of them. This morning, everyone's lives had been irrevocably changed. And there was no turning back now.

"I need to call Harrison," she said, not sure why she suddenly felt so urgent about it.

Surely he was at the *Times* office, dealing with verifying reports of Pearl Harbor and putting together the print run for the evening paper. When he answered, her heart rate zoomed. "Harrison, it's Julia."

"Julia, is everything all right?"

"Yes, well, except the obvious," she said, feeling a strange sort of comfort at the sound of his voice. Plenty of background noise filtered through—conversations, typewriters . . . "We've had quite a shock. I'm sure you're inundated."

"We are." He paused. "I'm glad you called. I've been worried about you. Wondering how you and your family are taking this. Especially your father."

Julia glanced over at Pop. He was finally eating something, as prodded by Dort. "He's been listening to the radio nonstop. We all have."

She could almost imagine Harrison's brief nod as he leaned forward, his shoulders in their standard hunch. "It's terrible news. And there's no relief in sight. We all have to buoy up."

"John's going to enlist tomorrow," Julia said. "He called a few minutes ago."

"I think most of America is." He paused, and Julia wondered if she should ask him about his plans. Would it be too much of a "girlfriend" question?

"I'll be enlisting in the navy," Harrison said. "No one's putting a fuss up about it here. Tells me my place, but I want to serve anyway."

A bubble of pride expanded in Julia. Maybe she didn't want to marry the man—well, she hadn't completely ruled it out yet—but she was proud of him, nonetheless.

After hanging up with Harrison, she called Katy Gates. They talked about what they'd heard, and Katy confirmed that her husband, Tule, was set on joining the navy. Others they knew were too. Everyone would be joining a military branch; everyone wanted to do something, including Julia. She just had to figure out what.

Hours later, Julia still felt numb with horror and disbelief, but she couldn't stand sitting around the house and listening to the increasing death toll. Images of burning ships, falling bombs, and trapped sailors wouldn't stop plaguing her mind. She headed into the back garden and found a bench to sit on. Despite the cool winter season, the bushes were still green, and tawny leaves dangled from the trees. The silence that should have been peaceful was somehow ominous.

And that feeling only grew the following day when it was reported that thousands of men were standing in lines, ready to enlist to defend their country against the Axis powers. She and Dort sat with Pop at the table again as they listened to President Franklin D. Roosevelt's declaration to the nation at 12:30 p.m. Washington, DC time: "With confidence in our armed forces, with the unbounding determination of our people, we will gain the inevitable triumph, so help us God. I ask that the Congress declare that since the unprovoked and dastardly attack by Japan on Sunday, December 7, 1941, a state of war has existed between the United States and the Japanese Empire."

After the declaration was brought to a vote, then passed by the Senate 82–0 and by the House 388–1, Roosevelt signed the declaration of war at 4:10 p.m.

Japan had already declared war on the United States, the United Kingdom, and Thailand.

The following day, December 9, Japan had twenty countries declaring war against them, including the US, the UK, the Netherlands, Australia, Greece, Guatemala, Canada, New Zealand, the Union of South Africa, and China.

On December 11, both Germany and Italy declared war on the United States of America.

CHAPTER 3

Pasadena, California
February–April 1942

"Radio Tokyo reported that Santa Barbara had been leveled. In truth, the most significant harm was psychological. California residents panicked. All kinds of rumors, even conspiracy theories, circulated. Some swore they saw large ships and other submarines flashing lights to shore to signal sleeper agents to begin the takeover of America. Others argued that the whole thing was a hoax, a 'false flag' attack, perpetrated by the US Navy to scare citizens and increase war bond sales."

—ON THIS DAY IN 1942: "THE BATTLE OF LOS ANGELES"

"We need to help beyond the Red Cross service, and we're needed by the AWS," Julia told her friend Katie Nevins over the phone.

The AWS, or the Aircraft Warning Service, had recently been formed and was recruiting civilian volunteers to act as spotters. California had been deemed a prime target should there be another attack from the Japanese military. The major aircraft plants and refineries, Lockheed and Douglas in Los Angeles as well as Consolidated in San Diego, were vulnerable to attack.

"What will we actually be doing?" Katie asked.

"I'm not sure," Julia said. "But we'll volunteer and find out. We can't let another Japanese submarine take shots at us." A few days ago, on February 23, during an evening radio address by FDR, a Japanese sub had appeared in the ocean north of Santa Barbara. The submarine had fired three shells at the refinery installments.

"All right, I'll come," Katie said.

The next morning, Julia drove Katie in her Ford to Los Angeles. Katie kept her window down, her blonde hair blowing in the warm spring wind. They parked across from a building on Flower Street, and Katie linked arms with Julia as they crossed the street.

"Doesn't look like much, does it?" Katie mused, her smile friendly.

The building was rather plain and boring, defying the name of the street, but that just made it all the more exciting. "It's like real undercover work."

They were let inside the building after identifying themselves to a clerk, who looked like she was eighteen years old.

The clerk led them to another room—without any windows. "This is the headquarters of the Information and Filter Center," she said. She motioned toward the large plotting map of the California coastline spread across a huge table in the center of the room.

After they'd made introductions to other volunteers, it didn't take long to be trained on the strategies. They'd receive radio calls from military personnel who would report on the movements of all seacraft so that the plotting map could be continually updated.

Once they'd completed several hours on their first day, the clerk asked them if they could report the following night for an eight-hour shift.

"Certainly," Julia said immediately, without looking at Katie. Katie could make her own decision, but Julia was likely her ride.

"I'll do it too," Katie said.

They headed out of the building into the orange glow of the setting sun. "Now, don't you feel accomplished?" Julia asked her friend.

"Yes, but I'm starving too," Katie said. "Those sandwiches from home only went so far."

"Let's stop somewhere delicious, then," Julia said. "I feel so important now that I know the position of every boat, ship, whale, or floating log along the California coastline. Just think, we're actually helping with national defense. It's the best we can do here in California. Otherwise, we'd have to join Katy Gates in Washington, DC to make any sort of dent."

"Or New York," current Katie said. "Gates is in DC because that's where her navy husband is stationed."

Julia shrugged. "I don't know about New York. Word is that it's passé."

"Sounds like government employee talk," Katie said. "I'll be much more up for debating after we eat."

Julia nudged her friend. "I'll start driving, and you pick a place." Even after spending worthwhile hours volunteering, it wasn't lost on Julia that the men she knew and cared about were already being stationed overseas. John had been sent to France.

But Katy Gates had planted the seed, and as the weeks of working for the AWS moved along and no real sightings of enemy aircraft occurred, Julia's persistent restlessness returned. She became as politically astute as her father, and often, they entered into long discussions about the war. He seemed supportive and impressed with her work for AWS, but she still felt like she was living in a bubble of bliss while so many of her friends were supporting the war effort in ways that mattered.

And meanwhile, things with Harrison were still dangling, like she had one leg off a cliff.

"You should marry that boy," Pop said one morning over breakfast. It was usually the only time she saw Pop. She had completed another night shift, and in an hour, she planned to be sound asleep, curled up under a soft blanket. "None of us are getting any younger, and who knows what might happen next in the war. Harrison could get shipped off somewhere."

Thus far, Harrison had been elbow deep in working at the *Times* with his father and brother. But he'd enlisted, and who knew when orders might come through. Disturbing news reports had been coming in about Nazi Germany putting thousands of Jews into concentration camps. If that weren't horrible enough, there were also reports of mass murders of Jews coming to light. Julia could hardly wrap her mind around it all, and it only spurred her to push aside the unnecessary extravagances of life and find ways to help end the war.

She refocused on the conversation with her father. "I'm not going to marry Harrison because he might get shipped off," Julia said, moving bits of her omelet about her plate. "I want to have a sure future in mind, not an unsure one. Besides, Pop, I don't think I love him."

JULIA

Her father set his napkin on the table with a flourish. "That's nonsense. You are still seeing each other, even after his proposal months ago. Obviously, you have some feelings for him, or you wouldn't keep him dangling like a rainbow trout."

Julia bristled but kept calm. "I've been busy, and so has he. We haven't had any proper conversations."

Pop muttered something about young people today and how they didn't know their hand from their foot.

Julia wasn't hungry anymore, and she cleared her dishes. Pop would linger over the newspaper, then probably listen to the radio most of the day. Dort would be getting up any minute, but Julia didn't want to talk to her or anyone else.

Her father's words had made her realize that she *was* keeping Harrison dangling. And for no real reason. She didn't love him last year, and she didn't love him this year. A conciliatory friendship wasn't reason enough for her to pledge her life to a man. Pledge her heart and her love.

She needed to break things off with him completely. Sure, they could be friends, but she couldn't have him thinking or hoping that no answer from her was a potential yes. She detoured into her father's home office and shut the door. The black phone on his desk seemed stoic somehow, resolute, as if it already knew its duty.

Without another moment's hesitation, she crossed to the desk and, still standing, picked up the receiver and called Harrison's home—hoping he hadn't left for the newspaper office yet.

When he came on the phone, relief battled with dread in her stomach, a tricky combination to keep locked in. "Harrison, I've finally made up my mind."

"Oh, what about, Julie?"

She tightened her jaw. His familiar tone couldn't dissuade her now. It was April 10, 1942, and she had to move onward with her life. Forward and upward. "Harris, I can't marry you. We need to step back from whatever it is we are to each other. I mean, I wish you all the best of course. You'll find a woman who will match you in every way, but that woman isn't me."

The silence was so long that Julia was about to ask if they were still connected.

"There's no rush," he finally said.

"I'm not rushing anything," she said on a sigh. "I've thought about it every which way, and we've been good friends for a long time, but marriage isn't on the table any longer."

He made a few more points, but his arguments were lackluster. He had to know that, had to feel that. Julia hung up feeling like she'd denied a puppy a treat, but in a few hours, or days, he'd be back, begging for another one. But she'd made up her mind. Finally.

In fact, she'd make it official and write about it in her diary before falling asleep. "And I hope I shall maintain this position," she scrawled in her diary once she was nestled in her bed. "It is a sin to marry without love. And marriage, while utterly desirable, from my point of view, must be with the right one. I know what I want, and it is 'sympatico,' companionship, interests, great respect, and fun. Otherwise and always—no."

Over the next few days, Julia was able to quite firmly put Harrison out of her mind. That was, after she told her father the news and he quit lamenting over it. The war was keeping everyone occupied, and there were times when, darkly, Julia felt grateful for something that gave her a greater purpose. But it wasn't enough.

The answer to her restlessness came in an unexpected way though. When Katie and Julia were sharing breakfast together in Los Angeles after a long night shift with the AWS, Harrison walked into the café.

"Harrison," Julia exclaimed. "What are you doing here?"

"Grabbing a bite to eat," he said, his gaze trained on her.

Had he tracked her down? Julia wondered. He was still part of every social event she attended, and she wasn't sure if it was always a coincidence or if he was hoping she'd change her mind. She never saw him bring another woman, or talk to other women, for that matter. He joined their table, and she was grateful to have Katie with her. She didn't want any private conversations rehashing their convoluted relationship.

"How is everything at the *Times* this week?" Julia asked.

"A madhouse," Harrison said. "We've been reporting on the Doolittle Raid. At least something is giving the American people some hope after the loss of Guam and the Philippines to the Japanese military."

Julia had read all about the first American attack on Japan. It had been a joint army-navy operation, where sixteen B-25Bs bombed Tokyo and other cities on Honshu. Specific targets had been hit and the mission considered a success.

Harrison changed the subject before either woman could respond. "What's new with the both of you?"

Katie took the lead and launched into their most recent work, with Julia only half-listening. She'd received a phone call the day before from her friend Janie McBain, who lived in Washington, DC. Janie was a San Francisco friend who now lived back east; her husband had recently been sent to Italy. Janie had offered Julia a place to stay if Julia was intent on moving to DC.

"You're far away," Harrison said, and Julia realized she'd completely checked out.

"Oh, sorry." She took a sip of her orange juice. The juice was a bit tart for her taste, but sugar rationing was in effect. "I talked to my friend Janie McBain yesterday. Do you remember her?"

Harrison tilted his head. "I do."

Julia launched into the conversation and explained everything about her friends who'd encouraged her to find work in DC.

Harrison nodded, his expression thoughtful, as if he were taking her seriously. Unlike her father, who continued to tell her to stay home and do good in her own community. "If you're truly determined to have a greater role, then maybe you should drop the volunteer work," Harrison said.

Julia stared at him. He *wanted* her to go to Washington, DC?

"You've heard of the newly formed WAC and WAVES Civil Service programs for women?" he asked. "You should take the Civil Service exam."

She blinked. Harrison was on to something.

"There's a shortage, you know, in the government agencies, with all the men leaving," Harrison continued with composure, although Julia's insides had tied into knots.

The WAVES was the navy division—Women Accepted for Voluntary Emergency Services. And the WAC was the army equivalent—Women's Army Corps. She'd apply for both while she was at it.

She just had to tell her family that she was moving to Washington, DC. Whether or not she was accepted in either the WAVES or the WAC, she was ready for a change.

Two weeks later, Julia arrived in Washington, DC. What she hadn't expected was the immediate boost of energy and morale she got the moment she stepped off the train at Union Station. Summer had hit DC with full force, packed with heat and humidity, tangled traffic, and professionals clogging the sidewalks. It seemed that everyone who wasn't eligible to enlist had congregated to this place.

She hurried off the platform, escaping the scent of oil smoke and bellows of steam.

"There you are," Janie gushed the moment the two saw each other at the curbside of the train station. "You look . . . wonderful."

"You're being kind," Julia said. "I look like I've spent a week on a train."

"Which you have." Janie grinned and pulled her in for an embrace, her familiar floral perfume scent enveloping Julia.

When Julia pulled away, Janie kept ahold of her arms. "Are you sure you won't stay with me longer? I'm happy to have you."

"Only the weekend," Julia said in a breezy voice that covered the deep exhaustion in her bones. She couldn't wait until she climbed into bed, any bed, tonight. "I've already arranged things with Brighton Hotel, the residence hotel on California Street."

Janie wrinkled her nose. "Well, if you change your mind . . ."

Julia linked arms with her friend as the taxi driver loaded her bags into the trunk of his car. "I appreciate everything, but I need to do this on my own. Prove something to myself, I guess."

JULIA

On the taxi ride to Janie's place, they chatted about their mutual friends who'd been shipped out to places such as Florida, Kansas, and Hawaii. The conversation only made the urgency stronger inside of Julia.

She spent a lovely weekend with Janie, catching up on everything and eating out at restaurants, which Julia insisted on paying for, and trying to get used to the dense humidity again.

Once she moved into the Brighton Hotel, she spent time sprucing up the mismatched furniture. The single window barely offered any view at all—unless she enjoyed looking out at the service alley and the brick wall of another building beyond.

Writing letters occupied some of her time, writing to her brother, her father, her sister, her sister-in-law, and a few of her friends. She didn't have much hope of John writing her back. Who knew how the mail service worked in France. And she didn't want to think of the other reason he might not be writing back.

She hadn't realized how much she'd pinned her hopes on the WAVES until she finally received a letter in reply to her application: *Denied.*

The naval reserve had listed the reason as "automatic disqualification" with a check next to "physical disqualification." Julia scanned through the document. The height requirement was that a woman couldn't be under five feet. Nothing was said for being too tall. But Julia knew that was it. She'd even altered her height to six feet one inch, but apparently, that was too tall to join the WAVES?

So when her rejection came later from the WAC, she wasn't surprised, although the disappointment weighed heavy.

In a phone call with Dort, her sister said, "Come back home. Pop misses you, even though he won't admit it, and I miss you. There's no reason for us all to be split up, especially with our brother over in France."

"I'm going to find something here, regardless," Julia said. "I might be too long for the WAVES or WAC, but there are typist and clerical jobs everywhere. I'm not too long to sit in a chair."

The following day, Julia met up with Janie at a café. They sat at an outdoor table with a folder of résumés between them. The spring air was unusually cool, and they stayed bundled in their coats while traffic crawled past—a cacophony of chrome and honking as a backdrop to their conversation.

"You can move in with me while you decide your next steps," Janie said, stirring the tea that she had ordered. "You don't have to keep living in that drab hotel."

Julia shrugged before starting in on her eggs benedict. She was ravenous this morning. "It's fine. I'm learning to cook quite well on a burner. I just have to keep splashes off the wallpaper."

Janie scoffed. "Well, the WAVES and the WAC have certainly lost out. Who would have thought you could be too tall to join up? There are more government jobs now than ever. It seems every time I turn around, a new war department has started up."

"Any that might take a tall woman who once went to Smith and enjoys golf and tennis?" Julia might be teasing, but she was still smarting from her rejection. It felt so . . . un-American.

"Sure." Janie sipped at her tea. "Let's see, there's the War Research Service, National Defense Research Committee, Office of Civilian Defense, Board of Economic Warfare, Alien Enemy Control Unit, National Defense Research committee—"

Julia cut her off with a laugh. "That's quite the list." She tapped the folder with her updated résumé. "I hope to make some headway today, then I'll sit by the phone and wait for the interview offers to pour in."

"You'll find something in no time." Janie picked up her fork and knife and proceeded to cut the waffle on her plate. "Keep me posted."

If only it were that simple, Julia thought as she spent the next few hours visiting multiple places of business, standing in job lines, dropping off her résumé, filling out application forms, and chatting up the clerks and secretaries. It seemed that everyone she had short conversations with were seeking anything, anywhere, that might get their foot in the door.

When a job offer came a few days later, it was with the Office of War Information. The OWI had recently formed that summer and were tasked with sending out propaganda.

"What do you have to do?" Dort asked over the phone when Julia called to report in after her first day of work.

JULIA

"I'm assigned to the Research Unit, behind the scenes." Julia turned to the burner she cooked most of her meals on and stirred the potato soup she'd prepared. "I guess this division is a combination of the former Office of Facts and Figures and the Office of Government Reports. I have to go through newspapers and other documents and spot names of government officials, then record the mention on a three-by-five card."

"Ow, that sounds tedious."

"It is, but I'm pretty sure I only got the job because Nobel Cathcart is the assistant director."

"You mean the Nobel who's married to our cousin Harriet?"

"Yes, that's the one, but I'm hoping this job can be a stepping stone to something better."

"Didn't you used to be in love with Nobel?"

Julia laughed and turned off the burner. The soup had started to boil, and she knew it would be only a couple of minutes before it began to burn at the bottom. "I did have a schoolgirl's crush on the man but deferred to Harriet. She's family, after all."

"You and your crushes," Dort said. "Either they're in love with you, or you're in love with them. And it's never mutual."

"In Nobel's case, I'm glad of that," Julia said. "I might not be the religious sort, but I do have morals."

"I know, and I'm lucky to have you as a sister," Dort said. "You've always been a compass for me in my life. Remember when you lectured me to get over myself and my height? To be proud of my long legs?"

"And I still believe that." Julia stretched out her own legs. "Us Mc-Williams women need to love ourselves first."

Talking to Dort always gave her a boost, and Julia spent the next few weeks keeping her head down at work, hyperfocusing on her job. She spent the evenings with groups of friends at cafés or bars as they discussed the parts of their jobs that weren't top secret and debated the progress of the war. Most of them had brothers or husbands who were now overseas, in the thick of the conflict, and there was a general feeling of anxiety, knowing that bad news could arrive for any of them at any time.

CHAPTER 4

Washington, DC
December 1942

"The great majority of women who worked for America's first organized and integrated intelligence agency, spent their war years behind desks and filing cases in Washington, invisible apron strings of an organization which touched every theater of the war. They were the ones at home who patiently filed secret reports, encoded and decoded messages, answered telephones, mailed checks and kept the records. But these were the necessary tasks without the faithful performance of which an organization of some 21,000 people, with civil and military personnel, could not be maintained.... Only a small percentage of the women ever went overseas, and a still smaller percentage was assigned to actual operations behind enemy lines."

—MAJOR GENERAL WILLIAM J. DONOVAN,
DIRECTOR OF THE OSS, WASHINGTON, DC

Julia had stuck out her job at the OWI as long as she could stand it. But being cooped up day after day, reading hundreds of documents, amounting to over ten thousand three-by-five cards, had taken its toll over the months. She wondered if what she was doing was the best use of her time—the best way to aid in the war effort. Newspapers had reported over the past month that two million Jews had been murdered. It was unfathomable to comprehend. She couldn't listen to the radio at night, otherwise she couldn't sleep. In the mornings, she was somehow able to bear it.

When she heard more and more about the Office of Strategic Services, she was eager to apply. The Office of the Coordinator of Information had been established the year before, in June 1941, when FDR asked William Donovan to form an intelligence-gathering agency.

JULIA

After Pearl Harbor, Donovan proposed that the COI become the Office of Strategic Services (OSS). This also switched the reporting chain from the White House to the Joint Chiefs of Staff. Some of Julia's friends were working for the different OSS divisions and had nothing but interesting things to say.

"The elite of the elite work there," Janie had told Julia. "You know, intellects and academics. People who've attended prestigious schools, like you. Besides, it's all cloak and dagger stuff—you'll love it."

"As long as they don't check my college grades," Julia had joked.

She'd been nervous in her interviews, then surprised and grateful when she'd been asked to report on December 14. She'd even bought a new leopard-fur coat to celebrate. So what if it made her tall frame attract more attention? She was celebrating no more three-by-five cards.

The morning finally came, and Julia walked in the brisk December weather, crossing the E Street complex to the OSS headquarters and heading up the stairs to enter the front doors. The building, with its stately moldings and polished hardwood floors, was impressive yet unassuming. When she was introduced to Alice Carson, Julia recognized her immediately as a girl from Smith who was a few years older and had graduated the year that Julia had started.

"First, fingerprinting," Alice said as she led Julia into a room with war posters decorating the walls. One of the posters sported a large ear, stating that the enemy was always listening.

Julia did the fingerprinting, marveling at how she'd just become a number on the military roster.

"Come with me to meet your boss. You'll be working directly under Wild Bill as his research assistant," Alice said in a hushed tone as they left the fingerprinting room.

"Wild Bill?"

Alice grinned. "You know, Bill Donovan. That's what we all call him—behind his back of course."

Julia wondered what sort of man she was about to meet. "What's so wild about him?"

"I'm not exactly sure, although he's a highly decorated World War I veteran," Alice continued as they passed a room with several typists clacking away. "He was awarded the Distinguished Service Cross, the Silver Star, and the Distinguished Service Medal, and rumor has it that he was injured multiple times. But I think his nickname comes from being stubborn and holding his own against people like the president of the United States."

"So, he's a Democrat?"

"Republican," Alice said. "Is that a problem?"

"Of course not."

"Donovan doesn't care about political affiliation." Alice kept her voice lowered. "He's even hired a few communists." This surprised Julia, but she didn't have time to digest the information because Alice continued, "I guess FDR was impressed with Donovan's prediction about the British withstanding the Nazi blitz and has now charged him with developing an organization equivalent to the Brits."

Julia remembered her father's ranting about how FDR could be so lackadaisical and staying out of the war when the Brits were getting pummeled.

Alice stopped in front of a closed door, numbered 122, but with no other markings. Before Julia could ask any more questions, Alice knocked.

"Come in," the answer was immediate and self-assured.

Alice opened the door, but instead of entering the office, she motioned for Julia to step in.

Julia walked into the office that smelled of old coffee and came face-to-face with William Donovan. He rose from his chair on the other side of his large mahogany desk stacked with files. He didn't look wild at all. In fact, Julia thought he looked unassuming, almost dumpy. His shirt was rumpled, and it looked like he might have a coffee stain on the cuff of his sleeve. If anything stood out about him, it was his piercing blue eyes.

He reached out his hand, and Julia gave it a firm shake as Alice slipped out of the office.

"Miss McWilliams?" Donovan said. "Welcome to the OSS."

JULIA

That was all the formality she received because he held up a finger while he leafed through a file, seeming to read it at superspeed. Then he looked up at her again. "Tell me about yourself."

She began, halting at first, not sure how much was too much. When she told him about graduating from Smith College, he said, "You're looking to help in the war effort, but you aren't doing it to earn money, correct?"

This was a strange question, but she answered, "Correct. I have my own money."

Donovan nodded. "Excellent. It's my philosophy that those from wealthy families aren't bribable. I'm sure you've heard rumors that I hire only the elite and wealthy, and while that has some merit, I want you to understand why."

Julia folded her hands together, curious at this line of conversation.

"Like you, they're educated, they've experienced more of the world, often overseas. They aren't intimidated to try something new. They have some brass, if you will. A few dollars or even a few more won't persuade them to break a trust. Besides, surrounding myself with academics and people who are smarter than me has never led me astray."

Julia had to set at least one thing straight. "I'm about as far from an academic as you can get, Mr. Donovan, but I can play a mean golf game or school you in tennis."

Donovan cracked his first smile. "This is a job where you'll learn that we have to cross many lines in order to infiltrate our enemies' boundaries. Espionage, organizing resistance groups, cryptography, forging documents, and initiating propaganda are only some of the tasks your sister spies have been engaging in. Because of that, I need someone completely trustworthy, and I've no doubt you fit the bill."

Julia felt like she'd grown another few inches, which would be a feat in and of itself.

"Now, I need to head out for a while," he said, picking up the file he'd scanned and tucking it into his briefcase. "Alice will show you around." He tapped a piece of paper on the desk. "Go over this financial statement and then determine the budget for ordering more office supplies."

"Yes, sir," Julia said, because what else could she say? He was clearly on his way out of the office.

He paused again, his blue eyes locked on hers. "I can trust you, yes?"

"Yes, sir," she echoed.

Then he walked out, and over the next weeks and months, Julia saw Donovan rarely. In fact, their conversations consisted of Julia parroting, "Yes, sir," or, "No, sir," most of the time. It seemed that each day, Julia was given more and more responsibility until she was personally overseeing eight people and indirectly supervising the office of forty people.

She thrived on the work. Not only did she handle sensitive information, which meant that she'd set up files on the information she received, then route the files to the right contact. She also hired people, oversaw financing and office purchases, and ensured office security. When a particular assignment came into her jurisdiction, she was told to investigate what could be done.

Since the OSS was entrenched in all main European cities and across Southeast Asia, by the end of 1942, reports were coming in at all hours from the various agents. It was no small task for Julia and her team to cross-reference and file the details on supply routes, arsenals, munitions storage, and industrial plants. Each word of each message had to be sorted and filed, then routed to the correlating office for further identification. One never knew when the smallest detail might be what led to a battle triumph or a life saved. The reports came through encoded cable messages or dusty pouches containing even dustier reports. Julia spent hours identifying code names, flagging critical words or phrases, analyzing photographs, searching for contacts, and labeling charts and maps.

In one instance, an assignment had her investigating the number of merchant vessels that were being sunk before reaching Europe. The supplies had been lost before they could be used. And now those supplies needed to be replaced.

"Julia," Alice said, coming into her office. "Your appointment is here. And he's handsome." She waggled her eyebrows and hurried out of the office.

JULIA

Curious but not interested in any handsome men at the moment, Julia headed down the hallway to meet Lieutenant Commander Earle F. Hiscock, who was part of the Coast Guard Reserve, in the supply room. Julia had wanted to meet him where she'd have more visual aids. She wasn't prepared to see such a short man inside the supply room. She supposed he was handsome to someone as petite as Alice.

Thinking fast, Julia snatched a wastepaper basket, turned it upside down, and sat on it. This brought her eye level with Lt. Cmdr. Hiscock.

After he left, Alice teased Julia. "I'm certain he'll never forget meeting you, Julia. I mean, he even asked for my number."

"That has nothing to do with *me*."

Alice only grinned. "Well, I think I'm in love, but that's beside the point. Want to catch dinner tonight?"

"That would be swell. I'm thinking of cooking tonight," Julia said. "Do you like chicken?"

"Can you cook in that single room of yours?"

"All I need is one burner, and I have two."

Julia might not be a noteworthy cook, but there was something to be said about having friends over for dinner and drinks, then lingering for hours' long excellent conversation. Yes, she could whip out a meal with only two burners, but the surrounding wallpaper would never quite be the same. Especially after her fabled fried chicken.

"What can I bring, then?" Alice asked.

"Something sweet for dessert. Just ignore the chicken fat splotches on the wall," Julia informed her. "I'll get that scrubbed off later."

That evening, when Alice arrived, she scanned the place and set down the fruit pie she'd brought to share. "You've fixed up the room."

Julia had invited Alice over a few times, along with other friends. She'd bought hothouse flowers on her way home, and flowers always made any room look brighter.

"I wasn't sure if I should come over tonight," Alice said, settling into a chair when it was apparent that Julia had the cooking mostly under control. "Earle might call when I'm not home."

"Earle, is it?" Julia teased. "First names already?"

Alice's cheeks pinked. "Not exactly, but I like to think of him as Earle rather than the stuffy sounding Lt. Cmdr. Hiscock."

Julia smirked. "So, I guess we'll be talking about him all night?"

Alice leaned forward, a gleam in her eyes. "Do you mind? I did some research on him—it was too tempting not to—and he's a fine man. Straight shooter."

Julia began to portion out the chicken, then gave a final stir of the potatoes she had boiling on the second burner as she listened to Alice rattle on about her crush. Julia wondered if it would happen for her like that. An instant attraction. An instant devotion. Of course, Alice had a long ways to go before anything could be concrete.

Over the next few weeks, it seemed that Lt Cmdr. Earle Hiscock did return Alice's interest, and they quickly became an item.

Julia was happy for her friend, and she was even happier with her job. Julia loved listening to the chatter in the Research and Analysis Department. Nothing was ever casually discussed, but theories were peeled apart, layer by layer. Half the time, she felt like her brain was only catching on to about half of the debates over variables, but she loved the intellectual stimulation. Such a far cry from her Smith days and anything she'd ever had at home. She didn't even mind reporting in six days a week.

By early 1943, OSS agents were stationed in all major European cities as well as throughout Southeast Asia. Each day, Julia dealt with the incoming reports from various agents, sorting, prioritizing, and rerouting the information to the applicable department. She never knew what to expect when opening a dirt-stained pouch or envelope that looked like it had been stepped on multiple times. Even if Julia couldn't always decipher the messages, she knew they were important and had to be handled with the utmost secrecy.

One morning, Donovan appeared in her office doorway. "Good morning, Julia." His words were clipped. "You're being promoted to senior clerk and will oversee my administrative support staff."

Julia's mind whirled, but all she said was, "Yes, sir."

"Oh, and a new department has been created—the Emergency Rescue Equipment Section. We're working against the clock on this one. We need to prepare pilots with emergency resources in case they are shot down."

"Such as rafts and flares?" Julia asked. She read about some of this in various reports. Planes were equipped with emergency transmitters, wet suits, flares, and flotation rafts.

"We need to think beyond that," Donovan said. "How will a pilot survive if he's stranded in a jungle or on a beach? What food can he resource?"

Julia had no answers, but that was why an entire department was devoted to its research. She learned later that Harold Coolidge and Henry Steel had started the department. And they were dedicated in their research. In fact, she and Alice were sent to the fish market to buy fish one day. Apparently, the researchers wanted to see if it was possible for a soldier lost at sea or a downed pilot to squeeze the liquid from a fish into his mouth and survive that way. Julia was game to buy the fish, but their other research projects of creating rescue kits, developing exposure suits, and inventing shark repellent were probably more worthwhile.

She and Alice carpooled to the fish market, and Alice filled her in on all the gossip. "You know that people outside the OSS are calling us Oh So Social or Oh So Secret, or even Oh Such Snobs?"

"Because there are so many Ivy Leaguers, professors, and academics?"

Alice grinned. "That's it. Also, we do have great parties and dinners."

It was true, and Julia's evenings were always filled with get-togethers if she wanted an evening out.

"But that's not all . . . We have some big names criticizing Donovan."

Now Julia was truly interested. "Like whom?"

"Well, J. Edgar Hoover and Charles Lindbergh. Lindbergh says we're full of politics, ballyhoo, and controversy."

"Hmm." Julia shrugged. She'd read some criticisms in the paper, so this didn't feel like shocking information. "What else?"

"Herr Goebbels said we're a staff of Jewish scribblers."

Julia winced. "Well, I'm not Jewish, and neither are you."

"I think after the war that everyone will realize how many brilliant advancements we're making."

"It's hard to reveal our 'oh so secrets' when we still have a war to win."

CHAPTER 5

Washington, DC
June 1943–February 1944

"We worked from nine in the morning often until eleven at night, sometimes for fourteen consecutive days before we had duty lay-offs. I was just twenty-three at the time. New York was very exciting during those war years. Emigrés were pouring in from Europe, and Mr. Dulles was developing a staff of experts on foreign affairs who interviewed refugees, built up data banks on personalities, industry, and political developments."

—ELINORE GRECEY WEIS, OSS STAFF, NEW YORK CITY

Purchasing fish wasn't a one-time affair, and by the summer of 1943, Julia had been transferred out of Donovan's office and into the Information Exchange of the Emergency Rescue Equipment Office. After one of her fish-buying excursions, she headed to the naval yard to pick up some graphics for the department. She stopped in at the office, her paper bag of fish in her hand, to find another OSS man already there. She recognized him by sight but hadn't officially met him.

"Oh, they sent you, too, Ms. McWilliams?"

"They did." She gave the friendly-faced man a smile. "You are?"

"Oh, sorry about that. I'm Jack Moore." He stuck out his hand, and she shifted the fish sack, then shook his hand.

"Are those . . . fish?"

"They are." Julia knew it was impossible to disguise the smell coming from the sack.

"For your lunch?" he asked.

Julia wriggled the sack. "Not quite. They're for the fish-squeezing unit." When Jack's dark brows tugged together, creating a deep line of confusion, she elaborated. "The ERES. You know, their experiments get quite out of hand sometimes."

A laugh boomed from Jack, and Julia decided she liked his easygoing manner.

"You'll find me boring compared to those in the ERES. I'm a map developer for the Presentation Division," he said.

Julia knew his division operated under Research and Analysis and reported to the State Department. After collecting what they'd both come for, Jack ended up walking Julia back to the office. She didn't mind in the least. The man was entertaining to talk to.

"I know my job is cushy, and I should be grateful for it," Jack said as they waited to cross a street. "I don't like the idea of twiddling away in DC while friends are overseas, putting their lives in danger every moment of the day."

"Surely you're too old to be a soldier," Julia quipped.

He chuckled. "I am, but not too old to serve the OSS in areas where I can make more of an impact."

"Where would that be?" she asked, truly curious as they crossed the street together.

"Well, my boss, Paul Child, has relocated to India, where he's setting up a War Room that will serve the Supreme Allied Commander, Lord Mountbatten."

"Ah." Julia had read about the British commander Mountbatten who headed up the Southeast Asia Command, but she hadn't heard of Paul Child.

"We call our boss Dr. Paulski as a nickname," Jack said as they navigated the E Street complex in the early summer heat that had burned off the remaining wisps of the morning fog. "He doesn't have any college degrees, but he's probably the most well-read man I know. We go way back, and Paul assures me that working in India is enough removed from any war action that it's perfectly safe, so I feel like I can be more productive over there."

"Besides, it's India."

JULIA

Jack met her gaze, brightness in his eyes. "Exactly. It's India. An exotic adventure, if nothing else."

They paused before entering the OSS building.

"I understand your perspective," Julia said. "I feel like I'm treading water most of the time while my brother, John, is stationed in France. I've not heard from him in a long time."

Jack's expression turned grave. German-occupied France wasn't on the top of anyone's list to serve or live, unless perhaps a person served in a medical unit. "I'm sorry. I hope he's all right." Which meant in translation—*I hope he's alive.*

"Thank you. I hope so too. I'll do almost anything to make the time pass and end this war as soon as possible."

"You should apply for India," Jack said, his gaze carefully searching hers. "I don't think you're one to shy away from a post abroad. Other women are heading over, like Betty MacDonald. Her husband is a journalist and is already stationed in Kandy, Ceylon."

Julia had met Betty a time or two. The thought of serving overseas hadn't entered Julia's mind in a way to actually be reality. Sure, she knew the OSS operation had expanded into India and China, but she'd never traveled anywhere outside of the United States, save for one trip to Tijuana.

Over the next few months, she put serious thought into Jack Moore's suggestion. She also received another promotion—to be the administrative assistant in the registry of the OSS, which put her back in Donovan's sphere. More often than not, Donovan wore an army uniform now. Julia appreciated the promotion since it had also come with a $600 raise, but she couldn't help feeling like she was treading water, so to speak, as she watched colleagues head overseas and become more directly involved in the war effort. Jack Moore had already left, and after discussing the idea with Dort, who wasn't too thrilled about an international assignment for Julia, she applied to work in India.

When her acceptance came, Julia was thrilled. She'd be going on a real adventure, and ironically, now that she'd been accepted, she'd operate under the WAC—the organization that had once rejected her for being too tall.

Her orders came with a departure date of February 26, 1944, leaving from Newport News, Virginia, by troop train. She'd been given a long list of vaccinations to get, including yellow fever, smallpox, cholera, diphtheria, and typhoid. She'd also have to take quinine pills weekly once they reached India.

"You're going to be surrounded by soldiers, you know," Alice told her as they sat across from each other in Julia's new office, both of them sipping tea. Alice had recently married her sweetheart, who was none other than Lieutenant Commander Earle Hiscock.

"Surrounded by nineteen- and twenty-year-olds." Julia grimaced, lifting her cup of tea and letting the warm fragrance wash over her. "You know I'm thirty-one, practically ancient."

"You're still youthful," Alice said. "And beautiful. Energetic. And have a million friends. What's not to love? A younger man might do it for you."

Julia had to laugh. "All right, my romantic friend. I'll be sure to keep you posted on all my love interests."

"I'll be counting on it." Alice sighed. "It's all going to be so fantastic and romantic. Just you wait."

Julia was certainly excited, but she also knew that she'd be working like a dog and trying to figure out an entirely different life.

It turned out that she wasn't the only woman on the troop train, thank goodness. Two other civilian women, Eleanor Thiry and Dr. Cora DuBois, had been assigned the same travel plans.

When Julia arrived at the train station, she wrinkled her nose at the familiar scent of steam and oil smoke. The station was indeed filled with young men in uniform, standing about, their conversations and laughter blending into a noisy din. She was surprised to see the dark, curly-haired Eleanor ignoring everything going on around her while she sat on a bench, scribbling in a diary.

"Are we allowed to bring a diary, Eleanor?" Julia lit a cigarette and settled on the bench. She'd been instructed not to keep a diary because it could be stolen and fall into enemy hands, with the potential of revealing confidential details.

JULIA

Eleanor lifted her chin. "I keep it with me always, so if something happens to me, my diary will go with me. And call me Ellie. Only my mother calls me Eleanor."

"Will do." Julia glanced over at Cora DuBois, who stood a few paces away and didn't seem to care that one of their own was already breaking the rules. Cora was a thin, pretty woman who wore glasses. They'd all been told to keep their OSS status a secret and only say they were file clerks if anyone questioned them.

"Come on, ladies," Cora said in a brisk tone. "Time to face the wolves."

Wolves was perhaps an understatement. When the women climbed on board and made their way along the narrow aisles and corridors to their train compartment that would be home for the next week, they encountered plenty of men asking questions, more than one whistle, and a few catcalls. The men who seemed more respectful hushed up most of the others.

"We'll be sticking together, right?" Ellie asked, linking her arm through Julia's and holding tight.

"Of course." Julia didn't feel threatened by these young men, but Ellie was closer to their age. Cora didn't give any of them the time of day, except for a polite thank-you to the couple of soldiers who'd carried their baggage.

For the next several days, Ellie stayed glued to Julia's side for every meal and appearance outside of their compartment. Cora didn't seem affected and came and went as she pleased. Julia had learned that Cora was an anthropologist, educated at Columbia University and University of California, specializing in Southeast Asian affairs.

Ellie loved to sing, and often, Julia would wake up to Ellie humming softly.

"There are sure a lot of good-looking men out there," Ellie said one afternoon, her arm resting over her eyes as she lounged on one of the narrow cots in their compartment, "but there are so many of them."

Julia paused in writing a letter to her father. "More handsome men than we can shake a stick at."

Cora laughed from where she was also writing a letter.

Ellie peeked out from under her arm. "I suppose, but I'll certainly be glad when we're off this train." She moved to prop up on an elbow. "You'll have to show us around in California when we get there."

"Sure thing," Julia said. "We'll use up all our free time sightseeing. We can even visit my home in Pasadena if we have time."

Julia didn't mind trains all that much, but she'd never been so grateful to get off one as when they pulled into their final stop. After the huge task of sorting luggage and organizing into groups, they were trucked to the barracks they'd been assigned.

It felt strange to be back in her home state but not in her neighborhood. She called Dort and her father on the first night in the barracks to report.

"Have you changed your mind yet, Julia?" Dort asked.

"Far from it," Julia said, sitting at a small table in the office where they'd been given permission to use the phone. "I wouldn't call the train ride ideal, but it's one week closer to my final destination." She noticed her father's silence—so dense it could be cut with a knife—because she was pretty sure he still didn't approve of her new assignment. But that argument had long been hashed out. This was the first time in her life that she'd made a choice by herself and for herself and not for someone else.

"Can you come home to see us?" Dort continued.

"I'm planning on it," Julia said. A soldier appeared in the doorway. Seeing that she was on the phone, he nodded, then stepped into the hall, likely waiting for his turn.

"We have a couple of days' leave coming up," Julia continued. "We're in the middle of lectures." It was all she felt she could share with her sister. Julia didn't mention how they'd been practicing how to use gas masks and evacuate ships by climbing down ropes over the side.

"Sounds quite dull," Dort teased.

"Oh, lectures are always a hoot," Julia said.

"Well, come on home when you can," Dort said. "It will be a nice change from the revolving door of widows visiting Pop around here. He's the prime catch of Pasadena."

Her father scoffed. "I can't very well be rude."

JULIA

Julia smiled, even though no one could see it. "That's worth coming home for. Fill the ice box with food. The army rations are lacking."

A couple of days later, Julia and her new friends were able to take two days of leave while the converted cruise ship underwent final preparations to become a troop transport. They arrived at her father's home in Pasadena, and Dort was delighted to see everyone. They spent the next two days telling stories, eating everything they could, and laughing late into the night.

The time came all too soon, and on March 8, they reported to Wilmington to board the SS *Mariposa*, wearing their army fatigues. Julia brought along a gremlin good-luck charm in her pocket, which Dort had given her. Julia named it Chester. They climbed out of the bus that had brought them, then shouldered their canvas military packs containing a bedroll, a pith helmet, a gas mask, and a canteen. It seemed like half the city had turned out to give them a rousing send-off. A band played cheerful music, and soldiers and sailors turned to see Julia and her friends approaching the dock among whistles and wolf calls.

"Thank the stars, there are more women," Ellie said, beads of perspiration standing out on her forehead from the weight of the canvas pack.

A group of six women wearing fatigues stood together on one side of the dock. One of them waved, and Julia said, "Looks like we're supposed to meet them."

They all made quick introductions, and Julia tried to commit their names to memory—Virginia Durand, Rosamond Frame, Virginia Pryor, Louise Banville, Mary Nelson Lee, and Jeanne Taylor. Three of them stuck out: Virginia Durand, Rosamond Frame, and Mary Nelson Lee.

"Since we have only nine women compared to three thousand men," Julia began, "maybe we should spread the word that we're traveling missionaries."

Cora smirked. "I'm game if everyone else is."

Ellie touched the curls that peeked out from beneath her beret hat. "That would be wonderful." Her gaze shifted. "Oh, look, it's the captain of the ship."

Sure enough, a man in a decorated navy uniform approached and shook hands all around. Then he stood, hands folded behind his back, and surveyed the small group of women. "Your group will be in cabin 237. The fit will be tight, but we've accommodated with three triple-decker bunks."

Julia felt like laughing until she realized the captain was completely serious. The other women were quiet—probably too stunned to speak.

A couple of sailors approached, their uniforms pressed and speck-free.

The captain introduced the sailors, who were to escort them to their cabin. Julia was grateful for the escort because the sailors had no problem clearing the way for them to make it below decks.

When they entered the cabin, Julia drew in a breath as she gazed about. There were indeed three triple bunks in a room that should fit only two cots. One corner was a bathroom of sorts, containing one tub, where they'd have only salt water to bathe in, one sink, and one toilet. Life jackets hung on a row of hooks near the cabin door. A couple of bureaus stood against the far wall, and Julia calculated that they'd each get one drawer to themselves.

"How long is this voyage?" Rosamond Frame asked. She was a petite, dark-haired woman.

Cora tossed her canvas bag onto a lower bunk. "Thirty days, girls. Time to settle in."

Julia set her stuff on another of the lower bunks. She figured her age gave her some perks.

Ellie crossed to the single porthole that looked out to the sea beyond. "I hope I don't get seasick."

"Well, if you do, I'm sure there will be plenty of others who will commiserate," Rosamond said. "I don't imagine many of us have been to India?"

"I've heard stories." Virginia fluffed out her hair in front of the lone mirror. "By the way, call me Peachy. Virginia is such a stuffy name. Anyone else have nicknames?"

"I'm Ellie," Ellie said. "I won't answer to Eleanor."

Everyone laughed.

JULIA

"I prefer Rosie," Rosamond said. She'd already taken out her compact and was touching up her lipstick.

Julia sat on the edge of her bed to give the others more room to move about and start unpacking. She could wait a little while. The women unpacked and debated on where to place certain items. Julia supposed they'd all be close friends by the end of thirty days. She'd lived with roommates before, both at Katharine Branson School and Smith College, but this would be a bit more intense than that.

"If anyone wants to get a head start in learning Chinese, I'm offering lessons," Rosie said. "I speak Mandarin, Cantonese, and French."

That caught Julia's attention. She'd taken years of French in high school and college but hadn't excelled past the awkward phrasing stage. "I'd love to learn some Chinese."

"Me too," Mary Nelson said.

Rosie flashed them a smile. "Excellent. You'll both have a spot in the class."

With a good deal of fanfare, the ship embarked, Julia standing at the railing with the other women, the brisk wind tugging at their clothing. They waved to those on shore, and Julia's heart felt a little pinch. Not that she expected anyone from her family to be there to see her off but that she was leaving her beloved country—for who knew how long. She could only imagine what was going through the sailors' and soldiers' minds.

So many fresh faces surrounded her, boys ten years or younger than herself. It wasn't hard to pick out those destined for OSS jobs—they were the older men.

"Is this spot taken?" a male voice asked, primly accented.

She turned to look over at the man who'd joined her at the rail and found she had to look *up*—a rare thing indeed. The man was probably six foot five and was as skinny as a beanpole.

"Gregory Bateson," he said, extending his hand, his accent definitely British.

She guessed him to be OSS.

"I'm Julia McWilliams, file clerk."

That earned a laugh from the man. They both knew what that meant. "Where you from, Miss McWilliams?"

"Why, just down the road in Pasadena, although I've been in DC for the past year working."

Mr. Bateson nodded. "Ever been to India?"

"No. What about you, Mr. Bateson?"

"Call me Gregory. We'll be chums soon enough." He leaned on the rail and lit a cigarette, looking toward the fading stretch of California coastline. "My wife, Margaret, and I have been to India a few times, as well as New Guinea and Bali. She speaks Malay, so that came in handy. She's home in England with our daughter, Mary, who's four years old."

Julia was impressed. "What took you on all your travels?"

Gregory glanced over at her, the wind tugging at his hair. "I'm an anthropologist, and we were studying the effects of outsiders on the islander culture and people."

"Interesting," Julia said, and it was. Cora was the first anthropologist she'd been around, and at the moment, Julia was feeling a bit undereducated. "Do you speak Malay or any foreign languages?"

"You mean besides proper English?"

She laughed.

"Not well, although I hope to change that with this trip."

Julia brightened at this. "My roommate Rosie Frame is teaching Chinese. You should join us."

Gregory straightened from the railing and turned toward her. "I think I will. Thanks for the invitation, Julia."

Pleased that she'd contributed something, at least, happiness bubbled up inside her.

CHAPTER 6

Pacific Ocean
March 1944

"In one day I would be asked to identify bombing targets in Southeast Asia; produce a plan to weaken the Japanese economy on the home front; assess political changes the Japanese occupation army had made in Indonesia! More often, we spent days poring through masses of material, to find one clue that would tell us, for example, that the enemy's war machine was short of tungsten, vital to armament production."

—PATRICIA BARNETT, OSS STAFF, SOUTHEAST ASIA

"Our voyage is haphazard on purpose," Gregory Bateson informed the gathering of men and women who were eager students in Rosie's Chinese language class. They'd picked an open spot on deck, which was sometimes distracting with all the activity. Chinese was coming along mind-numbingly slow, at least compared to Gregory and the others.

"Japanese submarines have sunk nine troop transports," Gregory continued.

The news shouldn't have been surprising to Julia, but it was—mostly because she was literally on a troop transport—despite its previous status as a cruise ship. Her ship comrades discussed this at length, and Julia marveled at how she'd become part of this intellectual, academic group. She'd been intrigued by all their discussions, especially Gregory's discussions on the relationships and connections between societies, national character, and genetics.

She'd discovered that Gregory worked for the OSS division of Morale Operations and was tasked with developing psychological warfare, something the British had been doing for years. It all sounded fascinating to Julia.

To pass the time on the voyage, Julia had joined the newspaper staff, which earned her a place at the center of all the gossip and otherwise inside information on how some of the sailors really felt about the war. Julia did her part and wrote up sketches of the women for the newspaper, which fostered an abundance of comments and attention—for better or for worse. The one woman who didn't mind attention was Rosie. In fact, Gregory had called her a little minx behind her back, and Julia could see why. Rosie flirted with every man she came across—which was a lot. If Rosie were a flower, she'd be a rose, and Julia would be a dandelion.

"I'm always up for an adventure," Rosie chimed in. "Did I ever tell you the time that my parents gave me two thousand dollars and told me to make my own way to Switzerland, where I attended school?"

Julia had heard the story before, but she didn't mind a repeat. Rosie had been raised mostly in China, where her father worked as a Christian college dean. Julia found Rosie's personality charming. All the men did, too—married or not, most seemed to be a little in love with her.

"After Switzerland, I attended school at Heidelberg University, followed by the University of Chicago."

"So now you speak English?" Gregory quipped, and everyone laughed.

Rosie only smiled her endearing smile.

"We'll be docking in Australia tomorrow," Gregory told their group, "if anyone needs a change of scenery from the endless blue ocean."

Rosie heaved a happy sigh. "Finally, we can wash our clothing with fresh water. No more dipping things into sea water collected in our helmets."

Gregory chuckled, and the conversation veered to what they might do for their brief stop in Australia.

The following day turned out to be a glorious event indeed. Julia followed her friends off the ship, her legs making her feel like she was a toddler learning to walk. Not only was Julia fascinated by her brief visit to Australia, but their cabin was also strewn with newly washed clothing. No one even minded the drying lines. The next items they'd be dressing in would be fresh smelling.

JULIA

Visiting Australia reignited her excitement for touching land again—even if she'd heard plenty of stories about the rough living conditions of Calcutta. They had to be better than sharing a single room with eight other women. Still, she'd miss the long days filled with endless sunshine, the rising and falling of the seas that sparked her imagination, and the intellectual circles she joined, comprised of the brightest minds she'd ever encountered. Where else would she be able to learn from scholars, photographers, economists, cartographers, historians, and anthropologists all in the same day?

And no matter the inconveniences of living on a ship, the gorgeous sunsets that lasted for what seemed like hours, and the night sky filled with millions of stars took her breath away time after time. She knew deep down that she'd embarked on the greatest adventure of her life, and she was ready for it.

A few days before they reached the India coast, a military escort came to lead the ship in. That knowledge only upped the anxiety among most of the women, but Julia figured that if they'd all survived this far, surely they'd make it all the way to Calcutta.

Cora came into their cabin as everyone was preparing to turn in for the night. "The ship's being redirected."

"What's happened?" Ellie asked.

Julia swung her legs over her bed and sat up.

"New orders are sending us to Bombay," Cora said. "That's all I know."

"Bombay?" Julia echoed, trying to remember all that she'd heard about Bombay from their shipmates.

The next couple of days were filled with discussions and theories about the redirect to Bombay. All anyone knew was that they'd sit tight in Bombay until the orders came in, then they'd be located to their new assignments. Finally, after thirty-one days at sea, the ship neared their destination. Julia was nursing a bad cold, but she resolutely stood between Peachy and Gregory at the railing, with practically everyone else on the ship, as they watched the nearing shoreline.

"What is that hovering over the shoreline?" Julia asked.

"Haze," Gregory said. "Can you smell it, or are you too stuffed up?"

Julia grimaced. "Is that what I smell? I thought someone was smoking behind us."

"It's a combination of India's blowing dirt, their leafy cigarettes, and their endless burning of incense."

"It's awful," Peachy commented.

Julia wouldn't go that far. Perhaps she was too fascinated, but her eyes began to water the closer they grew to the shoreline. "What have I gotten myself into?" she murmured as she wrapped her fingers around her good-luck charm, Chester.

"Amen," Peachy said.

When it was finally time to disembark, Julia's legs felt like gelatin again. Whether from being on a ship for so long or being unsure of where exactly to step among the chaos of the docks, she couldn't tell. It seemed that thousands of people had crammed themselves into the space of the harbor. Merchants, cart drivers, sailors . . . Was the entire city like this?

"Stay close, everyone," Cora commanded.

Gregory had valiantly volunteered to accompany the women to their new lodgings, along with a few other sailors, who carried the bulk of their luggage.

Julia became quickly engulfed in the chaos that didn't let up even as they traveled the streets. People were staring at them—perhaps they'd never seen a large group of white people. Or were they staring at *her*—a towering American woman?

New smells struck her first, despite her clogged sinuses—both sickly sweet, which Gregory said was opium, and foul smelling, making her wonder what sort of sewage system they had in place. The use of incense and its cloying scent to cover the more unpleasant smells seemed logical now. There was also dirt everywhere . . . dust in her eyes, her mouth, on her skin.

Julia couldn't look away from anything or anyone. Children ran around barefoot in dirt-stained clothing that may have never seen a speck of soap. A group of them swarmed her, staring at her—likely her red hair was something they'd rarely seen.

One of them spoke in English, "You desire to sit?"

JULIA

Gregory shooed them off.

Gharries moved passed them—small cabs drawn by horses, which weren't in any hurry to get anywhere. Men in white jackets, dark skirts, and squeaky shoes carried black umbrellas with crooked handles. Julia had so many questions, but the crowds made it a feat just to keep pace with the sailors and the luggage. They passed vendors with carts laden with colorful fruits and vegetables along with live chickens that eyed them with suspicion.

Julia supposed her group was a sight to behold, even for the Indian chickens.

"Here we are," Gregory announced as the sailors stopped in front of a small house. "Your home for the next week or two while everything gets sorted."

Julia could have hugged him, and she might have if she weren't carrying her canvas military bag and weren't about ready to melt into a puddle from the heat and humidity.

"I'll be around in a couple of hours, and we'll find some food and take in the sights."

At least the women had more than one room in the small house. Julia shared with Peachy, and they took turns washing and changing clothes.

Soon, they met Gregory in front of the house, along with Rosie, Ellie, and Mary. The other women had come up with a different agenda, which probably included napping. But Julia was too keyed up to sleep.

"You're an eager beaver," Gregory said.

"I look like a tourist, I'm sure," Julia quipped, patting the large bag she'd brought and the camera she'd hung about her neck. "I'm no photographer, but I'm not going to miss a thing. Oh, and don't tell anyone, but I've been keeping a diary. Nothing that reveals my country's secrets though."

Gregory laughed at this. He'd freshened up too. If possible, he was skinnier than when she'd first met him, and his trousers nearly hung off his tall frame.

"I've been a bad influence about keeping a diary, I see," Ellie said.

Julia linked arms with her friend. "I'm totally and completely blaming you."

They found a restaurant that smelled delicious, and although Julia wouldn't exactly call the place sanitary, she was too hungry to care.

One of their OSS friends met them—the cartographer Joseph R. Coolidge—along with his friend John Bolton-Carter, who was South African and had already been in Bombay for a while. The dinner party created a merry group.

Gregory cautioned them to eat in moderation though. "You don't want to get the Delhi Belly, especially if you have to share a toilet."

"You can't really avoid it," John said with a lopsided smile. "Everyone will succumb sooner or later."

Julia winced as she speared another piece of what looked like chicken in red curry sauce. They'd been served plates of rice with various meats and curries, and Gregory had pointed out the chicken, shrimp, and lamb—at least he'd assumed that was what they were eating. Then he'd insisted they doctor up their servings with condiments, such as paprika, chutneys, crumbled bacon, and crumbled fried bananas. All to make an interesting flavor.

"Thanks for the warning about our portions," Julia said, "but we have to acclimate, right?"

"Right." Gregory took a sip of his canned orange juice. He'd already recommended they drink only from cans or bottles. Never from a water tap.

"We've got John's car for whoever wants to go on the red-light district tour," Joseph said.

Julia's eyes about popped out.

"You mean you aren't brave enough to *walk* it?" Peachy teased.

"I don't think I could handle it," Ellie said with real concern. "I mean, it's terrible that those women are selling themselves because they feel like they have no choice."

Gregory nodded somberly. "I'll walk you back to your house. My wife will hear about it if I take any sort of tour."

"We're driving straight through," Joseph countered. "Not stopping."

JULIA

Julia didn't know what made her do it, but she said, "I'll come along." She was curious, if nothing else. She wanted to see everything she could about Bombay; who knew if she'd ever return.

So that was how Julia found herself with Mary, Peachy, Joseph, and John, driving through the red-light district. She couldn't exactly say she regretted the experience, but she knew she'd never return again. "I suppose every city has its seedy side."

"Bombay has more than its fair share," John commented. "Tell me about where you ladies are from and what your assignments will be."

They chatted, and by the time John dropped them off at the rented house, Julia had agreed to go golfing with him—curious to see where the golf course was within this bustling city.

Over the next eighteen days they spent in Bombay, Julia took advantage of every experience available. She quickly became used to the stifling heat, and the other women told her it was because she was so thin. She'd found everything enjoyable—eating new foods, golfing, shopping, dancing, and sightseeing.

Their stay had lasted longer than expected, which was fine with Julia, and they finally found out that it was because there was confusion over their US military division in Bombay. Apparently, the military hadn't been aware that some of the OSS agents were women. Rosie received her orders first. She was being sent to New Delhi instead of China, like she'd hoped. Julia's and some of the other ladies' orders came next. Apparently, Lord Mountbatten, who both oversaw the Southeast Asia Command and consulted for the OSS, was moving the OSS headquarters from New Delhi to Ceylon, which had become a vital Allied outpost since the fall of Singapore in 1942.

When Julia's orders arrived, she learned that she wasn't staying in India. She'd be reporting to Colombo, on the island colony of Ceylon, on April 25.

CHAPTER 7

Kandy, Ceylon
April 1944

"I find Kandy has a delightful climate, skin-warm all the time. Life is pastoral. Our office is a series of palm-thatched huts connected by cement walks, surrounded by native workmen and barbed wire. It is somewhat primitive, but airy and far from dressy."

—LETTER FROM JULIA TO HER FAMILY

If there was one thing to be said about a long, heat- and dust-filled train ride across India, it was the education that Julia received from a Sinhalese police officer on board who told her all about the one-hundred-fifty-year oppressive colonization that Ceylon had endured by the British. And the previous colonization of first the Portuguese, followed by the Dutch. He also educated her on the virtues of Buddhism.

Julia didn't even know if she could adequately capture all that she was experiencing in her letters back home, or in her clandestine diary, for that matter.

Peachy, Cora, and Mary moaned about the cruel heat, and they were all grateful when they boarded the ferry, enjoying the breeze as they traveled from Madras to the island of Ceylon. Its capital city of Colombo was very different from Bombay. Gone was the polluted haze and dusty streets and overcrowded buildings. They had been replaced by a tropical paradise. The heat was still sweltering, though, being so close to the equator, and she couldn't wait to swim somewhere—anywhere.

Gregory Bateson didn't seem too bothered by the heat, but he didn't seem bothered by much. Julia wondered what his wife was like—probably much the same if she spoke other languages and had traveled so much.

JULIA

S. Dillon Ripley, an OSS man, met them in Colombo, and Julia liked his open and frank manner immediately. He was a Yale and Harvard biologist and ornithologist, but he wasn't pretentious.

"Now, Celyon is not considered a hardship or dangerous post," Dillon said as he escorted them away from the harbor toward the waiting motorcars. "But mind you, your work here will be integral to the progress of the war. We have OSS posts in southern Burma, Malaysia, Siam, Sumatra, the Andaman Islands, and French Indochina. Our post on Ceylon has become the collector and distributor of intelligence on the enemy. Getting the right information regarding bomb targets, troop locations, and projected movements to the right people is essential."

His gaze fell on Julia. "Among the group of you, you probably have thousands of intelligence secrets in your heads right now. So while you'll be in a fairly protected and secure location, your letters home need to be completely free of any military information."

"Noted," Julia said.

A group of gnats swarmed them as they neared the cars. Julia batted them away, though most of them seemed interested in Dillon.

He grumbled as he shooed the gnats for a few seconds before climbing into the car. "I might be an expert on birds of the Far East, but I can't, for the life of me, understand how all these clouds of gnats seem to survive on the humid air alone."

Julia looked up at the blue, blue sky, marred by what looked like a moving cloud of hovering gnats. "Maybe they smell our perfume or ladies' cigarettes?"

"I'll have to add that to my notes," Dillon teased. "See if the gnats favor the ladies over the gentlemen."

"I don't think any of us even knows what perfume is anymore," Peachy said, fanning her face with a newspaper.

Their car pulled away from the harbor and onto the city streets crowded with carts, bicycles, trishaws, and tramcars attached to overhead powerlines. Julia's gaze was glued to the people and the carts and the animals.

"There's a cow on the sidewalk," Peachy said at the same time Julia saw a rust-colored cow with long horns.

It was the skinniest cow that Julia had ever seen. She could have counted its ribs. Up ahead, another cow wandered as well.

"Cows are sacred in Ceylon," Dillon said. "They go where they want and do what they want. We don't eat beef here."

"Like India?" Julia asked.

"Correct."

Her gaze stayed glued to the window as she watched the people—some of the men in sarongs, and many women wore brilliantly colored saris—again reminding her of India. The women walked behind their husbands—something that Julia had read about. Then she saw several Buddhist monks wearing orange robes, moving along the sidewalks with an air of serenity. She watched them stop near a beggar who seemed to be living on the sidewalk. Occasionally, she saw women with a red dot on their forehead, indicating their Tamil religion.

Dillon began to explain the different ethnic groups in Ceylon, which included Sinhalese, who were mainly Buddhist; the Tamils, who followed Hinduism; the Muslims; and the Burghers, who were a mixed race descended from Europeans.

"Oh, wow, is that a snake charmer?" Julia asked as they drove past a man crouched on the ground, a basket before him. A crowd had gathered, and he was playing a flute. A cobra's head poked above the basket.

"It certainly is," Dillon said. "Do you want me to pull over?"

"No," Peachy said immediately. "I think we can keep driving."

Dillon chuckled. "Cobras are revered in Hindu tradition. You don't have anything to worry about. Just make sure you check your shoes and under your bed each night."

Peachy shuddered, then she began to fan her face. "Is it always this hot?"

Dillon chuckled again. "Every day. And every night. You'll be hot unless you're swimming."

"Is there a swimming pool nearby?" Julia asked.

Dillon raised his brows. "Sure, the Indian Ocean."

Maybe he expected Julia to backtrack, but she said, "Sounds wonderful."

And she did swim in the ocean a few hours after they settled into their hotel. All the women joined her. The men lounged on the shoreline and chatted, drinking juice out of cans.

Peachy splashed around like a little kid. "I love this place already," she gushed. "And the gnats apparently don't like the ocean."

Julia smiled as she floated on her back, letting the undulations of the warm ocean water move her gently about. She could get used to this very quickly.

But their stay in Colombo was only one night, and the following morning at 8:00 a.m., they boarded an old-style train set for headquarters in Kandy.

"We Americans call this the Toonerville Trolley," Dillon said, overly cheerful this early in the morning, "but it's run by the British."

"So maybe we should call it the Mountbatten Special," Julia quipped.

"I'm not opposed to that."

They settled in their seats to take in the lush tropical vegetation outside the train window. The journey to Kandy was seventy-five miles from Colombo and was 1,600 feet above sea level, and every mile of it was gorgeous—like any imagined paradise a person could dream up.

"It's breathtaking," Cora said, glued to the window as much as Julia was.

And Julia wholeheartedly agreed as the train climbed the green hills and wove through jungles, around tea plantations, along palm tree groves, and across mountain streams. In the distance, Adam's Peak majestically rose. Julia had been told by her police-officer-train-ride friend that Adam's Peak was where Buddha had spent time.

"The headquarters in Kandy is newly established," Dillon informed the group. "Mountbatten has only been here since mid-April. He's staying in the King's Pavilion. It's like a miniature palace."

"At the top of these mountains?" Peachy asked.

"Yes, we're going to the tea plantation called Nandana, which is a colonial estate," Dillon continued. "You'll be housed at the Queens Hotel. Kandy used to be the stronghold of the ancient Sinhalese kings."

It was all very interesting, so Julia began to ask questions about the political strategy behind this location since she was sure the others were curious as well.

"I can't speak to the exact nature of your jobs, of course," Dillon said, "but the Allies needed a relatively safe stronghold for the intelligence headquarters. This supports SEAC's operations in Siam, or Thailand now—which holds the seat of our organized resistance—while the country is under Japanese occupation."

Julia had read enough reports to know that Japan had pressured Thailand into allowing them to pass through the country in order to invade the British colonies of Malaya and Burma. Then, on December 8, 1941, Japan had invaded Thailand. Now there was a military alliance treaty between the two nations. This allowed the Japanese military access, and in exchange, Japan had promised to help Thailand regain territories previously lost to France.

Once the Allies won the war—at least Julia could only assume so—the political state of the Southeast Asia countries would be in turmoil. It was like watching a materializing war brewing beneath an existing war.

The train slowed, bringing them into a station surrounded by exotic vegetation. Above the station rose a terraced rice paddy, and in the higher foothills, Buddhist temples stood out from the greenery.

"Look at the monkeys," Mary said with a laugh as they climbed off the train.

Julia looked toward the nearby banyan trees, and sure enough, monkeys scrabbled around in the branches. Some of them stopped to stare at them with comical dark eyes.

"Don't feed them—ever," Dillon warned. "They won't leave you alone if you do."

The air was different this high above sea level. No longer the stifling humidity of Colombo, it was the perfect warm temperature, and it was drier too.

When a couple of black limousines pulled up to the station, Julia was surprised that they were for them.

The group split up, and Gregory said he'd see them all later.

JULIA

"No expenses spared?" she asked Dillon when he led the women to one of the cars.

"You'll find that Kandy is like its own empire," he said. "You don't swoon over British accents, do you? Because if so, you'll be swooning all day here."

"I haven't swooned yet," Julia said, "so I'm sure I can stay on my feet."

The man who climbed out of the limousine was indeed British, indicated by his uniform.

"Now, don't let his charming accent fool you," Dillon murmured in an undertone. "While the British and Americans are collaborating on OSS operations, methods aren't always agreed upon."

The driver greeted them, then everyone piled into the limousine.

As they headed to the Queens Hotel, Dillon told them more about Kandy. "Kandy is the home of the Hinayana Buddhists," he said.

Outside her window, Julia caught glimpses of monks walking along the streets, heads shaved, wearing saffron yellow robes. As in Colombo, the women here wore saris, which looked very comfortable about now. Beggars seemed to be camping on the sidewalks—their permanent home. And there were more cows wandering about. And, oh, the elephants. Smaller elephants than what Julia had seen in American zoos, but here they were diligent beasts of burden. Julia watched as an elephant lumbered along one street, carrying bundles on its back.

"It's quite the sight to see the elephants bathing in the lake at the end of the day," Dillon said.

"Can we ride them?" Julia asked.

"Of course," Dillon said. "Offer a little money and you can ride all you want. Wait until you see the Kandy Esala Perahara festival, which takes place in July and August. We call it the Festival of the Tooth."

"What is that?"

"The processions happen several nights in a row to pay homage to the sacred tooth relic of Buddha. You'll see decorated elephants, fire dances, the peacock dance, cannonball firing, drummers, and music.

The festival's end is marked with a water cutting ceremony called *Diyakepeema*."

"Sounds interesting," Julia said. She should still be in Kandy to see it.

As the limousine stopped at the Queens Hotel, Dillon said, "A truck will be by in an hour to pick you all up and bring you to the plantation—where you'll be fed lunch and shown around the plantation."

Julia and the others thanked him, then Dillon offered a final warning, "Don't drink any water that hasn't been boiled yet. And that includes brushing your teeth."

Julia and the women climbed out, and once their luggage had been delivered to their rooms, Julia finally took in her surroundings. She and Peachy were roommates, and their beds were impressive—four-poster canopy beds draped with mosquito netting.

Julia parted the netting and sat on the edge of her bed as she watched Peachy unpack. Julia wasn't in any big hurry. She was just looking forward to a meal.

A knock sounded on the door, and Peachy answered it.

Ellie strode in. "Did you hear about the cockroaches? They're four inches long! I don't think I'll ever walk anywhere barefoot in this place."

Julia laughed, and at that moment, Peachy screeched.

Julia jumped off her bed. "What is it?"

Peachy backed away from the open drawer of the bureau in front of her. "There's a scorpion in there."

Julia moved close enough to see that, yes, indeed, there was a scorpion in the drawer. It was small, so maybe it was young—but that didn't mean it wasn't dangerous.

"I think we should head outside and wait for the truck to take us to the plantation," Julia said. "At least outside, the scorpions will stay hidden."

Slowly, the women moved out of the room, and Peachy reported the scorpion to the hotel clerk, who promised to take care of it.

JULIA

By the time a two-ton truck rumbled to a stop in front of the hotel, Gregory had joined them, and Peachy had finally calmed down enough that she was no longer perspiring.

"Always check your bed before climbing in each night," Gregory said.

"That's not helping, Bateson," Peachy said with a sniff.

He chuckled. "And your shoes." Peachy glared at him, but Gregory wasn't deterred. "The mosquitos are noiseless, so you won't be forewarned," he said. "There are also tarantulas; cockroaches; snakes, such as cobras; oh, and leeches—if you walk through the underbrush after it rains."

Peachy shuddered. "This should have been in our training."

"Would you have still come?" Gregory asked, sounding curious.

"I don't know, honestly." Peachy's tight tone had softened though. "I hope I never come across a scorpion again. I mean, I'm going to have to shake out all my clothing from now on."

"Give it some time," Gregory said with an easy smile. "The beauty of this place will soon outshine any pesky scorpion."

Dillon climbed out of the truck. "Are we waiting for something? Climb in."

"After you, girls," Gregory said.

Julia joined everyone inside the truck. The bumpy ride was less than ten minutes, thankfully, and they trundled past terraced rice paddies, flowering trees, and a pristine lake. Soon, they were escorted past a barbed-wire perimeter surrounding the tea plantation and toward a thatched-roof building at the top of a hill. Low lounge chairs lined the porch, and Julia imagined sitting in one and watching the sunset.

"This is the mess hall," Dillon said. "People will be arriving soon for lunch, so you'll be first in line." He pointed down the hill, where a spread of small thatched buildings were scattered among crisscrossing walkways. "The offices are down there, about three hundred yards. Office hours are over by 5:00 p.m., and then you'll still have two hours of sunlight to enjoy sports or whatever you prefer. We have tennis courts and a small golf course."

Julia perked up at that information. She'd fit right in.

They entered the mess hall to find a buffet table set up. Julia could have eaten almost anything at this moment.

Peachy was busy telling anyone who'd listen about the scorpion in her drawer when in walked a familiar face: Betty MacDonald, whom Julia knew from DC.

"Julia!" Betty cried out. They embraced, then Betty drew away, her eyes dancing. "Look at you. Fresh off the train?"

"Nearly," Julia said. "Do I look it?"

Betty was too polite to comment further; instead she said, "You'll adjust in no time. Now, tell me how you got assigned to Ceylon."

Julia sat with Betty at one of the tables after loading up a plate of food. She wasn't about to take polite portions. She was starving. Betty was a former journalist with Scripps-Howard, and she'd drawn notice from the OSS because she spoke fluent Japanese—after living with a Japanese family in Hawaii. So she'd been brought over from New Delhi to Ceylon to work with the Morale Operations Division.

"You're so tanned," Julia commented.

Betty grinned. "Tennis. You play, right? I'll take you on. Or maybe we can play doubles."

Julia grinned back. "It's a date."

A man sat across from them, and Betty introduced him as Colonel Richard P. Heppner, who oversaw the registry office where Julia had been assigned.

"What's your pedigree, Colonel Heppner?" Julia asked bluntly while keeping a smile on her face.

His eyes creased at the corners. "First of all, I go by Dick, and I suppose you mean, Where did I go to school?"

"I do."

"Princeton, then Columbia Law School," he said. "I'm an old associate of Donovan."

"Ah, I was a research assistant to Donovan."

JULIA

"I've already heard. You'll be working with me, Ms. McWilliams." Dick tilted his head. "You must meet the other officers. I'm sure they'll be more than happy to give you a rundown of their Ivy League credentials."

Julia laughed and decided that teasing broke across all academics.

Dick called over Lieutenant Colonel Paul Helliwell and another officer named Byron Martin, who Julia discovered was from Pasadena too. Then a man by the name of Fisher Howe stopped by their table. Julia had heard of him since he'd been an assistant to General Donovan—but mostly had worked in London.

"I heard you were sent overseas," Fisher said to Julia.

They chatted for a few minutes about what it had been like working directly for General Donovan, then Fisher headed out of the mess hall.

Over the next few days, Julia discovered her job was rather mundane. Sure, she had top security clearance at her registry job, but really, it meant running the files. Organizing. Cross-referencing. Updating master cards for Secret Intelligence on the names of the secret agents, their student recruits, and their assigned code names.

Julia's memory had always served her well, and she continued to add to her memory the identity of all the undercover agents and their locations in jungle hideouts, where they could report on troop locations and bombing targets. She reviewed and funneled through their next set of instructions, knowing that everything was timely, and if she failed, lives would be lost. She was, quite literally, a keeper of the secrets, which identified her as a senior civilian intelligence officer, but at the very core, she felt like a filing clerk.

But when Heppner walked into her office one afternoon, things took a turn. "We're sending men and equipment into Bangkok, where they can be our eyes and ears tuned to the Japanese troop movement."

"Do you need the locations of the jungle hideouts?" Julia asked. There was a significant resistance growing.

"That's exactly what I need," Heppner said. "The indigenous resistance is gaining ground, but they need more support."

"We'll get it to them," Julia said. "Give me about an hour, and I'll have the locations for you to encode."

"Perfect." Heppner strode out of the office.

It was afternoons like this that Julia felt the value of her work.

A few days later, Julia met Peachy in the mess hall. Lunch consisted of egg hoppers with a coconut sauce called *kiri hodi* and a spoonful of creamy *dhal*. They rarely went outside of the mess hall because they didn't have a lot of time for lunch, and they couldn't be sure if the meat on another restaurant's menu was actually cat—one thing Julia refused to try.

"I've found a way out of my daily tedium," Julia said.

Peachy raised a brow. "Oh? I'm intrigued."

Julia grinned.

Peachy leaned forward. "You're in a festive mood. Are you in love? I saw you dancing a lot at the American officers' club last night."

Julia laughed, a bit too loudly, and a few heads turned. Peachy was a like a kid sister—too pesky sometimes. Dancing at the officers' club was fun—the music ended at midnight, but many stayed on, singing beneath the bright moonlight, songs like "Lili Marlene," "I'll be Seeing You," and "Don't Sit Under the Apple Tree."

"Not exactly," Julia said in a lowered tone. "I've pulled some jokes on the bureaucrats."

Peachy's eyes widened. "Oh, do tell."

"Well . . ." Julia looked about the cafeteria to make sure no one was paying them any mind. "I've sent out a few memos. One of them states that we're implementing a new filing system that will be organized by the first letter of the last word of each document."

Peachy covered her mouth to stifle a laugh.

"I've yet to get that approved, of course. I also sent out a notice to a department in Washington, DC that is late in sending their report." She paused for dramatic effect. "I told them that if they're late again, I'd fill the next Washington pouch with itching powder and virulent bacteriological diseases, then change all the numbers as well as translate the material into Sinhalese. Followed up, naturally, with destroying the English version."

Peachy couldn't hold back her laughter this time. It burst out, and when she was able to speak again, she gasped. "You didn't. What will they think?"

Julia shrugged. "They'll get a good laugh, that's all, but I'd love to be a fly on the wall to watch their initial reaction."

Peachy was still grinning, her skin flushed from laughing so hard. "Or a cockroach on the wall."

Julia shuddered. She could handle almost any critter, within reason, but not cockroaches. She couldn't stand the thought of them.

"I feel like a trapped bug half the time," Peachy admitted. "Especially when I'm on night duty for cable traffic, either sending it to and from the Arakan, or the various OSS drops, and, of course, to Detachment 101."

"You're definitely underpaid," Julia quipped.

They both laughed.

"What's so funny over here?" a male voice interrupted.

Julia looked up to see Gregory and, next to him, Jack Moore—her friend from Washington, DC.

She leaped to her feet. "Jack! I didn't know you were transferred here."

He pulled her into a quick hug. "When I heard about a woman named Julia being among the new arrivals, I hoped it was the one and only Julia McWilliams."

"It will be so great to catch up with you," Julia said. "What's your assignment?"

"I'm still working under Paul Child in the War Room. I'll have to introduce you to him."

"We should all get together," Gregory said. "What do you say we all go on a picnic this weekend?" He eyed Peachy. "There's a clearing in the jungle that I've gone to quite a few times. It's safe—mostly."

She wrinkled her nose. "As long as you're planning on keeping the venomous creatures away, I'll come."

"I'll come too," Julia said. "I have some wacky stories to share."

CHAPTER 8

Kandy, Ceylon
May 1944

"I have a nice time with the office men—not Whee, but pleasant. There is Paul Child, an artist who, when I first saw him, I thought he was not at all nice looking. He is about 40, has light hair which is not on top, an unbecoming blond mustache and a long unbecoming nose. But he is very composed. I find him both pleasant, comfortable and very mentally get-at-able. We have dinner frequently and go to the movies."

—JULIA McWILLIAMS

Julia had to miss the picnic fun after all because she had a landslide of reports come in. Lately, she'd been putting in six-day work weeks, plus half-day Sundays. She'd even worked a few nights, constantly recording and filing.

Her boss, Heppner, was in and out of her office on a regular basis. She liked him, for the most part, and he listened to her concerns and suggestions.

"How are we coming on that report?" he said, appearing in the office doorway.

Julia straightened the five-by-eight file cards she'd been writing on. "Nearly finished."

Heppner came around her side of the desk to read her findings. "Those are the current bombing targets the Japanese army is going after in India?"

"With 90 percent accuracy," Julia said, which they both knew might as well be 100 percent. She'd spent hours cross-referencing and comparing messages coming in from intercepted Axis power intelligence that had been translated and decoded by the Communications Branch and sent to her office. She handed over the stack of file cards. "They're ready for the War Room."

"Thanks," Heppner said, grasping the file cards. "I'll be back to help with the Thailand industrial plants."

After Heppner left the office, Julia stood and stretched, taking a few moments to clear her head. She had only a few moments, though, because they had received reports only a couple of hours before about some industrial plants in Thailand that the OSS believed the Japanese military was using. Julia needed to comb through all her references to those industrial plants to determine the layouts of the buildings, their sizes and capacity, and what bomb damage had been done to those buildings. Were the buildings now being used to house an arsenal? Chemicals? Lumber? Rubber? Should these industrial plants be next on the target list?

The sheer cliff of all the tasks stacking on top of each other was mind-numbing, to say the least. She'd practically lived on rushed meals and endless cups of tea, but it had turned out that Ceylon had wonderful teas, and one of her new favorites was Cheericup Ceylon.

Despite the long work hours, she loved the social aspect of her Kandy colleagues—she found being around so many academics an exhilarating experience. The people here were adventurous, opinionated, competitive, witty, and sophisticated, and she took to calling them her "ologist friends" because there was every sort of expertise floating among them, from anthropologists to cryptologists. She enjoyed all the activities that happened at night: dancing a couple of times a week, swimming, tennis, and golf . . . She just needed more time to join in.

Her mood lifted when she received a packet of letters from her family later that day. Several letters from Dort and a couple from Pop. She read through them quickly, hungry for news from home. But her stomach coiled when she read that John had been seriously wounded by field artillery in France when he'd been on a bridge that had been blown up. Thankfully, the subsequent letter from Pop reported that John had been treated well at a field hospital, then sent back to the States, where his wife was now caring for him. Both Dort and Pop predicted he'd make a full recovery.

Her heart aching, Julia spent the next hour writing to her brother and his wife, giving them all her love and best wishes. The only bright side to all this was that John was now out of harm's way.

Throughout the month of May, Julia frequently joined a group of friends on the veranda of the main headquarters building, languishing in the shaded humidity and sharing tea before everyone went their separate ways for the evening. Often, Julia headed back to her office and stacks of paperwork. She enjoyed the temporary break and the good company.

Jack, Gregory, Peachy, and Ellie made up the usual crowd, and sometimes more joined.

"Oh, here comes Paul now," Jack said, glancing past Julia. "He finally broke away from the War Room before dark. He's always double-checking everyone's work."

Julia couldn't help but look over to where a man walked toward them. Jack had mentioned Paul so many times, yet she'd never actually met him, so she wondered if he were a phantom creation.

This man was blond, the setting sun glinting off his receding hairline. He had a camera strapped across his shoulder, and Julia guessed him to be about forty years old. He wasn't particularly striking or handsome, with his blond mustache and rather long nose. Yet Julia was intrigued because of how he carried himself, walking with assurance and a sort of elegance that was hard to describe.

"I thought you were going to pull an all-nighter," Jack said as the man neared.

"I'm getting too old for that," Paul said in a smooth baritone as he arrived at their table and set down his camera. "What are we drinking tonight?" He nodded to Gregory, then glanced at Peachy and Ellie.

When his gaze settled on Julia, she introduced herself. "I'm Julia—the one who knows everyone's secrets around here."

Paul's brows lifted slightly, as if he couldn't decide whether she was being serious or not.

JULIA

"She hasn't stooped to letter reading just yet," Jack chimed in. "So your love correspondence is safe for another day."

Paul settled himself in the empty chair next to Jack, and again, Julia wondered how he sat so precisely. He was shorter than she was, that she could tell without standing. But sitting, there was no height discrepancy.

"Unless you count my letters to my brother, Charlie, as love letters," Paul said, "I'd say Julia will be sorely disappointed."

He'd spoken so matter-of-factly that she wasn't sure if he was teasing her.

"Charlie's your twin, right?" Gregory asked, lighting his second cigarette.

"Right," Paul said. "He's an artist, too, though he went through a lot of formal training." He lit a cigarette for himself too. "Unlike me, who dug it out of the dirt."

"Plus," Jack said, "you have to do double the work in art and photography since you only have one working eye."

Julia frowned. Both of Paul's eyes looked the same if she were to compare them. "What's wrong with your eye?" she blurted out before she could determine if the question was too personal. But Jack had brought it up.

Paul tapped his left temple. "My left eye only has partial sight from an accident as a child. Charlie was holding a needle when we were horsing around, and I stumbled into him."

Ellie gasped, and Julia winced. Peachy went nearly white.

Paul flicked a hand. "Our father died when we were only six months old, so we ran our mother ragged. We were always getting into scrapes. Two brothers tied at the hip but fighting like wolves all the same."

Jack's smile was still in place. "You wouldn't know by Paul's sophisticated demeanor that he's a black belt in jujitsu."

Another surprising revelation. "That's impressive," Julia said. "Although I must admit that I have no idea what jujitsu is."

Everyone laughed, and even Paul smiled—if only politely.

Had Julia put her big foot in her mouth?

"Give us a demonstration, Paul," Gregory urged.

"I have my best trousers on," Paul deadpanned, but his clear gaze moved to Julia. "If you were hoping for a demonstration out here on the veranda, you're out of luck. If you're familiar with martial arts, jujitsu uses few or no weapons. We focus on holds, throws, and calculated blows."

Paul Child certainly looked like a man who took his physical fitness seriously. She'd have never guessed it was through martial arts though.

The next hour passed lazily and companionably, with Jack and Gregory pulling out a few stories from Paul and that man becoming more and more fascinating by the moment. He was definitely a sophisticate—something Julia would never be. And he spoke French and Italian, a talent that had always fascinated Julia.

"You lived in France?" she asked when the conversation turned. "So you're fluent in French?"

"*Oui, mademoiselle.*"

His accent even sounded authentic, not that she was any expert. "I took years of French in school, but I never got the hang of it."

"Where did you go to school?"

"Smith College."

"Ah, it's difficult to become proficient in a language when you're not surrounded by it."

Julia completely agreed. That must be why she had such poor grades on her pronunciation. "How long were you in France?"

"Let's see . . ." He took a drink from his glass. "Five years. I began living there in 1925."

"Ah, that sounds amazing. Before coming here, I'd only been to Tijuana," she said. "I'm rather boring compared to those around this table . . . well, pretty much everyone here. Just a homegrown Pasadena girl who's been back east a few times."

Paul tapped his fingers on his armrest, studying her as if he had a microscope. "You've been across the Pacific, and now you're working for the OSS in Ceylon. I don't think that's boring."

Paul Child certainly had a way with words—his vocabulary seemed as large as the ocean—and something told her he didn't dole out compliments freely. She couldn't decide, though, if that made her feel intimidated or inspired. Maybe she could ask him for recommendations of subjects to study or books to read. She was suddenly fiercely envious of her group of friends and their easy shifts through such a broad range of topics and their seamless switches into other languages. Even her month of learning Chinese had only cemented a few dozen words and phrases in her brain.

"You're not boring, Julia," Peachy added. "What you might lack in language skills, you make up for in enthusiasm. You should have seen her in Rosie's Chinese class on the ship."

Paul's brows shot up. "Rosie Frame?"

Julia held back a groan. Of course Paul would know Rosie Frame—every man did. Were all men instantly besotted by a beautiful woman?

"Do you know her?" Peachy asked. "Don't tell me, you fell in love at first sight."

Paul had the decency to redden. "I do know her. And we are friends . . . only. I met her in New Delhi on one of my trips out there."

Julia marveled at the coincidence, and she studied Paul a bit closer, wondering if there had been something between Paul and Rosie. Why should it matter to her though?

"Come on, Paul," Jack said. "You can admit that you and Rosie dated."

Paul didn't seem too fazed at Jack's teasing. "We did go out a couple of times, but I wouldn't call it dating. She was always looking elsewhere."

Jack snapped his fingers. "Who was the woman you were dating, then?"

Paul seemed to hesitate, then said with a faint barrier in his tone, "I dated Marjorie Severyns, but we've decided to remain friends."

"Marjorie, that's the gal I was thinking of."

The conversation turned then because Gregory and Peachy came up with the idea to night swim at the lake. Something that Julia refused to do. There were too many creatures to watch out for in the daylight hours, and she wouldn't risk it at night. She didn't care if the others thought she was a ninny.

"I have to put in a few hours tonight anyway," she defended when Peachy begged her to come with them.

"You're working more than Mountbatten," Peachy said.

Julia released a breath. "Once I get through the current pouch from DC, I'm going to take an entire weekend off."

The conversation switched again to war news and how the Soviets had retaken Sebastopol and the American advancement in Italy as they drove their way toward Rome. Julia tried to focus on the conversation, but she found her thoughts drifting back to Paul Child. How many women had he dated over here? It was going on all around her, that she knew. Relationships flaring up, then burning out just as fast. Julia had some minicrushes of her own but nothing that she'd seriously pursue. No . . . she didn't want a repeat of Harrison Chandler, or Tom Johnston, for that matter.

"What if we go to the pool instead?" Peachy asked Julia. "Surely you can skip off work a little."

Julia didn't hesitate. "Sure, I'll come to the pool."

"Did someone say swimming?" Guy Martin asked, walking up to their table with a grin on his face.

Julia loved Guy, in a platonic way, of course. He was much younger than she, more like a kid brother, and from Pasadena too. As a naval officer, he was here in Kandy for a while, and Julia found him fun to pal around with. He was the younger brother of Byron Martin, who was formerly a bomb navigator and Air Force Intelligence before working in the OSS.

When they finally made it to the pool, the sun had set. Julia swam for a bit, then sat at the edge of the pool, watching the others.

Peachy sidled up to her. "Our new friend Paul has been watching you all night."

Julia waved a hand in dismissal. "He's been watching everyone—observing, I guess, since he refuses to swim. Photographers watch the world through a different viewpoint. I'm sure Paul's no different."

Another thing she'd learned about Paul Child. The man currently sat on a lounge chair, still fully dressed and smoking.

"You should go talk to him," Peachy continued. "He looks lonely."

"Jack's over there talking to him now," Julia said.

Peachy only smiled. "Well, they're old friends and work together. I meant that Paul would probably like someone new to talk to."

Julia looked at her friend. "Why do you care so much?" she teased. "Paul Child is ten years older than me." She'd found over the course of the earlier conversation on the veranda that he was forty-two.

"You ladies swimming?" Guy asked, dropping down next to them. He had yet to get in the water.

"I've been swimming already," Julia said. "Go on. Show us your backstroke."

"Water looks cold."

"It's perfect," Peachy said, then nudged Julia.

It was their signal.

Julia rose to her feet. "I think I'm going to grab a drink." But instead of leaving, she moved behind Guy.

He was too quick, though, and stood as well. "Oh no." He raised his hand as if to ward her off. "I know what you're planning. You're not pushing me in."

Julia shoved him in the side. Guy dodged her, then tried to push her over the edge. Julia wrenched away from him and spun, then grabbed him around the torso and threw him into the water. But she lost her balance and fell in too.

They both came up laughing.

"I know now to never sit by you at a pool," Guy said.

"Unless you want to get wet," Julia said.

Peachy dove in, and soon, they were playing an improvised game of pool tag.

Julia was pretty sure she'd proved to Paul Child—who may or may not have been watching—that she was too juvenile for him. She didn't care though. She wasn't going to get caught up in all the matchmaking going on about the plantation.

She'd have fun, sure, but nothing would progress with anyone.

After everyone tired of the tag games, Julia stayed in the pool, floating on her back, gazing up at the stars appearing in the darkening sky. When she was the last one in the pool, she finally climbed out and wrapped a towel about her. She was surprised to see Peachy sitting next to Paul. They seemed to be in an intimate conversation, with Paul smiling a lot . . . and Peachy laughing.

Well, Peachy could pursue the man all she wanted. She was petite, beautiful, enthusiastic, and would hang on Paul's every word. Julia was completely fine with that. Peachy fit better with a man like Paul anyway—a man who was five nine and wouldn't be interested in a woman who was six two.

CHAPTER 9

Kandy, Ceylon
June 1944

"We are wakened at 7:15 by our room boy who knocks heavily at the door, murmurs 'Morning, Missie,' and paddles into the room in his bare feet carrying morning tea and fruit. We leisurely dress, leaving 5 minutes for breakfast, and at 8:05 our 2-ton truck is at the door of the Queens Hotel and we are off, at the fast clip of 19 to 24 miles an hour to our office, 7 miles away."

—JULIA McWILLIAMS, DIARY

Peachy had been talking nonstop about Paul Child for days, and Julia had grown tired of it. She couldn't complain, though, or she might let some of her true feelings escape. Yes, Julia liked Paul. She didn't know how it had happened, but over the past couple of weeks, he'd become a permanent fixture in their group.

She told herself she was just drawn to his interesting conversations. The way he spoke, his choice of words, his deadpan sense of humor. Oh, and he was a poet. She found that out through Peachy because, apparently, she'd read a couple of his poems on one of the nights Julia hadn't been with the group. Paul hadn't even gone to college—but he'd read everything, it seemed, and he knew music, art, language, and culture.

Today, they were all going on an excursion together. Julia was taking the entire day off—even though it was Sunday, and she should have had the day off anyway.

"He said he's bringing his camera," Peachy said, slipping on yet another cotton dress. She'd changed so many times getting ready that Julia had lost count.

Julia didn't even need to ask who "he" was—it was always Paul.

"That sounds great," Julia said absentmindedly. She'd been attempting to write Dort a letter, but she couldn't focus in the cloying heat of their room. If only a breeze would start up and come in through the windows.

"There." Peachy turned from the mirror. "How do I look?" Her lilac dress was belted at the waist, and she wore small pearl earrings with a matching necklace.

"Lovely," Julia said honestly.

Peachy's nose wrinkled. "Are you wearing that?"

Julia looked down at her person. She wore a cotton dress that could use a good pressing. "I was planning on it."

Peachy shrugged and said nothing else. Julia wasn't any sort of fashion icon. When she'd first arrived at Smith College for her freshman year, she'd discovered that she was woefully out of style among the other girls. Her mother had put that to rights on a visit for Thanksgiving, and they went on a shopping spree to purchase the requisite Brooks Brothers crewneck cable-knit sweater, brown-and-white Spaulding shoes, pastel tweed skirts, camel's hair coat, and strand of five-and-dime pearls. Only then had Julia felt like she fit in with the girls at Smith.

"They're here," Peachy said, leaning toward the window. "Looks like Jack brought a Jeep. It's covered in mud."

Julia rose from her place and crossed the room. "Want to rethink your pretty dress?"

"Never," Peachy said.

They headed out of the hotel where they met up with Gregory and Ellie. Paul was already inside the Jeep with Jack.

Julia paused to feed the stray cat that lingered outside the building. She brought back morsels from their cafeteria meals for this purpose.

When she dropped the bits of food and gave the cat a friendly scratch, she looked up to see Paul watching her. She couldn't read his expression, but Peachy said, "Are you coming or staying?"

"Coming," Julia said, then crammed into the back seat, feeling as though she were about three feet too tall for the vehicle.

"Where are we going again?" Peachy asked, nestled in the front between Jack and Paul.

Jack stepped on the gas. "North to Dambulla."

"We're visiting the ancient cave temples," Paul added. Sure enough, he had a camera strap around his neck.

Julia kept her gaze out the window as they traversed the jungle roads. The terrain was beautiful, with deep greens and yellows interspersed with tropical flowers, and it kept her mind busy. She shouldn't be focusing on Peachy's flirting at all. No good would come of that, and Julia was determined to keep her mood light. She had the day off, after all, so why waste it on sulking?

When they arrived at the exhibit of five shrines, Julia quickly forgot about any petty feelings she might have toward who was flirting with whom, because she became caught up in the artistic displays of murals and statues inside the caves. Even the ceilings were beautifully painted.

"I've never seen such a collection," Julia said to Ellie as they gazed at a row of Buddha statues in one of the caves. The air was cool inside and the atmosphere serene. The place smelled of incense and damp stone. "There has to be dozens of Buddha statues in this cave alone."

"It makes me feel dizzy somehow," Ellie said. After a moment, she headed to another section.

"One hundred fifty-three," Paul said. "Amazing, hmm?"

She turned, surprised that he stood nearby, apparently having ditched Peachy.

"It's breathtaking." Julia shifted her gaze to another statue. "I could stand here all day. I'd need a bathroom break, but then I'd return right here, to this spot."

Paul chuckled, the warmth of his laugh making her feel lighter.

"I feel transcendent somehow," Julia mused. "As if I'm not really standing here at all, yet everything in my life has led to this exact moment."

"It's the power of Buddha," Paul said, his voice quiet, contemplative.

He'd moved closer, and she watched from the corner of her eye as he raised his camera and clicked a photo.

When he lowered his camera, he stayed next to her as they both gazed at the statues. Julia couldn't begin to guess his thoughts, but no matter, just sharing this experience with another person was somehow significant.

"Are you a religious man, Paul?" she asked. The moment the words flew out of her mouth, she wished she could take them back.

A couple of heartbeats passed, and finally, he said, "I'm not traditionally religious. I don't attend a specific church, if that's what you mean. My mother took us to church when we were young, but that soon dropped off."

She felt his gaze on her.

"How about you?" he asked. "Are you staunch something or other?"

This made Julia laugh for some reason. "Far from it," she said, then corrected, "I mean, I'm old-fashioned, I guess, and I grew up in a Presbyterian household, but once I hit college, I gave up the once-a-week sermon." She drew in her breath. "My mother might be turning over in her grave right now, and my father would probably have an aneurysm if he heard me say this, but I've quite put my childhood religion behind me."

Paul gave a brief nod, then asked, "When did you lose your mother?"

"July 21, 1937."

"I'm sorry," Paul said with quiet sincerity. "My mother died in 1933."

Julia faced him then. "Oh goodness. I'm sorry too. You've lost both your parents."

Paul's gaze was steady upon hers, observant as always.

Julia wasn't sure where their group had gone, but it seemed she and Paul were completely alone among the Buddha statues. "What was your mother like?" she asked.

Paul's forehead creased, and Julia wondered again if she'd asked a question too bluntly.

"Artistic," Paul said after a moment. "We were young when my father died—it was my older sister, Mary, who we called Meeda, then me and my brother, Charlie. We were a handful, and my father had left my mother financially destitute. Mother moved us around a lot. She became involved in the Boston social scene, as a disciple of Theosophy, but through it all, she insisted her children take lessons in singing, music, drawing, and languages." He took out his pack of cigarettes and lit one.

Julia waited because, somehow, she sensed he had more to say.

"Mother started us in a family musical performance group—mostly to bring in some money," he said. "She called it Mrs. Child and the Children. She sang while I played the violin, Charlie the cello, and Meeda the piano."

Julia tried to imagine Paul as a boy performing at weddings and ladies' luncheons. He was certainly a man of all trades.

"My sister died in 1941," he said.

Julia drew in a breath. "Oh, I'm so sorry. She must have been young."

"She was forty," Paul said quietly. "She has two children. A son named Paul with her first husband, and Fiona with her second husband. She was married to her third husband and living in Paris when she died."

"What a terrible loss," Julia murmured.

Paul nodded toward a path leading through the statues, and they began to walk together, with no real destination in mind.

She was surprised when Paul said, "After my father died, Mother found a man to take care of her—a boyfriend, I guess. Edward Filene, who was the general manager and president of a women's fashion store. We used to call him Uncle Ed."

Julia blinked. "I've heard of Filene's."

Paul tapped ash from his cigarette. "Uncle Ed sent Charlie to Harvard. It seemed he could only pick one twin, and Charlie was it. He was considered the 'real artist' in the family."

Julia scoffed and covered her mouth. "I'm sorry," she said. "I'm sure your brother's wonderful, but I don't see how anyone could overlook your talents."

He met her gaze, and for a long moment, he didn't look away. When he finally did, he added, "I felt insecure because of Charlie's education. I sort of went crashing through life after that. Finding odd jobs, from everything like digging ditches in California to building furniture reproductions in Cambridge. I worked as a photographer at a New York advertising agency. And I've done several stints teaching in private schools and public schools."

"You seem to be a Renaissance man."

Paul laughed, and Julia decided she liked to make him laugh, even though she was awkward compared to his refinement.

"That's certainly a polite way to say it." He paused in front of another statue, and Julia stopped too. "I'm old—that's what's going on here. I'm forty-two." He looked over at her. "How old are you?"

Julia swallowed down her surprise at the question. "Thirty-one."

Paul gave a brief nod, then raised his camera and took a picture of something just beyond Julia. She turned to look, spotting an elephant past the exhibit, standing at the edge of a pond.

"Come on, let's get closer," Paul said, walking toward the elephant.

As they started over, Julia bent to give a cat perched on a bench a scratch.

"You like cats, huh?" Paul asked.

Julia straightened. "I do. We always had dogs growing up, like Eric the Red, but I think when I'm on my own someday, I'll get a cat."

Paul didn't comment, his attention caught by Jack waving for their attention. He and Ellie stood on the perimeter of the pond, watching the elephant. The creature seemed oblivious to its audience as it proceeded to bathe itself.

"Have you ever ridden an elephant before?" Paul asked as they walked together.

"Not yet," Julia said. "But I'd love to."

He flashed her a smile. "We'll have to rectify that."

Julia's heart stuttered at his smile. His eyes were crinkled at the corners, and everything about him seemed warm and welcoming.

All that was quickly replaced by a jolt of envy when Peachy called out, "Oh, there you are, Paul. I thought you'd turned into a statue with all the Buddhas."

Julia hated that she was jealous of a woman years younger than herself, and she hated that she was finding Paul Child attractive. And intriguing. And easy to talk to, even when she said blunt and awkward things. Her intrusive questions didn't seem to faze him, and she liked that he answered honestly from his heart. He didn't provide the quick and easy answers. Now, if she were really fortunate, this growing crush of hers would quickly burn out. She was too good of friends with this group to let hurt feelings ruin their excursions.

She and Paul joined the group, and Paul took several photographs. Julia was determined to enjoy the day, no matter what happened. She was in a beautiful, captivating location, and there was an elephant bathing itself only steps away. Her letter to Dort would certainly contain this experience, although Julia didn't know what she might say about Paul Child. Watching his patience in photography, his waiting for the right movement or angle of the elephant, was intriguing. She supposed that all artist types were like that—patient. Valuing the right colors and hues and lighting, whereas other people in the world rushed through life's experiences.

Julia settled on a bench not far from the group, and while Paul continued to walk about, photographing, the others wandered off. She hadn't realized she was quite alone with Paul again until he sat next to her. She wondered why he hadn't followed after Peachy.

"What brought you to the OSS?" he asked.

The question felt out of the blue but was one she'd been asked many times by others—just not by Paul.

"I was working for the Red Cross and the Aircraft Warning Service, but I wanted to do more," she said. "My friend Janie was in Washington, DC, so I decided to give it a try." She told Paul about her first job, then finally landing at the OSS, then going through different job titles. "Jack was the one who talked me into applying for an India post—well, it didn't take much talking me into it. The news coming out of Europe was horrific, and I wanted to make a real difference, you know?"

Paul's gaze was still upon her. "Are you glad you came?"

His question felt so genuine that Julia wondered if there were a deeper meaning.

"Oh, yes, I'm very glad. The food isn't great, and the work . . . well, it's important but quite tedious. I've pulled my hair out many times." She patted her hair. "It's growing quite thin."

Paul smiled.

"But where else can I live in such a tranquil place while contributing toward the war effort?" She motioned toward the elephant. "This is absolutely paradise."

"I can help with the food choices," Paul said. "Chinese food is delectable—if you know where to eat."

"I'd never turn down a good meal," she said. *Or an invitation by this man*, she thought. "What about you? What led you to the OSS?"

"Oh . . . well, heartbreak actually."

This answer, Julia hadn't expected. Was this about his mother and sister? Or . . . about another woman? "I'm sorry," she began.

Paul lit a cigarette, and Julia recognized his pattern. He smoked like most people around here, but he also smoked when he was speaking of personal things.

"Her name was Edith," he said, a weight to his voice.

Julia noted how he referred to Edith in the past tense, and her stomach knotted. What had happened to this woman he obviously cared about?

"Our families knew each other in Boston when she was married to her first husband," he continued. "Edith was an artist—a painter, writer, and musician."

He paused, and Julia let him take his time. She wasn't going anywhere.

"When I was in Paris, I bumped into her. She'd been through a divorce and was going through a difficult time." He shrugged. "Then irony of ironies, a few years later, when I was back in America, her son became one of my students when I was teaching art and French at a school in Avon, Connecticut."

He paused as a group of people walked past them, heading toward one of the caves.

"I was in love," Paul said. "Looking back, I wonder if she was in love as much with me as I was with her. She refused to marry again. She was the life and blood of our social circles, which consisted of accomplished artists, creative types, and Harvard scholars. I always felt like I was on the wrong side of the eclipse in those circles."

JULIA

Julia found it hard to imagine Paul feeling small and ill accomplished when she saw him in a completely different light.

"Edith lived life to the fullest, never slowing down despite her precarious health condition. I had to force out of her that she suffered from heart disease, and by then, it was advanced."

The pit in Julia's stomach grew.

"By June 1942, she was extremely ill," Paul said, his voice taking on a stilted quality, as if he were merely reciting impersonal facts. "Her breathing became labored, she tired quickly, and her skin grew pale, like the moon. When she began to hallucinate, I begged her to get treatment. But all she wanted was to be left alone. She told me to take a break and visit my brother. I hadn't seen Charlie for a while, and he and his wife, Freddie, had just bought a house in Lumberville, Pennsylvania . . ."

He broke off, and after a moment, he continued, "Word came a few days later that Edith had died. She . . . she wanted it that way, I think. To not have me hovering and grieving over her."

Maybe Paul wasn't crying, but Julia wiped at her eyes.

"She was older than me by ten years, but she was only fifty years old. Too young to die." His voice faltered.

Julia heard heartbreak in his story, and she rested a hand on his arm. He didn't seem to notice. "I'm really sorry, Paul."

He lowered his head for a long moment, his breathing steady. "At the time, everyone was signing up to fight in the war. Charlie and I both wanted to do something, although we knew we'd be turned down for the armed forces because of our age. But we moved to Washington, DC regardless. Charlie found a job at the National Planning Association, and I landed at the Visual Presentation Branch."

"And Ceylon was next?" Julia asked.

"Not quite," Paul said. "In the summer of 1943, I went with my brother to visit an astrologer—Jane Bartleman—and I wasn't prepared to believe much of what she said . . ." He glanced at Julia.

She raised her brows. "But she saw into your soul," she quipped.

His mouth twitched. "Something like that. She said that I'd be involved in a secret mission, which would require a lengthy journey to the Far East."

"Oh." What else could she say?

"I didn't think much of it, but a few months later, I received a call from General Donovan asking if I'd consider a position as the OSS representative to Lord Mountbatten. In New Delhi, of course."

"And the astrologer was suddenly correct?" Julia asked.

"Well." He spread his hands. "Here I am. So you'd better believe I was in Jane Bartleman's office the very next morning."

"You went back?"

Paul's smile appeared. "I did. And she told me that I'd get the job, and it would be highly secretive work. I'd make many invaluable friends. There would be adventure and excitement, and to top everything off, I'd fall heavily in love in about a year."

Julia's mind reeled. "Well, you've still got time."

Paul laughed. Loud and long. Which made Julia laugh too.

When they both caught their breath, Julia added, "Is that what all this dating is about? Rosie? Marjorie? Peachy?" She went absolutely still. Surely she'd gone too far.

But again, his answer wasn't what she'd expected. "The astrologer's prediction rattled me a bit, sure, but do I really believe her? Maybe? Maybe not. It did give me hope that one day I'll not feel so heartbroken all the time. I don't know if I'll ever stop missing Edith, but I need to move on. And it would be wonderful if I could fall in love again."

Julia had never had such a serious and frank conversation about love with a man before. Paul Child was keeping his heart wide open.

"I think people can fall in love again," she said, not sure where her conviction was coming from. "Just as completely and deeply as the first time."

Paul straightened and ran a hand over his head as the breeze picked up around him. "There's one thing I've learned about myself," he said in a wry tone. "Women in their twenties are certainly not for me." His gaze was on her again, his expression seeming to blink between past and present. "I don't know why I'm telling you all this," he said matter-of-factly. "I suppose you're an easy woman to confess private matters to, Julia McWilliams. You're not a judgmental person, and I admire your zest for life. Somehow, being around you has lightened this old curmudgeon's soul."

Julia was determined not to let his compliments go to her head . . . but they did anyway.

CHAPTER 10

Kandy, Ceylon
July–October 1944

"Ceylon was an Elysium far removed from reality where everyone had an academic interest in the war but found life far too pleasant to do anything too drastic about it. To the red-blooded Americans ... Ceylon [was either] another form of British tyranny—frustration without representation [or] ... a palm-fringed haven of the bureaucrat, the isle of panel discussions and deferred decisions."

—LETTER FROM JANE FOSTER TO BETTY MacDONALD

Julia wasn't sad when Paul eased off his flirtation with Peachy, or with other women, for that matter. And yes, Julia noticed. She noticed everything about Paul Child, which was easy since they spent almost every free moment together—either in groups or the two of them. And their mutual friends were noticing.

Julia repeated what she told every person: She and Paul were *friends*. There was no indication that he thought of her romantically—he'd never tried to kiss her or said anything that could be considered deeper than friendship. So, she'd wait. And if the wait proved fruitless, she'd move on. Realistically, everyone knew the flings and flirtations taking place in their bubble of paradise would likely not transfer to the real world once the war was over.

Julia wasn't blind to Paul Child's faults; they were just eclipsed by his attributes. Paul could be stubborn, to say the least. Cora had called him "difficult"—and Julia understood her viewpoint. Cora had worked with Paul in DC, but they'd never become great friends. Julia was more compassionate toward his nature because she knew the tragedies he'd experienced. He was also a bit of a perfectionist, whereas Julia was far from that. It created a sort of mad pairing between them. Yet Paul seemed to

JULIA

enjoy explaining things when Julia asked questions. He possessed endless teaching patience, and she supposed it was because he had a lot of experience teaching.

Spending time with Paul was her only bright spot during the evenings since she was back to working around the clock, including late nights and four hours on Sundays. So she was more than grateful when OSS staff member Patty Norbury arrived and was assigned to be Julia's assistant.

After introducing Patty to their boss, Colonel Dick Heppner, Julia led Patty into the registry office.

"Come in, come in," Julia said.

Patty was around five and a half feet tall, with a pretty face and friendly eyes behind her glasses. Now her eyes widened at the sight of the room crammed with stacked files.

"Believe it or not, it's all very organized." Julia pulled out a chair on one side of the central desk. "Where are you from, Patty? Tell me a little about yourself. We're going to be spending dozens of hours a week together."

"I'm from Ohio," Patty said. "I asked to be transferred here so I can find my fiancé."

Julia frowned. "Is he with the OSS too?"

"No," Patty said. "He was shot down by the Japanese and pronounced missing in action. I'm certain he's still alive, and I'm going to figure out a way to locate him."

Normally, Julia would have inwardly scoffed at the notion of a woman thinking she could track down her fiancé in the middle of a war. If he was alive, he was in prison somewhere. There had been rumors of prisoner-of-war camps throughout Japan holding captured Allied pilots. But Patty's gaze was fierce and determined, almost challenging Julia to disagree with her.

"We'll keep our eyes out for any information that might lead to your fiancé's rescue," Julia finally said. "Once you learn my filing system, you'll be an expert researcher yourself."

Patty folded her hands atop her lap. "I'm looking forward to it." Her gaze strayed to the stacked files.

Over the next hour, Julia walked Patty through her code-number system and how to cross-index. "This work takes the utmost seriousness and astuteness. You have to be completely transparent in the cross-referencing and not make any errors—an error can cost a life. There's also suspicion of spying between the Americans and the British—so nothing inside this office can be discussed outside of it."

Patty nodded, her demeanor somber.

"Not to say I don't play the occasional trick on Washington or on our comrades here." Julia waved a hand toward the files. "Keeps the boredom away."

Patty looked at Julia then. "I thought the British are our allies."

"Of course they are, but we are still allegiant to America first and foremost, even though our commander is British." She drew in a breath. "For instance, our American OSS are the most fluent in Japanese, but the British have other attributes. Together, we're cutting through Japanese supply lines and creating underwater sabotage. One of the main focuses of Admiral Lord Mountbatten and US Army Major General Stilwell is to reopen a land route to China since Japan controls the Burma Road."

"Is that possible?" Patty asked.

"If they can recapture all the Ledo Road, which will provide the alternate route. But there is a portion of that territory that the Allies will have to retake. And once we retake the land, someone will have to build the road itself."

Julia cleared off a place at one of the tables for Patty to sit down. "Our priority is to cross-index without any errors," Julia said. "We've been working hard to establish a foolproof system so that when needed, we can locate the right information for the right entity, whether it's the Office of War Information, the theater commander, or the air force. With intercepted messages and encrypted commands disrupting the flow of information between entities, our office's intelligence has to be the one to tie everything together."

JULIA

By lunchtime, Julia assumed that Patty's head was swimming. They'd been working on information about the day's Japanese rail and troop movements, which had been received by shortwave radio, then translated by the Communications Branch, so that Julia could file the information on index cards.

"Let's grab some lunch," Julia said to Patty, "and I'll introduce you around."

They headed to the mess hall, traipsing in the stifling humidity, and stood in line to get their plates of food.

"There you are," a peppy voice said.

Julia turned to see Jane Foster. She was as short as Julia was tall. Jane's blonde hair and freckles and jolly personality made her seem younger than she was. They'd become fast friends over the past couple of weeks, with Jane easily integrating herself into their group. Her smile focused on Patty. "You the new girl?"

"This is Patty Norbury from Ohio," Julia said. "She requested the transfer so she could track down her fiancé, who's MIA."

Jane slipped an arm through Patty's. "Sorry to hear about your fiancé, Patty. Don't you worry, though, we're your gals, and we'll help you find your man."

And that was how Jane Foster integrated herself with people.

Next thing Julia knew, they were sitting at a table together while Patty told them every piece of intel she'd collected on her fiancé. Jane listened in rapture, although Julia wasn't surprised. Jane Foster had an interesting background. In 1938, she'd joined the Communist Party in California, though she'd later dropped out. She'd lived on Java Island while working on her master's thesis on the Batu Islands. Languages came easy to her, and she spoke Malay as well. Jane was on her second marriage, currently to a Russian-American man, George Zlatovski.

Paul brought his plate over and sat across from Julia. He nodded at her but didn't interrupt the current conversation. Soon, Gregory and Jack joined them, along with Ellie and Mary.

Peachy sat at another table, chatting up a couple of officers. Thankfully, Peachy had abandoned her crush on Paul and now pined for another man, but at the moment, Julia wasn't sure which one.

As the conversation swirled about the table, Julia noticed that Paul was unusually quiet. Maybe he didn't have anything to add to Patty's plight?

"Are you feeling all right?" she asked him after several moments.

Paul looked over at her as if realizing he was surrounded by conversation. "It's a migraine, I'm afraid. I felt it coming on this morning, and it's not letting up."

"Oh, I'm sorry," Julia said. "Is there anything I can get you?"

"Nothing really works except for quiet," Paul said with an ironic smile since they were currently surrounded by noise. "I'm going to try to leave the War Room a little early this afternoon."

It was a good plan and should have eased Julia's worry. He'd told her once that he'd been in a serious accident in 1941, and ever since then, he'd come down with random migraines. But the pain seemed to have chiseled fine lines about his mouth and eyes.

With Patty's help the rest of the afternoon, Julia finally saw progress in her workload. Since it was Patty's first day, Julia let them end on time. But instead of hanging out with the group for the evening, and knowing Paul would be absent, she decided to visit him to check on how he was doing. She brought along some canned orange juice. Maybe at the very least, it would be refreshing.

She might have spruced up a little by changing into a pressed cotton dress and adding a strand of pearls. And she might have also quickly painted her nails and put on a fresh coat of lipstick.

When she arrived at his hut, he answered the door with a book in hand.

"You're feeling better, then?" she asked.

"Much." Now he ushered her inside, and he motioned to the single chair next to a table stacked with books and a pile of photographs.

JULIA

"Oh, don't let me take over your evening," Julia said, perching on the edge of his army cot. "I've brought you some orange juice, but I don't want to intrude."

"You're not intruding." Paul settled into the chair and picked up a stack of developed photographs. "Remember the elephant?"

Julia took the photographs. "He was adorable. So talented in bathing himself."

Paul smirked. "I suppose if something that should be natural to every animal could be called a talent."

Julia leafed through the rest of them, then handed them back. "You're a gifted photographer. I mean, you pick the best angles and are patient enough to wait for the right lighting."

"If something intrigues me, I'm willing to wait." His gaze had locked onto hers, and she realized how alone they truly were—probably for the first time.

Her heart did a little leap, but she ignored it. "What have you been reading?"

Paul tapped the book he'd set on the top of his stack. "*Dubliners* by James Joyce."

"Sounds frightfully above my intellect."

"Nonsense." Paul picked up the book and held it out. "Here, you can borrow it. Then we can discuss it. I've read it more than once, so I'll not miss it . . . much."

Julia took the book and opened it to the first page. "There was no hope for him this time: it was the third stroke. Night after night I had passed the house (it was vacation time) and studied the lighted square of window: and night after night I had found it lighted in the same way, faintly and evenly. If he was dead, I thought, I would see the reflection of candles on the darkened blind for I knew that two candles must be set at the head of a corpse. He had often said to me: 'I am not long for this world,' and I had thought his words idle. Now I knew they were true . . ." She paused. "Well, I'm intrigued."

Paul picked up another book. "Do you like poetry?"

Julia peered at the title. "I haven't read much since college. Who's the poet?"

"Edna St. Vincent Millay. Have you read her?"

She shook her head, then he did something unexpected. He opened the book and began reading aloud. "This is from *Renascence* . . .

> *All I could see from where I stood*
> *Was three long mountains and a wood;*
> *I turned and looked another way,*
> *And saw three islands in a bay.*
> *So with my eyes I traced the line*
> *Of the horizon, thin and fine,*
> *Straight around till I was come*
> *Back to where I'd started from."*

Julia tried to remember when a man had ever sat and read a book to her—there wasn't a time. Paul seemed perfectly content to read to her, and well, she liked the sound of his voice. He made the words interesting—adding inflection and different tones. So, she settled back on his cot and listened. But mostly she watched him read.

After turning a couple of pages, he looked over the top of the poetry book and eyed her. "Are you going to fall asleep?"

Just then, a yawn rose, and Julia covered her mouth. Then she laughed.

Paul didn't laugh though. Instead, he said, "Don't move. I want to take a photograph. I've been meaning to send my brother a photograph of the layout of my room."

"With a woman on your cot?"

Paul didn't even crack a smile. He simply collected his camera, found his aim after a couple of moments, and took her picture.

Julia couldn't help but smile because it was rather absurd to pose on his dumpy army cot, with her in a dress and pearls, her long legs stretched out.

"What will you say to your brother about the photo?" Julia asked, sitting up straighter and facing him.

JULIA

Paul settled again in his chair. "Oh, I'll tell him all about my hut. The typical ten-by-eighteen-foot space, the woven Cadjan walls, wooden shutters, and an army bed with a folded-up mosquito net above."

"I mean what will you tell him about *me*?"

Paul gazed at Julia for what seemed like a very long moment, then he said, "He already knows about you."

"What? What did you say?" Julia felt both surprised and pleased.

"I told him that you're a six two *bien-jambée* from Pasadena and that you have a ragged but pleasantly crazy sense of humor."

"Are those compliments?" she asked, trying to remember what *jambée* meant—it was French, she at least knew that much. And did Paul *like* her sense of humor? They seemed to laugh together plenty, so maybe?

"Do you want me to read more, or are you too tired?"

So, he wasn't going to answer her? "Read more. Unless *you're* too tired?"

His mouth quirked, but his smile stayed hidden. He continued to read, and she was perfectly content listening to him.

Eventually, he lit a cigarette. "Do you want one?"

"Sure," she said.

"When did you start smoking?" he asked.

"Technically?" She paused. "As a kid, I had a friend named Orian Hall, whom we all called Babe. We would sneak my father's cigars, climb our oak tree, and try them out."

Paul's brows lifted. "Did you get caught?"

"Of course we got caught," Julia said. "The smoke rising from the tree was a big clue. I'll never forget when my father sat me down with my younger brother and sister. Told us if we didn't smoke until we reached twenty-one, he'd give us each a thousand-dollar bond."

Paul lowered his cigarette. "Did it work?"

Julia grinned. "It certainly did. I didn't smoke again until one minute after my twenty-first birthday."

Paul chuckled and shook his head. "You were a precocious daughter, I see. What's the craziest thing you did as a child?"

Julia had a long list to choose from. "Well, everything seemed to involve Babe. She was a year older than me, and we brought out the wild side in each other the moment we got together. My poor brother, John, got dragged along on most of our adventures." She paused. "I'm not boring you?"

"Far from it."

She took courage at that. "We once sent for a mail-order blank cartridge gun under Babe's brother Charlie's name, which we fired from the roof and, of course, got into trouble. Another time, we dropped rocks on the Santa Fe passenger train. And more than once, we sneaked rides on milk wagons and streetcars."

Paul was laughing now. "You were incorrigible."

"I grew out of it, mostly."

His smile was still in place. "I've heard about the pranks you've played around the plantation. I don't think you've grown out of it at all. My brother and I were well-behaved in comparison. We only did injury to each other."

This reminded her about his partial blindness. "Does your eye ever hurt?"

"No . . . at least, not directly." He tapped his temple. "I didn't start getting migraines until after that accident."

She was still curious about one thing and had to ask, "What else did you write to your brother about me?"

Paul took a drag from his cigarette, his gaze on her, as if contemplating whether to tell her more.

"Never mind, I don't want to know." She rose from the cot, the book still in her hand. "I should head to my place. I'm glad you're feeling better." She crossed quickly to the door and stepped out.

Paul caught her hand before she could get very far. "Julie."

She didn't know if he'd called her *Julie* before, but a few others about headquarters did. Beyond his hut, the sun had sunk low, disappearing beyond the horizon, creating a maze of violet and peach colors above the tree line.

"I told my brother everything about you," he said, his hand still holding hers, his gaze intent. "I told him that Julia McWilliams is very tall and has lovely legs. She's thirty-two years old, and she's a darling, warm girl."

"Oh." She breathed out and looked down at their clasped hands. "That's . . . sweet of you."

"It's the truth." He released her hand, but he didn't move away. "You're beautiful and lively and intelligent, and any man would be fortunate to have you in his corner."

At this, Julia couldn't even come up with a reply.

Fortunately, Paul was never short on words. "You know that I've been dating off and on while over here. Nothing has been serious since Edith though. I don't know if I have it in me. And I don't want to get in too deep when who knows how it will translate to life after the war. So if you feel like you're wasting your time on me, I understand, since I can only offer friendship."

He'd cracked open everything, right then, right there. She swallowed against the tightness of her throat. "I want friendship too," she managed to say. "Friendship is worth a lot more to me right now anyway. None of us knows when this war will end or what will happen when we all return stateside."

"Agreed." Paul's gaze didn't leave her, and even though they were both agreeing on the same thing, she saw a flicker of longing in his eyes.

She only recognized it because she knew she was half in love with him. Friendship would have to suffice for now, and if that was all their relationship amounted to, it would ease the heartache later on. He was a man with plenty of experience with women, while Julia had never gone beyond kissing a man. She knew somewhere, deep down, that Paul could truly break her heart if she gave it to him and he rejected it.

"Good night, then," she said.

"Good night." Still he didn't step away, and she didn't either.

Paul grasped her hand again, and he squeezed her fingers. Then he did the most extraordinary thing. He kissed her. It was light and brief. More of a friendly peck on the mouth, but it was something.

What it meant, Julia couldn't guess or define. But she was going to cling to their friendship and be ever so grateful for Paul's absolute honesty.

She didn't want games or pretty platitudes, because those would absolutely lead to a broken heart. As she saw things now, she might be casting her net over the wrong man, but she was willing to be patient. If there was one thing she'd learned from Paul Child, it was patience.

CHAPTER 11

Kandy, Ceylon
December 1944

"There are three curries: one meat, usually lamb; one fish, usually shrimp; and one fowl, usually chicken. One first lays down a good bed of rice all over a plate, takes generous helpings of each of the three curries, and then covers this all over with as many condiments as the human imagination can devise: chopped coconut flavored with curry powder, paprika, pepper, cardamom, crumbled bacon, crumbled fried bananas, and chutneys of every hue and flavor."

—LOUIS HECTOR, OSS STAFF

Julia awakened to a dim and muggy bedroom, which could only mean it was a cloudy morning. She felt so well-rested that she knew something was wrong. She sat up and parted the mosquito netting.

"The electricity's gone out again," Peachy said, sitting at the vanity table she'd rounded up from somewhere.

"What time is it?"

Peachy checked her watch. "Nearly noon."

Julia's head spun. It was a Saturday, but still, she'd been planning on working a full day today. "Why didn't you wake me up?" They'd had this routine for months. Peachy woke up Julia in the mornings because Julia struggled to crack her eyes open.

Peachy turned to look at her. "You've been exhausted all week. You work too much. I thought Patty was going to help you cut down on your crazy hours."

Julia stifled a yawn. "She has, but I still need to get through some paperwork today." She swung her legs over the bed, and a crack of thunder pealed overhead. "More rain?"

It had rained most of the past two days, and Julia was sure that if she tried, she could drink from the sky. According to Gregory, it was the start of the monsoon season, so they wouldn't see any letup soon.

"There's flooding at the end of our road." Peachy turned back to the mirror and applied lipstick.

"Plans?" Julia asked.

Peachy flashed a smile. "Yes." Her gaze met Julia's in the mirror. "You and Paul sure spend a lot of time together."

"He's a friend, like I've told you and everyone else."

Peachy shrugged. "Whatever you say."

Julia quickly washed and dressed, then headed out of the room with her umbrella.

"Wait for me," Peachy suddenly called after her.

"You're not getting picked up?"

"No. I'm meeting a certain someone at headquarters, but I don't want to walk through this rain by myself. Plus, I'm hungry now. I'll come with you to the mess hall."

The two of them hurried along the street as the rain started in earnest. More than their road was flooding. "Should we be worried about how high the water is getting?"

Peachy gingerly stepped around a large puddle of water. "I don't know—I mean, the rain has to stop sometime, right?"

The wind had started, tugging at Julia's clothing and blowing rain into her face, despite the umbrella. She could appreciate the beauty of the monsoon weather, with mists surrounding the mountain peaks and making the trees look like they were out of a fairy tale. Oh, except for the four-foot lizard she saw climbing one of the trees. Another reason, in addition to leeches, to avoid walking under all trees.

When they reached the plantation, they veered toward the mess hall, and Julia shook off as much rain as possible before entering. The heavenly smell of curry greeted her when she walked in. She dished up a plate of rice, topped it with curry, then added the toppings of paprika, cardamom, and crumbled fried bananas, with Peachy making her selections behind her.

JULIA

A group of OSS huddled near the radio, listening to the reports coming in about the Battle of Leyte Gulf that the US had fought a few days ago. The air and sea battle had severely crippled the Japanese Combined Fleet, and the US, Australia, and Mexico had invaded the Philippines, removing Japan from their stronghold.

"Join us," Jane Foster called out over the radio broadcast.

Julia looked over at the table, where Jane sat with Jeanne Taylor and Paul. Julia pushed down the rising questions she had about Jeanne, who chatted easily around Paul—Julia didn't know how to read that. Jeanne was her same age, an art school graduate, and much more sophisticated than Julia would ever be. Was she more Paul's type?

"We're sharing the geranium jelly that Paul's brother sent him," Jane continued in a cheerful tone. "It's delightful."

Paul's gaze settled on Julia, and she wondered what he was seeing—besides her rain-soaked clothing and wind-blown hair.

"Looks delicious," Julia said as she neared their table with Peachy right behind her.

Paul pushed the jar of jelly toward her, then a plate of flatbread. "Have all you want. Might as well use it up in one sitting."

Jane and Jeanne both laughed, and Julia tried not to prickle.

"Oh, this is amazing," Peachy said as she helped herself.

Julia slathered some onto a piece of flatbread, then took a bite. "Delicious. I must have the recipe."

"I'll write to my brother right away," Paul said with perfect sincerity. "I'm sure his wife, Freddie, won't mind sending it along."

Julia felt everyone's attention on her. Had she said something odd? Had Paul been too generous, too openly friendly? Peachy nudged Julia's foot, and Julia did her best to ignore the fact that heat had risen in her cheeks.

"Well, I have an appointment," Peachy said. "I'll leave Paul with his three Jays." She nudged Julia again, then rose from the table, and headed off.

"Watch out for rats," Paul called after her. "Word is that rats invaded one of the offices, trying to escape the flooding."

Peachy waved a hand in dismissal, as if the thought of rats running around didn't faze her.

"Her head must be in the clouds over some man," Jane said, a playful smile on her face, her brows quirked in amusement. "Do we want to guess who it is?"

Jeanne and Jane bantered for a few moments, while Julia's mind floated off as she enjoyed the geranium jelly. When she caught Paul's eye, he only smiled at her. "Anything new from the War Room?" she asked, knowing he couldn't really tell her a thing.

"There is some news," Paul said.

This alerted Julia.

"General Joseph Stilwell is being recalled from China."

Julia blinked. Earlier that month, there'd been a series of top-level meetings in Mountbatten's pavilion that had included a visit from General Donovan, and she'd been wondering what the fallout would be. General Stilwell spoke both Mandarin and Cantonese, and he clashed heavily with Chian Kai-shek, the current leader of the Republic of China.

"And you didn't hear this from me, but my boss, General Wedemeyer, is taking over as chief of staff from the Sunday School Teacher, so Heppner's going to be over all operations in Kunming."

"Big changes for the Sunday School Teacher," Julia said, smiling at Paul's nickname for Stilwell, because the man wore wire-rimmed glasses. She wondered if *she* would get a new boss. "Does that mean anything for us?"

"It does," Paul said.

Jane and Jeanne were listening in now as well.

"Fresh strategies are being put into place in China. We need to keep them in the war, on our side. I'm going to be increasing my hours in the War Room for the next few months." He paused and lowered his voice. "We're coordinating air-supply drops, paratroop operations, and counterespionage activities."

"If anyone can handle this, you can, Dr. Paulski," Jane said, using the pet name that had grown on everyone. The OSS staff called him either Paulski or P'ski. He didn't seem to mind.

JULIA

Paul gave a nod, but Julia sensed his apprehension.

"What more?" Julia asked.

"Heppner wants me to transfer to Chongqing with him," Paul said in an undertone. "We need to set up a new War Room. I could be reassigned in weeks or months. Heppner will get there and decide."

"Well, that's incredible," Jane said. "You're the perfect man for the job."

He obviously was, Julia very well knew, but her feelings battled inside her chest. The tides of the war were obviously changing—for the better? But if Paul was transferred, when would she ever see him again? It wasn't like she could make a weekend visit. Besides, they weren't in that sort of relationship anyway.

The rain outside increased its pace, coming down in droves, and the thundering and pounding rain only added to the feeling of doom growing inside Julia. Paul might be sitting across from her, regaling them with OSS updates, but she was already missing him. She felt like her heart was being painfully torn in two.

She was no stranger to heartbreak; Tom Johnston's cruel rejection had introduced her to that . . . and she was not a freshly graduated college girl anymore. She no longer wore rose-colored glasses, so to speak. And she wasn't the social butterfly of Pasadena that she'd been before the OSS. Paul Child was a man she could see herself with long-term, for a lifetime, even. And he was about to disappear from her life.

Sure, they could write letters, but to what end?

Tears burned in her eyes, and she hated that she was about to cry over Paul being transferred. His leaving might be weeks or months away, like he'd said, yet she was about to make a fool of herself in front of her group of friends. Pushing to her feet, she said, "I should get to the office so I can be done before dark."

"I'll walk you over there." Paul rose to his feet as well. "It's getting fierce out there."

But the last thing Julia needed was for Paul to see her crying . . . about him and about this war. She knew she couldn't hold out much longer, so she said, "I'll be fine. I'll hurry and be there in no time." She strode away, hoping he wouldn't follow. Thankfully, Jane asked him something, and he stayed to answer.

Julia increased her speed and snatched the umbrella she'd left by the door. She pulled on her poncho that was still wet. Paul was right. The rain had increased, and the wind lashed against her as if it were trying to mold her as she ran to the registry hut. Her tears fell immediately, but if anyone saw her, they wouldn't be able to tell her tears apart from the spitting rain. Blinking furiously and wiping at her face, she couldn't avoid all the puddles, and her feet were soaked by the time she arrived.

Opening the door let in a gust of wind and scattered papers about, so she spent the next while reorganizing, then working by the heather gray of the stormy day.

Somehow, she made it through the next hours, and when she was ready to call it a day, she opened the door to more flooding. The rain had let up, barely, but there was no way her shoes weren't getting soaked again.

She was surprised to see Paul sitting on the veranda of the mess hall when she hurried over to it. He was smoking and watching the rain as if he had nothing better to do. She thought he'd be buried at the War Room until late.

He stood as she approached, slipping one hand into his pocket. "Are you finished for the day?" he asked.

"Yes, and you?" She closed her umbrella. She didn't need to look in any mirror to know that she looked frightful.

He stubbed out his cigarette. "No, I'll be going back after I eat something."

"Is everyone inside?" She didn't need to explain to him that "everyone" was their usual group of friends.

"They are, but I wanted to talk to you alone."

Julia's pulse jumped. Was this a good thing or a bad thing? Paul had never issued such an invitation before. The times they'd been alone together had been more happenstance, and they'd never revisited their kiss.

"Is this about my opinion on the Hemingway book you lent me?"

Paul's smile was faint. "Let's go around the corner. Less interruptions."

JULIA

No one else was on the veranda, but she knew that could change at any moment, with someone leaving or arriving. So Julia walked with Paul around the veranda, where he stopped just past the corner, positioning them out of sight from the main door. The rain dripped off the roof only a foot away from them, and beyond, the rain had softened to almost a mist.

"I wanted to talk to you about my transfer," Paul said, both hands in his pockets, his gaze on her.

"Oh? Did you find out more information?"

"Not any more than I had earlier, but I saw your surprise."

Julia swallowed against the growing tightness in her throat. "Sure, but it's to be expected, right? Things are always changing in a war, and at some point, we'll all be sent home, back to our regular lives. You in the east, and me . . . well, probably in the west. I really have no idea."

Paul's expression turned sympathetic. "There's no need to plan all that out now."

Julia touched her unruly hair. Was her hand trembling? "Yes, I know. It's just that . . . I wanted to have an adventure and help in the war more than anything. I didn't expect to gain so many dear friends, and the thought of you leaving is probably the first step in all of us breaking apart."

Paul looked out at the rain for a moment. "I'll write to you and keep you updated."

Julia nodded. Writing wasn't the same, and they both knew it. "That would be wonderful, and I'm sure you'll be dying to know about all the goings-on here."

Paul turned his head. "I will." He hesitated. "I guess what I wanted to say is that I've enjoyed our friendship. You've been a real friend, Julie. You're tough and full of character, and you're always pleasant to be around. Not like my moody old self."

Julia released a soft laugh. "You have a lot of responsibility and weight on your shoulders. I'm a superfluous cog in the wheel over here."

He shook his head. "Hardly. You're the keeper of secrets, and you keep them well." He paused. "So, we'll write to each other? See where life takes us next? I'm not going to be a Tom and ditch you or a Harrison and bore you."

Julia's skin prickled with warmth. "That would be appreciated." She'd told him about Tom and Harrison during one of their evening talks. But how *would* Paul define their relationship? Or was it fruitless to try to do so? At this moment, all she could hope for was staying in touch. Maybe secretly, she longed for a future that included Paul Child. But right now, right here, they couldn't make promises because they wouldn't hold up.

Julia didn't know what she was hoping for at this moment on the veranda. Maybe it was for him to kiss her? To hug her? Instead, he stepped toward the corner. "Let's go eat, and then you can tell me all about your opinions on Hemingway."

Julia would take whatever moments she could get with Paul Child, whether it was alone or in a group, so she smiled like she didn't have tears threatening to appear again. Following Paul into the mess hall, she imagined a ticking clock beginning its countdown.

CHAPTER 12

Kandy, Ceylon
March 1945

"Julia and I managed to borrow a jeep from a friend last Sunday afternoon and, after buying a bottle of mulberry wine, struck off into the great unknown, for about 40 miles. The weather was incredibly inspiring: hot sun and cool air, sparkling sky, breeze enough, scattered clouds. The great mountains lay around us like back-broken dragons. God what beautiful country—the mud villages with their green-tiled towers, the herds of black swine, the blue clad people, the cedar smoke, the cinnamon dust, were all eternally Chinese, and connected us with the deep layers of past time."

—LETTER FROM PAUL CHILD TO HIS BROTHER, CHARLIE

Everything felt different when Paul left just after New Year's in 1945, and at first, Julia tried to carry on without missing a beat. It was only at night, as she tried to fall asleep, that she missed him the most because she couldn't distract herself with work or other activities.

They wrote letters back and forth, sure, but it wasn't nearly the same. And finally, she put in a request for a transfer. She didn't expect to end up in the same place as Paul, but she was ready to move on from Kandy. She'd been there ten months, and Patty was doing an excellent job at the office. Patty had yet to find out news on her fiancé, but she hadn't given up hope yet. Julia's new assignment would be in Kunming, China.

Her goodbye to Jane, Cora, Mary, and the others was bittersweet, but they all promised to stay in touch. Julia would hold them to it. Ellie and Peachy were both being reassigned with her to Kunming, while Paul remained in Chongqing.

Their first stop after flying out of Ceylon was Calcutta. Julia had heard plenty of negative stories about the British-colonized city, but she wasn't there to make friends.

On March 15, she and her comrades loaded onto a C-54 transport plane to fly "the Hump"—the route from Calcutta, India, to Kunming, China. It was a 500-mile trip that took them over the 15,000-foot peaks of the Himalayas. The C-54 wasn't equipped with pressurization and had no heat. So they were all instructed to wear warm parkas, strap on parachutes, and carry oxygen masks.

"Well, if it's our time, this will be it," Julia said after settling into her seat. She felt no fear, though, so she hoped that was a good sign and her intuition was working properly.

Peachy already looked like she was about to hurl. "How can you joke about any of this?"

Betty MacDonald, who'd boarded after them, paused by their seats. "If you can't joke about this, then you'll pass out from fright." She nodded toward the man coming up the aisle. "This is Louis Hector."

Julia introduced herself, and Betty and Louis settled across the aisle. Seeing everyone bundled up so tightly was a bit comical, but Julia refrained from mentioning it.

As the plane lifted off the ground, Julia asked, "Have you taken this flight before?"

"Oh sure," Betty said. "It's mostly safe. Did you know a female aviator Nancy Love piloted this route a couple of months ago? She did great, but we've heard some wild stories too." She leaned closer to be heard over the noise of the engine. "One OSS officer, Lieutenant Colonel Duncan Lee, and a journalist named Eric Sevareid had to parachute out on one of these trips, but before jumping, they grabbed a bottle of gin. Just in case, I guess . . ."

Julia didn't want to ask, Just in case of what? Capture? Serious injury?

Betty continued with a few more stories, then when she seemed to run out, Julia pulled out a Hemingway book from her bag. Paul had left her a few books and told her she could keep them.

JULIA

Suddenly, the plane pitched forward. People jolted in their seats. Everyone gasped. Someone behind them started quietly crying.

"What's happening?" Peachy asked.

"We've hit turbulence," Betty answered. "The pilot needs to find a hole in the clouds."

Julia glanced out the window, where bits of ice were clattering against the pane. She pulled her parka closer as her breathing came out in visible, cloudy puffs inside the plane.

Then the lights snapped out.

"That's not good," Peachy said, her voice rising in pitch.

"Here, take my lucky charm," Julia said, pulling it out of her pocket. She handed over the gremlin figurine, Chester.

Then she returned to her book, focusing on the words that she could still see from the muted light coming through the window. There was nothing she could do about the plane, and focusing on reading would stave off the panic.

Finally, the plane broke through the tattered clouds and leveled out. Peachy returned the good-luck gremlin with a trembling hand.

"You're one cool cucumber," Betty told Julia. "I can't believe you kept reading your book through all that."

Julia shrugged. "I think I read the same paragraph over and over." Now looking out the window brought a different visage. They were heading toward the Roger Queen Airport north of a gorgeous blue lake.

"That's Kunming Lake," Betty said.

"It's so beautiful." Julia's gaze stopped on a group of Chinese men dressed in blue jackets, grading the field at the edge of the runway. "What are those men doing?"

"Expanding the runway probably," Betty said. "And those children are running to greet us."

Once they disembarked, Julia marveled that a plane ride could place them into such different weather. The March temperature was cool and dry. She smiled when she saw children with their red cheeks from the cold, calling out cheerful greetings. Farther down the runway sat a row of planes that had been painted to look like Tigers.

"Tiger planes?" Julia said to Betty.

"Curtiss P-40s," Betty said. "This is the AVG base, which we call the Flying Tiger base. The Japanese attacked this base a couple of weeks after Pearl Harbor, so China recruited American pilots to help fight against Japan. They were called the First American Volunteer Group and later became known as the Flying Tigers."

"So interesting," Julia said. She turned to Peachy. "Are you feeling better?"

The woman still looked pale, but she offered a weak smile. Ellie didn't look much better.

A couple of men in OSS uniform drove up in a Jeep. They climbed out, and Julia recognized her former boss, Dick Heppner. He greeted her enthusiastically, then introduced her to the other OSS officer, Paul Helliwell.

"You were so late, we started to worry," Heppner said. "Come on, let's get you to your quarters."

As they drove along the bumpy roads, Betty filled the men in on their flight.

Julia gazed out the window as they passed rice paddies, millet fields, and even a large brood of ducks. In the distance, she saw what looked like pigs? A herd of black creatures running toward a group of eucalyptus trees. "Oh, are those pigs?"

"You don't want to get in the way of a herd of swine," Betty said with a laugh, then pointed up ahead. "And there's Kunming."

The city was walled, which shouldn't have surprised Julia since it was a medieval city. As a gateway to the Burma Road and the end of the supply line to China, it had become a political center of the war.

"It's really beautiful here," Julia said. "The blue mountains and eucalyptus trees remind me of California."

"Except we're 6,000 feet above sea level," Heppner said.

He turned onto another road, and they drove past mud-caked homes. "Don't worry, you aren't staying in one of those. OSS women are outnumbered twenty to one here, and we give the women the nicest living accommodations."

JULIA

He said this as he slowed the Jeep in front of a building with a red-tiled roof. The building looked newer, as did the surrounding buildings. Balconies made the place look elegant.

The men helped unload the women's luggage, then Heppner shook Julia's hand. "Great to be working with you again. I think you'll know some of our other transfers who just arrived. Rosie Frame and Paul Child."

Julia's words disappeared for a moment. Paul was here too? It had to be new because her last letter from him—last week—hadn't said anything. And Rosie too? She was excited to see Rosie, and she pushed down the memory of Paul saying he and Rosie had gone on a couple of dates . . . But more importantly, what would it be like to see Paul again? Would they fall into their easy friendship again? Would they be pairing off like they had at Kandy? Or would new distractions and new people keep them firmly in the casual friend corner?

"It's getting late," Heppner continued. "We're having food delivered here so you can unpack. Tomorrow morning, be ready to get to work."

"We will," Betty said.

The next morning, Julia's roommate, Betty, somehow commandeered a truck, and Julia jumped in with her. Ellie and Peachy were roommates, and Julia didn't know what their schedule would be. As Betty drove, Julia saw Kunming with fresh eyes. Most of the buildings had red-tiled rooftops, which created a harmonious picture. Once they were out of their nicer neighborhood, they drove along muddy roads crowded with people and wagons and trishaws.

Many of the Chinese wore padded blue coats, and to keep their hands warm this early in the morning, they tucked them into the opposite sleeves. "Look at the beautiful embroidery of that woman's slippers," Julia said as they drove past a shop woman setting out her wares on the sidewalk.

Then something foul filled the air, and Julia wrinkled her nose. "Oh, what's that smell?"

Betty held a scarf to her nose. "Well, it looks like sewage and smells like sewage."

"Down the *middle* of the road?"

"You're not in Kandy anymore."

They certainly weren't. The truck passed seedy alleyways that Julia was pretty sure she'd never dare step foot in, and after they left the walled city, they arrived at the Detachment 202 compound, which was also surrounded by high walls. Regardless, Julia was more than happy to be out of the mud and stink. She was also a little happy that Peachy and Ellie weren't with them right now—Julia didn't know how she'd react to seeing Paul. Or better yet, how he'd react to seeing *her*. Did he know she was here? He had to.

She wouldn't have to explain anything to Betty, and Julia wanted to keep it that way. For now.

Heppner was there to greet them, and he led Julia to her new office. "We're in desperate need for your talent, Julia," he said. "I've told Helliwell all about what you accomplished in Kandy."

"I hope I can live up to it, then," Julia said, all the while wondering if she'd turn the next corner and see Paul. Of course, he wouldn't be wandering around. He'd be neck deep in setting up another War Room.

"Here we are," Heppner said, opening a door.

Inside the room littered with desks and stacks of files, Helliwell rose to his feet. It was early in the morning, and he looked like he hadn't slept at all the night before. His hair stuck out on end, and he sported dark circles beneath his eyes. "Welcome, welcome," he said. "Did Heppner give you the grand tour?"

Julia looked at the man. "Did you?"

He grinned. "Not yet, but there's work to be done right now."

"Yes, sir." She turned to Helliwell. "What can I start on?"

Relief crossed his face, and over the next couple of hours he showed her the ins and outs of how their division served the intelligence branches. He explained that once he trained her, he'd be turning over the operation to her. "Don't worry, there are nine other staff members who will work directly under you."

"Nine?" Had Julia been promoted?

"It's a large operation, and information has to be sorted, labeled, and distributed immediately."

JULIA

Julia could understand that. After only a couple of hours with Helliwell, she could also see that a new system for code names and filing confidential paperwork needed to be implemented. The way Helliwell was doing it was much too tedious.

The other staff began to arrive, and after brief introductions, everyone set to work.

Julia familiarized herself with the index files system, and it didn't take long to spot where improvements needed to be made. She found a stack of reports that had come in from the OSS field missions—which included the coastal cities of China. The field reports detailed the locations of prisoner-of-war camp sites, and some of the reports were months old.

"Have any of these reports been categorized or indexed?" Julia asked Heppner.

By the look on his face, he didn't even need to answer. "It's in the queue. We're getting more every day, and it will take time to verify the locations and the number of prisoners."

"I think it needs to be prioritized," she said. "These prison camp locations can't be estimates only. We need to cross-locate them with other field reports on the movement of the Japanese army and the prisoner estimations in each of these locations."

Heppner sighed. "Yes."

Yes? That was his only answer. Julia noted the expectation in his eyes. She now knew why she'd been reassigned here. "I'll start organizing the system. When the OSS rescue teams are allowed to perform rescue operations, we need to provide them with accurate information so those prisoners don't spend one more day in camp than they have to."

The next hours passed quickly, and when Louis Hector, the man from the plane, entered, Julia was happy to see him.

"I need some currency," Louis said to Heppner.

The man nodded. "This way. Julia, you come too. Since you'll be doling this out."

Julia, curious, followed the men into the adjoining office. In one corner sat a steel footlocker. Heppner turned the combination then opened it. He reached inside and drew out squares of grease paper that looked like small pieces of chocolate had been wrapped inside.

"What's that?" Julia asked.

Heppner glanced over at the open door, then up at Julia. "Secret currency that we pay the spies for their work. Money is not all that valuable to them."

Julia frowned. "And that is . . ." Then she realized what she was looking at. "Opium? We pay them in opium?"

"Correct." Heppner counted out a dozen pieces, wrapped them, then handed them over to Louis.

After the transaction and Louis had left, Heppner explained their currency method of what he called *operational opium*. "Kunming is an opium stronghold. We tell all OSS, especially the women, to only travel to designated and approved areas. And never travel alone."

When Julia got over the shock of the opium payments, she returned to work, pushing through. She probably would have continued straight through lunch if Helliwell hadn't stopped her. She was so deep in her work, she hadn't even heard him talking until he came over to her desk.

"You have to eat, or Heppner will have my hide."

"I'll never complain about stopping for a meal," Julia said. When they stepped outside the main building, the wind pummeled around them. "Is this normal weather?" she asked, touching her hair—knowing it was too late to save it.

"It's normal for spring, or so I've been told," Helliwell said. "Word of advice: Don't talk until we're at the cafeteria. There's a lot of dust in the air."

Julia had just noticed that a reddish-brown dust billowed around her, making her eyes water. She kept up Helliwell's pace and hurried to the cafeteria. Once inside, she brushed off her clothing. Helliwell didn't even seem to notice that his hair was peppered with reddish-brown dirt.

"Julia!" a voice called, and she turned to see Rosie Frame.

The petite woman flung herself at Julia and hugged her. "I heard you were coming." Rosie drew back. "You're as beautiful and statuesque as ever. I think China suits you."

JULIA

Julia laughed. "You're as flattering as you've always been."

"I'm stealing her, Helliwell," Rosie said and drew Julia toward the cafeteria buffet. They walked arm in arm. "Tell me everything," Rosie continued. "As soon as I found out you knew Paul Child, I drilled him with a thousand questions. I think he's been hiding from me the past couple of days."

"What did Paul say about me?" Julia asked, then regretted being so transparent.

"Oh, I'll let him answer that himself," Rosie said lightly. "He just walked in the door."

Julia couldn't help but turn and look. Sure enough, Paul headed toward them, an easy smile on his face. She couldn't explain the relief she felt at seeing him safe and sound after three months apart. She didn't expect him to fall over in raptures, but his smile was nice.

"Julie, you're here," he said.

"I'm here. I didn't know you'd be here though."

He stepped close, kissed her cheek, then stepped back.

Julia's skin warmed at his touch and attention. She tried to keep her voice mellow though. "When did you get reassigned?"

Paul motioned toward the line that had moved forward. "Let's get our food, and I'll tell you all about it."

Julia frowned as she inspected the large platters of food. "What is all this?"

"Rice, potatoes, water buffalo, and canned tomatoes. You'll get used to it."

Julia's stomach recoiled. "I hardly think so." She looked over at Paul and asked, "Is it really water buffalo?"

"It is."

Their table ended up being crowded, with Paul, Rosie, Ellie, Peachy, Heppner, and Betty. It was like no time had passed at all, and there were only a couple of different faces mixed in. Everyone had a story to tell, including Paul about his challenges of securing needed equipment and waiting for his full team to arrive—which would include Jack Moore and Jeanne Taylor.

Rosie regaled them about her great crush on a man named Thibaut de Saint Phalle. "He's OSS, too, but he's French. With a name like that . . ." She blushed. "He's from a famous French family, you know."

A family Julia had never heard of, but that didn't matter. She was happy to see Rosie so obviously enamored, and secretly happy that it wasn't Paul she was after. Because, even now, knowing Paul for almost a year, and seeing him in two different settings, Julia could honestly say that her feelings for him were only growing stronger.

CHAPTER 13

Kunming, China
April–August 1945

"In the closing days of the war, the Office of Strategic Services was given the vital humanitarian and military assignment of locating, contacting and protecting Allied prisoners of war and civilian internees at camps scattered throughout China, Manchuria, Korea and French Indochina. The highly efficient manner in which simultaneous airborne landings were carried out after the aerial distribution of psychological surrender leaflets prepared and printed in China by OSS personnel was a glowing tribute to careful planning, excellent teamwork and unremitting devotion to duty of all personnel."

—OSS UNIT COMMENDATION

Julia stayed in Kunming for just over a month, then she was transferred again. To Chongqing this time. Paul had been able to fill her in on a few details about what to expect in Chongqing, and they'd spent more time together, but it was always in groups.

Julia's impression of Chongqing was that it was beautiful in a wild, chaotic way. The city was built atop hills and cliffs, and the Yangtze River flowed through the center of it. The temperature was warmer and more humid than Kunming, and Julia enjoyed the contrast. And the population was dense. Julia stood out like a towering statue among all the people, and gaggles of children followed her everywhere in the brown streets. In fact, everything was brown—the clothing, the water, the buildings, the roads.

Amid the beauty, though, there were harsh reminders of Japanese bombings everywhere, from the crumbled houses to the destroyed roads.

When Julia found out that her assignment was only short-term and then she'd be returning to Kunming, she was overjoyed. She'd been tasked with organizing the file system, which mostly meant reducing redundancy. She was more than happy to be overseas and helping with the war effort, but why did it always have to be attached to spending tedious hours cataloging and filing?

The day she finally returned to Kunming, she learned that President Franklin D. Roosevelt had died. It was April 12, 1945. However, the nation's sad news could not overshadow the joy she felt at being back. Even though the US's politics were in an upheaval and Kandy was the paradise she truly missed, her dearest friends were here—and that made Kunming feel like a second home.

She wasn't too happy about the cafeteria food, despite rumors that said the OSS base had hired some Chinese cooks, but there was only so much that could be done with army food, it seemed.

"Is anyone up for exploring the city for other options to eat?" Paul asked as a group of them entered the cafeteria together.

"Me," Julia said immediately. Everyone else had an excuse, but she didn't mind.

"Let's go," Paul said. "We'll take the OSS truck."

Julia was more than thrilled to find herself riding along with Paul on a narrow dirt street until they found a restaurant he said he'd been to a few times, one their mutual friend Theodore White, who'd been in China since 1939, had recommended. Julia could only hope that something inside would be tastier than what they'd left behind in the mess hall.

They parked at the far edge of the road, and Paul held the door open for her. Then they waited for a couple of trishaws to pass before crossing the street and entering the restaurant.

Everything inside was noisy, hectic, and smelled amazing as the cooks chopped vegetables and meat, then stirred the food in sizzling woks.

A server ushered them to a table next to one of the open windows. The noises from the street only made the dining experience more striking.

JULIA

The server lavished them with dish after dish of tasty food, and Julia was pretty sure she was in heaven.

"What *is* this?" Julia asked, taking another bite of some sort of fragrant chicken stew. "I could eat it every day. Can we come back tomorrow?"

Paul smiled. "It's called *qi guo ji*." He reached for his drink, then said, "I'm not sure about all the spices they use, but they cook the stew in a clay pot."

Julia took another dreamy bite. "It's incredible. What else have you eaten here?"

Paul described dishes such as *ba jiao y zheng yu* and *guo qiao mi xian*. It all sounded delicious, and she wanted to try everything. Besides, it was nice to have Paul along since he was the driver and he knew Chinese better than she.

Over the next weeks, she and Paul visited more restaurants. Once in a while, others would accompany them, but mostly, it was the two of them. When the news came that Adolf Hitler had died on April 30, Paul wanted to celebrate, so they headed out to find another restaurant. Apparently, Kunming was the capital of Yunnanese cuisine, and Julia couldn't get enough. She loved to sit and watch the chaotic preparations all around them as their waiter yelled their order to the cook and the cook threw the dishes together in adept fashion. Julia was completely entertained and only wished she could speak the language better.

Paul got by very well, and she watched as he picked up chopsticks and artfully began to use them.

The chopsticks in Julia's hands wouldn't quite cooperate.

"Don't grip so hard," Paul said. "Here. Think of them as an extension of your fingers. Just as your fingers might pick up that piece of meat, so can the chopsticks."

Julia drew in a breath, then tried again. She successfully picked up the meat, but it wobbled as the chopsticks rose. With Paul watching, she felt self-conscious. She managed to get it into her mouth, but some of the sauce escaped.

Paul only laughed and handed over a napkin.

"Does it get easier?" she asked. "I'm going to starve at this rate."

"You'll become an expert in no time," he said.

The next hour sped by, and Paul ordered more food. If he wasn't in any hurry, then neither was she.

"Word is that transfers are coming again," Paul said.

Julia had heard this too. She both dreaded it and wanted to see more of the world. Mostly she didn't want to give up Paul again. Yet she couldn't ever tell him that. He hadn't kissed her in Kunming, even though they'd spent more time together than ever before.

"Tell me about your sister," Paul said.

The question was surprising, but the other day, he'd asked about her father and brother. She'd told him about her father's extreme political views and his general stubbornness, and she'd also mentioned John's war injuries and his wife, Jo. Then Paul had shared more about Charlie and their childhood rivalry, which Julia suspected was still going on. Paul seemed to obsess over the things Charlie had that Paul didn't, such as an education, a steady job, marriage to the love of his life, and children—although Paul had said he wasn't keen on having a brood of children since he'd had his fill teaching school.

"Dort is impulsive," Julia said.

"Knowing her older sister, that doesn't surprise me."

"My sister is . . . well, she's the typical younger sister, copying everything I did as a kid. But she's more creative than I am—more passionate and really talented in all aspects of the theater. I know she's putting things on hold while I'm over here. Someone has to look after our father."

"It's noble of her, certainly," Paul said. "But you're doing something noble too."

Julia wouldn't argue with that, but she also worried about Dort's becoming resentful. "She and Pop get along well. Dort doesn't push his buttons as much as I do." Julia shrugged and took another bite of her steamed fish. She took a moment to chew and enjoy the taste.

"You're an entertaining eater," Paul said, amused. "And I mean that in the best way."

Julia's eyes widened. "And how is that *in the best way*?"

"You enjoy your food, and it's enjoyable to be with you when you eat."

"Well." Julia was probably blushing, but the warmth of the restaurant hopefully hid all that. "I have you to thank. No more army dinners for me." She gave a mock shudder.

"Do you like to cook at home?"

Julia paused at this. She could cook . . . basic things and some of her mother's recipes. "I do like to cook, actually," she said. "Although I wouldn't be what you'd call a domestic. I grew up rather pampered, as you know, having a cook at the house. But Dort and I would steal into the kitchen and make a few things."

"Too bad they don't have Chinese restaurants in Pasadena."

"It would be amazing if they did," Julia said. "I might even be able to convince my father to try it." She glanced over at the kitchen and the busy cooks. "Do you think they'll share their recipes?"

"I don't think they follow recipes," Paul said.

They both laughed as one cook yelled at another cook, obviously unhappy with his choice of ingredients or cooking method.

Before Julia knew it, they'd spent three hours at the restaurant, talking about the impending German surrender, the end of the war in the European theater, and what might happen with Japan next. They also discussed how Julia would probably be relegated to caring for her father in Pasadena after the war, and Paul would be scrabbling for another government position and living with Charlie until he became established.

Julia cherished their conversation about what to do after the war ended, especially when a week later, on May 7, Germany surrendered to the Allies. While in Reims, France, German General Alfred Jodl signed the unconditional surrender of all German forces, with General Ivan Susloparov of the Soviet Union and French General Francois Sevez signing as witnesses. General Walter Bedell Smith, General Eisenhower's chief of staff, signed for the Allied Expeditionary Force. The surrender document stated that all German forces would stop fighting on May 8, 1945, at 23:01 hours. The Soviet Union then mandated that they would accept only a separate surrender from Germany to the Red Army. Field

Marshal Wilhelm Keitel signed the surrender on May 8 in Berlin in the presence of the commander in chief of the Soviet Army, General Georgi Zhukov.

Despite knowing the Allies weren't out of the woods with Japan, both Julia and Paul accepted a transfer to Chongqing, along with several of their OSS staff friends. There the work continued, Paul setting up another War Room and Julia getting the registry in shape. They spent time together and with groups of people, working all hours but also finding gaps to enjoy dances on the base and the occasional weekend excursion to the hot springs or the temples.

Julia was looking forward to exploring more restaurants with Paul, but a cholera breakout prevented that. And before the end of the summer, Julia and several OSS friends were transferred back to Kunming.

Then the news came.

On August 6, the United States dropped an atomic bomb on Hiroshima. Two days later, the Soviets invaded Manchuria and Sakhalin Island. Then, if that news wasn't enough to send everyone reeling, on August 9, the US dropped another atomic bomb on Nagasaki.

"The Japanese Empire has no choice but to surrender," Jack Moore said as they all gathered around a table at the cafeteria, the scents of food and cigarettes intermingling.

Paul tapped his cigarette against an ash tray, then took another grim drag. "Our work will change once again. There's much to wrap up here, and transportation back home will take weeks or even months to arrange."

Julia didn't contribute to the conversation, only listened, as a deep sense of melancholy wrapped around her—not only because of the immense loss of life that had forced the war to end but because of the losses that had been occurring for years. And now . . . despite the relief that this war would finally be over, she'd miss her tight-knit group of friends. She'd miss the purpose she'd felt for the first time in her life.

Was it selfish to feel so glum about her future? Yet she had no real skills beyond her experience. She knew a few dozen phrases in Chinese, she knew a lot of OSS secrets that wouldn't matter anymore, and she'd seen parts of the world she could have only imagined before. She'd been

JULIA

part of a unit, a cause, but once she was back in Pasadena, she'd be back to her old life of wiling the days away at a country club, listening to her father's extreme political rants, and telling Dort that it would be fine for her to leave—to go live her life.

Over the next several days, Julia and her friends stayed up late talking about the coming changes. On August 10, Japan offered to surrender to the Allies, the only condition being that the emperor be allowed to remain the nominal head of state. But the US countered on August 12, saying that the emperor could remain as a ceremonial figure only. Air raids continued on August 13 as the Japanese government delayed their decision.

With Julia's birthday approaching, rumors about Japan's impending surrender flew about headquarters. Then, finally, on her birthday, August 15, the Japanese emperor announced by radio broadcast that Japan was surrendering.

"We have much to celebrate," Paul told her as the group gathered to discuss all the changes coming. He'd sat next to her, and the others were deep in conversation about something else.

"My birthday?" Julia teased.

"Yes, and that's why I wrote you a sonnet."

Julia stared at the folded paper he held out. She was almost afraid to open it. She hadn't expected any recognition or fanfare . . . not today of all days.

She opened the folded page, but Paul put a hand on her arm. "Not here. Read it somewhere else."

"Is it private?"

He shrugged. "More like . . . personal. Besides, my artful words should be read with appreciation and not amid all this discussion."

Julia lowered the paper and held it in her lap. Were her hands trembling? She drew in a slow breath, trying not to grin with giddiness. She had no idea what Paul had written, but the fact remained, he'd written a sonnet to *her*. Only her.

"We'll be organizing commando teams to retrieve the POWs from the Japanese prison camps," Gregory was saying to the group.

That comment made Julia sober, and she wondered if there might be news of Patty's fiancé in such a place.

"I'm probably going to Java since I speak Malay," Jane Foster said. "The Dutch have been in prison camps since the bombing of Pearl Harbor, after which Japan invaded the Dutch East Indies in defiance of the Netherlands."

Theodore White nodded. "There will be thousands of refugees to relocate. It's going to be a colossal undertaking."

This sobered everyone at the table. "What's been going on in Europe will be going on here too," Theodore continued, "but with more complications. China was in the middle of their civil war when they paused to join forces with the Allies against Japan. What's going to happen now?"

"They'll resume because both sides will still want control," Paul said.

"It's what I believe, too," Theodore said.

"So the killing will continue," Jane said. "Revolution, refugees, and everyone trying to rebuild."

Everything was changing, yet again. Important changes but also devastating changes on all fronts.

The discussion continued, turning to the military occupation of Japan that the US had led under the direction of General Douglas A. MacArthur. Intelligence had already been collected on how the Japanese people might react to the occupation and the mountain of rehabilitation and restoration work that would be taking place over the next few years.

It wasn't until Paul suggested a walk outside that Julia was finally able to breathe a little more freely. It had been raining off and on the past couple of days, and right now, the clouds weighed heavy, but the rain was holding off. She and Paul ended up sitting on the veranda because the ground was mostly mud.

"I know the war is officially over, but it seems like the news coming in is still devastating."

"Recovery will take a long time," Paul agreed as he lit a cigarette. "That doesn't mean your birthday shouldn't be celebrated."

Julia gave him a small smile. "Thanks for this." She held up the folded paper. "Can I read your sonnet now?"

JULIA

"You may." His voice was soft, almost affectionate, but Julia didn't want to assume anything.

She unfolded the paper, then read.

> *How like the Autumn's warmth is Julia's face*
> *So filled with Nature's bounty, Nature's worth*
> *And how like summer's heat is her embrace*
> *Wherein at last she melts my frozen earth.*
> *Endowed, the awakened fields abound*
> *With newly green effulgence, smiling flowers.*
> *Then all the lovely riches of the ground*
> *Spring up responsive to her magic powers.*
> *Sweet friendship, like the harvest-cycle, moves*
> *From scattered seed to final ripened grain,*
> *Which, glowing in the warmth of Autumn, proves*
> *The richness of the soil, and mankind's gain.*
> *I cast this heaped abundance at your feet*
> *An offering to Summer, and her heat.*

CHAPTER 14

Kunming, China
September–October 1945

"We have been asked by the War Crimes Commission to cooperate in obtaining evidence against some of the principal Nazi leaders in Germany. I should like to ask my trusted contacts in Stockholm to determine what happened to labor leaders in Germany after the seizure of three trade union associations in May and June of 1933. The best qualified evidence should be gathered as soon as possible. Find out the nature of the arrest, confinement of leaders, assaults, maltreatment, murders, 'suicides after arrest,' 'killed while trying to escape,' etc. Clear evidence will go far in explaining the guilt of these disappearances."

—LILLIAN TRAUGOTT, OSS STAFF, STOCKHOLM, SWEDEN

Each morning and evening, Julia and her friends glued themselves to the radio broadcasts in the cafeteria to hear updates on the progress of Japan's surrender and the liberation of prisoners of war throughout the Pacific Rim. Finally, on September 2, 1945, the formal surrender ceremony took place on the deck of the USS *Missouri* in Tokyo Bay.

That morning, Julia sat next to Paul as they listened to the broadcast. "The Japanese envoy's Foreign Minister Mamoru Shigemitsu and General Yoshijiro Umezu signed their names on the Instrument of Surrender at 9:04 this morning."

Julia felt both overjoyed and exhausted. The war was truly over, although it still felt surreal.

"Next, General Douglas MacArthur, commander in the Southwest Pacific and supreme commander for the Allied powers, also signed," continued the radio broadcaster, "accepting the Japanese surrender for the United States, Republic of China, United Kingdom, and Union of Soviet

Socialist Republics, and in the interests of the other United Nations at war with Japan."

Everyone in the cafeteria broke out in cheers.

Paul hugged Julia, and she hugged him back. Then she hugged her other friends. Things between she and Paul had changed since her birthday. Perhaps it was a weight off everyone's shoulders that they had finally won the war. Or perhaps it was spending the last eighteen months off and on in each other's company that had allowed them to get to know each other's true selves . . . and Paul appreciated what he found in her.

She could only hope.

As more changes came down the line and the OSS staff began to receive reassignments, Julia spent more time with Paul than ever. They frequented the regional restaurants, trying every bit of Yunnanese food they could find, and they sat on the main veranda in the evenings, which had become their favorite spot, and Paul read to her—something he seemed to enjoy, and something she loved.

They were currently working their way through Hemingway's short stories. Paul had such a way of reading with emotion that Julia wondered if he could ever truly see her as an equal. She'd read books over the years, but she'd never read simply for the visceral pleasure of falling into the story through the words.

Some OSS staff were already going home, like Peachy and Betty. Betty had been sent home to begin work on an assignment to write the history of the OSS in China. She'd also told Julia she was going to start on her memoir.

It was a surprise to Julia when she found out that Heppner had recommended her for the Oak-Leaf Cluster award, with the official description reading as: Julia McWilliams's "meritorious service as head of the Registry sections of the Secretariat of the Office of Strategic Service, China Theater. Important job calculating and channeling a great amount of classified documents. Her drive and inherent cheerfulness served as a spur to greater effort by those working for her." Certainly an honor, but changes were happening so fast, she didn't have time to appreciate her award.

President Harry S. Truman had announced the dissolution of the active-war-duty OSS starting on October 1. Time had just shortened. But over the next weeks, the workload of the OSS staff changed to postwar assignments.

On the night of October 5, Chiang Kai-shek's army infiltrated Kunming and fired upon Long's troops in a push to resume the Chinese civil war and establish political dominance now that Japan had been neutralized. For four days, Julia was sequestered with the women in their house, not allowed to go anywhere. They couldn't even sit on the balcony, for fear of getting struck by one of the stray bullets.

When the Kunming Incident ended, Julia and Paul both had their new assignments. Paul was leaving on October 12 for Peking, where the army wanted to establish its presence before the Communist Party had time to dominate. In the meantime, he'd been kept busy drawing maps for the humanitarian teams working to recover prisoners from POW camps.

And Julia received the news that she'd return to Calcutta on October 16.

"I can't focus on one word," Julia told Paul one evening as they enjoyed the velvety night air beneath a lantern on the main veranda. "You're reading it beautifully, but I feel like Hemingway is turning over in his grave right now."

Paul didn't laugh. He lowered the book and asked, "What's wrong?"

Julia closed her eyes, feeling frustration bubble up. She hated how her voice warbled up and down in pitch when she was upset or excited. She dragged in a deep breath, then opened her eyes. "What's going to happen to us back in America? I mean . . . will your departure to Peking be the last time I see you?"

Yes, they'd talked about this, but now it was a reality, and Julia couldn't stop agonizing over it. Perhaps she was being dramatic, but they were literally running out of time.

Paul scooted his chair closer, then reached for her hand. She watched as their fingers entwined together. They'd only kissed once, but despite all the time they'd spent together, there had been no ardent declarations made. They'd already discussed how friendships might not be the same stateside and how life would pick up again for each of them, pulling them even farther apart through living on opposite sides of the country. It was why their relationship hadn't progressed to physical intimacy. Julia supposed she could be flattered that Paul didn't see her as a throwaway girlfriend, someone to have a fling with. And of course Julia was fine to wait—she wanted to wait—but she wanted that wait to be for Paul.

Julia's eyes burned. Her heart would probably fail if Paul told her that they'd write to each other and wait and see . . . It was the *waiting and seeing* that was killing her now. She lowered her chin, unable to look him in the eye as her tears brimmed.

"How about we meet in Washington, DC once we both arrive?" Paul asked in a gentle tone. "We'll have to fill out our formal discharge forms, and then you can meet Charlie and Fredricka."

"I would love to meet them," Julia said. Meeting his family definitely seemed like something that would happen if Paul had serious feelings for her. Yet she didn't allow herself to feel too much hope.

"What are your plans for Thanksgiving?" he asked.

She bit her lip. "I suppose spend it in Pasadena. Do you have a better idea?"

"I do." Paul smiled, and she decided it was her favorite expression of his. "We'll likely both end up in Washington working anyway. That is, if you can get out of babysitting your father."

Julia smirked. She wouldn't know until she got home what the real situation would be with her father.

"My brother will tire of me soon enough," he continued. "So . . . why don't you come to Pennsylvania for Thanksgiving? We'll celebrate the holiday together at my brother's house, and then . . ."

Julia blinked, and a tear fell, but she lifted her chin anyway. "And then . . . ?" She prodded.

"And then we'll go from there." He squeezed her hand. "I can't make a promise when anything can happen at any moment. But right now, right here, I'm saying that if we are both stateside toward the end of November, we now have a plan, and we're sticking to it."

Julia wiped at her cheek with her free hand. Paul procured a handkerchief and offered it over.

"Charlie already knows you're warm, funny, understanding, and darling," Paul added. "They'll love meeting you, and I'll love you meeting them."

Julia really had no answer, but one thing was clear: She had to kiss this man. So she did. It was too brief, in her opinion, but she wasn't sure how public Paul wanted to be with affection. Anyone could walk out onto the veranda at any time.

"Did you really tell Charlie all that about me?" Julia asked, drawing away but keeping his hand in hers.

"I've written pages about you to my brother," he said. "But it's time to stop talking about my brother. We only have a few days until I leave. Let's go splurge at Ho-Teh-Foo."

Ho-Teh-Foo had become their favorite restaurant in Kunming, and since Julia was pretty much a Chinese food fanatic now, she agreed without a second thought.

As they drove, they got onto the subject of French food, which Julia said she'd never tried—at least nothing authentic.

"You haven't lived until you've eaten French food," he said.

Julia laughed because his tone was so serious. "All right, I'll have to take your word for it since I've gotten along fine so far."

"One day, I'll prove it to you," he said in a lighter tone.

Julia knew he was teasing, but a small thrill ran through her nonetheless at the thought of any future world that might feature eating French food with Paul Child.

By the time they reached the restaurant, she was good and hungry with all their talk of food—Chinese, French, or otherwise.

The place was busy and crowded and smelled delicious.

"I think I'm hungry enough to order everything on the menu," Julia said.

"Go ahead," Paul said. "I'm buying, and we can take the leftovers to our friends. They're probably huddled over the radio as we speak."

So they ordered until their small table was crowded with steaming dishes. Julia tried it all, from the egg-drop soup to fried spring rolls, Yunnan ham mixed with cabbage, and Peking duck on a platter of noodles to beets, mushrooms, and the list went on.

The meal was absolutely perfect, and in Julia's mind, so was Paul.

She didn't realize how much she could miss a person until Paul left for Peking. She'd known it was coming, but that didn't make it easier. Nothing was sufficient enough to distract her from the aching longing that seemed to plague her night and day. Was this love? True love? She didn't know what else it could be.

She wrote letters to her family and friends back home at night, knowing there wouldn't be time to receive replies from them. Still, she'd hoped for something from Paul but wasn't surprised when no letters arrived. Before she knew it, she had been given her discharge order, and soon, she'd be on her way back to the United States.

She flew back over the Hump to Calcutta and ended up getting stuck there for over a week, where she had to live in a small room with five other women. The living conditions were so tight that she looked forward to getting on a ship soon—any ship.

Julia was relieved to set sail with two of her best friends, Ellie and Rosie, and discovered Rosie was newly engaged to Thibaut.

Their journey aboard the troopship *General Stewart*, transporting 3,500 people, had very sparse accommodations. Reveille was at 5:00 a.m., and taps sounded at 9:00 p.m. Julia and her friends wore the most basic, worn-out clothing and didn't care a fig about their hair or makeup. Nothing like the journey on the SS *Mariposa*.

"I can't believe we're finally on our way," Ellie said to Julia, coming to stand beside her by the railing. "We have to plan something once we land."

They both glanced over at Rosie, who was ignoring the approaching shoreline of Colombo, Ceylon, and reading a book.

"You're right," Julia said. "Rosie will only have eyes for her fiancé. What should we do?"

"I know." Ellie smiled. "We'll take a cab to New York City's famous restaurant, the 21 Club."

"Sounds delightful to me." Julia gazed at the Colombo bay before them as the ship moved toward the harbor to refuel. The docks were packed with all types of ships, including freighters and warships. She watched the bustle of activity and felt the warm breeze tickle the hair at the nape of her neck. It had been nearly eighteen months since she'd first arrived in Colombo. She had been a different girl back then.

"Oh, and I'll need a perm straightaway," she said, touching her flyaway hair. "If any of it is even salvageable. I don't want to attempt visiting Paul in DC until I look human again."

"You'll look wonderful in no time, well before Paul makes it to Washington," Ellie said.

Julia released a sigh. "He probably wouldn't recognize me if I do too much. Besides, who knows if Paul of Washington will like Julia of Pasadena."

Ellie linked their arms. "I'm rooting for you both."

So was Julia. "And I'm rooting for you and your major."

Ellie's cheeks pricked pink. She'd met British Major F. Basil Summers in Chongqing, and Ellie was hoping for a proposal and a ticket to England—sooner rather than later.

Once they reached New York Harbor, both Julia and Ellie made good on their promise. They didn't care if they were bedraggled or ship worn. They wanted something to eat that wasn't out of a can. But the news that greeted them on US shores was sobering, with reports detailing the indictment of twenty-four Nazi government officials and organizations. The Nuremburg trials were set to start November 20. Julia would be happy to see justice served, but reading about the terrible war crimes made her soul feel heavy.

Her first night spent at the Brighton Hotel in Washington, she slept fitfully. When she awoke, she felt tired and foggy-brained. But Ellie reminded her that they were going to get perms, and by the end of their hair appointment, Julia had recovered somewhat.

Together they made their way to the Q Building and found the structure familiar yet strange at the same time. Had the past two years really happened overseas? Nothing here seemed different. She and Ellie filled out their triplicate discharge forms and took their final physical exams.

When they walked out of the building together, they paused on the sidewalk, with traffic inching its way along the street and pedestrians bustling about them.

"Do you want me to come with you?" Ellie asked.

"I would love it, but I think I need to do this myself." Paul had given her Charlie's address and said that when she arrived, she should stop by in the evening. He'd be staying there once he made it to DC.

Julia could only guess if he was in DC right now, but she'd find out soon enough.

"Oh, wait," Ellie said. "I picked up our mail."

"Mail?"

Julia stared as Ellie drew out a battered envelope from her bag. "One letter from Paul."

Julia snatched it, and Ellie laughed. The envelope looked like it had been around the world twice.

"I'll leave you to it, and don't worry, Paul will think you look like a confection all dolled up." Ellie grinned. "See you back at the hotel." She gave Julia a brief hug and walked away.

That left Julia to find a cab and time to read the letter alone. Inside the envelope was a short, hurried note, but the words were a balm to her aching heart.

> *Beloved Julie,*
> *At the risk of sounding trite, I wish you were here. I need you to enjoy these marvels with, and I miss your companionship something awful. Dearest Julie, why aren't you here, holding my hand and making plans for food and fun!*
> *Love, Paulski*

The letter was dated a month ago. He must have written it soon after arriving in Peking. She read the letter again, and a third time, then analyzed the salutation. He'd used their nicknames, he'd written "love," and he missed her.

She smiled the entire ride into Georgetown, and when the cab pulled in front of 1311 Thirty-Fifth Street, she said, "Can you wait for me? I won't be long."

It would give her an excuse to have a short stay, and if Paul was there, he could visit her later at the Brighton Hotel. She didn't want to feel like a bug under a microscope around his brother and family.

Knocking on the painted door, she felt her pulse zip higher and higher. She heard footsteps, then a woman's voice, and suddenly, the door swung open. The woman standing on the threshold was probably in her thirties and had to be Freddie. Her red hair was as bright as a sunrise, and her freckles nearly matched Julia's. She was several inches shorter than Julia, which most people were.

"Hello, I'm Julia McWilliams, and I've come to introduce myself. I'm friends with Paul Child."

The woman's face broke into a wide grin. "Julia! We've been waiting for you."

Right there on the stoop, Freddie gave her a tight hug.

"Come in, come in. Dinner is about to start, and I'll set an extra place." Freddie turned halfway toward the hallway. "Charlie! Paul! We have a visitor."

Paul. She'd called for Paul. He was here? He was here!

Julia barely had time to register the information and draw in a breath when two men walked into the hallway—twin men. She could tell them apart immediately, but the likeness was still uncanny. Charles was a bit stockier, and more of his hair had receded compared to Paul's.

And Paul . . . He was deeply tanned.

"What did you do? Sunbathe all day while on the ship?" Julia blurted out.

Paul laughed and crossed to her, then kissed her cheek.

Julia's heart warmed at his familiar scent of musky soap.

Paul turned to his brother and sister-in-law. "Charlie and Freddie, I'd like you to meet Julia McWilliams."

Charlie extended his hand. "The famous Julia. So pleased to finally meet you." His tone was warm, his gaze earnest.

JULIA

"Please, stay for dinner, won't you?" Freddie said.

But Julia couldn't bring herself to say yes. She wanted to, but she wanted more to have Paul all to herself. Until she knew what was going on between them, she didn't want to become invested in his family. She sensed it would only bring more heartache.

"My cab is waiting since I have another appointment," she said. "Tomorrow, I'm going to Pittsfield to see my brother and his wife, along with a visit to my mother's sister, Theodora. I wanted to meet everyone before I head back to Pasadena. Paul has told me so much about you both."

She could see the disappointment in Paul's eyes, and that made her feel both guilty and pleased at the same time. Maybe his letter to her, with its endearments, was still true?

They chatted for a few moments, then Julia insisted that she had to leave.

"I'll walk you out," Paul said.

Well, she couldn't turn down that offer. They headed outside, with Paul closing the door behind them. The neighborhood was quiet, and only a handful of cars were on the street. The cab driver was waiting, his windows rolled down as he smoked and read a newspaper.

"I'm so glad you came," Paul said, stopping at the bottom of the steps. "Do you really have to run off?"

Julia stopped, too, and faced him. "I do. I'm glad I was able to meet some of your family though. Your brother and his wife are lovely people."

Paul touched her arm. "You aren't upset with me, are you?"

"No—no, nothing like that." Julia smiled, trying to reassure him. "I received your letter, dated a month ago. They were sweet words and gave me a lot of hope, you know."

Paul dipped his chin. "They're still true, if that's what you're asking. This isn't goodbye, Julie. I still hope you'll come for Thanksgiving. Make it a proper visit next time."

Julia's heart soared, and she had to ask, "Is stateside Julia all that you expected?"

Paul's brows rose. "Whether or not your hair is styled or your shoes are polished doesn't matter to me. I think we're beyond first impressions."

"I should hope so."

He grasped her hand, and somehow, Julia's heart rate spiked higher than it already was.

"By the way, you do look beautiful," Paul said. "Perhaps I should have led with that, and then you'd be convinced to stay."

She looked from him to the front door of the home. "I just . . ." She drew in a breath. "I want to visit with you, but being with the entire family is a bit overwhelming."

He didn't say anything for a moment, then he nodded. "I understand." He leaned close, kissing her cheek. "Until next month, fair Julia. I'm counting on it."

Julia wouldn't be surprised if her heart jumped out of her chest then and there. She wanted to wrap her arms around this man and never let him go. Was he too good to be true? She certainly hoped not. "I'm planning on it," she said.

Moving toward the waiting cab, she suddenly felt reluctant and weepy. Could she really say goodbye to Paul once again? He hadn't moved. He was watching her, hands in his pockets, his gaze keen, the edges of his mouth lifted. Then she couldn't wait anymore. She hurried toward him and threw her arms about his neck.

Paul's arms came around her, and he pulled her close.

"It's good to see you, Paulski," she whispered.

"It's good to see you too." His voice rumbled against her ear.

And then her self-consciousness kicked in, and she released him. Stepped back. Gave a little wave, then climbed into the cab.

CHAPTER 15

Pasadena, California
January–May 1946

"I do love to cook. I suppose it would lose some glamour if I were married to a ditch digger and had seven children, howsoever."

—LETTER FROM JULIA TO PAUL, APRIL 22, 1946

Julia hated that she was in Pasadena and Paul was back east. She'd applied for a government job before leaving Washington, DC, saying she was happy to locate anywhere, but she only wanted to work in public relations, and have *nothing* to do with filing. Oh, and she'd stated she was only six feet tall.

Before returning home, she'd visited her brother and his wife in Pittsfield—the reunion was bittersweet. John had aged, although she supposed they'd all aged. He also walked with a limp; otherwise, he seemed as active as ever. And Julia took solace in seeing her brother in person and being assured of his well-being.

Once she finally reached Pasadena, her reunion with Dort and Pop was equally sweet. Although the very next day, her father's caustic political remarks dug into her skin like a burrowing beetle because now she knew better. She understood other viewpoints since being exposed to other beliefs and traditions.

Mostly, she let her father's comments slide off her back. She was trying to figure out her next steps in life—like the rest of the country. The war was over and, with it, the purpose that Julia had held close the past couple of years too. Marriages of her friends seemed to be happening left and right, and though Julia hadn't ever exactly walked a traditional path, marriage to a specific man was certainly appealing. After all, she wasn't getting any younger—and Paul certainly wasn't—and if she could see herself doing something five years from now, she wouldn't mind being a wife and mother. Perhaps she could become a housewife after all.

If only to confirm her affection toward Paul, later in the week, she ran into Harrison Chandler at a social function. Luckily, her friend Katy Gates was with her, and Julia could use her as a bit of a buffer. Because it was clear that Harrison was still interested in her. But Julia didn't feel even one spark of interest for him. He would probably laugh if he knew all her domesticated thoughts toward another man.

She offered Harrison condolences on his father's death, who'd passed in September 1944. Harrison talked briefly about his brother Norman taking over as publisher and how Harrison would stay as the vice president of the Times Mirror Printing and Binding House.

After he asked about her family, he added, "I'd love to take you out—the two of us—so I can hear about all your OSS adventures."

Julia hadn't exactly committed, but she hadn't exactly turned him down either. Frankly, she hadn't been prepared to see him or to be asked out.

The very next week, she learned that Harrison had been talking to her father since her return, hinting that he would love to start dating Julia again.

By the time February rolled around and Harrison had dropped too many hints, all of which her father had encouraged, Julia had to finally put a stop to it. First, she called Harrison early in the morning when she knew he'd be starting his day at his office.

"Harrison," she said without bothering with a polite greeting. "I'm sorry to bother you at work, but this is a serious call, and I don't want you distracted. I'll be speaking to my father this morning, too, but I want you both to know that I won't be marrying you."

She heard his bluster on the other end of the phone.

"You haven't proposed—yet—but you're intruding on my privacy, and you're including my father—giving him hope where there isn't." She dragged in a breath. "I should have said something earlier, even written you a letter during the war, but I'm in love with another man. I can only hope it will result in marriage. Even if it doesn't, you and I aren't right for each other."

Harrison spent the next few minutes telling her he hadn't been pressuring her, and he wasn't trying to butter up her father, but it was all white noise as far as Julia was concerned. After hanging up with him, she went to find her father, who'd be a harder person to speak to.

He was finishing his breakfast in the dining room, looking over a copy of the *Washington Post* she'd recently subscribed to.

"This is drivel, Julia," Pop said, looking up at her, his graying brows furrowed. "Cancel your subscription. I don't like it in my house. The only trustworthy reporting is the *Los Angeles Times*, you know that."

She sat across from her father and took the newspaper he handed over. Their opinions were still a mile apart, but that could be an argument for another time. "Pop, I just spoke to Harrison Chandler."

She hated the way his entire expression lit up.

"I've turned down any future with him," Julia said. "He's not the right man for me, and he'll never be my husband. I told him that he shouldn't be chumming with you behind my back either."

With every word she spoke, her father's face grew redder and redder.

"That was a mistake!" he burst out. "You only need to get to know each other again after such a long separation. You shouldn't throw away years of friendship, and don't forget, you were in love with him enough to become engaged."

"I wasn't exactly in love—"

"You're a good match—the best match," Pop continued as he gripped the edge of the table, his knuckles turning white. "You don't understand how wonderful your life will be by marrying a steady fellow with a future legacy mapped out for him. Security and trust are more important than silly feelings of love that burn out like fire."

Julia knew that her parents had been in love, and they'd waited for years to marry until her mother's ill sister had finally settled with her own husband, so Julia didn't understand how her father could even think he had a leg to stand on here. Maybe he wanted her to be financially secure, but she could work if needed, and she probably would. She was done being a social butterfly who spent her days at the country club and evenings at parties. She wanted something real and substantial, and that was Paul.

"I have full trust in Paul," Julia told her father, using every ounce of calm she could muster. "And the two of us will create the security we need for each other. I know your intentions are good, Pop, but I can't marry a man I don't love, and I won't be changing my mind."

"You need to consider the whole picture," he continued as if he hadn't heard a word she'd said. "Paul is a liberal, and he flits from job to job. That's no way to support a wife or family. A man his age should be well established and—"

"If you'll excuse me. I'm not willing to listen to you cutting down a person I care deeply for," she interrupted. Julia couldn't stomach her father throwing mud at Paul and his political beliefs and his line of work.

She hurried out of the room, tears burning in her eyes as her father stared after her.

The next days were filled with silent tension between her and her father, though she'd heard his rants—to Dort, mostly, or anyone else who'd listen to his tale of woe about his ungrateful and naive daughter.

Julia told herself to rise above her father's needling complaints and focus on her letter writing with Paul. Throughout the past month, Paul's letters to her had become sweeter, even amorous, with one of his recent letters saying, "Whether we do or do not manage to live a large part of our future lives together, I have no regrets for the past, no recriminations, and no unresolved areas of conflict. It was lovely, warming, fulfilling, and solid—and one of the best things that ever happened to me. *Affectionately, Paulski.*"

He told her of his brother's second home in Lumberville, Pennsylvania, which they called Coppernose. Freddie had inherited a nearby house, and when the owner of Coppernose had died, Freddie had bought the home, and it became their weekend retreat. Paul had described it as a beautiful home with a brick terrace that overlooked a garden with a brook running through, a small waterfall, and a swimming pool.

Julia would never admit to how many times she read each of his letters.

And they had a plan in place. Paul would come to Pasadena in a few months, in July, to meet her sister and father, then she and Paul would drive across the country to Charlie's vacation home in Maine. A month of driving together and spending nonstop time in each other's company would be the final valuation—would their relationship grow, or would it fall apart?

Whatever might happen, Julia had a few months to prepare herself, and one of the things she talked to Dort and her friends about was how she was not really wife material.

"If I'm hoping that Paul proposes and asks me to be his wife, what sort of wife will he be getting?" Julia lamented one day as she, Dort, and Katy Gates lazed on the veranda behind Father's home, surrounded by early spring flowers and budding trees. "I can barely cook. I can passably clean. I'm not afraid of trying new things or going on adventures. I can hold my own on the tennis court, but . . ."

"But what?" Dort asked, taking a sip from her glass. She'd been talking about going to New York City again to work in theater, and they'd had more than one discussion of how it was Julia's turn to look after their father. Dort had done her bit the past couple of years, working at the army hospital and looking after Pop. "What do *you* think Paul expects in a wife?"

"Well, his mother was a good cook," Julia said, "and he talks fondly about the food in France."

"And the two of you practically had an affair over the love of Chinese food," Katy mused.

If Julia were sitting closer to her friend, she would swat her. "That might be true, but the Chinese restaurants were affordable with the strength of the dollar over there. We'll go broke pretty quickly if we have to eat out every night here."

"I guess you need to learn to cook, then?" Katy asked.

Dort laughed. "*My sister*? In the kitchen? You must be head-over-heels in love."

"It's nothing to laugh over," Julia said, her face heating as she turned toward Dort. Maybe she was head-over-heels, but it was nothing to debate. She wasn't about to tell them she thought of Paul night and day, and sometimes she missed him so much, places deep inside her ached. Regardless, right now, she had a real dilemma. "I've been plagued night and day over this. Besides, I've made a few of Mother's recipes."

Dort didn't seem impressed. "Speaking of Mother, you could use your inheritance from her for all your restaurant visits."

Julia released a sigh. "I've thought of that, but it won't last forever."

"Find another job, then?"

"I'm afraid if I'm following Paul's career, I'll end up with one of those filing jobs again." She winced.

"Then, I guess you'll have to take cooking lessons," Katy said, smiling at both sisters as if she'd just had the most wonderful idea in the world. "I'll take them with you. We could go to the Hillcliff School of Cookery in Beverly Hills."

Julia straightened. She'd thought of shadowing their father's cook for a couple of weeks, but that might become intrusive; besides, she wanted to learn to cook more things than basic stews and roasted meat and potatoes. Cooking lessons sounded like a much more reasonable plan.

"All right," she said without another moment's thought. "We'll go together. How about you, Dort? Are you coming?"

Dort scoffed. "I'm staying right here. You go become domesticated for your man—I have no such plans in my immediate future."

Julia knew her sister was teasing, but she wasn't about to press her. Besides, if Katy was willing to come, it would make it all the more fun.

Over the next weeks, Julia fully enjoyed the cooking class, although she might have been frustrating to their instructors, Irene Radcliffe and Mary Hill. It wasn't that Julia didn't follow directions, because she did, but disasters happened anyway. Usually because Julia forgot one small step or made a substitution that ended up not being a wise choice.

When she prepared a duck, she forgot to puncture the skin, and the bird exploded in the oven. Another time, she ran out of butter, so she thought it logical to substitute lard in the *béarnaise* sauce, and well, that was a mistake because the sauce hardened into a solid lump. She couldn't figure out how to smoothly blend in the eggs with a pancake recipe, so they came out mostly eggs in a couple of the pancakes and mostly flour in the others. She also somehow turned a soufflé into a brick-like dish, both in weight and density.

Fortunately, Paul seemed vastly entertained by her letters about her cooking attempts and always wrote something encouraging back. "You'll be a wonderful cook in no time since you enjoy food so much," he'd written once.

It made her laugh because it was so true. She did enjoy food, but how does one turn an eating passion into a cooking talent that would impress the likes of her Paul? Yes, he knew all sides of her personality and never seemed exasperated with all her dabbling, but was he just being indulgent and not really being serious about their future?

She supposed that if he actually did show up in Pasadena in July, she'd know—she'd know that Paul cared for her beyond a friend. And they'd be another step toward a possible future together.

Until then, she'd expand her culinary skills—as well as her mind— by reading intellectual books. Her latest read was *Language in Action* by S. I. Hayakawa, a book that Paul had mentioned in one of his recent letters. He'd told her that Hayakawa's work had helped him discipline his mind and writing style. She'd even taken the book, in addition to a few of Paul's latest letters, with her to the hospital when she'd had surgery to remove a goiter inside her neck.

Also, much to her father's verbal complaint, she'd kept her subscription to the *Washington Post* and added the Sunday *New York Times*. She wanted to read more viewpoints of political policies and theories. It wasn't that she stopped reading the *Los Angeles Times*—she did have some loyalty to the Chandler family after all—but she was more open-minded now.

When Paul's letters began to include more endearments, Julia wondered if she were reading into things too much. Her heart felt like it was in a constant tug-of-war, and she knew a rejection from Paul would be a crushing blow.

"What swoony thing did he say this time?" Dort asked coming into the kitchen, where Julia languished over a late breakfast of toast and fruit.

Pop had already left for the Annandale Country Club, with some comment about a tee time. Julia knew she should join him. Things had finally mellowed between them, although she'd turned down the last couple of invitations. But she liked to work on her recipes when everyone was out of the house.

"He says he's kissed no one since he's kissed me," Julia said.

Dort sank into the chair next to her. "Oh, that's an interesting thing for him to say. Does that mean he's been around other women who want to kiss him, but he's gallantly turned them down?"

Julia frowned. "I don't know . . . Should I worry about that?"

Dort nudged her arm. "No, I'm teasing. I think—knowing Paul only through his letters and your stories—he's trying to tell you that you're the only woman on his mind and in his heart."

Julia sighed. "Do you really think it's true?"

Dort placed a hand over Julia's. "The two of you write each other almost every day. There's not one thought that goes through your head that you don't share with him." She tapped the letter. "His letters are pages long—so he's spending significant time on writing to you. He's even sent you poetry."

"That's true," Julia said. "But he's a poet, so he can't help himself."

Dort folded her arms. "Really, Julia. I think you need to have more faith in all of this. I know you are hoping and cooking and reading all those boring books, but you're already a catch. Reread those letters of Paul, and you'll start to see yourself as he does. As we all do."

Julia's chest felt as tight as a new shoe. Her sister was saying magical words—could Julia really believe them though? Could she stop her hopes from going into a tailspin? "I'm so different from the last woman he was in a relationship with."

Dort released a sigh. "Yes, well, Edith shouldn't be your competition or comparison. She was what Paul needed for the years they were together. And don't you think that sometimes memory isn't the same as history—that we remember people better than they really were?"

JULIA

Dort was probably right.

"But you have your own qualities, and you're what Paul needs *now*." Dort slung an arm about Julia's shoulders. "Stop being so doubtful. This should be a magical time of your life—falling in love. Just let yourself fall, and enjoy the slide along the way."

Julia wrapped her arms about her sister. "Thank you, Dort. Maybe you can help me with my response to this last letter, then. I'm a bit bothered by it."

The two sisters drew apart, and Julia read aloud the portion where Paul had gone with Charlie back to the astrologist Jane Bartleman.

"The astrologist made a prediction about me," Julia said. "I guess Paul told her about me—which is flattering, but she was certainly snippy."

"What did she say?" Dort asked, clearly holding back a laugh.

"It's not funny," Julia said. "Paul puts stock in the woman's words, and she predicted that we'd both fall in love with other people."

Dort snickered. "That's ridiculous. I'm pretty sure my sister isn't going to stand for such a prediction."

Julia straightened. "I'm certainly not." She reached for the paper and pen she'd brought to the table and began to write.

Dort sat close, reading every word.

"Dear Paul, I read about the prediction from Jane Bartleman, and I'm going to make my own prediction. The woman is probably in love with you herself, so she is trying to distract you." She drew in a deep breath.

"It's perfect," Dort said. "Setting everyone in their place."

Julia wasn't listening though. She was fully invested in writing a small sermon to Paul. He could be upset with her, but she wasn't going to hold back on this opinion.

The front door opened, and moments later, Pop strode into the kitchen.

"I thought you were golfing, Pop," Dort said.

Julia gathered the letters strewn about the table as Pop paused in the kitchen.

Without any preamble, he said, "I'm getting married. In May."

Julia tried not to fall off her chair. Sure, she knew Pop was seeing women. Baked goods dropped off at the house was a good indicator.

"Her name is Philadelphia Miller O'Melveny," he said. "She goes by Phila."

"Donald O'Melveny's widow?" Dort asked.

Julia's mind was still trying to catch up.

Pop nodded and finally took a seat. Phila was about fifteen years younger than Pop, which might be a good thing. She'd have the energy to care for him as he aged.

"She's Roman Catholic, and she's been widowed for nine years," Pop continued.

"I love her," Dort burst out. "Her son went to school with me. Oh, Pop." She rose and hurried around the table to hug and kiss him.

Pop's ears reddened.

Julia, mostly recovered, rose, too, and embraced her stiff father. If Pop was marrying . . . disbelief combined with excitement bubbled up in her. He'd be taken care of—and happy—and Dort could follow her theater passion in New York, and Julia . . . well, she wouldn't feel obligated to stick around Pasadena. Unless Paul wanted to?

"How did this all happen?" Julia asked, her mind humming with so many thoughts and questions. "I mean . . . how did you choose each other?"

"She's a fine woman," Pop said. "And most importantly"—he swallowed back emotion that Julia was surprised to see. Her own heart softened. Had Pop fallen in love? Was that possible for a man as cantankerous as he'd become?—"she cares about my family too . . . Said that she would treat each of you as if you were her own daughters."

Tears blurred Julia's vision. It was as if her father had become a different man—a softer man. A man who appreciated what was before him in the here and now.

"Besides, her father is a true Republican," Pop added.

Well, the different man had lasted only half a second, and Julia wanted to swat her father now. Yet she was happy for him and even more happy for herself. Pop would have a companion, someone to care for him, someone else to love him. And he looked pleased about it.

JULIA

Until his gaze narrowed as he spotted the latest copy of the *Washington Post* on the sideboard. Julia would have to take it to her room to read to avoid an argument because right now, she didn't want to ruin the celebratory mood in the room.

The next weeks were spent in a flurry of wedding preparations, and the more Julia got to know Phila, the more she liked her. Julia felt no need to compare Phila to Julia's mother or to resent any replacement. Julia was, perhaps selfishly, appreciating another woman around to be a companion to Pop.

Pop and Phila were married on May 8, with Phila's children in attendance and both Julia and Dort, along with John and Josephine. The event only turned Julia's heart more toward Paul because a future between them had become even more of a possibility. There was nothing that would hold her back from following him to wherever he found employment.

Julia's elation took a small dive, though, when she received Paul's next letter while spending the morning at the dining table reading newspapers. He complained about his job's bureaucracy and how he was struggling to get five weeks off starting in July.

"Do you think he's trying to back out?" she asked Dort after showing her what Paul said.

Dort read the lines a couple more times. "I think he's being honest. Look." She pointed to the opening salutation. "*Dearest* Julie. Besides, he's complaining about a headache, too, so he's obviously suffering some pain. But the fact that he still made an effort to write you tells me that you've become both his confidante and comfort."

Julia decided to agree with her sister. When headaches hit him, they could last for days. And really, his letters had grown increasingly romantic—that was something that couldn't be denied. "I wish I could show up on his doorstep with a jar of chicken soup."

"Do you even know how to make chicken soup?" Dort teased.

"I'll learn today." She rose from the dining table and headed toward the kitchen. "Surely one of our cookbooks will have a good chicken soup recipe. I'll have to go to the market and get the chicken."

Dort's laughter followed her.

Julia did go to the market, and though she didn't consider her chicken soup experiment a success on the first attempt, she proceeded to make another batch, then a third.

"I think if you keep adding spices, it will taste good no matter what," Dort suggested, perched on a chair, watching with amusement and not offering a helping hand in the least.

"I think you're right." Julia added another dash of rosemary, then some thyme, for good measure. "Although the goal of making chicken soup for the ill is to not make them *more* ill."

CHAPTER 16

Pasadena, California
July 1946

"Julie is a splendid companion, uncomplaining and flexible—really tough-fibered, a quality which I first saw in her in Ceylon and later in China. She has great charm and ease with all levels of people without in any way talking down to anybody. She's got a much tougher stomach than I have, and in the 3 years I've known her in War and Peace, in tropics and in USA, has never been sick from anything. She also washes my shirts! Quite a dame."

—LETTER FROM PAUL CHILD TO HIS BROTHER, CHARLIE

Julia hadn't forgotten a thing about Paul when she met him at the train station. But seeing him walking toward her, bags in hand, his clothing somehow neat as a pin instead of rumpled from the train, his open smile and those intelligent eyes, she was sure her heart had burst from her chest. He set his bags down as she hurried toward him, her newly coiffed hair blowing in the summer wind.

She'd pushed aside the worry of how to greet him after so long apart—a hug? A kiss? A handshake? Heaven forbid. Her reserves and worries had completely melted at his endearing expression. He had her heart completely and fully.

"Julie," he said a half second before she threw her arms about his neck.

He chuckled, the sound warm and low, and then his arms came around her.

She could only sigh and breathe him in—his scent familiar and exhilarating all at once. "Welcome to Pasadena. I've missed you." There, she'd said it, laid it out.

Paul drew back and cradled her face, then kissed her soundly.

Who cared about her carefully applied lipstick?

"I missed you too."

It was all she needed to hear. Her heart felt like it had split, then come back together, beating stronger and with more confidence than ever. Even the worry about her father's reaction to meeting Paul took a back seat as she drove them to her home. Paul updated her on the adventures of the cross-country train ride, and she found herself laughing at every turn in the story.

Pop was polite when meeting Paul, Phila was delightful, and Dort was ecstatic.

That all changed at dinnertime when Pop couldn't keep any of his opinions to himself. His opinions about the newly elected congressman Richard Nixon and how he'd effectively shut down Helen Gahagan Douglas, who was a Communist sympathizer, only fueled Pop's lectures.

Julia wanted Paul's visit to be an introduction to her family and shared peaceful family dinners, but the days passed with agonizing tension as Paul had to practically sit on his hands and keep his mouth shut in order not to incite a full-blown argument.

"Why does he wear a scarf, for heaven's sake?" Pop had hissed to Julia in the hallway on their final morning. "Just because he's an artist doesn't mean he has to dress like that. He's not really a European, even though he seems to think he is."

Julia had seen Paul wearing civilian clothing many times and thought he was an elegant dresser. Today, he wore an open-necked dress shirt with a scarf.

Julia had been counting down the hours, literally, until they were leaving. So now, she simply set a hand on her father's arm and said, "I think he looks handsome that way."

Pop scowled, but thankfully, Phila joined them in the hallway.

"Are you all packed, Julia?" she asked, having become the master at defusion and peacemaking this past week. "I can help if you need me to."

"Oh, that would be wonderful, thank you."

The two women moved away from Pop, and Phila whispered, "Don't mind him. He's going to miss his little girl, and every father sees their future son-in-law with critical eyes."

JULIA

Inside Julia's bedroom, she turned to face Phila. "Do you really think Paul will propose?"

"He's besotted with you. That much is clear." Phila smiled. "I've never seen a Democrat spend so much time with your father and not make for the hills like his feet are on fire."

"Paul definitely gets a lot of credit for taking all those verbal lashings," Julia said. "Pop shouldn't get away with treating another person so poorly. His biases are so caustic, and we're supposed to be the people he loves the most."

Phila grasped Julia's hand. "Leave him to me. There's been a lot of changes in his life, and I'm sure that letter writing will bring the pair of you on better terms."

Julia pulled Phila into a hug. "Thank you so much for your kindness. And thank you for marrying Pop."

Phila drew away. "I only wish you all the happiness in the world. Please have a safe trip driving back east. Drop us some postcards and letters."

"I will." Julia stepped toward her suitcase perched at the end of the bed. "I'm all packed, but it was nice to have a private chat with you. Let's get this out to the car before Pop can rope Paul into any sort of political conversation."

They headed down the hallway and out the front door with Julia's suitcase and extra bag. Outside, Paul stood talking to Dort next to her Buick. Thankfully, Pop was nowhere in sight.

Julia had watched Paul deflect Pop's comments over and over, like a hero wearing armor in a novel. Now, watching Paul smile and chat with Dort made Julia feel warmth and appreciation for him all over again. In one of her letters, she'd confessed that she loved him. He'd responded by saying, "I want to see you, touch you, kiss you, talk to you . . ." And she supposed that would happen, once they were away from her father's house.

"Ah, there you are, Julie," Paul said, noticing her arrival. "Is that everything?" He moved toward her and took the suitcase from her hands. With easy deftness, he loaded everything into the open trunk.

Pop came outside then, watched in silence, then said goodbye as if he hadn't just been criticizing Paul's clothing moments before. Julia hugged both Pop and Phila, then she hugged Dort extra tight.

"I'll write to you every step of the way," Julia told Dort.

"Not too much," Dort said with amusement. "Have fun with your man. Enjoy the drive and the sights. You can catch me up at the end of it all."

Julia squeezed her sister again, then rounded the front of the car to where Paul was holding the door open for her. She slid into the passenger seat, having designated Paul as the driver for the first leg of their trip. They'd be visiting a series of friends along the way. First up would be joining Katy Gates and her husband in Ojai Valley at their mutual friends' ranch. This would be followed by a visit to Paul's longtime Boston friends, Tommy and Nancy Davis, who'd moved to San Francisco and now had a baby daughter.

The first few moments on the drive were silent, and Julia began to worry that maybe Paul had overheard Pop's unkind remarks, or maybe he was burned out from her family's drama. She reached for his hand, and was pleased when he linked their fingers.

"You've put up with a lot," Julia mused. "Do you still like me, despite my father's political opinions?"

They both knew that her father's political views were only part of his gruff personality. But Paul squeezed her hand.

In that moment, Julia felt flooded with gratitude that her family dynamics hadn't driven off the man she loved.

"I'm glad I met your family because they are what shaped and molded my dearest Julie." He smiled over at her, and her heart skipped several beats. "Both of us had upbringings we've grown from, and now, together, we can grow again. This old dog is learning new tricks every day."

Julia laughed. Yes, Paul was ten years older than she was, but she only viewed him as being more sophisticated, not old.

"Your father might be right about one thing," Paul said as they drove.

"I'd be shocked if that were true," she quipped.

"Sticking with me won't be easy sailing," he said. "My career has been a kaleidoscope of jobs. I don't own a home; I don't even have a home, technically. I have very little family left, as it is. I had to turn down the teaching job at Yenching University in Peking because the political situation in China is teetering. So it seems I'm going to be reinventing myself again."

Julia knew about the teaching job and how it had been a disappointment to him, but she couldn't let this remarkable, talented man feel down on himself. "You'll find your niche, Paulski. You have so many skills and such a breadth of experience that any government department would benefit from your expertise."

He cut a glance to her. "Even a foreign appointment?"

"Of course." Her mind raced. What was he saying? That he wanted to apply for a foreign post?

"Would you be able to stand living out of the country again after being back for only a few months?"

Julia's heart lodged in her throat. He wasn't proposing—far from that—but he was being open with his thoughts and words and including her in the equation.

"These past few months living back at home have shown me that I'm ready to completely cut ties with Pasadena," she said. "I'd visit, but my father is settled with Phila, and I wouldn't be surprised if Dort made her move back to New York in a short time." She took the plunge. "One thing that working for the OSS taught me is that I love to travel and try new things, especially Chinese food."

"Wait until you try French food. The authentic kind."

Paul spent the next several moments describing dishes she'd never heard of, let alone be able to pronounce herself. She allowed herself to believe in Paul's words. She couldn't predict the status of their relationship a few weeks from now, with spending so much time together, but she hoped it would remain intact. Both for her and for him.

The next weeks proved to be a whirlwind, time both speeding by as they stopped to visit friends along the way and slowing to a crawl as they drove the long, scenic stretches of road in between.

Julia told Paul of her grandfather McWilliams, who'd come westward to California in 1849, and how he'd declined Chief Alikit's offer to marry his daughter. They discussed the landscapes and vistas her grandfather must have encountered traveling in a wagon train and sleeping beneath the stars, whereas Paul and Julia were staying in trailer parks and motels. The driving hours passed as whoever wasn't driving would read aloud from either newspapers or the *Time* and *Life* magazines.

Paul had to change a blown-out tire once, and Julia set to work on washing their clothing by hand. They found they could sit for hours together and still want to be in each other's company.

When they at last reached Maine after nearly a month of traveling, Paul seemed quiet and pensive, his temperament matching the darkening gray clouds above as they drove through the small town of Bernard. He was the one driving, and Julia didn't question him about his mood. When they reached the peninsula of Lopaus Point, Paul slowed to a stop before they crossed the knotty, unfinished road that was more of a lane.

"This is what I call Burma Road," Paul said and pointed up ahead. "Soon, we'll be surrounded by my family, and there'll be no going back."

"What do you mean?"

Paul reached for her hand. "I mean that I need you to know something before we're surrounded by the chaos of my family and their one-room cabin."

Was this good or bad? He was holding her hand, and they'd come all this way with hardly a disagreement.

"Julie, I love you dearly, and I want everyone to know it."

Julia felt like the sun had burst through the clouds. She scooted close and slipped her arms about his neck. "It's about time, P'ski."

He laughed, then slid his hand behind her neck and kissed her.

She could have sat with him for hours, kissing him, letting the world pass her by.

But when Paul drew away, he said, "If I weren't starving, I'd stay parked with you all day."

Julia smirked and reluctantly disentangled herself, then primly folded her hands in her lap. "Drive on, Mr. Child."

JULIA

They bumped along the rutted lane, then Paul parked in a clearing in the middle of a group of tall trees.

Julia scanned the area for the cabin Paul had told her about, but she couldn't see anything that looked like a cabin. "Where are we?" she asked.

"We'll walk there on foot," he said, opening his door. "You'll get the full view if we do that. Besides, I want to surprise them and not warn anyone with the sound of the motor."

He stepped out of the Buick and walked around the car to open her door. He took her hand to help her up and didn't let go. She wasn't even sure her feet touched the ground as they walked slowly along a path through a collection of trees. Paul had said he *loved* her. He'd said there was no turning back from here . . . Did that mean what she thought it meant?

As the trees thinned, a partially finished cabin came into view. The setting was serene, idyllic, with the Atlantic Ocean surrounding the forested peninsula—the deep blue of the water sparkling in the presence of the majestic trees. The breeze smelled heavenly and fresh.

"They're here!" a young voice called.

Paul tightened his hold on her hand. "That's Rachel. She's twelve now."

Julia hadn't met Charlie and Freddie's children in DC, and now a young, willowy girl, who could only be the daughter of Freddie, ran across the front yard and disappeared into the cabin.

Moments later, the entire family tumbled out: Charlie, Freddie, Rachel, Erica, and Jon.

"You're here at last," Charlie said, embracing Paul.

Freddie got to Julia first and pulled her into a tight hug. "We're so happy to see you." She drew back. "You're in one piece, I see, and you have a smile on your face. Did Paul put it there?"

Julia laughed with the smiling, warmhearted woman. "He did."

"Come in, come in," Freddie said. "This time, you can't escape. I'm starting dinner preparations now, and you can catch me up on your trip while you help me."

Julia loved Freddie's frankness. She walked into the cabin with her, while the men trailed behind and the children asked Paul question after question.

The cabin was a single room with a back porch. "We sleep on the back porch," Freddie said. "Did Paul tell you about the summer that we dug this place out? He helped us clear the land and do the framework."

"I worked on it too." Erica followed them to the kitchen corner with a coal stove and a huge fireplace made of stones.

Freddie squeezed Erica's shoulder. "You sure did. We all did."

"I helped cut down trees," Erica said. "Then we'd peel off the bark and saw them into planks. Rachel and I hauled all the stones for the fireplace."

"That's truly wonderful," Julia said, looking around at the humble but sturdy beginnings of this cabin. "I love it already."

"Here," Freddie said. "You chop the vegetables. You do know how to chop, don't you?"

"I can chop." She paused and peered at Freddie. "What did Paul tell you?"

Freddie raised her hands. "Don't get upset with me—Paul made it clear that you've had a few disasters in the kitchen, so I wasn't sure if knives were forbidden."

"I've had plenty of disasters," Julia said. "None involving knives, though, so I think we're safe. But what did Paul say?"

Freddie's eyes twinkled with mischief. "He said that you could burn water."

Julia's mouth dropped open. She was going to give that man a talking to when he came back into the cabin.

Freddie started to laugh, and Julia said, "Well, I can't go much lower than that, so I'm sure to impress you. But I must say, whatever is baking in the oven smells delicious."

"I'm baking bread. We're rudimentary here, but we eat well." Freddie nodded toward the shelf in front of the kitchen window that let in the ocean breeze. "No refrigerator since we don't have electricity yet, so we use nature to keep the milk and eggs cool."

"We don't have a bathroom either," Rachel announced, joining them in the kitchen corner. "We go on the beach." She pointed at a protruding

JULIA

peg on the wall that held a roll of toilet paper. "Be sure to take that when you head out."

Julia laughed. There was nothing else to do but find humor since they were staying here at least a week. "This is like luxurious camping. You're all so lucky."

Both Rachel and Erica beamed.

"We bring in water from the spring"—Freddie nodded toward the large pot on the stove that was starting to boil—"then heat it on the stove. Like the pioneers."

"Like your grandpa," Erica piped up. "Father read Uncle's letter about your grandpa crossing the country in a wagon."

"That's true," Julia said as she moved on to the next task of cutting chicken after a short tutorial by Freddie on how exactly she wanted it done. Since Julia felt confident that she could cut up chicken and talk at the same time, she told the young girls more stories. And when they asked about China, she told them about the monkeys, the elephants, the monsoon season, and all the tropical bugs.

The girls sat enraptured, and when a bit of chicken fell to the floor, Freddie said, "Just throw it in the pot. Any germs will get boiled away."

So Julia picked up the chicken pieces and dropped them into the boiling pot of water and vegetables.

"Here," Freddie said, handing Julia a glass of wine. "Cooking should never be stressful."

"Wine for the cook?"

"Exactly." Freddie winked and took a sip from her own wine glass. "It's the French way, which is the best way."

"Paul has told me all about his favorite French dishes," Julia mused. "Do you know how to cook any?"

"Certainly," Freddie said. "I learned some things while we lived in Paris. Charlie studied art there, you know. Tomorrow, we'll drive into town, do some shopping, and I'll teach you to make coq au vin." She leaned close. "That will really impress Paul."

Julia had to admit that she was enjoying herself immensely—how could she not. She loved the energy of this place, the friendliness of Freddie's family, the coziness of the cabin, and the smell of good food.

She felt like she could talk to Freddie about anything and everything, and the time flew as they shared stories. Julia hadn't even noticed Paul and Charlie returning to the house with young Jon until Paul laughed at one of her stories. She turned to see him watching her, amusement on his face. His mood had shifted, brightened, and she knew that this reunion with his brother was good for him.

"Look, I'm cooking," she told Paul. "And it's going to be delicious." She lifted her glass of wine as if to toast him.

He crossed to her, and rested his hand on her waist and kissed her. "I don't doubt it."

Julia was shocked that he'd been so boldly affectionate in front of his brother's family, but she didn't mind in the least. She noted the exchanged looks between Freddie and Charlie. Were they happy that Paul had brought her for a visit?

"Now, girls, set the table," Charlie said, then turned to Jon. "Bring in some more of the chopped wood for the stove."

Freddie opened the oven door, letting out a cloud of heat. "Come and look, Julia."

She bent and peered into the oven. The loaf of bread had started to brown.

"It's ready, don't you think?" Freddie asked.

"It looks perfect to me."

Freddie grinned, then used a linen cloth to take out the bread.

As they sat around the table, Julia soaked in this family life of Paul's. He might have often complained about the competition with his twin brother, but Julia could see that their bond ran deeper than any disputes.

And another interesting thing happened. Paul, whom Julia always saw at the center of their friend group since everyone looked to him for his opinions, was now eclipsed by his brother. Paul was quieter around Charlie, and Julia surmised it was because Charlie was so gregarious. She was pretty sure that Charlie could walk into any room, in any sort of crowd, and command attention.

Yet Paul seemed resigned to his role, if not content. And it was clear he was still gunning for his brother's favor as they both talked about art and photography.

When Paul's hand found Julia's beneath the table, she suddenly knew. She knew that Paul had brought her here because he wanted her to feel welcomed by his family. He wanted her to be a part of his family. And she would be saying yes.

CHAPTER 17

Lopaus Point, Maine
August 1946

"She has deep-seated charm and human warmth which I have been fascinated to see at work on people of all sorts, from the sophisticates of San Francisco to the mining and cattle folk of the Northwest. She would be poised and at ease anywhere, I should say; she tells the truth, and for the most part uses balanced rather than extravagant language. In this connection I believe that her thinking has become much more careful, logical and objective in the last two years, and I find her interesting to talk to at any time. And I love her dearly."

—LETTER FROM PAUL CHILD TO HIS BROTHER, CHARLIE

"He's different around you, you know," Freddie said as they browsed the produce at the local grocer in the town of Bernard.

"Different how?" Julia asked. She was glad they'd come into town without all the children. Paul and Charlie had taken them to the beach. This gave Julia more time with Freddie to have a heart-to-heart.

"He's lighter somehow, happier." Freddie picked up a couple of cloves of garlic and set them in their basket. "I love that he hugs and kisses you in front of everyone."

Was that notable? Hadn't he been this way with previous girlfriends—such as Edith? "I've been wanting to ask you something, and I don't know if I should . . ."

Freddie zeroed in with her astute gaze. "You want to know about Edith?"

"I do," Julia admitted. "I mean, Paul has told me plenty. Especially when we were in China, and he was still grieving over her loss. She seemed

JULIA

to be a perfect match for him. Artistic, intellectual, experienced . . . all the things I'm not."

Freddie began picking through the mushrooms, selecting specific ones to add to their basket. "He was never openly affectionate with her," she said. "He always seemed careful around her—like he was trying to please her or impress her all the time. With you . . . he's *himself.* He's more carefree, more expressive, and I can tell he's crazy about you."

Julia released a careful breath. This was what she needed to hear in order to move past the last stumbling block in front of her heart. She understood that Edith was dead and long gone, but Julia also knew it was impossible to compete with a sainted memory.

"Julia," Freddie said. "You're the best thing that's ever happened to Paul. We all see it, and I believe he knows it as well. He's happier than I've ever seen him, and besides, he and Charlie haven't had one disagreement since you arrived."

"It's only been a day," Julia said.

Freddie chuckled. "That's plenty of time for at least a dozen."

They both laughed, but inside, Julia was swooning. Was Freddie right? Was Paul at his happiest—because of *her*?

"Now," Freddie said. "Let's get back because this coq au vin will be a process. Ready to be my sous-chef?"

Julia straightened. "Ready."

The cabin was still empty when they returned, and Julia had no idea how long the men would keep the children at the beach, but she gamely joined in her first French cooking lesson. And while she thought there should be a recipe somewhere, apparently, Freddie had it all in her head.

They'd brought home bacon, chicken, tomatoes, mushrooms, garlic, and pearl onions. Everything else, Freddie said she already had at the cabin.

"Now," Freddie said after they'd unloaded the groceries. "Cut the bacon rind and then cut the bacon into rectangles about a quarter inch wide and one inch long. We're going to simmer the bacon pieces in water for about ten minutes, then we'll rinse and pat dry."

"How much water?" Julia asked, pouring water from one of the buckets into the cooking pot.

Freddie paused. "A quart? No, two quarts. Estimate. You don't need to measure."

Estimating and improvising had led to most of Julia's disasters in cooking school.

"We'll sauté the bacon in hot butter until it's lightly cooked," Freddie continued.

While Julia worked on the bacon, Freddie dried the chicken. Then she added it to the casserole pan heating on the stove. Next, she seasoned the chicken.

"Add the bacon to the casserole now," Freddie said, "and we'll cook it for five minutes, then turn the chicken and cook for another five minutes."

While they waited for the chicken to cook, Freddie instructed Julia to make a tomato paste and add in mashed garlic and herbs, such as thyme and bay leaf. Julia wished she could write everything down as they prepared, but she didn't want to slow the process.

"We're going to uncover the chicken and pour in some cognac," Freddie said.

Julia watched her remove the chicken from the oven, douse it with cognac, then light a match. "You have to turn your face when you do this to save your eyelashes."

Julia gasped as Freddie touched the match flame to the chicken and ignited the cognac. Flames leaped up, and Freddie jiggled the casserole dish until the flames died out. Next, she poured in red wine. "This should be a Burgundy, or a Chianti. Some chefs use Beaujolais or Côtes du Rhône."

Julia wasn't really a wine connoisseur and usually left any wine ordering to Paul.

"Bouillon is next," Freddie said. "Then you'll stir in the tomato paste mixture, and we'll let everything simmer for thirty minutes."

Julia could do that. She added in the next ingredients. "And then what?"

"Boiling the onions and sautéing the mushrooms."

Julia set to work, and Freddie skimmed the fat from the chicken as it progressed in cooking. Then she raised the heat until the liquid was boiling. "Once the liquid is reduced to about two cups, we remove it from the heat. Add flour and butter, blending it into a paste right inside the casserole pan."

Julia watched as Freddie used a wire whip to do the blending.

"More simmering and stirring until the sauce thickens." Freddie motioned toward Julia. "Place the mushrooms and onions around the chicken, then baste with the sauce. We can either move to a platter or serve from the casserole. I prefer the casserole. Less cleanup."

Julia laughed. They'd dirtied every pot and pan in the cabin.

"And a final touch—which really makes the entire dish," Freddie said, breaking off sprigs of parsley and adding them in strategic places. "What do you think?"

"It smells like heaven," Julia said.

"And the men and children are back just in time," Freddie announced, looking out the kitchen window. "They probably smelled it cooking."

The door opened, and in walked the rest of Freddie's family.

Julia felt pride in her contribution to preparing the meal as everyone sat to eat and exclaim over the deliciousness. She could tell that Paul especially appreciated the French meal. Julia found every bite delicious, and she vowed to write down the recipe the next day so that she'd always have it.

Over the length of their stay, Julia stuck close to Freddie for all meal preparations, trying to learn as much as she could. Freddie was such a natural around cooking, and Julia knew she'd never forget how Freddie effortlessly threw together salivating dishes with a glass of wine in one hand and a spatula in the other.

On their final morning at the cabin, Paul asked Julia to go for a walk with him after breakfast. As they stepped outside the cabin, she realized that she'd miss this place, this family, and the constant action. Yet it would be nice to be with just Paul again.

Paul grasped her hand, his with paint flecks on it since he'd been working on a landscape. They walked toward the rocky bluff that overlooked the beach. The wind felt cool, but the sun would soon warm them. When they reached the bluff, Paul settled on one of the larger rocks, setting his sketchbook on his knee. He'd already drawn a few renditions of the landscape and the distant village of Blueville.

Julia took out her diary that she'd faithfully kept on their trip and wrote about the happenings of the day before when she'd gone swimming with the children and made sandcastles on the beach.

A seagull landed close to them, but they had no food to interest the bird as it artfully circled them, hoping for a morsel. After a moment, it flew away with a low squawk, then joined other birds down the beach as they perched on rocks, watching the incoming tide. Another gull took flight, sailed over the water, and snatched a fish from its surface.

Julia wondered if she'd ever be in such a quiet, peaceful cove again. Every inch of California beaches seemed to be occupied, but here, it was like a private paradise.

"Have you enjoyed the visit?" Paul asked.

She tugged her gaze from the seagulls. "Yes, absolutely. I love your family. Their cabin is in the perfect location. And no tourists, which makes it better."

Paul set aside his sketchbook and reached for her hand. "I'm glad you love my family."

She laughed but felt a bubble of nervousness too. "And I love you too."

"I love you, Julie." Paul leaned close and kissed her as the wind seemed to tug them closer. When they drew apart, he said, "Do you think your father and Phila might make a trip to Pennsylvania? And, of course, your brother and your sister, but they'd have less distance to travel."

Dort had ended up leaving Pasadena a couple of weeks after Julia and was already settled in New York.

"Why Pennsylvania?" she asked. Charlie lived there, but Julia wasn't sure why Paul would even want her father to come out east. Unless . . . her voice stuck in her throat as she stared at Paul.

His smile appeared as he shifted to his knees in front of her. Two thoughts pricked her mind—first, that Paul's knees were going to hurt, and second, the only reason he'd be on his knees was to propose.

JULIA

Julia placed her free hand over her heart. "Paul?" she whispered.

"Julie—you're the only woman for me, and I've known it for some time. I don't have roots, though, or a flourishing career, but I can't wait another day. Or another moment to ask you to be my wife."

Julia's eyes filled with tears, but she didn't bother to try to stop them.

"Will you marry me, Julia McWilliams?" Paul said, his tone earnest, sincere.

"Oh, Paul." Julia threw her arms about his neck, and they almost fell over. But to Paul's credit and years of jujitsu, he kept them upright.

"Is that a yes?" he murmured against her ear with a chuckle.

Julia drew away, grinning. "It's a big yes! It's a yes that I would have said months ago. Or even a year ago."

Paul didn't look surprised at all. Then he pulled her close again and kissed her soundly.

When he released her, Julia didn't know if she wanted to keep kissing him or make wedding plans. Her energetic brain won out. "So you want to marry at Charlie's place?"

"I think that would be best, don't you?" Paul asked.

Everything sounded wonderful right now, and if Paul suggested they marry on the moon, she would say yes.

"Charlie will be thrilled. He's been pestering me this whole time about when I'm going to ask you to marry me."

Julia's skin heated as she thought about the brothers discussing *her*.

"I know what you're thinking." Paul sat next to her again and wrapped his arm around her shoulders. "I almost proposed to you in Pasadena so that your father could give us his blessing." He paused. "But I wasn't sure if he'd do that, so I thought a little distance might be better."

Julia nestled against him and leaned her head on his shoulder. "You're right. A phone call with this news is much better than delivering it in person. Oh. Dort is going to be tickled. And all our OSS friends. They'll think it's a hoot."

Paul laughed, his chest vibrating against her. "Maybe, but I think they all saw it coming."

Julia lifted her head and gazed at her future husband. "Truly?"

He kissed the tip of her nose. "Truly. Now, you must also know that I don't want this to be one of those long engagements. Winter will be too cold and dreary, and next spring feels too far away. Besides, I'm certainly not getting any younger."

"Because you want children?"

Paul squeezed her hand. "If you want children, we'll have children. If you don't, I think we can keep ourselves fully occupied."

"We'll see where life takes us." She leaned against Paul again. They hadn't had a serious talk about whether either of them wanted children. During their OSS service, he'd only sounded frustrated when he'd spoken about the misbehaviors of the students when he'd taught school in Connecticut. Julia might have been a terror as a child, but she'd enjoyed being with Charlie's children the past week. She was happy to hear Paul was amenable to having children. She only worried that perhaps she'd passed her optimal child-bearing years.

"How does September 1 sound for a wedding date?" Paul asked. "August is your birthday month, so September can be our anniversary month."

Julia straightened and stared at him, excitement bubbling inside her. "That's less than a month away. Do you think we can pull everything together by then?"

"I don't see why not," Paul said. "We don't need to book a church."

"Lumberville it is, then," Julia said. "Now I can't wait to find a phone to tell everyone."

He pulled her close again. "Well, I think we'd better head back since it's almost lunchtime, and we have news to share." Paul made a move to stand, then helped her to her feet. When his arms came around her and pulled her close, she breathed in the scent of his sun-warmed skin and his musky soap.

Being married to Paul would be wonderful, and come rain or sun, she'd give it her all.

Entering the cabin a short time later, Julia's heart thundered with anticipation. She wondered when Paul would make the announcement. But he didn't say anything as Julia joined Freddie in last-minute sandwich

JULIA

preparations. Charlie and Paul set the table with the children, then poured the wine.

They all sat and started to eat, with the discussion revolving around their packing and leaving. Julia caught Paul's eye more than once, but he'd only smile and continue on with the conversation. Then, finally, Paul picked up his wine glass and raised it.

Everyone fell silent and looked at him—probably expecting him to say how much he'd enjoyed their little vacation and thanks for the hospitality. Instead, he announced, "We're going to get married—and right away. And if it's all right with all of you, we'll marry on September 1 at Coppernose, in your backyard at Lumberville."

Freddie squealed, and Charlie cheered. The children clapped in excitement.

"We thought you'd never come out with it," Freddie said, then came around the table and hugged them both.

Charlie raised his glass. "It's about time, and don't worry, our house works perfectly."

Julia should have guessed that the next weeks would be a whirlwind. After informing everyone in her family, they made travel plans. Pop and Phila would fly in from California, and everyone else would be driving to Philadelphia. Paul had rounded up some of his friends and extended family.

The days felt surreal, and there were a lot of unanswered questions about their future, but Julia still wanted to spend every moment with Paul. On August 30, they headed to the Doylestown town hall to apply for their marriage license.

"Do you have your blood test results with you?" a receptionist with horn-rimmed glasses asked them.

Paul looked over at Julia, surprise on his face. "Blood test?"

"It's required by the state of Pennsylvania," the receptionist said, her tone peevish. "You can get it done at the clinic around the block, but I don't think you'll have the results back"—she looked at the line on their application that read September 1—"in two days' time."

Julia noted the flush on Paul's cheeks, and she reached for the application and tucked it inside her purse. "We'll get that taken care of. Thank you."

Then she grasped Paul's hand, and they walked out of the building.

"I had no idea," Paul said, his jaw tightening. "I don't think any of us knew—Did you?"

"It didn't cross my mind," Julia said. "I guess we'll be sweet-talking a nurse at the clinic."

They only hit another roadblock at the clinic though. "Results will be back in five days, maybe seven," the clinic's nurse told them without offering any other options.

Julia couldn't fault anyone though. She and Paul could have come the week before, and none of this would have happened. As they left the clinic, Julia looped her arm through his. "We could push the wedding back a few days?"

Paul rubbed the back of his neck. "What will we tell everyone? Your father is already in New York City, and everyone else is currently traveling. Most of them have to be back to work on Monday."

Julia knew he was right, but what else could they do?

"Your father will laugh me out of the state," Paul muttered.

She squeezed his arm. "Maybe Charlie will have an answer. This is his state, after all."

Paul looked over at her. "You're right. Charlie might know a workaround. Surely this isn't the first time a couple has run into this situation."

Even after Charlie called those he thought might be able to help them rush through the marriage license, no one was able to get around the blood-test requirement.

Julia was sitting with Paul on the front porch when Charlie delivered the news. "No luck. You're not getting married in Pennsylvania on Sunday."

Freddie joined them outside. "Nothing?" she asked Charlie.

He leaned against the porch railing. "Nothing."

Paul took out what was probably his tenth cigarette of the day and lit it.

JULIA

Then Charlie's expression cleared. "You know, New Jersey is only a couple of miles away, and they don't require a blood test for their marriage licenses."

Paul's head snapped up. "New Jersey?"

Freddie clapped her hands together. "Our friends live in Stockton. The Seymours. What if we call them up and see if you can marry at their place? Then we'll all come back here for the reception?"

Paul rose to his feet and stubbed out his cigarette. "Well, let's call them up." He grinned down at Julia. "Do you want to marry me on Sunday?"

She laughed, renewed hope bouncing around in her chest.

Moments later, they had their answer. They were getting married in New Jersey. Paul kissed Julia in celebration, then he whooped.

"It will be a surprise to everyone who shows up, but it will be a good surprise." Paul grasped Julia's hand. "I'm glad you said yes."

The next day, Julia was still basking in the change of fortune when she and Paul climbed into the car to drive to New York City. Her father was throwing them a wedding rehearsal dinner at the River Club. It would be filled with a lot of superficial chatting, but it was a grand gesture from Pop, so Julia wasn't complaining.

Paul drove, as usual, and the two-hour drive was beautiful. They couldn't have picked a more serene day.

Just a few miles out of town, Paul slowed the car when they reached an intersection where the lanes were reduced. Then he suddenly said, "Oh no." His eyes were on the rearview mirror. "That truck isn't slowing down."

Julia turned to look behind them, and to her horror, a large truck was barreling toward them. It was going way too fast.

Paul accelerated and tried to turn out of the way, but it was too late.

The truck careened toward the driver's side, and the last thing Julia remembered was hitting the windshield.

CHAPTER 18

Lumberville, Pennsylvania
August–September 1946

"I was not much of a cook when we first married. I was using magazines and the *Joy of Cooking*. We would not eat dinner until around ten because it took me so long to cook. I was doing fancy things. Paul would help. He would do anything. He was a wonderful companion; he was never, ever boring."

—JULIA CHILD

Julia heard Paul saying her name, but she wasn't sure why she couldn't answer. And why couldn't she see anything? Was it the middle of the night? She heard more voices. People she didn't know. Talking to Paul.

Then she remembered. They'd been hit by a truck, and she had slammed into the windshield and then been thrown from the car. About the moment her memory returned, the pain hit her like a boulder. She groaned and dragged her eyes open.

Everything was blurry, but she could see Paul. Hovering over her. Blood, a livid red, streaked his face. The muted sounds around her sharpened.

"Julie," he breathed in obvious relief. "You're going to be fine. We're on our way to the hospital. Just rest, and don't try to move."

"My arm," she croaked. Her mouth tasted bitter, and her arm felt like it was on fire. They were in another car right now. Not an ambulance. Who was driving them?

"You have some cuts on your arm," Paul rasped. "Nothing that can't be easily fixed." He placed a shaking hand on her cheek. "We'll be at the hospital soon, and you'll be fine."

JULIA

Why did he keep saying she'd be *fine*? It made her wonder if she would be fine. Her head was throbbing now, and her ears hurt. Was that a strange thing to notice?

A woman spoke, telling the driver of the car where to turn.

Julia slowly turned her head to look out the window and saw that they were pulling up to a hospital.

"We're here," Paul said. "We're going to get someone to carry you inside. I'll be right by you the whole time."

A couple of hospital orderlies came out to the car, and while Julia was loaded onto a gurney, Paul limped beside her. But he wasn't allowed into her room because, apparently, he had to get X-rays to see if his ribs were broken.

As the doctor and a couple of nurses hovered over Julia, she closed her eyes. She was supposed to be in New York City, celebrating with her father.

"Hold as still as possible," one of the nurses said. Julia had already forgotten the woman's name. "We need to extract the glass shards."

Julia drew in a breath as pain seared through her, but she was able to hold still. "Where's Paul?" she asked more than once, and the answer was always the same: he was getting checked over, but he'd be fine.

Fine. She was starting to hate that word.

More hospital staff bustled in and out. Once her arm was taken care of and set into a sling, the doctor with a tidy mustache said, "You have a wound on the side of your forehead that needs stitching."

Julia exhaled. "I'm going to live?"

"You're going to live," the doctor said, "but I must say, you're lucky things weren't worse."

"Well, make sure the stitches are pretty—I'm getting married tomorrow."

The doctor didn't speak for a moment. "You might want to reschedule your wedding. You'll be wearing a sling, and your head will be bandaged."

Julia didn't even have to think about it. "Brides can wear white on their wedding day, right? Mine will be my bandages."

The doctor chuckled, and beyond him, she heard the door open. Without seeing the person entering, Julia knew it was Paul. She simply felt his presence, but she couldn't turn her head because the doctor had started his stitching.

When Paul came into view, he grasped her hand. "How are you?"

"The doctor promised that I'm going to live," she said. "Are you ready to have a bandaged bride?"

Paul squeezed her hand. "We can see how you feel."

"I'm feeling *fine*." At least she thought she did. "And you promised I'd be fine, so I will be."

She didn't know if Paul would have argued with her, because at that moment, another nurse came in. "You have visitors in the lobby. I told them they had to wait."

"Finished here," the doctor said. "I'll send you home with aspirin, but I do recommend taking things as easy as possible for a few days. In a week, we can take out the stitches."

After the doctor left, Paul pulled her into a careful hug, being mindful of her arm sling and head bandage.

"Are you all right?" she murmured against Paul's cheek.

"Bruised, nothing more." Paul held her for another long moment. "I think my life flashed before my eyes, and I was terrified that we wouldn't escape. I found out that the truck lost its brakes. I wish I would have seen it sooner and gotten out of the way."

"It was all so fast," Julia murmured. "I don't think you could have gotten out of the way. There wasn't anywhere to go." She drew away and held his gaze. "It was an accident, nothing more. Not your fault."

Paul nodded, but there was a pained expression on his face.

Julia looked past him to the cane propped against a nearby chair. "They gave you a cane?"

"Got some good bruising on my hip and leg, but nothing is broken." He paused. "Ready to marry a man with a cane?"

Julia laughed. "We'll make a unique bride and groom tomorrow."

Paul dropped a kiss on her cheek, then pulled her into another embrace. Julia wanted to stay in his arms the rest of the day. The accident could have been much worse, and she was grateful that she had her Paul fully intact.

When they finally made it to the lobby, Charlie and Freddie greeted them, then asked a thousand questions. And after an adamant discussion about tomorrow's wedding, in which Julia insisted she would be all right, they piled into Charlie's car and drove back to the house.

In the late morning, Julia commandeered Mrs. Seymour's elegant dressing room, and Dort helped Julia dress and do her hair. She hadn't wanted a fancy wedding dress that she'd wear only once; besides, she didn't want to bother with fittings or to be persuaded into what might be fashionable—it felt extravagant after coming through a major world war. She wanted to be comfortable in her own skin. So she'd chosen a brown-and-white polka dot dress with a belted waist. She'd ditched the arm sling because she could move her arm well enough.

"Despite the bulky bandage on the side of your forehead, you look beautiful," Dort said, stepping back from the vanity table. "You're wearing high heels?"

"I am. Paul already knows I'm tall, and I like these shoes."

"And we both know that finding a good pair of shoes to fit our large feet is always a chore," Dort said.

"I think if my house—when I have a house—ever burned down, the only thing I'd grab is my shoes," Julia said with a teasing grin. "Plus, we all tower over the Child family since you're six five and John is six four. We'll have the tall side and the not-so-tall side."

Dort hugged Julia. "You're such a good sport. If you weren't wearing a bandage on your head, no one would even know about the accident. I can't believe you're keeping your original wedding date."

"Well, thanks to our hosts, Whitney and Lola Seymour, today is still possible," Julia said. "I'm not letting an accident stop us."

"You really love him, don't you?" Dort asked.

Julia's heart expanded, and there was no hesitation on her part. "I really do."

"Let's get out there, then," Dort said. "You have a groom waiting for you."

It was nearly noon—time to get married.

As Julia stepped out into the beautiful backyard, fragrant with foliage and framed with leaves beginning to turn autumn colors, she glanced at the gathered guests—her father and Phila, John and Jo as well as Paul's close connections from Paris and Connecticut. Richard Myers and his family, the Kublers, and the Bissells.

But it was Paul who captured and held her attention. He might be standing at the end of the makeshift aisle, leaning on a cane, but his pleased demeanor made him seem another foot taller. Julia smiled as tears burned her eyes. The moment was finally here. She took her place across from her beloved Paul, flanked by Dort as her single bridesmaid and Charlie as Paul's only groomsman. The ceremony was short, which was perfect since Julia had waited long enough.

Paul had carefully prepared his vows, and Julia knew her heart would be devoted to him the rest of her living days. After their "I do's," Paul stepped close to kiss her. Yesterday, a runaway truck had almost ended their lives before they could really begin.

Today was a second chance for them—and the happiest chance of their lifetime.

Everyone headed across the state border, back to Coppernose, where Dort and Freddie had outdone themselves with the food preparation. Tables had been set up in the backyard and on the bricked terrace, and the women brought out dish after dish and set them on the long tables for a sumptuous lunch. In Julia's opinion, the location couldn't have been more beautiful, with the fully bloomed gardens edging a brook and small waterfall. One side of the yard held a swimming pool that sparkled blue in the sunlight.

When everyone was full from all the delicious food, Dort announced, "It's time to cut the wedding cake."

Julia wanted to groan at the thought of taking one more bite of anything, but she and Paul climbed to their feet, hand in hand, and crossed to where Freddie proudly displayed a layered cake she'd baked. Maybe it was because they were both sporting injuries from the car wreck, but their shared taste of the wedding cake was perfectly sweet and polite.

JULIA

Paul leaned in for another kiss, his eyes smiling at her. "Thanks for going easy on me."

Julia laughed.

Despite there being some grumbling on her father's part about how the Child family had planned all the wedding details—when Julia knew he didn't want anything to do with the planning anyway—Pop came through with a generous wedding gift of a new car—a 1947 Buick—which would replace their wrecked vehicle.

They immediately nicknamed it the Blue Flash in honor of the color.

Pop made a point of disparaging the French when he presented them with an original gift: a gas refrigerator. "You don't want to buy one of those new-fangled French iceboxes. We should only patronize American businesses."

Julia didn't exactly agree, but it was her wedding day, and she wasn't going to turn down her father's wedding gifts.

The first week of marriage to Paul was everything Julia could hope for, and she pinched herself more than once to make sure she was really and truly married to him. But reality soon set in as the weeks turned into months, and Julia felt adrift when faced with what her role should be while Paul continued to work for the government in Washington, DC. She toyed with the idea of finding a desk job—because that was what she was qualified for, and there were plenty of those available with the State Department—but she couldn't bring herself to commit to more secretarial work, even though she also didn't want to blow through her mother's inheritance. Paul was making a passable wage, and they weren't desperate, but the future felt narrow and limited if they relied on only his income.

Paul gave her the autonomy to decide whether she wanted to work, so while she was making up her mind, she determined to be content with setting up house and enjoying their social circles. Through Charlie, they'd found a house at 1677 Wisconsin Avenue in Georgetown. The place needed attention and love, and Julia loved the small, cozy rooms. She didn't mind diving into the work of plastering, putting up wallpaper, painting, and watching Paul do the rewiring. Slowly, it began to feel like a home—*their* home.

"It looks like you're getting ready to cook up a storm," Paul said, coming home from the office one day and finding stacks of cookbooks and magazines on the kitchen table and every pot and pan and cooking utensil strewn across the counters.

Julia set her hands on her hips. "I'm getting ready. Like, to really cook. We can't survive on soup from a can or going out to eat every night. But cooking dinner probably won't happen until tomorrow. Fortunately, Freddie invited us over for dinner tonight."

Freddie and Charlie owned a house only a few blocks away on Thirty-Fifth Street. They ended up eating together a few nights a week—Freddie cooking something delicious and Julia bringing a measly side dish of canned vegetables and a bottle of wine. Eventually, Julia planned to start inviting their OSS friends over for dinner and socializing. Several of them lived and worked in DC, including Betty MacDonald and Dick Heppner, who'd married each other after the war, and Guy Martin.

"Then, what's all this?" Paul waved a hand.

"All this?" Julia echoed. She rested her hand on the stack of women's magazines. *Ladies' Home Journal* was on top. "I'm learning to be a homemaker, and this has recipes. Plus . . ." She picked up a copy of *Joy of Cooking* by Irma S. Rombauer. "I'm going to make you the most delicious and joyful meals. Irma guarantees it."

In a couple of strides, he crossed the room and pulled her into his arms. "I think a *joyful* meal sounds wonderful. When will it be served?"

Julia scoffed. "That's the real mystery. You've heard about all my cooking mishaps. You might want to brace yourself."

Paul leaned in for a kiss and lingered. "I'm not in any hurry."

His stomach grumbled then, and they both laughed.

"How about you help me hang the pots and pans on the peg board," she said, "then we'll head over to your brother's for some real cooking."

Paul released her and surveyed the peg board. "We don't have much to fill it."

Julia crossed to the counter and picked up a frying pan. "I want to be able to see what I have to work with, even if there's not much."

Over the next hour, they organized the peg board until they had everything in a neat order. Paul used a marker to outline the pans and pots on the board, so they could be replaced in the same spot without second-guessing. Then he set the cookbooks on the shelf above the stove. "Anything else?"

Julia picked up one of the *Family Circle* magazines. "Let's go. I'm going to ask Freddie about one of the recipes in here. Maybe she can help me work through it."

"Which recipe?" Paul asked.

"It will be a surprise. For tomorrow night's dinner."

Freddie proved to be very helpful and even offered to do a trial run in her own kitchen. But Julia felt confident that she couldn't mess up the simple recipe of broiled chicken. The recipe seemed straightforward—put the chicken into the oven, broil it, then take it out of the oven. She just had to ask Freddie about the sauce since her last attempt had turned out too runny. And she knew better than to add lard.

"You can always add more stock to the sauce," Freddie told her. "Or even wine. If it's weak-tasting, add more spices. Not much to it. Or you can simply glaze the chicken beforehand or even partway through cooking."

Julia hung on to those words. It seemed there were many options in cooking, and it didn't need to be an exact science. Clearly, Freddie treated it more like an art—ever fluid and changing. Once Julia was by herself again the next day, she made a careful list of all the items she'd need at the grocery store. She didn't want to go overboard, but she wanted everything delicious. For both her and Paul. If she'd learned anything in working for the OSS overseas, it was that eating food could be enjoyable. An event in and of itself; a reward after a long day's work. Food had been a major connection between her and Paul when they'd first become friends, and she wanted to continue that. Besides, her new husband deserved something to smile about and please his stomach and palate when he returned home from a job of drudgery. And Julia would take pride in providing it.

Returning home to her small kitchen that was now organized was only a boost to her confidence and determination. She flipped to the recipe pages she'd earmarked, calculated the time when she needed to start glazing the chicken—because she decided to skip the sauce altogether—roasting red potatoes, and making apple tarts for dessert. This wasn't like cooking on a small burner like she'd had in Washington, DC, as a new OSS agent. She had to wrestle with a full-sized oven and a full-sized meal. Pretty soon, she was sure, she'd be proficient enough to invite company over.

Thankfully, she hadn't invited company that evening, because by the time Paul walked in the door, the chicken had burned beyond saving, the apple tarts were an incongruent combination of too-browned crust and apples that hadn't softened enough, and the potatoes had shriveled to rubber.

"It smells delicious . . . ?" Paul said in an expectant tone, looking about the kitchen, then at her, his smile in place.

Julia held up a hand. "Before you say anything else, dinner is ruined. At least, this dinner. I can make something different, but it might take a while. Maybe you'll need a sandwich to tide you over?" Tears sprung to her eyes, despite making every effort to keep them back.

Paul set down his carrying case and walked to the stove, where Julia had left the abandoned, burnt evidence. "What was dinner going to be?"

"Well . . ." Julia drew in a breath. Paul didn't sound upset—why should he be? It wasn't like he'd ever come home to a fantastic meal she'd made. In fact, his voice had sounded like he might be trying to hold back a laugh. "Broiled chicken cooked in a lovely glazed sauce."

Paul lifted the aluminum foil she'd covered the chicken with. "Ah, there it is."

"The recipe didn't say how long to broil, and I was only gone about twenty minutes." Even as she said this, she knew that she could get caught up in conversations with others and not realize how much time had passed. But this time, it hadn't been a neighbor who'd distracted her. It had been a cat. "I heard a yowling. I guess the cooking chicken attracted a stray cat."

There was no surprise on Paul's face as he said, "Ah, so you went out and fed it?"

"Something like that."

Paul nodded, apparently resigned to the fact that Julia could never *not* feed a crying cat. "What else do we have here?" he asked, turning his attention back to a baking sheet covered with a dish cloth.

"Tarts with golden-brown sugary crust and sweet apples straight from the market."

He lifted a corner of the dish cloth and picked up one of the extremely crispy tarts. After biting off a corner, he chewed, then swallowed. He didn't wince, at least. "And this?" He lifted the lid off a pot.

"Boiled New England potatoes seasoned with fresh parsley."

"Hmm." Paul picked up a discarded spatula and poked at the shriveled lumps. "We could mash this and make some gravy to drench it."

He looked over at Julia, then seemed to notice the expression on her face. "No gravy?"

"Definitely no gravy," Julia said. "There's not enough chicken stock left in the burned pan, and you have to bring it to a slow roiling boil—whatever that is, exactly—then add things like cornstarch and flour and milk and seasoning. In what amounts, I have no clue. And the recipe says that it can't be left unattended."

Paul tilted his head. "I can attend to the gravy and whatever you need help with." He paused. "Or soup is fine. We'll finish off the bread. Do we still have bread? For dessert, we'll eat the centers of the apple tarts." His mouth twitched.

"This isn't funny," she said, teetering between laughing and crying.

"It's a little bit funny," Paul said, his smile appearing.

Julia allowed his smile. "Should I apologize for a ruined dinner? Resign myself to being better at filing than filleting? Maybe I should apply for a secretarial job. This housewife thing has more twisty turns than a Ceylon jungle road."

He crossed to her and took her hand. "No apologies, dearest, ever. Want to go out? Or stay here and scrounge up something?"

"You've had a long day, and I've had a long day." Julia nodded toward their disaster of a kitchen. "I do like to cook, and I love having a kitchen of my own. I need a bit more hand holding, I think. Recipes can be so vague, and they assume I already know things that I don't. It's like the steps happen too fast, and before I know it, things are overboiling or burning or—"

Paul cut her off with a kiss. When he drew away, they were both smiling. "You'll become better and better, if that's what you wish for, but right now, I'm taking you out for dinner. It's my treat."

Julia's heart felt lighter. "Can we really treat each other if we share the same bank account?"

"Oh sure," Paul said with a grin. "I'll make sure I only use the money that's from one of my paychecks."

"Perfect."

Julia leaned into him, and he pulled her close.

"Tomorrow," she said, "I'm going to make cod chowder. What could go wrong? You boil a few things together, then simmer, then eat. But first, let me feed the cat."

"The stray cat that distracted you earlier?" Paul asked, leaning away to look her in the eye.

"The cat lives here now," Julia quipped. "It's napping on your office chair. The coziest place in the house, it seems."

PART TWO

1948–1962

CHAPTER 19

Paris, France
November 1948

"Paul and I floated out the door into the brilliant sunshine and cool air. Our first lunch together in France had been absolute perfection. It was the most exciting meal of my life."

—JULIA CHILD

Stepping off the SS *America* in Le Havre, France, should have been a banner moment, but Julia felt like she'd been dragged along railroad tracks behind a train. The five-day ocean crossing had been treacherous, with rough weather that included towering waves and dense fog. Paul had spent most of the time in their stateroom, suffering with agonizing stomach pain. Julia had made it to the observation deck only a handful of times.

For the duration of the journey, she'd been glad that she wasn't pregnant and that they hadn't been wrestling with a small child. Two years of marriage hadn't brought them any signs of children, and Julia was beginning to wonder if it would ever happen. Maybe she or Paul needed a doctor's checkup? Paul had said he was perfectly happy with just the two of them. Julia agreed, but there had been times when she'd let her mind wonder about the possibility of becoming a mother. Was there still a chance, or was her body not capable?

So, yes, standing on solid ground was certainly a blessing, allowing both of their stomachs to settle, and then they could appreciate their surroundings. Her first glimpse of fabled France was murky, at best. The predawn darkness was broken up only by a scattering of lights from buildings under construction. As they disembarked and waited for the Blue Flash and their luggage to be unloaded, the sky lightened to a pale gray, outlining the evidence of a city being rebuilt after the destruction of the war.

Some of the buildings beyond the harbor still showed the scars of war, crimson and savage, with brick rubble and a patchwork of broken windows. Farther up the harbor sat a rusted-out ship—or part of a ship—that looked like it had been in the process of disassembly, then had been forgotten for a more urgent matter.

Paul set an arm around her. "What do you think?"

"It's beautiful in a sad way," Julia said as the sky brightened more, revealing additional war scars of this harbor city. "Is it hard to see it this way?"

He was quiet for a moment, then said, "It only demonstrates the resiliency of the French people. Once we get in the car, I'll show you the beauty of the Norman countryside."

Julia stifled a yawn. She was tired, aching, a bit wobbly, and possibly homesick. But she was happy for Paul's new assignment as a Class 4 Foreign Reserve officer. He'd be working as the attaché for the US Information Service Department founded about the same time at the Central Intelligence Agency. Paul's department replaced the Office of War Information division, and he was in charge of photography and putting on exhibits that would show American life, such as photographs of Hoover Dam, with the purpose of spreading goodwill and combating the spreading influence and misinformation of communism. Anything to push against the Soviet Union's aggressive campaign in Eastern Europe and Asia.

So, here they were. Back in Paul's beloved France, and Julia was missing her darn cat, of all things. She'd had to rehome the former stray. And it was all fine. She just needed a moment to get her legs under her again.

Paul squeezed her shoulder. "Once we get settled in Paris, with our personal belongings around us, we'll find you another cat."

Julia gasped. "How did you know?"

Paul chuckled and pressed a kiss against her temple. "We've been married for more than two years. That's how I know."

They'd shipped their belongings overseas—fourteen suitcases and seven trunks. The rest had gone into storage, and they'd rented out their Olive Street house. Their first house, on Wisconsin Street, had burned down that February in a terrible fire. They'd awakened at four in the morning to the smell of smoke and the sound of wood collapsing from flames. They'd thrown out some of their things from their second-floor bedroom window, including a good number of Julia's large-sized shoes, then they'd belly crawled through the smoke and pitch blackness until they could find a ground-floor window to escape through.

The whole experience had taught Julia that as long as she had Paul and they were both healthy, not much else mattered. She'd been thrilled with Paul's assignment to France, although she didn't know the language—years taking French in school hadn't stuck in her mind—and she didn't have any sort of job lined up. At this moment, she had no idea what the next weeks would bring, but she was with her Paul, and they were in a new place.

Paul was true to his word, and once they were driving in the Blue Flash, they were surrounded by the beautiful French countryside. Marred as it was with sightings of centuries-old châteaux that had been bombed during the war, beauty had won. Fields of cabbages spread far and wide, along with flax plants bursting a riot of blue color, like an intricate medieval rug.

"We're almost to Rouen, the capital of Normandy," Paul said. "We'll stop there for lunch." He glanced over at her. "You hungry?"

"Always," she said. "I feel like my stomach shrank on the boat from such paltry food." In truth, she wanted to eat, then take a long nap. The sights were fascinating but overwhelming, too, as her tired mind tried to take in everything.

The road now turned into cobblestone as they entered the town that straddled the Seine River. "You'll remember Monet's painting of the Cathédrale Notre-Dame de Rouen," Paul said. "An Allied bomb hit the Saint Romaine tower just before D-Day."

"I remember the newsreel about that," Julia murmured, humbled at the sight of so many burned buildings, including the famous cathedral. So much had changed during the war, and now, more things were changing because of the war. The Central Intelligence Agency had been organized the previous year, in 1947, taking up the reins that the OSS had started. Even though there was a gap between the ending of the OSS and the creation of the CIA, Donovan had been recognized as the original founder.

In fact, several of their former OSS friends had been invited into the new CIA, including Clark McGregor, Douglas Dillon, Arthur Schlesinger, and Stewart Alsop.

"We're going to the place du Vieux-Marche," Paul said, bringing Julia out of her musings. "It's where Joan of Arc was burned at the stake. Despite that grim history, the oldest restaurant in France is at the side of the town square. It's an inn with dining on the ground floor, called La Couronne."

"Anything sounds lovely," Julia said.

"This place has the three-forks-and-spoons rating from the *Guide Michelin*, so your first authentic French food will be the best of the best."

"Can you drive any faster?"

Paul laughed. "Not unless we want to drop an axel on this car."

Julia would eat anything at this point, but she could see that Paul was excited about this particular place, so she kept quiet about the many other places they probably could have stopped at much sooner.

Once they parked and Julia had unfolded her stiff body from the car, she walked with Paul to the restaurant. The building was multistoried with timberwork on the outside of the building in the *fachwerk* German style, which Julia had noticed a lot in France so far. Paul had corrected her in calling the architecture *colombage*—the French interpretation.

Paul opened the door, and Julia stepped into the dim, cozy interior. Tables covered in white cloths, chinaware, and wine glasses dotted the room. A maître d'hôtel led them to a table. Paul spoke to him in French, impressing Julia with his easy switch into another language.

"Madame," the maître d' said, pulling out her chair.

She sat in the plush chair and marveled at the romantic and intimate feeling of the place. She almost forgot her grumbling stomach.

Within moments, a waiter appeared with a platter of oysters and a bottle of wine. He presented both with a flourish, then after Paul's approval of the wine, a chilled Pouilly-Fuissé, the waiter poured.

Julia ate one of the oysters; she'd never tasted anything better in her life.

"These are Portugaises oysters," Paul said.

"Delicious. Are they from Portugal?"

"Originally, yes, but France also produces them."

When the waiter appeared, Paul spoke with him in French as Julia scanned the menu. Nothing sounded familiar, and she could pick out only an occasional word. Her years of French lessons had utterly failed her.

"Order for me, Paul," Julia said.

After a brief discussion with the waiter, Paul said something about "*Sole meunière.*"

Julia at least recognized that "sole" was fish.

When the waiter left their table, Paul said, "We should enjoy the *sole meunière*. It's a traditional French dish that most restaurants offer. There wasn't any duck on the menu—which is odd because that's pretty much a staple at the nicer restaurants. And the steak and potato soufflé seemed too heavy for lunch, even though we're practically starving."

Julia was less starving now, thanks to the oysters, but her stomach still wanted more. "What does *sole meunière* mean, exactly?" she asked.

Paul looked up from the oyster shell he'd discarded. "'Sole as God.' It's a rather simple dish, cooked in Normandy butter, which is incomparable to other butters."

Julia didn't know there could be more than one type of butter.

When the waiter finally arrived with their plates, the smell alone of the still-sizzling fish fillets lightly browned by the Normandy butter almost sent Julia into a swoon. That was nothing compared to the first bite of the delicate, textured fish. The taste seemed to burst in her mouth in a combination of lemon, parsley, creamy butter, and supple fish.

She closed her eyes and swallowed, then opened her eyes to find Paul smiling at her.

"Do you like it?" he asked.

"Paul . . . this is . . ." She shook her head because she wondered if she was dreaming. Maybe she'd fallen asleep on their drive. She took another bite, finding the second bite was as heavenly as the first. She moaned as the flavors startled her senses.

"I guess I should stop worrying if my wife will like French food. I mean, we're going to be living here a few years."

"I don't think I've ever tasted anything more delicious in my life," Julia said, forking another portion. "In fact, I know I haven't. This is divine. Absolutely made by the gods." She took another bite, then another. When she finished, she hadn't left a speck behind.

Her stomach had registered as filling up, but she knew she could eat plate after plate of *sole meunière*, and she'd happily go broke doing so. "I feel like I've just been born on earth. As if I've never truly eaten before. Tell me, what makes the Normandy butter so delightful?"

Paul dabbed at his mouth with his napkin, proper as ever. "It's made from Normandy cream that's unpasteurized and unprocessed. Churned by hand."

"And the sole? I've never had such tender fish in the States."

Paul nodded. "And you won't," he said. "This is Dover sole. In the States, they serve flounder and call it sole."

Julia shivered, in a good way. "Now what is he bringing?"

The waiter appeared at their table again to clear their plates. He presented a green salad, a cheese course, a dessert that Paul called *crème fraîche*, followed by *café filtre*.

Julia had certainly entered another existence, one in which she didn't want to leave. As all good and beautiful things come to an end, though, so did their meal, despite their having eaten slowly. As if they'd had all the time in the world. It reminded her of their meals in Ceylon, which had never been in any rush, and every bite had been pleasurable. And now, Julia was pleasantly satiated and more than ready to declare her devotion to the town of Rouen.

"Let's walk for a bit," Paul said, grasping her hand and bringing her to her feet.

After settling the bill, they stepped outside and strolled along the cobbled streets, taking in the Rouen cathedral and the rest of the war-torn city. The old structures and the damages and the rebuilding seemed

JULIA

to spark a fire inside Julia. She turned to Paul and kissed him, not caring if they were in a place full of strangers.

"I love you, and I love that you brought me here," she gushed. "I love everything about this place."

Paul pulled her close, into a warm embrace. "We're not even in Paris yet, dearest. Just you wait."

They arrived in Paris at twilight. The horizon outlining the Parisian buildings in a lush magenta color took Julia's breath away. "Is that the Eiffel Tower?" she asked, pointing to the icon in the distance. Of course it was, but it was hard to believe it was real—that she was truly here.

Paul grasped her hand briefly as he navigated the narrow roads. "Yes, she's watching over her city."

"It's beautiful, Paul," she said, reverence vibrating through her. "Absolutely gorgeous." Her gaze didn't know what to settle on next—the majestic buildings, the bridges over the gently flowing Seine River, the graceful statues, the people, the shops, the scents from the cafés coming in through the car windows.

When they arrived at the Hôtel Pont-Royal, which the embassy had temporarily booked for them, Julia was still reeling from all the sights and sounds. While Julia waited in the lobby for Paul to park the car on rue Montalembert, she tried to decipher the buzz of conversation from other guests around her. She could pick out only a word here and there, but she loved the melody of the language.

Paul strode in through the lobby doors, scanning for her. When he reached her, he said in a rush, "There's news from the States. Harry Truman defeated Thomas Dewey in the presidential election."

"That's an unexpected upset," Julia said. When they were leaving the States, all speculation was pointing to Dewey for the win. "I'm more than happy about it."

Paul squeezed her hand. "Me too. Now, let's get settled, then walk through the city until we find a café where we want to have dinner."

Julia couldn't think of a better plan.

CHAPTER 20

Paris, France
November–December 1948

"On November 5, a banner headline in the *International Herald Tribune* proclaimed that Harry S. Truman had been elected president, defeating Thomas Dewey at the eleventh hour. Paul and I, devoted Democrats, were exultant. My father, 'Big John' McWilliams, a staunchly conservative Republican, was horrified."

—JULIA CHILD

The first weeks in Paris were dreamlike, that was the best that Julia could describe it. She awakened bright and early with Paul for the routine they'd established: having their morning *café complet* at a literary café in St. Germain des Prés, a place Paul had frequented when he'd first lived in France. Julia tried not to think of the fact that his previous stay had included Edith—someone Julia never found productive to mull over.

Julia was making new memories with Paul, and she jumped in with both feet. Paul's working hours were long, so they had free time only on the weekends, in which they explored the city, with Julia loving every moment of it. They'd walk along the Seine, visiting restaurants and finding new favorites like *sole à la normande* at La Truite and shellfish au gratin at Lapérouse. They wandered through museums, medieval churches, theaters, and the Louvre. Paul told her of his work on the stained-glass windows of the American Church on the Quai d'Orsay, though some things had changed in the eighteen years since Paul had lived there, due to both time and war.

The effects of war were still felt with the gasoline and food rationing, as evidenced in the long lines for ration coupons for items such as coffee, butter, milk, cheese, eggs, and sugar. Every so often, they'd come across streets and buildings surrounded by rubble, and occasionally the electricity cut out at a restaurant or their hotel. Every time they saw a plaque commemorating a fallen French citizen, they'd stop to read it.

Their evenings were filled with diplomatic dinners and getting enmeshed in the social life, which, for Julia, meant a lot of standing around and politely smiling while others spoke French. They also spent time apartment hunting, but with Paul's long work hours, it was Julia who did the legwork and had the conversations—in very rough French—with potential landlords. They wanted to live on the Left Bank, where most of the university professors, artists, and publishers lived. The embassy was on the Right Bank, where businesses and shops lined the streets.

If it was possible to fall in love with food, with each passing day, Julia was falling headlong in love with French cuisine. And buying fresh baguettes every day only helped cement her growing affection. Each time they went out, Paul ordered something different so Julia could try all sorts of dishes, from *rognons sautés au beurre* to *poulet grantiné*, because if a restaurant menu included sole, that was what Julia ordered, which Paul took upon himself to tease her about. But she knew he was pleased with her response to France since he'd shown her the letters he'd written to Charlie.

Julia determined, with all the social events, to take French lessons right away, so she enrolled at Berlitz three times a week. And on most days, she tried to speak only French when she was out and about, taking buses about the city and shopping and eating out by herself. The French people seemed to appreciate her efforts and were more than patient.

She gushed about her days to Paul over dinner, many times at their favorite restaurant, Michaud, where the dishes weren't extravagant, but every bit of food was delicious, many of them with sauces containing butter and the scarcer cream. "I know people have warned me that the French might be dismissive of Americans and difficult to communicate with, but everyone I've met here is delightful."

Paul smiled. "You turned this old curmudgeon around, so I'm not surprised that every French person you meet becomes your friend."

Julia smirked. "I don't know about that, but I do know that the French are charming and so very wonderful. I wouldn't mind living here forever. Of course, my sister and brother need to come for visits. And maybe my father?"

Paul didn't comment on that as he took another bite of escargot d'or, which Julia had also come to love. "What was your favorite part about today?"

"Only today?" Julia sighed in rapture as she cut off a bit of brie from the cheese platter between them. She popped it into her mouth, savored it, then chewed, and swallowed. "I suppose it was speaking to a craggy fisherman on Ile S. Louis. His accent was a bit hard to follow, but we managed, somehow, to have a few laughs."

Paul shook his head.

"Oh, I'm also getting to know one of the chestnut vendors," she continued. "I buy chestnuts almost every day, you know." She glanced out the restaurant window, where a woman was passing by, walking her pristinely groomed white poodle in the light of the fading embers of sunset.

"The white poodles are so adorable," she added. "Paris must be full of them. They're everywhere. Oh, and the cats. They hang out on street corners, like newspaper boys."

Paul chuckled.

As they headed back to their new lodgings that Julia had secured in the Left Bank, she looped her arm through Paul's, enjoying the brisk night air. Their apartment was on the third floor of a townhouse at 81 rue de l'Université, owned by Madame Perrier. At a hiked-up American price of eighty dollars a month for their apartment, they considered themselves fortunate. Julia called the place Roo de Loo for short.

Here Paul could park in front of their building or drive under the front of the building and into a stone courtyard. Parking was always scarce, and there was always the risk of another car passing too closely and nicking their car.

Once they reached the building, they stepped into the cage elevator that creaked as it ascended, and Paul talked about the struggle to organize his office with little money. "The Marshall Plan is funneling money into Europe by the millions, yet I don't have the funds to fully do my job."

"You can only do what you can," Julia soothed as they unlocked the door to their apartment. The Marshall Plan, named after US Secretary of State George C. Marshall, and also known as the European Recovery Program, was a US program that provided aid to Western Europe, with billions of dollars funneling into rebuilding efforts. "And you're the best man for the job."

Paul opened the door, and she stepped inside first. "Perhaps," he conceded. "I have photo archives enough to put on dozens of displays, but everything is lagging because of such a sparse staff. We've been promised Marshall Plan funds for the USIS, but nothing has come in."

Julia heard the frustration in his voice, and it was the first time he'd talked about the complications of his job. Without turning on any interior lights, he walked through the apartment to the window overlooking the night skyline. Lights twinkled from various buildings, breaking through the fog that had started to gather. Their view included the twin green spires of the church of St. Clotilde, and Paul had already begun a painting of their view of the Paris skyline, which was now propped against an easel in the corner of the room.

She joined him at the window and leaned against him. The moon had cast a spell over the city—like a translucent web of hope and possibility.

Paul slipped his arm about her. "We're in Paris. Despite all the frustrations of my job, I'm happy to be here, happy that you're here too. It really is the City of Light—attracting people from all over the world."

And it was true, Julia and Paul had heard of so many artists and creatives in Paris. Some of them they'd met. Despite the city being a juxtaposition of beauty and light contrasting with crumbling buildings, cracked plaster, and burned wood, Julia discovered new wonders each day.

Even their apartment was a hodgepodge of the old and the new—well, mostly the old. The walls were covered in aged and faded leather, and the thick brocade curtains were in need of a good cleaning. Julia had moved out several of the rundown furniture pieces and stored them in the attic, which Paul called the "forgettery." Otherwise, Julia loved the open spaces and how the windows bathed the upstairs kitchen in full sunlight during the day.

"Everything will smooth out eventually," Julia said.

In the late evenings, he often became melancholy. It didn't bother Julia, not really, because she understood the feeling. He was probably homesick a little for his brother too. They'd had a great time living so close to Charlie and Freddie the past two years.

"What are you doing tomorrow?" Paul asked idly, his hand stroking her arm.

"After French lessons, I'm going to the market with Hélène. I think I learn more from her and interacting with the shop keepers than I do in class." Hélène Baltrusaitis was a new friend of theirs, recommended by George Kubler. Her husband was teaching at Yale for the semester, so she had plenty of free time on her hands. "Besides, I need to be cooking more things than eggs and toast for breakfast and lunch. The only time we eat something exciting is when we go out to dinner."

"I don't mind eggs and toast," Paul said.

Julia scoffed. "I don't either, but we're in Paris, surrounded by the most beautiful foods. I mean, they cook with fresh vegetables here, not out of cans, like in the States. Their turnips are huge, and their asparagus unmatched, and you can buy beans still in their shells."

Paul chuckled, but Julia continued in her excitement. "The potatoes are the creamiest I've ever had, and there are so many new things I've tried here, like chard, leeks, truffles, and zucchini flowers—who knew we could eat flowers? It can't be that hard to learn to cook like a French chef, right? Freddie can cook wonderful things. She'd be so impressed if I came back to the States with an entire arsenal of dishes I can prepare."

"You've had some successes."

Julia winced. "I think they were more good luck than actual successes." She moved to a lamp and turned it on. "I forgot to show you this. Hélène loaned me her *Encyclopedia of Practical Gastronomy*." She held up the well-read tome.

Paul crossed to her and took the book in hand. "*Gastronomie pratique: études culinairs* by Ali-Bab." He thumbed through a few pages. "This is serious business." He lifted his gaze. "You're going to read this?"

"I've already started."

Paul looked impressed, as he should. "You know that the author's real name is Henri Babinski."

"Hélène told me," Julia said. "Just look at the index. There are thousands of recipes. He includes variations of standard dishes, then variations of those. It's endless."

"You're getting pretty serious about this, aren't you?" Paul asked. "I really don't want you thinking you need to outdo anyone in the cooking department. I knew who you were when I married you."

Julia laughed and shoved at his shoulder, which almost caused him to lose his balance with the heavy cookbook. "This wouldn't be for you, Paulski. It would be for me. I mean, what else am I good at, except eating?"

Paul set down the cookbook and drew her into his arms. "You are good at eating, and I love eating as well. You have my blessing, even though you don't need it, to buy out the markets and try every recipe in that book."

"Maybe I will."

Over the next weeks, Julia began to experiment with cooking more and more at home. Not to replace dinner. Never to replace dinner since there were simply too many exquisite restaurants to be tried and to be patronized again and again. They often met friends for dinner, including the Mowrers, who were in their fifties and quickly became close friends. Paul had known Hadley Mowrer from his previous time in Paris—back when she'd been married to Jack Hemingway. Hadley's second husband, Paul Mowrer, was the foreign editor of the *New York Post*. But Julia wanted something decent and exciting for Paul to eat when he came home for lunch. It was a nice reprieve for them both.

And Julia felt inspired to create good food at home when she was surrounded by good food wherever she turned in Paris. Every corner, every street had a bistro or café or restaurant that turned out mouthwatering dishes—*terrines, cassoulet, boeuf bourguignon, veal blanquette, ragoûts* . . . the menus were endless. The smell of freshly baked French bread was her favorite scent in the entire world now. She could spend years and years in Paris and never tire of the food.

Of course, eating out so much put a tight grip on their pocketbook, with Paul's income at ninety-five dollars a week, which covered their rent and a few basics. So Julia frequently dipped into the inheritance from her mother, and did so happily, knowing that living in Paris was something that might not last forever.

But making ends meet remained at the back of her mind, which was probably why she enjoyed speaking with a produce vendor named Marie des Quatre Saisons. Not only was it good for Julia to better her expanding French, but Marie was also a cook who knew her vegetables. She instructed Julia on which vegetables were in season and how to prepare them correctly. Through Marie, Julia was directed to other vendors and grocers whom she eventually became friends with and could trust their choices, including the butcher and the *crémerie* and *fromagerie* as well as the wine merchant. She alternated between her neighborhood market on the rue de Bourgogne and the market on the rue de Buci, a short walk away. Then, a couple of days a week, she'd walk to the large outdoor market off the Pont de l'Alma across from the Eiffel Tower.

She was further inspired when she and Hélène took a five-day excursion to Nice, where they also visited the vacationing Mowrers. Seeing more of France only added to Julia's appreciation of the food and culture. Once back in Paris, she found herself testing the recipes in Ali-Bab's cookbook. And instead of feeding Paul something boring for lunch, most of her experiments weren't half bad.

"What do I smell today?" Paul asked, coming into the apartment on a lunch break, a fresh loaf of French bread under his arm.

Julia turned from the stove, where she was whipping up a sauce that might be overcooking. It was hard to tell exactly. "I'm making sautéed cauliflower, and there's duck à l'orange in the oven." The bulky oven was temperamental, but Julia had grown accustomed to it.

Paul set the bread on the table, then stepped close to her and wrapped his arms about her waist. "Smells heavenly."

Just then, Julia caught a whiff of something . . . burning. "Oh no." She moved away from Paul and opened the oven. No smoke billowed out, so she took that as a good sign.

"It looks perfect," Paul said, crossing to her, hot pads in hand. "Let me."

She stepped aside as he removed the duck from the oven. It looked . . . well, not exactly burned but quite crispy.

"When did you start this?" Paul asked, picking up the boning knife.

"Right after breakfast," Julia said. "I knew I had to start early, or it wouldn't be done in time for your lunch."

He began to slice pieces off the duck, and Julia fetched a platter.

"The cauliflower—almost forgot." She set to work on stirring the cauliflower. She wasn't exactly sure what it should look like when it was done, so she popped a small piece into her mouth. It was sizzling hot, but she rolled it around until she could stand to chew it. "Why, that's pretty good."

Paul turned off the gas element. "Let's eat, then."

"Good plan." In minutes, they were seated at the table, Paul having poured wine for each of them.

Julia took a tentative bite of the duck. It was a bit dry, that was all. So she dipped the next piece into the extra sauce—which was a tad too bitter.

Paul ate with relish and only offered compliments. "I think you've nearly mastered duck *à l'orange*," he said magnanimously.

"It certainly tastes better than it looks," Julia said, "but I've learned a few things that I'll do differently next time."

Paul set a hand over hers. "It's wonderful, dearest. Thank you."

His soft words went straight to her heart. "You're my biggest fan, P'ski, I'll have you know. Even when I ruin something, you find a way to make it enjoyable."

He merely shrugged and leaned over to kiss her cheek. Well, she couldn't let him stop with just a kiss on the cheek. She scooted her chair to loop her arms about his neck and gave him a real kiss.

"You'll make me late for the office if you keep that up," Paul murmured.

She kissed him again. "Maybe that's the plan."

"If only I didn't have to return today. You and your lunch have been the only bright spot."

Julia drew away. "What's going on?"

Paul rubbed his temple. "The usual bureaucratic red tape. Every decision has to go through a chain of command, even the simplest ones. Nothing I haven't complained about before."

She stroked the side of his face. "Everyone's trying to figure out their roles with this new division, and you're probably overqualified."

He seemed mollified for the moment, but the issues would start to bother him again soon enough. Julia felt fortunate to be surrounded each day by the people she wanted to interact with. Shop owners were always willing to answer her questions, and the growing brood of friends she and Paul had made were preferable to any embassy society connections.

"Did I tell you that Dort is coming in April?" she asked.

"Is it certain now?"

"Yes, she's bought her ticket," Julia said. "She'll be so impressed with my French speaking and French cooking."

"I'm already impressed with both." Paul pulled her close again.

"Oh, and I've made a doctor appointment."

Paul's expression filled with concern. "What's wrong? Are you ill?"

"I'm not quite sure." Julia pressed a hand to her belly. "I feel different, and I've had some cramping and weight gain . . . so I wondered . . . or I suspect . . ."

When she didn't finish, Paul said, "Are you pregnant, Julie?"

His gaze was intense, concerned. They hadn't exactly discussed when they wanted to have children—Paul had lamented once that he was probably too old, but it had never turned into a serious discussion. Julia wasn't too old at thirty-six, but she was definitely on the riskier side.

JULIA

"I don't know," Julia said. "That's why I wanted to see the doctor. I don't want to keep waiting and wondering."

Paul cradled her face and kissed her. "When's the appointment? I'm coming with you."

CHAPTER 21

Paris, France
March–June 1949

"Parisian restaurants were very different from American eateries. It was such fun to go into a little bistro and find cats on the chairs, poodles under the tables or poking out of women's bags, and chirping birds in the corner. I loved the crustacean stands in front of cafés, and began to order boldly.... As we explored the city, we made a point of trying every kind of cuisine, from fancy to hole-in-the-wall. In general, the more expensive the establishment, the less glad they were to see us, perhaps because they could sense us counting our centimes."

—JULIA CHILD

It wasn't that Julia had been desperate to have a child. She liked children and imagined she'd enjoy motherhood. Paul got along well with Charlie's kids, although Julia could see that his patience ran thin as a twig sometimes; surely that would change with his own child.

But tears stung her eyes as she lay in bed with darkness surrounding her, listening to the sound of Paul's relaxed breathing as he slept and a light rain pattered against the window. She hadn't known how much she wanted children until she'd thought she was pregnant. Only to have a Paris doctor tell her that she was not pregnant. Her stomach cramps were from too much indulgence. Imagine! She'd overeaten. She hadn't been limiting her desserts. She'd been indulging in sauces full of cream and butter.

Sure, she'd felt foolish, but she'd laughed it off when she'd been with Paul. He'd hugged and kissed her, although she didn't know if it was in relief or comfort. She wasn't pregnant. And she'd be thirty-seven in a few months. Perhaps she'd missed her chance. Or perhaps there was still time.

Would she want to have a baby in France though? Would she be able to manage mostly on her own with Paul's intense work schedule? These questions swirled in her mind as she finally drifted off to sleep.

The next morning, when she awakened to the scent of brewing coffee and the sound of Paul's humming in the kitchen, she decided to be grateful for each day. No matter what it brought. She had a happy marriage, a wonderful husband, a family who was well and answered her many letters, and an entire world outside her window.

It wasn't like she'd had a miscarriage or anything. She'd simply misunderstood her symptoms. It would be funny one day in the future, and maybe that future would include an actual child. A child with her hazel eyes and Paul's intellect.

She turned her head when she heard Paul's footsteps.

He took a seat on the edge of the bed, coffee cup in hand, its warm aroma filling the room. "I made you this. I think you should take the day off. Keep off your feet. Rest or read or do nothing. Skip your French class. I'll bring something for lunch."

Julia pushed up on her elbows. "I'm not sick."

Paul's smile was gentle. He'd already showered, shaved, and dressed. "I know, but the doctor didn't give you the news you wanted."

Her throat went tight. "Was I that obvious?"

He set the cup on the bedside table, then leaned close and kissed her. "You don't need to be obvious. We've been married long enough that we can practically read each other's minds."

Julia sat up more fully and wrapped her arms about him, breathing in his familiar scent of musky soap. "I love you."

"I love you too," he murmured.

After a long moment, he finally pulled away and left her in bed to wait for his return at lunchtime.

She tried to stay in bed, tried to rest, tried to read, tried to let her mind coast, but she began to feel agitated about twenty minutes after Paul left. The best time to shop at the markets was in the mornings when everything was fresh. Besides, Marie's daughter was due with a baby any day. What if the baby had been born the night before? Julia wanted to hear all about it.

And the wine merchant Nicolas would want to tell her about his son's upcoming wedding. Julia would miss out on all the morning chatter on the streets. And she knew her instructor wouldn't be happy if she missed class right before a long weekend. Plus, she wanted to try a new recipe. Paul could bring home lunch, but that wouldn't stop her from experimenting with dessert, and today felt like a good day to make a chocolate cake—*un gâteau au chocolat*—and indulge.

Julia's feet hit the floor less than thirty minutes after Paul left, and she stayed busy the rest of the morning. Perhaps it was a coping skill to mask her disappointment, but she could truthfully admit that she felt better when she was kept occupied and didn't let her thoughts take a deep dive off a cliff.

By the time Paul arrived with lunch, the apartment was filled with the aroma of a baking chocolatey deliciousness.

"You're not in bed," Paul said, a teasing chastisement in his tone as he set a couple of paper sacks on the table.

"I've been too busy," she said.

He pulled her into his arms, his gaze locked on hers. "Feeling better?"

"I'm feeling grateful. For you. For this old apartment. For a beautiful spring morning in Paris. For flowers."

Paul's brows arched. "I did notice quite a few vases about the apartment on my way to the kitchen."

"I was in the mood to buy flowers," she said with a shrug.

He chuckled, then was interrupted by a meow. He dropped his hands immediately and turned to see a small furry creature walk into the kitchen as if she owned the place. "Who's this?" Paul asked in a tentative tone.

"Her name is Minette. We met about an hour ago, and well, she was hungry and needed a place to stay."

He bent to pet the cat, but it sauntered past him, straight to Julia.

JULIA

"She'll warm up to you, don't worry." Julia scooped up the cat, who immediately began to purr.

"So . . . we have another cat."

Julia flashed her husband a smile. "We have another cat."

Paul unpacked the lunch he'd bought. "Frankly, I'm surprised it took you this long."

She set the cat down, and it hopped up on a nearby chair, content to watch the activity. The cat kept her company during Paul's long work hours, and the weeks flew by as she waited for her sister's visit to France.

On April 8, Dort arrived in Paris, becoming the perfect distraction for Julia. Reuniting with her sister was delightful. It was also wonderful not to feel like the tallest woman in Paris. With Dort by her side, they attracted a lot of attention, especially at the markets.

"Perhaps I will stay in Europe," Dort told Julia on one of their weekend picnic excursions. They'd finished their meal and were lounging on an old blanket, surrounded by wildflowers, with Paul a few dozen feet away, taking some photos of the blooming cherry trees beyond. "There's an English-speaking theater group here, and it might be fun to get involved."

"You should do it," Julia said. "You have nothing stopping you right now."

"You mean I don't have a husband or father to care for?" Dort teased.

"Exactly."

Dort stretched her long legs in front of her. "Anything specific I need to pack for Lyons?"

"No, just a raincoat for England."

After they visited the exhibit that Paul had been working on for months, which demonstrated how the Marshall Plan had made improvements in Europe, they'd drive to England in the Blue Flash for a ten-day excursion. They'd be visiting friends and acquaintances along the way, including Nigel and Sally Bicknell, who they'd known in Georgetown.

"Paul wants to see the University of Cambridge," Julia told Nigel and Sally one night over dinner with the couple. It was, in fact, a goose dinner that Julia had proudly prepared.

"Nigel's brother Peter and his wife, Mari, live there," Sally said. "You should visit them. Mari is a ballet instructor. We'll ring them up and let them know you're coming."

Within a short time, it was all arranged, and Julia, Dort, and Paul were on their way to Cambridge. Julia connected immediately with Peter and Mari, who loved to cook. They spent time in the kitchen, Julia showing Mari some of the dishes she'd learned, including veal *blanquette* and *navarin printanier*.

"These are excellent dishes," Mari said, leaning against the kitchen counter as Julia poured broth over the veal.

"I've mastered only a few things." Julia turned up the heat and continued skimming the broth over the meat. "I have trouble following recipes sometimes—or maybe it's more coordinating the preparation and cooking of a meal to have everything ready at the same time. Poor Paul has sometimes waited hours for his dinner when I cook at home. It's why we eat at restaurants most nights."

Mari only smiled. "It does take time to learn, and you said that you didn't cook much growing up?"

"Rarely." Julia enjoyed visiting with the Frenchwoman, which helped because even though England was a lovely adventure, Julia missed France already. "But I've fallen in love with French food, so that's all I'm attempting right now. It gives me immense satisfaction when I get a dish right and when my husband compliments it."

Mari's brows shot up. "Is Paul really so picky?"

"Not at all," Julia said. "He's helpful in the kitchen, and he's also a very good sport when I overcook things, or simply mess something up."

"I know that feeling," Mari said. "You know . . . if you really want to learn French cooking, you should enroll at Le Cordon Bleu cooking school in Paris. I graduated from their course."

"You did?" Julia added chopped vegetables and an herb bouquet to the veal, then partially covered the casserole. "This isn't all intrinsic?"

"Maybe some of it is since I grew up helping my mother, but I learned so much more at Le Cordon Bleu," Mari said. "The famous chefs Claude Thilmont and Max Bugnard were some of the instructors. Bugnard

JULIA

trained as a boy with Escoffier in London, at the Carlton Hotel. His specialties are fish, meats, and sauces. Le Cordon Bleu is a pretty intensive course, so you need to be able to commit the time."

Julia gave a slow nod. She'd heard of the famous cooking school. Jean Friendly and her husband, Paul's associate, had suggested it. But Julia hadn't thought to enroll because although she was getting better at speaking French, she wasn't exactly fluent.

Mari seemed to read her mind. "Your French is coming along fine. You'll just have to work harder to impress the instructors. But something tells me you'd be a great student."

Julia had to laugh at that. "I wasn't a great student in college, but I'm much more grounded now."

"We all grow up, and then we figure out what we really want to do with our lives." Mari picked up one of the pearl onions that Julia had set out and began to peel it. "Now, what are these onions for?"

"*Oignons glacés à blanc*, of course," Julia said.

"Of course," Mari said. "Dinner will be divine."

That night, after everyone had retired and Julia was alone with Paul, she said, "What do you think about me taking classes at Le Cordon Bleu? They start in the fall."

Paul paused in pulling back the covers of their bed. "The cooking school in Paris?"

"Yes—Mari suggested it," Julia said. "She's a graduate."

Paul didn't say anything for a moment. "Are you really that serious about French cooking?"

Julia grinned. "I think I am. Every morning when I wake up, my first thoughts are what I should cook next, and when I fall asleep, I'm cataloging recipes in my head."

He climbed into bed and patted the space next to him. "You mean you aren't dreaming of me?"

Julia slipped in next to him and nestled against him. "I dream of you first, then cooking second."

Paul pulled her close and kissed the top of her head. "I think you'd sail through the cooking school. They'd be lucky to have you, and my stomach wouldn't complain if you wanted to test recipes at home."

"Of course I'll be doing that." She moved up on her elbow. "I just thought of something: Maybe Freddie should come over and take the course with me. She'd love every minute of it."

"Perhaps, although it would be a big move for her family," Paul said. "But it wouldn't hurt to ask, and with your combined skills, you could open a restaurant together."

"Funny," Julia said, although she was pleased at the idea, even if Paul was joking. She moved out of bed, and he groaned in protest. "I'm going to write to her now and mail it in the morning. I don't think I'll be able to sleep if I wait on this."

Paul reached for a book that he'd set on the nightstand, resigned to Julia's late-night letter writing even when they'd both had a full day. Julia was too keyed up to sleep quite yet, both about heading back to Paris and about possibly enrolling in the most reputable cooking school in all of France.

Once they returned to Paris with Dort, who was still staying in their apartment, Julia set up a tour of the school. Dort had no interest in accompanying her. Dort had joined a theater group, which kept her busy most of the time, and somehow managed to speak her own version of French, which no one minded.

Julia toured the school on June 2, once she found the drab-gray building at 129 rue du Faubourg Saint-Honoré, on the corner up from the American Embassy.

The sign on the front of the building was barely legible and read École de Cuisine. Julia opened the weather-beaten door and stepped inside. What she might have expected of a world-renowned cooking school wasn't much to look at inside. The building contained four small classrooms, and the two kitchens were in the basement. Not a modern appliance in sight, not even a mixer or an electric blender.

Despite the confusion she felt at the actual interior, she promptly enrolled in the cooking school's six-week course that would start in

JULIA

October. The rest of the world outside of France might be heading toward the more modern conveniences of packaged meals and making sauces from canned soup, but Julia wanted to re-create the layers of flavor and freshness that she so heartily enjoyed. And Le Cordon Bleu was where it would start.

CHAPTER 22

Paris, France
October 1949

"At 9:00 a.m. on Tuesday, October 4, 1949, I arrived at the École du Cordon Bleu feeling weak in the knees and snozzling from a cold. It was then that I discovered that I'd signed up for a yearlong Année Scolaire instead of a six-week intensive course. The Année cost $450, which was a serious commitment. But after much discussion, Paul and I agreed that the course was essential to my well-being and that I'd plunge ahead with it."

—JULIA CHILD

"You don't need to walk me," Julia told Paul as she pulled on a short jacket. The morning was cool, and rain clouds threatened a decent downpour. She then collected her white apron, white cap, a notebook, a kitchen towel, and a set of knives. All of which she'd been asked to bring.

"Of course I'm walking my wife to her first day of class at the famous Le Cordon Bleu," Paul said.

Julia smiled as he pulled her close and kissed her neck. "Come on, then; I can't be late." The cat meowed and rubbed against her leg. Julia bent for a final pet goodbye. "See, Minette agrees."

The class started at 9:00 a.m., and nothing in the world would make Julia late, so she was leaving extra early.

Thankfully, Paul was ready, and as they headed out onto the street, he said, "We'll meet for lunch and celebrate your first successful day of class."

Julia linked her arm through his. "That would be delightful. And delicious. I'm sure I'll be starving after a few hours of intense instruction."

Paul laughed.

JULIA

The early-morning sunrise breaking through the clouds painted the buildings lavender, while scents of baking bread wafted around them. Julia breathed in her favorite smells of Paris, but by the time they reached Le Cordon Bleu, she was feeling jittery. She wasn't nervous to take the class, but she was nervous about falling behind when most of her cooking skills were self-taught.

"You'll do well, dearest," Paul said, kissing her. "Do you want me to walk you in?"

"I'll be fine." Julia patted her hair as the wind picked up. She squeezed his hand, then headed inside. She'd probably be the first student to arrive, but it was better than being late.

Once she found her class, she stepped into the room where hundreds of hopefuls before her had breathed the air. Two other young women, her fellow classmates, joined her. One was French, the other English. They greeted each other, made introductions, then Julia asked them, "Is this your first class? What are you hoping to learn?"

The English woman said, "Well, I'm hoping to make a good pot of tea."

The other woman smiled. "I'd love to learn that as well. But isn't that what all English know from birth?"

"Not me."

They all laughed, but Julia's stomach sank. Were these ladies really here to learn such basic knowledge?

Before Julia could ask more questions and determine if these two women really didn't know how to make tea, the instructor strode in.

"Gather around," the instructor said in French.

The instructor wasn't one of the famous chefs whom Mari had told Julia about. Julia joined the other women at a table that looked as though it had endured decades of knives.

The instructor set down a container with several items in it, garlic cloves among them. With a flourish, he picked up the garlic cloves, handed them each one, then proceeded to instruct them how to peel the cloves.

Julia followed along, wondering if it was really necessary to spend so much time on peeling garlic. Even she knew how to do it, but from the other women's comments, apparently they hadn't learned this either.

Julia wasn't sure whether to be pleased that she already had foreknowledge or disappointed that this was part of the curriculum.

Once they had all apparently mastered peeling a garlic clove, the instructor announced, "Now we'll learn to hard-boil an egg."

Julia waited for the other two women to laugh, but no one laughed. Should she say something? Ask if this class was meant for housewives who'd never cooked a day in their life?

When she met Paul for lunch, she was stewing over the first day of lessons. "Do you think it will continue like this?" she asked him. "The other ladies are perfectly content, but I feel like I'm crawling out of my skin."

Paul patted her hand. "Maybe it's just the first day? You've been so excited about this school. Let's see what happens tomorrow."

But by the time class ended on the second day, Julia was more than done. They'd learned only basic skills that should be commonsense. She might not have a lot of expertise, but she was miles ahead of her two classmates, and she absolutely could not endure this for an entire year. When she spoke to the instructor after the class about transferring into a higher-level class, he told her she'd have to make the request of the director, Madame Élisabeth Brassart.

That, Julia was happy to do. Once she found the woman's office, which was in one of the narrow hallways that seemed busier than a train station with all the comings and goings and doors opening and closing, Julia met the petite, elegant Madame Brassart for the first time.

It wasn't lost on Julia that Madame Brassart wasn't interested in a friendly conversation. The woman spoke in such rapid French that Julia probably missed more than half of what she was saying, yet some things were *very* clear.

"You have no experience in sophisticated French food preparation," Brassart said, her eyes narrowed and intent. "Not only are you American and barely speak our language, but you've also nothing to recommend you." Julia opened her mouth to respond, but Brassart plowed onward. "The *haute cuisine* course is for competent cooks, and you're not even close to that."

"I can do some demonstrations to prove which dishes I'm proficient in," Julia cut in.

Brassart waved her off. "It's a six-week, complete-immersion class, and you've paid for a year's tuition. It's out of the question."

Julia tightened her jaw, then said, "I can't take a beginning class. Surely there's another option."

Brassart's mouth pinched so tight that her lips disappeared. "There's *one* other option. Another class started this week that's for professional restauranteurs, and it's taught by Max Bugnard. You'll also have afternoon demonstrations by Claude Thilmont."

Julia had heard of these famous teachers. Claude Thilmont had been a pastry chef at Café de Paris, and he was known for his wonderful desserts. She'd heard of Max Bugnard, too, who had worked in many restaurants in Paris before the war and had been teaching at Le Cordon Bleu the last several years. "What's the schedule like?" Julia asked.

"It's a ten-month course." Brassart hesitated. "Twenty-five hours a week, organized by morning hands-on cooking and afternoon demonstrations."

"I'll take it," Julia said.

The following morning, she arrived early once again and stepped into a classroom filled with eleven men—all wearing white aprons and white caps.

"Bonjour," Julia said immediately to the men staring at her. "I'm Julia Child."

"You're American?" one of the burliest men asked in English.

Julia grinned. "I am."

In moments, she discovered they were all American GIs, and the US government was covering their four-thousand-one-hundred-francs-a-week tuition. She told them about her service in the OSS, and they all seemed duly impressed. There was enough teasing and comradery among the men that Julia felt like she'd gone back in time to her OSS days.

"So you all want to open restaurants?" Julia asked.

"That's a bit of an overstatement," one of the men said. "I want to open a bakery."

"A hot dog stand for me," another man said, and everyone laughed.

"We're mostly mess hall cooks," a third man said. "And sure, maybe some of us will end up in the restaurant business. We'll see where the next ten months take us. What about you, madame?"

"Oh, please call me Julia," she said. "I'm—" She cut off when a stout man who had to be at least seventy walked into the room, wheeling a cart behind him, stacked with . . . dead pigeons.

He wore chef whites and a wiry mustache. His step slowed when he peered at Julia through his round, horn-rimmed glasses. "You must be the new student," he said in French.

"I'm Julia Child," she said, extending her hand.

"Max Bugnard." He shook her hand, and Julia found his grip warm and inviting.

"Welcome," he said, then turned to the other GIs. "Today, we'll dress pigeons."

Julia wanted to clap with glee, but she restrained herself. She'd be learning something, at last. The next hour was spent learning about how to properly prepare a pigeon, stuff it, and cook it. Julia's turned out nearly perfect, and she was so proud of herself, she couldn't stop grinning. After cleaning the preparation table with salt and vinegar, she rushed home to prepare lunch for Paul. She'd return later for the afternoon demonstration, and she couldn't wait.

"Tomorrow night, I'm making dinner since Dort will be home early enough for it," Julia announced to Paul when he walked into their apartment. "*Pigeons rôtis délicieux.* You're going to love it."

Paul crossed to her. "Good class this morning?"

"The *best* class. Sit down and eat, and I'll tell you all about it."

Paul listened, laughing at the interactions with the GIs, and Julia realized that she was in heaven with such an instructor as Chef Max

Bugnard. "He's a darling little man. Very dignified yet warmhearted. He told me he knows every French dish imaginable. Did you know he worked with Chef Escoffier?"

Paul had been the one to tell her about the famous Escoffier.

"Bugnard has all kinds of experience in restaurants, galleys of steamships, and London's Carlton Hotel," she continued.

Paul listened to every word, asked a few questions, and fed Minette a few scraps at her perch on one of the kitchen chairs.

Julia told Paul how Max Bugnard began each morning with a flurry of instructions, demonstrating everything, including proper chopping techniques, like how to make the seven-sided cut on all vegetables. Bugnard explained everything he demonstrated, unloading volumes of details that made Julia's mind spin. He laid out the elements of creating sauce bases, including *soubis*, *madère*, *béchamel*, *bordelaise*, *hollandaise*, and *béarnaise*, for starters. Then he moved on to the custards—the delectable *crème anglaise* and *crème caramel* . . . And the students didn't just listen. They interrupted with questions, and the conversations twisted and turned, buzzing around Julia like a horde of bees. She fumbled to write everything down in her notebook.

Bugnard didn't just cook one dish and have them learn it, but he cooked entire meals, from the appetizer to dessert. This helped the students balance their time while preparing multiple dishes and illustrated how to break down the steps, making them simple to follow.

After the morning sessions, she'd rush to the market, purchase everything, and experiment at home. Then she'd hurry back for the afternoon sessions that lasted until dark. Some nights, she made the recipes more than once until Paul had to drag her off to bed.

"Is it possible to be a Cordon Bleu widower?" he murmured against her ear as they lay in bed one night only a few weeks into classes. "We never go out anymore. I come home to a tornadoed kitchen, a wife elbow deep in stuffing a chicken, a duck, or a goose, and a mewing cat who can't wait to sample what you prepare next."

Julia laughed. Her stomach was full from all the cooking and eating that night, and she could have easily fallen off the cliff of sleep to Paul's soothing baritone voice if he hadn't expected an answer. During some cooking sessions, he'd help her in the kitchen, but mostly, she told him to read to her. Just as he had in Ceylon. His most recent picks had been Faulkner's short stories and Boswell's London *Journal*. "I'm right here, dearie," she murmured. "You're not a widower." She turned to face him and looped her arms about his neck. "I'm . . . so thrilled to be in this class. I can't learn everything fast enough. And the reward is eating the wonderful food after all the work."

"And my stomach and palate thank you," Paul said with a chuckle.

"The afternoon demonstration class today had my head spinning," she said. "It's like watching an orchestra of one person playing each musical instrument—and keeping the melody going. The instructors start everything from scratch; nothing is chopped or mixed beforehand. I took pages and pages of notes, although my handwriting is barely legible."

"What was on the menu today?" Paul asked in a murmur.

"A woodcock roasted with vegetables, glazed carrots, rouget *en lorgnette*, and a dessert of hand-mixed chocolate ice cream with ganache spread between layers of cake. Oh, and buttercream icing, of course."

"Of course." Paul pulled her closer. "Your cooking is improving with each meal, and you have a new air of authority about you. In the past few weeks alone, you've made quiche Lorraine, rabbit terrine, Alsatian-style choucroute, chicken Marengo, spinach gnocchi . . . just for starters. If you're going to keep up all this cooking, we need to do more than give our neighbors leftovers. We need additional people to join us at our little La Maison Schildt. Otherwise, I'm going to double in size."

Julia nestled against him. "You're probably right. Why don't you invite a few people for tomorrow night. I'm going to make my best *boeuf bourguignon* yet."

CHAPTER 23

Paris, France
November–December 1949

"In late 1949, the newspapers informed us that something called 'television' was sweeping the States like a hailstorm. People across the country, the papers said, were building 'TV rumpus-rooms,' complete with built-in bars and plastic stools, in order to sit around for hours watching this magical new box. There were even said to be televisions in buses and on streetcars, and TV advertising in all the subways. It was hard to imagine."

—JULIA CHILD

"What's all this?" Paul asked when Julia led him to where she'd parked the Blue Flash in front of their building. He'd come home for lunch, but she needed some manpower first.

"I stopped to buy a few kitchen supplies at the BHV," she said, opening the trunk with a flourish. The rainy day had morphed into a cloudy day, making the perfect shopping trip.

The trunk teemed with new pans, pots, casseroles, knives, choppers, a timing clock . . . and that was only the trunk. In the back seat, she'd added a scale, jars, skewers, grater, rolling pin, double broiler, and a marble slab.

It wasn't her first shopping trip to Le Bazar de l'Hôtel de Ville and wouldn't be her last.

Paul scratched at his forehead. "Where is all this going? The counters already look like a science lab."

"It will fit," Julia said in a cheerful tone. "You'll see."

Paul didn't move for a moment, and she finally nudged him. "I have lunch to prepare, so the sooner the car is unloaded, the sooner you'll eat."

This sent Paul into action, and after multiple trips, Julia was happily preparing seafood risotto with her blue denim apron secured about her waist and a dish towel tucked under the apron strings.

Someone knocked on their door, and Paul went to answer it. Moments later, Dort arrived in the kitchen, a new polka-dotted scarf about her neck and smelling of Chanel N°5. "Just in time for lunch, I see?"

Julia set a hand on her hip. "Just in time to set the table. Paul's been busy."

Paul huffed. "Carrying stacks of kitchenware up from the car. Have you ever seen so much stuff?"

"No . . ." Dort picked up one of the bowls. "Is that a new copper bowl?"

"It's for beating eggs," Julia said without looking up.

She sensed the exchanged silent looks between her husband and sister.

"Want a tour?" Paul asked. "Don't touch anything, or it will all come tumbling down. Who knew we needed a long needle for larding roasts, three small frying pans that can be used *only* for crêpes—"

"Mmm, crêpes sound delicious." Dort set the bowl down. "And of course they'd need their own pan, or three of them, it seems."

Julia grinned at the interchange.

"Don't forget the pewter-liter measures." He pointed. "We have demi-liters, quart-de-liters, and deciliters and enough knives for an entire gang of pirates, should they choose to storm a nearby ship."

"Whatever it takes to produce that." Dort nodded toward the casserole Julia was carrying to the table, fragrant steam rising.

Julia untied her apron and drew it off. "Lunch is served. *Bon appétit.*"

Paul leaned close and kissed her, then he pulled out her chair. "Looks wonderful." He scooped the cat off the next chair so he could sit down.

Minette protested and scurried away.

Dort took the first bite of the seafood risotto. "Absolutely delicious," she said, giving a half moan. "You get better with every meal, I swear."

JULIA

"Not every meal," Julia said, looking over at Paul, who only smiled his encouragement. She'd already told him about the lunch disaster the day before when he'd had other business and she'd invited her friend Winnie Riley. "Yesterday, I made eggs Florentine for Winnie, and let's just say it didn't turn out."

Dort paused before taking another bite. "I've had your eggs Florentine before. What happened?"

Paul chuckled, and Julia nudged him under the table with her foot.

"I got ahead of myself," Julia said with an ironic smile. "Since I've made it more than once, I didn't dig up the recipe to follow the exact measurements. I thought I could eyeball it."

Another chuckle came from Paul.

"I should have known it would be a disaster when I couldn't find spinach at the market and substituted it for chicory."

Both Dort and Paul winced.

"It sounds awful already," Dort deadpanned.

"I discovered that chicory doesn't soften like spinach, and it was too wiry and tough." Julia took a sip from her glass, then said, "I didn't exactly measure the flour for the sauce Morney, and it became a gluey paste. Awful."

"So, what did you do? Throw it out and serve something else?"

Paul snickered, and Julia cleared her throat. "No, I didn't throw it out. I have a little pride, after all, especially while being a student at Le Cordon Bleu."

Dort stopped eating and stared at Julia.

"We ate the darn meal, and it was awful," Julia said. "I had to gag down each swallow. Bless Winnie, but she didn't say a thing. She ate what I served her as if gooey glop were the most delicious lunch in the world."

Dort scoffed, then began to laugh. Paul joined in.

"It's funny, I guess," Julia said with a shrug. "I didn't even apologize. I was the cook, and I decided to grin and bear it."

"I'm sure that Winnie will never forget those eggs Florentine," Dort said, still chuckling.

Julia sighed. "I'll have to invite her again and hope for better luck."

"Don't be disappointed if she turns you down," Paul said.

Julia grimaced. "Well, I'll be redeeming myself with a dinner party this weekend. There will be at least eight of us. Do you want to come, Dort? I'm going to attempt to make French bread too."

"I have rehearsal with my theater troupe, and then I have a date." She'd most recently started working for the American Club Theater in Paris.

"A date?" both Julia and Paul said at the same time.

"With whom?" Julia asked.

Dort's cheeks pinked. "Ivan Cousins. You remember him—he's done theater in New York and some modeling."

"Yes, I remember him." Julia was a bit surprised Ivan had caught Dort's attention. He was a full head shorter than she, and his personality was larger than life. Julia also knew what Paul would say about him without a word even being spoken. Paul thought Ivan drank too much and was more interested in men than women. With Dort staying with them, her theater friends frequented the place a couple of nights a week when they didn't have rehearsal.

But by the light in Dort's eyes, Julia could tell her sister was looking beyond all the warning signs. Maybe a first date would change Dort's mind.

"He's an overgrown child, Dort," Paul said. "You can do better."

Julia had been hoping Paul would keep his opinion to himself, but that rarely happened.

Dort didn't seem bothered by Paul's criticism since she was probably used to his opinions.

"He's not boring," Dort said with an easy smile, as if she'd expected to defend her choice. "I like that he's open and vulnerable—maybe that's childlike, or maybe it's refreshing. He's brilliant in front of an audience, and we have a lot of things in common."

Julia was quite impressed that Paul held his tongue, at least for now.

"Going on a date might give you a chance to know the real him," Julia said to soothe all parties.

JULIA

"Oh, we've been on several dates, and I do know him." Dort turned her gaze on Julia, ignoring Paul's grumpy expression. "He's really a dear man, JuJu. You just need to give him a chance."

Julia reached for Paul's hand and squeezed since she could practically see waves of frustration rolling off his shoulders.

"Well, if you want to invite him to the dinner party," Julia said, "that would be fine too."

Dort nodded. "Thank you, but we already have our own plans." She rose and cleared her place, then started in on cleaning the dishes, which was appreciated but also meant the conversation was over.

Paul stood as well, and the three of them worked in silence until it was time for everyone to go back to their regular day.

Julia's next weeks were consumed with creating the perfect tried-and-true recipe for mayonnaise when she had a batch not turn out on a cold, wintry day. She'd realized that cooking wasn't just throwing ingredients together and hoping for the best outcome. There was technology involved—which justified her collecting kitchen gadgets—and there was also science involved—which meant she had to understand the chemistry of how the ingredients interacted when combined.

Why hadn't the mayonnaise recipe turned out when the weather was colder? She'd made tubs of mayonnaise, beating salad oil into egg yolks until the creamy mixture had thickened. She only had to add some salt and vinegar, and the mayonnaise was perfect. Until it wasn't. In the winter months, her mayonnaise was too thin and not creamy at all.

So she began to experiment with different measurements and proportions, with making sure the egg yolks were room temperature, with changing up how hard she was beating the mixture. She wanted to truly understand how the ingredients combined and what made the recipe successful. What was the quality of the oil? How many egg yolks were needed to bind to the oil? And how much salt and vinegar was needed to break down the yolks in order to absorb the oil?

"I don't think I can put mayonnaise on one more thing," Paul said one evening after their shared dinner. His gaze was locked on the three tubs of mayonnaise she had made that day.

"I think I almost have the recipe perfected," she said. "I want to create something fool proof—where every person can use the recipe, no matter the weather or temperature or city they live in—and come up with the perfect mayonnaise. Wouldn't that be something?"

"It would be something," Paul said. "Maybe you can submit the recipe to one of the ladies' magazines once you have it down. But count me out as your taste-tester."

She laughed. "You don't even know about all the batches I've flushed down the toilet."

Her experimenting continued and with different foods too. For a couple of weeks, she attempted to make French baguettes at home. It turned out a disaster each time. Her oven at the Roo de Loo was nothing like the bakery ovens in the cafés.

But she also learned that her obsession with perfecting recipes was sometimes over the top.

"You don't need to marinate the veal in so many herbs," Chef Bugnard told her one day. "Veal is simply veal. Bring out the flavor, don't mask it."

Julia looked down at her creation of probably 200 spices.

"Watch me," Bugnard said, and he proceeded to dress veal by salting and peppering the meat, then wrapping it in a salt pork blanket. "Adding in your sliced carrots and onions in the pan, then a tablespoon of butter on top for the basting becomes all you need to create the burst of flavor."

When Julia tried the veal after Bugnard's demonstration, she was sold. French cooking wasn't just about learning technique and starting with fresh ingredients; it was also about simplifying the process and, more importantly, mirroring Bugnard's confidence.

"Surely there's never been a student as hardworking as you," Paul commented one night after a successful dinner party for which Julia had made *sole meunière* for everyone. They'd invited their former OSS friend Jane Foster and her husband—who were currently living in Paris. Despite the good company and nostalgic conversation, Julia had felt frustrated because she hadn't gotten the sauce exactly right and was close to marching into one of their favorite restaurants and demanding the recipe from the cook.

"Probably not," Julia said as she sat at the table while Paul did the cleanup. He insisted on it most nights, and Julia was more than happy to let him take over. After cleaning the kitchen, he often turned to painting or reading. "In class, we've made quiche Lorraine sixteen times, and veal *blanquette* twelve times, and that doesn't count the many times I've made it here. The program is ten months, but I'll be done much sooner at this rate."

Paul crossed to her, wiping his wet hands on a towel. He bent and kissed the top of her head. "What does Chef Bugnard say?"

"That I am doing fabulous," she said. "I still have to get approval from Madame Bussart to take my final exams. Once I pass, I'll get my graduation certificate."

Paul sat across from her and took one of her hands. "You're truly remarkable."

Julia thought her husband was particularly handsome tonight. Folded towel over his shoulder, his smile soft, his constant support and encouragement, his patience with her commandeering half of their apartment for her cooking experiments. His mild-mannered grumbling of their stacks and stacks of cooking gadgets. The way he artfully debated politics with their dinner guests, carefully dissecting the Marshall Plan, British socialism, and the state of the global economy. His brotherly friendship with Dort, despite her on-again, off-again relationship with Ivan Cousins.

"I don't know how wonderful I'll be when I graduate, because I plan to write up my complaints about Le Cordon Bleu," she said.

"Like what?" he asked, although he'd heard them all along.

"For the most prestigious cooking school in France, it's remarkable how Madame Brassart has run it into the ground. Starting with the knives—none of them are sharp. I have to bring my own knives, or I can't even cut a tomato. She's started to check everyone who is taking the extra food home with them. And she tried to tell us we can't cook with butter anymore—only margarine."

The food rationing had been lifted, but some items were still in short supply.

"It's why some of your dishes turn out differently at home," Paul mused.

"Exactly." Julia released a sigh. "I can't create an exact recipe if I can't rely on the ingredients. I have to create more than one recipe for the same dish. The equipment is either hopelessly outdated or works on its own fickle schedule. Only a few of the electric ovens even operate."

"And the GIs?" Paul said. "They're not complaining?"

"Sometimes I think they're just there to horse around," Julia said. "They aren't really progressing and refuse to even clean a chicken in the French way. None of them can even prepare *béchamel* sauce. They aren't serious about the class."

"Like I said, you're remarkable, and not everyone—in fact, few people—take cooking as seriously as you do."

"I love it," Julia said. "I think I've found my passion."

Paul chuckled.

"What are you laughing about?"

He waved a hand about the room that was indeed cluttered with every pot and pan and cooking implement imaginable. "I think you just made the biggest understatement of the year."

Julia shrugged. "Now the question is, What will I do after I graduate from the famous Le Cordon Bleu?"

CHAPTER 24

Paris, France
March 1950–April 1951

"The sight of Julie in front of her stove full of boiling, frying and simmering foods has the same fascination for me as watching a kettle-drummer at the Symphony. (If I don't sit and watch I never see Julie.) . . . Imagine this in your mind's eye: Julie, with a blue denim apron on, a dish towel stuck under her belt, a spoon in each hand, stirring two pots at the same time. Warning bells are sounding off like signals from the podium, and a garlic-flavored steam fills the air with an odoriferous leitmotif. The oven door opens and shuts so fast you hardly notice the deft thrust of a spoon as she dips into a casserole and up to her mouth for a taste-check like a perfectly timed double-beat on the drums. She stands there surrounded by a battery of instruments with an air of authority and confidence."

—LETTER FROM PAUL CHILD TO HIS BROTHER, CHARLIE

Julia decided that rising each morning at six thirty and walking in the rain only to attend a class full of GIs who didn't take anything seriously, nor did they care about progressing, was beyond her patience.

Chef Bugnard stopped her one day after class. "I see you're frustrated, madame. What can I do to help?"

Bugnard was a dear to even be concerned.

"I'm thinking of quitting," Julia said truthfully. "I want to keep learning, and you're an excellent instructor, but there are too many interruptions by the other students acting ridiculous."

Bugnard didn't deny it. "You're my best student. Why don't you take a leave of absence instead? You can still attend the afternoon demonstrations, and I could also do some private lessons at your own home if you wish."

Julia hadn't thought of that, but she was definitely interested. "Do you think I could still prepare for the final exam if I'm not in morning classes?"

"Of course," Bugnard said with confidence. "I don't know anyone who works harder than you."

Julia hurried home with a lighter step to report to Paul. She could devote herself in preparing for the final exam and curtail her involvement in embassy socials, which had lately become tiresome and boring. She found she had less and less in common with the embassy wives, who cared only about primping and preening and shopping all day. Oh, and she and Paul and Dort also had to prepare for her father and Phila's visit in March.

Julia had been quite blasé in her letters to her father after Phila told her that any mention of politics riled him up. His opinions hadn't mellowed with age. No, he still argued with anyone who had views different from his own, and he couldn't understand why any American would choose to live in Paris since he couldn't understand the language, not to mention that he detested the art and culture.

"We have a plan for Pop," Dort said that evening over the dinner table.

Julia looked from Dort to Paul. "Oh, what is it?"

"We need to keep Pop and Phila busy, that's what," Dort continued. "I don't want him to have too much free time, or he'll fixate on how I've traded my soul to the theater or how you've married an intellect who must be sympathetic to the Communist mind-set since all intellects are Communists."

Julia nearly spat out her drink. She wanted to defend Pop, but Dort was absolutely right. Once he started a tirade, it was impossible to stop him.

"What are we doing, then, for the month that he's here?" Julia asked.

"Paul is putting together the Paris itinerary for the first week," Dort said. "Then the four of us will travel through the south of France and end up in Italy. It will be a grand tour of sorts."

Julia looked at Paul. "The *four* of us?"

JULIA

"I can't take extra weeks off from the office," he said, "especially if you're traveling for three of them." He paused, a flash of guilt crossing his face. "I think it will be better for everyone if your father sees as little of me as possible."

"Or the other way around?" Julia prompted.

"Correct." He reached for her hand. "You know I love your family..."

He didn't need to finish. Julia squeezed his hand. "The week in Paris will be very much appreciated. We'll show Pop the beautiful city and people we've grown to love. We'll change his mind, you'll see."

"That would be a miracle," Dort said. "But you have a better attitude than me, JuJu."

"Whatever happens, we'll make some good memories," Julia insisted.

And they kept that mind-set until the day Pop arrived. Everyone was on edge when he and Phila stepped off the plane, but apparently, Pop had decided to be on his best behavior. Whether it was for the duration of the trip or his heart had really softened, Julia wasn't sure.

He refused to try speaking French, with the exception of his badly pronounced "Bahn Joor," which most people found charming. At every museum or restaurant stop, Pop would simply speak in English, expecting everyone they encountered to understand and converse with him. It was rather amusing.

At age seventy, he had lost the status of being able to intimidate others, and frankly, Julia enjoyed being around her father more than she ever had in her life. Dort felt the same way too.

Despite Pop's change of demeanor and withholding of insults, Paul still remained in Paris when they took their cross-country trip. Julia ended up feeling glad that Paul had remained behind because although Pop had softened, it was clear that he didn't much enjoy the history of the architecture and art, calling everything dank or cold. He remained unimpressed with European culture, and it made Julia sad to realize she had little in common with her father.

Once they returned to Paris, Julia cooked up a dinner fit for royalty. Both Pop and Phila were impressed with her newly acquired cooking skills, and when Phila asked her what her future plans were, Julia said, "I honestly don't know. Keep learning, I suppose? Talk my sister-in-law into opening a restaurant one day? I wouldn't mind teaching others as well."

"I think teaching a cooking class is an excellent idea," Paul said, joining the conversation. "You're excellent with people; the whole of Paris is friend to Julia Child."

Julia laughed. "That's because I feed everyone who walks through our door."

The distraction of Pop and Phila had been a good one and surprisingly less painful than she'd anticipated, but once they left, Julia threw herself back into preparing for the final examination at Le Cordon Bleu. She sent a formal request to Madame Brassart but received no reply.

Months passed, and even with Julia dedicating herself to cooking around the clock and Chef Bugnard's encouragement and endorsement, Madame Brassart dragged her feet.

"She hates Americans," Julia complained to Paul one night at their apartment. "Or maybe it's me?"

"What does Chef Bugnard say?" Paul asked.

"To stay persistent." Julia sat with a sigh, knowing that in minutes, she'd have to get up to check on the chicken breast she was making for dinner—*suprêmes de voilaille à blanc*. Paul would take over if she asked him, but she wanted things just right for this meal. Dort was bringing Ivan Cousins over, and good food would relax everyone.

By the time their guests arrived, though, Julia was still in a sour mood. While they ate the chicken with artichoke hearts, she explained to Dort and Ivan how she'd spent months going over recipes multiple times, testing them all. She'd memorized portions. She cut up a chicken in twelve minutes flat. "Everyone knows how hard I've worked, and everyone encourages me and appreciates eating my meals. Everyone but Madame Brassart. Doesn't she care about her students at all?"

"You're going on vacation to the States soon," Dort commented. "Maybe tell her that you need to take the exams before you leave?"

"That's an excellent idea," Paul said. "And it wouldn't hurt to let her know that the US ambassador is particularly interested in your culinary exam."

"And that's all true," Julia said. "The ambassador is always asking me how things are going."

So it was decided. That very night, Julia wrote her most stern letter to Madame Brassart, including mention of her travel plans and the ambassador.

Again, no response.

After another week of Julia's waiting and fuming, Chef Bugnard agreed to speak to the woman.

That did the trick, and Julia was finally granted an examination time.

On Friday, April 2, 1951, Julia reported to her exam in one of Le Cordon Bleu's upstairs kitchens. She was more than prepared and confident. And she'd brought her own set of knives.

The written portion was a breeze, and Julia raced through it, writing her answers out in her hard-practiced French. She had no trouble explaining how to make *fond brun* as well as the right method of cooking green vegetables to keep their color and flavor and, finally, the steps of preparing *sauce béarnaise*.

She'd surely finished the written portion in record time, and when the assistant walked in and handed over an index card of instructions, Julia eagerly read through the next assignment. "Write down which ingredients you want for the following for three people."

Julia's gaze fell to the list of dishes she was supposed to create, and her heart sank. These were not the classic French dishes she'd practiced over and over. She had no idea what *oeufs mollets* were. She'd never even heard of *mollets*. She could make the *sauce béarnaise*, but she was stumped over the *côtelettes de veau en surprise*. She could prepare veal—but *surprise* veal? And she didn't know the exact measurements for the *crème renversée au caramel*.

Julia closed her eyes, letting the frustration roll through her. How was she going to pull this off? She rose from the counter and headed to the basement kitchen that contained the most supplies. She didn't have to be told that she had a good chance of failing the cooking portion. She felt humiliated as she prepared the meal to the best of her ability. She'd been set up. None of these dishes had been part of her curriculum. Chef

Bugnard hadn't taught them, so why should Julia be expected to know them?

The hours passed, and Julia knew she'd botched everything. When she finally turned in her meal and stormed out of the building, she found Chef Bugnard waiting for her.

"I heard," he said without preamble, his face drawn.

"That I was set up?"

"You may or may not be able to make a case for that," he said. "The recipes were from the housewives course."

Julia's mouth opened, then she clamped it shut. "The one I spent two days in, then transferred to your class?"

"Correct."

"She knows I dropped that course," Julia said. "She only sees me as a housewife and has no respect for my dedication. I can make dozens of French dishes without a second thought. I'm the master of *cassoulets, chaucroutes, balantines, blanquettes de veau, soufflés Grand Mariner*—"

Chef Bugnard set a hand on her arm, stopping her rant. "You *are* a master, *ma chère*, there's no question. How did you prepare the meal in your exam?"

As she told him about poaching the eggs and sautéing mushrooms, he murmured, "The eggs should have been coddled and peeled. And the mushrooms should have been hashed."

Julia wasn't surprised that she'd messed up the simpler steps. "And the surprise? What was that all about?"

"It means that the meal is reheated in a paper bag for when your husband comes home."

Julia blinked. She could barely comprehend the ridiculousness. "Well, I guess I have truly failed the exam. What do I do now?"

Chef Bugnard had a ready answer. "Keep cooking. Don't let any exam stop you from doing what you love."

Julia nodded, her eyes burning with tears and her chest heaving with held-back emotion. She gave Chef Bugnard a quick hug, then wiped at her cheeks. "I need to get home to Paul. He'll be pacing our apartment, wondering how it all went."

Chef Bugnard set his hand back on her shoulder, making her pause. "Don't give up, my friend. I'll see you on your return from your vacation. You still haven't made your way through *Larousse gastronomique*, and I'll be around to answer any questions."

Julia had told the chef that she planned to try all the recipes in the French cookbook tome once she'd finished Le Cordon Bleu exam. And that had happened today.

She made it home in record time, bypassing the market where she usually strayed and found something to buy. She also wanted to avoid nightfall because of the recent strike that had been instigated in the Chambre des Députés. Several strikes were happening throughout the country, supported by the largest holding company for the unions, Confédération Générale du Travail, or CGT. This meant that dockworkers, telephone employees, electricians, and gas company employees were on strike, asking for higher wages.

Paul had taken to driving their Blue Flash all over the city, transporting embassy staff as needed since the bus and metro services were unreliable or impossibly crowded. Driving at night was dangerous since the streets of Paris were still reliant on gaslit lamps. The streets had become packed with bicycles, army trucks used for public transportation, and any type of vehicle that could be cobbled together and made to run.

Julia made it safely home just as the sun was setting, and Paul rose from a chair, where he'd been reading as she entered.

"How did it go?" he asked, anticipation lining his face.

"I failed."

"What?" Dort rose from another chair in the room. She'd recently moved out of their apartment to live with Ivan Cousins in a flat on the boulevard de la Tour-Maubourg but had been waiting with Paul to hear the news tonight.

"Impossible," Paul said, his eyes wide as he stared at her through his reading glasses.

"It's true." She flopped onto an upholstered chair across from him and told Paul and Dort everything, including her conversation with Chef Bugnard.

"We need to file a formal complaint," Paul said, his voice tight with anger and disbelief. "That woman knows your worth."

"I'll deal with that later," Julia said. "I'm going to do as Bugnard told me to: Focus on my own cooking, my own path, and keep working at it. Eventually, not even someone like Brassart will be able to look down on me."

Paul crossed to Julia and kissed her. "That's my Julie."

She smiled up at him, even though she felt like crying, grateful for this dear man who supported her through everything.

"I'm so sorry, JuJu," Dort said. "I hoped it would be a happy occasion when you came home since I have an announcement."

For the first time since Julia had walked into their apartment, she noticed the high color on Dort's cheeks. Should she be worried? No, Dort was smiling, although she was twisting her hands with nervousness.

"What is it?" Julia asked.

"Ivan and I are getting married," Dort announced. "Right away, at the end of June. We'll all be in the States, so you can be at our wedding in New York."

Julia was truly stunned. She knew her sister was dating Ivan, but they were on-again, off-again so frequently that it was hard to believe they were really serious about marriage. Julia pushed to her feet and crossed the room to embrace Dort. "Congratulations, dearie. I'm happy for you." And she was because she'd seen the devotion that Dort had for Ivan, and perhaps this would bring Dort the most happiness.

"Thank you," Dort said, hugging her back. When they drew apart, she said, "Also, we're all invited to Ivan's boss's cocktail party tonight. Remember, I told you about George Artamonoff? He used to be the president of Sears International. He now works at the Economic Cooperation Administration and helps administer the Marshall Plan in the Far East."

"I remember," Paul said. "We can go if Julia is feeling up to it."

Julia reached for his hand, thinking it was sweet that he was willing to attend something with Dort and Ivan—even though the two men were polar opposites.

JULIA

"I'm fine." Julia pasted on a smile that would eventually be genuine. Life wasn't over. Only new adventures awaited. "We'll all go and enjoy every minute."

What Julia didn't expect was to know so many people at the party and to have everyone ask about Le Cordon Bleu examination. That was what she got for running her mouth off so much.

"You really failed the exam?" an elegant Frenchwoman asked, her eyes peering through her eyeglasses, her blonde hair impeccably coiffed. "How do you know if you took it only today?"

Julia turned to the woman.

"I'm Simone Beck Fischbacher, by the way," the woman continued with a warm, easy manner.

So Julia regaled her with the tale until they were both laughing. Julia supposed her story was becoming slightly exaggerated the more she told it.

"I've heard of your cooking talent," Simone said, lifting her wine glass and taking a delicate sip, "and that's saying a lot since I'm a cook myself. I'm writing a cookbook, in fact, with my friend Louisette Bertholle."

Before Julia could ask her about that, Simone plowed on in her lovely French. "You really should join our cooking club—Le Cercle des Gourmettes. It was started by an American woman named Ethel Ettlinger in 1927, and she's still the president all these years later."

"Really?" Julia asked. "What do you do?"

"We get together and eat, *bien sûr*." Simone winked. "If you're a true Gourmette, then I will sponsor you into the club."

"Are you sure you want to sponsor a Cordon Bleu failure?"

Simone moved closer. "Chef Bugnard has told me all about you, and I think you'll fit right in. You must follow the rules though."

Julia was intrigued. "What sort of rules?"

Simone took a sip from her wine glass, then said, "Each Gourmette must be able to cook well, and each should be able to cook the perfect dinner paired with the perfect wine, the table settings should complement the meal, and no discussion of politics or religion."

Julia could do that. "When's the next event?"

"I hear you have a vacation coming up, so you'll come after that," Simone said. "But I have something else to speak with you about."

This woman grew more interesting by the moment.

"The cookbook I told you about a moment ago—Louisette and I published the first version of it a couple of years ago with Ives Washburn Publishing in New York," Simone said.

Julia was both surprised and impressed. "What was it called?"

"Oh, we called it *What's Cooking in France*," Simone said with a wave of her hand, "but it failed, even though our editor Helmut Ripperger put his name on the book too. It contained only fifty recipes and was printed in a spiralbound book. It seemed that no one in America was interested—but that might be due to some of the faulty translations."

Simone put on a bright smile and continued, "I'm expanding that book into a new cookbook and am gathering more family recipes. Our friend in New York told me that the recipes needed to be written from an American viewpoint, so that's what Ripperger helped us with, but he doesn't understand French cooking at its heart."

Julia raised her brows, and Simone kept her gaze direct.

"So you're looking for an American to help you?" Julia ventured.

Simone maintained her eye contact. "I am. It wouldn't be a lot of work. Maybe a review of some of the recipes here and there—see if you think Americans could follow the instructions."

Julia exhaled. "Would you like to come to my apartment tomorrow? And we could talk over your ideas in more detail?"

"I would love that," Simone said.

Julia held out her hand, and Simone took it, giving it a vigorous shake. "Oh, and call me Simca."

Julia's mood was much improved by the time she returned home that evening. Her mind wouldn't shut off as she mulled over her conversation with Simone Beck Fischbacher—or Simca—so Julia stayed up reading long after Paul went to bed. Settling on the couch, she opened an issue of *Fortune* and happened upon an essay that Bernard DeVoto had written. He spent paragraph after paragraph complaining about how businesses were shortchanging consumers, more specifically the manufacturers of general household goods. Julia straightened as she read, glued to the man's words. He complained about cutlery and knives and how they weren't sharp, making them ineffective.

"That's so true," Julia nearly shouted into the night. But she didn't want to awaken Paul, so she quietly cheered.

"You're still awake?" Paul's voice came from the hallway anyway.

Julia startled. "I can't sleep."

Paul moved to the couch, and she shifted her feet to make room for him.

"It seems I can't sleep either."

Julia showed him the article. "This man is as frustrated as I am about the state of cutlery."

"What?" Paul said with a startled laugh. He picked up his reading glasses from the side table. "I've read Mr. DeVoto's articles before. There's another one in *Harper's* on his knife crusade." He shuffled through their magazine stack. "I think it's this issue."

Sure enough, Paul found the article, and Julia eagerly read through it, laughing and commiserating at his words: "They look wonderful, but they won't cut anything."

"That's it," she said. "I'm going to write DeVoto a letter and profusely thank him for standing up for the state of cutlery. In addition, I'm sending him a knife I picked up at Dehillerin so he can see what I'm talking about in person."

CHAPTER 25

Paris, France
June 1951–January 1952

"Chef Bugnard had told me that, despite my exam debacle, I was well qualified to be chef in a maison de la haute bourgeoisie. It was a nice compliment, but I was no longer satisfied with being 'just' an accomplished home cook. Cooking was so endlessly interesting that I wanted to make a career of it, though I was sketchy on the details. My plan was to start by teaching a few classes to Americans in Paris. My guiding principle would be to make cooks out of people, rather than gobs of money: I wouldn't lose money, but I'd dedicate myself to the teaching of gastronomy in an atmosphere of friendly and encouraging professionalism."

—JULIA CHILD

It was strange to no longer be associated with Le Cordon Bleu, but that freed up Julia to be open to whatever Simca had to say. When the woman knocked and Julia opened the door to her, Julia was greeted with another firm handshake.

"Come on in," Julia said. "We'll sit in the kitchen. I've made a chocolate mousse."

Simca followed her up the stairs to the kitchen on the next level, then stopped and stared. "I've heard that your kitchen rivals a restaurant, but this . . . This is marvelous."

Julia hung back, trying to see the kitchen from a first timer's point of view. It was quite the thing. The wall of cookery had grown by immense proportions to dozens of gadgets, which Paul had outlined on the wall with a felt-tip marker—each one.

"Where did you buy all this?" Simca asked with awe.

JULIA

"I brought some things from America," Julia said, "but the rest I acquired here."

Simca nodded and took a few more steps into the kitchen, then examined one of the shelves double-stacked with cookbooks. "Wonderful," she murmured, then turned to face Julia, her eyes bright. "Let's sit; I have much to say."

Julia served drinks and dished up the chocolate mousse.

Simca took one bite and said, "Excellent."

Julia soon learned that Simca was friendly, direct, and full of ideas—much like herself—and she was pleased to feel such comradeship with this woman.

"Now, our cookbook that failed in America received very little promotion. Nevertheless, we have great hopes for our newly expanded cookbook. It even has a title."

Julia felt like she was breathlessly waiting for the secret of life to be revealed.

"*French Cooking for All*," Simca said. "What do you think?"

Not exactly unique, but Julia smiled. "It's definitely inclusive."

"Oh." Simca grasped Julia's arm. "And we're self-publishing our own cookbook in a couple of months called *What's Cuisine in France*, which contains fifty recipes for Americans. But we need it translated into English."

Julia nodded.

"Perhaps you could help? Not with the translation but with reading it through after the translation . . ." Simca paused. "Since you're an American who is equally passionate and talented in French cooking. But mostly, we'd like to run some recipes by you for our cookbook with Ives Washburn."

Julia's heart felt like it would gallop out of her chest. Imagine! She had never thought of helping with a cookbook, but here was an opportunity to do just that. And with two Frenchwomen who were experts.

"You must meet Louisette, my . . . how would you say it? Sidekick?" Simca said. "She travels to America often and stays in Georgia with her uncle. She loves all things American."

"I'd love to meet Louisette," Julia said immediately. "After our trip, I'll come to the next Gourmette luncheon."

"Wonderful. And you must tell your husband that while we Gourmettes are meeting for lunch, the husbands also gather." Simca took a sip of her drink. "They call themselves *les Princes Consorts Abandonés*."

Julia had to laugh at that, and she knew Paul would be equally delighted.

The next couple of months sped by as they traveled to the States, visited friends and family, and attended Dort's wedding. All the while, Julia thought about Simca's invitation to help with a cookbook. She didn't know if it would go so far as getting her name on the cover, but she wasn't too worried about that. She was just thrilled to be invited.

Once they returned to Paris, it was an odd realization, feeling like she'd returned home. She very much looked forward to her first Gourmettes luncheon. Simca greeted her warmly, and introduced her around, most specifically to Louisette. Julia's first impression of Louisette was that the woman was vivacious and warm. She seemed overjoyed to meet Julia, and she gushed about American sports, citing statistics that Paul probably didn't even know. She spoke excellent English.

"Oh, don't look so surprised at my fluent English," Louisette said. "I had an English governess as a child. Now, what's this about Simca saying you might help us with our cookbook?"

"I'm very interested," Julia said truthfully.

"That is indeed good news," Louisette said. "There's no reason a French cookbook can't sell well in America. You know that after the war, all of your American soldiers returned home from France spoiled with our food."

Julia understood completely. "My own husband was spoiled when he lived here in the twenties. He shared some memories about French food while we were working for the OSS in China."

Louisette gave a knowing nod, adjusting one of her earrings. "French food is impossible to forget, so why shouldn't the best food in the world be available in America too?"

"I don't see any reason why that shouldn't be the case." Julia sobered then. "I have to be honest, I didn't know food could taste so wonderful until I came to France. The fresh markets add to the experience because I can shop daily for fresh ingredients. In America, I ate vegetables from a can."

Both Louisette and Simca shuddered, then they all laughed.

Louisette looked at Simca. "Have you told her about the cooking class idea?"

Julia's brows popped up.

Simca's smile remained in place. "We want to open a cooking school. Nothing too formal—it will be held at one of our houses. Teaching Americans how to cook French food. None of the stuffy lessons found at Le Cordon Bleu."

"And you think I should be an instructor?" Julia asked, feeling both flattered and intimidated.

"You're wonderful with people, and your cooking reputation is excellent," Simca gushed. "We'd all teach together. The students will get the best of all three of our viewpoints."

"And you can keep Simca on track," Louisette said. "She might claim she's following a recipe, but I've never seen her actually do it. Once she's finished, who knows what she put into her *tournedos sautés chasseur*?"

Simca gave a good-natured sigh. "Fine. You will both keep me in check."

"Now," Louisette said, linking arms with Julia. "We will meet several times a week and discuss the recipes we want for our cooking class."

Julia blinked. "I haven't exactly agreed yet."

Both women looked at her expectantly.

"All right. I will teach classes with you. Do you know when you want to start?"

Louisette waved a hand in dismissal. "We'll figure that out together."

"Let's meet tomorrow," Simca said. "Is that too soon? We'll cook up a storm for our husbands. See how we all get along in the kitchen while we make plans."

"Where should we meet?" Julia asked immediately.

"Your place," Louisette said. "You have everything a cook would ever need, and I'm planning a renovation for mine."

"I do have everything," Julia said. "Oh, by the way, I've officially graduated from Le Cordon Bleu. I received my diploma in the mail."

Simca gasped. "I thought you failed the exam?"

"I thought I had, too, but the date on the diploma is stated before I even took the exam," Julia said. "I suppose Madame Brassart wanted me to stop patronizing her school."

Louisette's eyes lit up. "She wanted to be *rid* of you?"

"Something like that," Julia mused.

"Perhaps that is true," Simca said. "But she also couldn't deny your talent, so she gave you what you earned."

The following days and weeks were like a dream for Julia. She'd entered into back-and-forth letter writing with a woman named Avis DeVoto, who lived in Cambridge, Massachusetts. Her husband was Bernard DeVoto, who'd written those diatribes on dull knives, but Avis had been the one to respond to Julia's letters. Julia had been so impressed and charmed by the woman's reply, which had not only thanked her for the knife but also reminisced about the time she'd spent in Paris, that Julia had written again. Avis was fascinating and wasn't afraid to state her opinion or become involved in causes important to her. Julia considered her a true Renaissance woman.

Also, Julia was tickled with her growing friendship with Louisette and Simca. A few times a week, the women arrived at her place with groceries in hand, and they spent hours together creating meals and adjusting recipes. They all agreed that they didn't want their class recipes to be full of the classic French food served in restaurants, but their recipes would be more reminiscent of family dishes one would prepare in the home, although still refined and excellent.

"We'll use my kitchen for the classes," Louisette said one afternoon as they sat together in a salon overlooking rue de l'Université. "The kitchen renovation is coming along, and it will be more spacious."

"Excellent," Julia said. "We should teach the class in English to set us apart from Le Cordon Bleu."

JULIA

When Simca began to protest, Julia said, "We're teaching *Americans*, and we'll have more students if we offer the classes in English."

Simca and Louisette exchanged glances, but both agreed.

"I'll post an ad in the *Embassy News*," Julia continued. "The families of the government employees will all see it—and we should get students that way."

"Excellent idea," Simca said, adjusting her glasses.

"Paul has access to an army discount on food staples," Julia added, "so we can get some things for a lower price than at the markets. What do you think?"

"I like it," Louisette said. "What should we charge for the classes?"

After some discussion, they agreed on 600 francs per lesson, which included eating what was prepared during the lesson.

The months of autumn sped past as the three women continued putting together their class curriculum. Small irritations crept in when the women had differences of opinion on measurements or ingredients, but Julia was able to hash them out with her co-cooks. Simca was an expert in desserts and pastries. And Julia would have to say she was most confident in fish, sauces, and meats—like she'd been taught by Chef Bugnard.

Their first class took place on January 23, 1952, and ended up in Julia's kitchen at Roo de Loo after all. The renovation on Louisette's kitchen continued dragging out. They'd decided on two sessions a week for two hours each, and they'd finish it with a lunch at 1:00 p.m. By that time, Paul would join them and educate everyone in the art of pairing wine with a meal. He carried out his one culinary duty with a flourish. And, of course, he was also on cleanup duty.

Julia soon learned that although Louisette was a wonderful cook and could pull anything off beautifully, she never used exact measurements. She was what Julia considered a "romantic" cook, whereas Julia and Simca were more organized and wanted to get details correct so that other cooks could accurately duplicate recipes. But Louisette was the originator of the idea to teach Americans how to cook French dishes, and she had an extensive network of social contacts.

"Come in, come in," Julia said, ushering the students into her apartment on a winter-cold day. The three American women, Mrs. Martha Gibson, Mrs. Mary Ward, and Mrs. Gertrude Allison bustled into the space and then ooh-ed and ahh-ed over the kitchen setup. Everyone was introduced all around, and Julia began to explain what was on the menu. Then she planned to start with some of the basics—just as Chef Bugnard had done at Le Cordon Bleu.

But Simca had other ideas, followed by Louisette jumping in and taking over.

Julia realized they'd never actually planned out *who* would instruct which portions, and now they were talking over each other. It wasn't like each of them couldn't teach on their own, but they all had different emphasis and order of what they did when. Was it really necessary to learn how to properly slice vegetables in the first hour? Julia thought so, but her friends didn't.

Somehow, they were able to hobble through the first lesson, and after their students left and Paul returned to his office, Simca faced both of them, hands on her hips.

"Something is wrong with your oven, Julia," Simca announced, her voice tight with frustration. "It's too large and bulky—it's like a monster. I put in my perfect pie, and the crust crumbles like a stack of pebbles knocked over by a toddler."

Julia winced. That had been a letdown during the class. Simca had made hundreds of pies—and Julia had been a witness and taste-tester of many of them. They'd all been more than perfect, except for today.

"The temperature was regulated," Julia defended. "We checked it constantly." She looked to Louisette for help, who thankfully nodded.

"We did check the temperature," Louisette said. "It must be something else."

The three women fell into a tense silence. Finally, Julia began to rummage through the ingredients, examining each one that had gone into the pie. She didn't want to criticize Simca's method of not measuring in advance. Sure, she'd made hundreds of successful pies, but she had the habit of not following her own recipes.

JULIA

Julia picked up the flour sack—Gold Medal flour—from the States that they'd bought in bulk with the army discount. Then her gaze shifted to the flour she'd bought the week before at the market—the flour she usually used when cooking for her own personal use. "It's the flour," Julia said in a thoughtful tone.

"What about the flour?" Simca asked, her voice strained.

Julia held up the sack. "American flour contains additives to extend its shelf life. The natural fats are processed out so that weevils can't survive."

"You're right," Louisette said, turning her gaze to Simca. "I've had many pastry fails in America when not using my French flour."

The women all stared at each other, then Simca clapped her hands. "Then I have not lost my touch and forgotten my roots?"

"Not at all," Julia said.

"I need to make a pie, right now," Simca said, reaching for her apron again. "Whatever else you have planned, change it. I need to prove that your theory is right."

The women settled around the table while Simca began making another crust, this time with French flour. It was a joy to watch her work, although more concerns plagued Julia's mind. While it was wonderful to have discovered the problem with Simca's piecrust, it also revealed that all their pastry recipes they'd tested with French flour for Simca's and Louisette's cookbook would now need to be altered and recalibrated for American cooks.

Simca's pie turned out perfect—a delicious, golden-brown crust that flaked and melted in their mouths.

"Oh, here's something that will cheer us up more," Louisette said, smiling like a satisfied cat. "Irma Rombauer will be visiting in July."

"Oh." Julia was truly surprised. Irma Rombauer was the author of *Joy of Cooking*, the cookbook Julia had relied upon when she'd been newly married. "Can I meet her?"

Louisette tilted her head, eyes bright. "*Bien sûr.* I want my best friends with me. She'll be delighted to hear all about our class. But first, you must meet Maurice Edmond Sailland."

Julia didn't know if she could take more good news. "Oh, I would love to."

Maurice Sailland, or known by his pen name, Prince Curnonsky, was an icon in France. As the coauthor of the thirteen-volume *La France Gastronomique*, he had encyclopedic knowledge of the history of French cooking. He'd taught one of the demonstration afternoon sessions at Le Cordon Bleu as a guest chef, and Julia had been awed by his skill.

When the meeting was agreed upon, Julia went with Louisette and Simca to Curnonsky's home at 14 Place Henri Bergson, and to Julia's surprise, Curnonsky greeted them wearing his pajamas and bathrobe. He made no apologies or excuses but simply ushered them in.

Julia was taller than his six-foot frame, which had grown rounded with the years. His pale-blue gaze was sharp—almost bird-like—which only matched his intellect. Julia knew she should feel intimidated to be personally meeting Curnonsky, a well-known reporter and food critic as well as a prolific author, but he was immediately welcoming.

His personality filled the entire flat, and he regaled them with story after story—some of them very fantastical. But he had them all laughing until Julia's sides ached. When he told them about his cookbook that would be coming out in January 1953, which he called *Cuisine et Vins de France*, the conversation turned to Simca's and Louisette's publishing endeavors.

"Bring me a copy of your cookbook," Curnonsky boomed. "I'd love to read it."

"Of course," Simca said, her eyes dancing with excitement.

Curnonsky shifted his bulk and leaned forward. "We all must agree that good cooking is when things taste of what they are."

"Yes," Julia said. "I've had to learn that the simpler the recipe, the better it tastes."

Curnonsky slapped his knee. "Exactly. I knew that's why I liked you."

Julia laughed, and Curnonsky joined in. She liked this spirited elderly man very much. She'd never thought that the world of cooking would bring her into such circles of wonderful people who became good friends. But here she was, a front-seat witness.

Another highlight came when, on July 4, Julia met Irma Rombauer. Julia's first impression was that she was a very personable, no-frills woman in her seventies.

When the discussion turned to the cookbook that Simca and Louisette had published in America, Irma said, "You have to be careful of publishers. They'll try to weasel you out of royalties. Did you know that my publisher owes me royalties for over 50,000 copies? They keep giving me the runaround."

She turned a stern gaze to Louisette. "Don't let that happen with Ives Washburn. Make sure you demand a complete breakdown of book sales."

"We will."

The talk turned to royalties and advances, something that Julia realized she had a lot to learn about.

"You know, I self-published *Joy of Cooking* in 1931," Irma said. "I was desperate at the time to do something with my life. My husband died by suicide in February 1930." She drew in a breath, her eyes reddening with tears. "The stock market had crashed a few months before, and I was now a widow at fifty-two years old, with no job."

Louisette handed over a tissue to their new friend.

"I decided to write a cookbook, and I used some of my savings to print 3,000 copies. The original title was *Joy of Cooking: A Compilation of Reliable Recipes, with a Casual Culinary Chat*." She lifted her brows. "A. C. Clayton Company printed the book, even though they'd never printed a book before."

"Was it successful from the beginning?" Simca asked.

"It took about a year to get the first 2,000 copies sold," Irma said with nonchalance. "My daughter Marion helped get copies into bookstores and gift shops. It seemed the number-one compliment was not the recipes themselves but my style of adding advice and anecdotes throughout the book."

"That's what I enjoy too," Julia burst out, "in addition to the recipes," she corrected.

Everyone laughed.

"It makes cooking feel more friendly," Louisette said. "Most of us are alone in the kitchen when preparing a meal, so having the cookbook written in such a personable way makes me feel like I'm cooking with a friend."

"You are a dear." Irma reached over and patted Louisette's hand. "Now you know why I stopped over in Paris to visit on my way to Germany."

Julia came away from her meeting with Irma feeling inspired—inspired to be a better instructor at their cooking school.

CHAPTER 26

Paris, France
August–November 1952

"I had been wrestling with the subject of butter in sauces when Paul took me to a little bistro way over on the Right Bank, off the Avenue Wagram, called Chez la Mère Michel. The Michels were extremely friendly and forthcoming, and during a lull, the chef invited us into her kitchen to show us how she made her famous sauce in a brown enameled saucepan on an old household-type stove. I paid careful attention to how she boiled the acidic base down to a syrupy glaze, then creamed tablespoon-sized lumps of cold butter into it over very low heat. When we sat down to eat a carefully poached turbot crowned with a generous dollop of beurre blanc we found it stunningly delicious."

—JULIA CHILD

"Our editor has left the publishing company," Simca announced one day in late August before their next cooking class. The number of students had doubled, and the three instructors now had a new name for their school: L'École des Trois Gourmandes. They all wore white chef coats with an official logo of a red number 3 in a circle.

Julia took the letter from Simca and scanned through the explanation from editor Sumner Putnam of how Helmut Ripperger had left Ives Washburn Publishing. Julia looked up and met Simca's and Louisette's frustrated gazes. Louisette had been the primary contact point with the publisher.

"Ripperger's been dillydallying on the pages I've sent him, so I don't even know what state the recipes are in right now." Louisette folded her arms. "Our publishing deal might be off completely, so we have 600 pages typed for nothing. We don't have an American as an editor or writer anymore."

Julia didn't have any direct connections to any publishers, so she didn't know what advice to give. She could reach out to Avis DeVoto just to get her opinion, she supposed. Avis's husband had plenty of publishing experience.

Julia had become so lost in her thoughts about writing a letter to Avis that she hadn't realized her two friends were staring at her.

"Well?" Simca asked. "Do you want to be our coauthor?"

Julia stared at both of them. "Me?"

Both of them nodded.

There was only one answer Julia could give. "I'd be delighted to."

Louisette and Simca both hugged her, then Louisette headed out of the kitchen, saying she'd be back in a moment. When she returned, she carried a copy of the 600-page cookbook.

"Here it is," Louisette said with breathless excitement, plopping it onto the table.

"This is the original?" Julia asked, thumbing through the manuscript pages.

"Ripperger never sent us anything he edited," Louisette said. "We were trusting that he was doing the work—but obviously, we're starting over now."

Julia continued leafing through pages. She could easily see that the tome needed a lot of work. She sank onto one of the kitchen chairs and paused to read the introduction to the sauces section. The writing wasn't even professional . . . Was it like this throughout the entire book?

Her throat tightened, feeling like someone was squeezing as hard as they could. She'd already agreed though . . . Besides, she'd love to publish a cookbook. This one though . . . needed to be wholly rewritten.

By the time she saw Paul in the evening, she'd made up her mind. Simca and Louisette were wonderful cooks, and it would be terrible to let this project disappear. She remembered her heavenly introduction to French food, and now she'd gained so much knowledge living four years in France. It would be a shame to keep that from the general American population.

She found Paul cleaning the kitchen. For a moment, she stood there watching him.

"What's wrong?" he asked, wiping his hands on a towel.

She exhaled slowly, then told him everything. About the letter from Ives Washburn Publishing and about her agreement to coauthor the cookbook. Paul sat next to her at the kitchen table, and they looked through the chapters of the hefty manuscript.

"They said it's 600 pages?" Paul asked, his tone tight.

"Yes."

"This job will be colossal, Julie," he continued. "Are you sure you want to commit?"

Julia was sure, but the weight of responsibility was feeling heavier and heavier. "It will be a challenge, sure, but the outcome could be amazing."

Paul leaned close and kissed her. "It will be amazing." He paused, and she sensed what he'd say next. "You know we're going to be transferred at the beginning of next year. It's only a few months away. Will this . . . be able to progress?"

Julia stiffened. If she didn't have easy access to her friends, the lack of communication would slow everything down. They saw each other almost daily. "There's no way to stay in Paris?"

"No," Paul said. "Four years is policy, and we're almost to four years now. I'm hoping for Bordeaux or Marseille since I'm French speaking. But there are also openings coming up in Madrid and Rome."

Julia knew this, but the reminder drove everything home. She wished they could stay in Paris one more year—that was all she'd need to get this cookbook into shape.

"There's always the possibility of returning to the States too," Paul said.

It had to be said, and although Julia would love to be back in Washington, DC, among their roots and closer to Freddie and Charlie, her heart was currently in France. Besides, the State Department was on a rampage and investigating every corner for possible Communist sympathizers, including some of their OSS friends in their suspicions.

Washington, DC was thrumming with accusations and investigations, everyone pointing a finger at someone else.

Staying away from DC might be wise at this point.

"I'll start right away and see how far I can get before we're relocated," Julia said. It was all she could do. Work on this an hour at a time, a day at a time.

By the following morning, she had a plan in place. She determined that the recipes had to be absolutely accurate, forward and backward, and for that to happen, she needed to test all the recipes. The recipes had to meet several requirements, including being a traditional French dish, usable in the States, and frugal with ingredients—meaning no ingredients were wasted because they could be used for other recipes in the book.

She began with the soups and, each day, focused on a new recipe. She'd consult with Louisette and Simca concerning questions she had but also referred to the classic cookbooks she had in her kitchen: Ali-Bab's, Curnonsky's, Flammarion's, Carême's, and *Larousse gastronomiuqe*.

She hit barriers from the very first day as she experimented, cooked, made notes, then started over. Measurements of "spoonful" or "medium carrot" weren't specific enough, and Julia had to rectify that for her cookbook. When she consulted the American cookbooks for any French recipes, such as her favorite *Joy of Cooking*, she found that some of the recipes weren't accurate at all. She made *béchamel* from the book but found that the measurements weren't precise.

"Sorry, Irma," she muttered as she worked, tediously weighing American butter and flour on a scale until she had the exact measurements tried and tested.

Paul came and went, pitching in during the evenings, and half the time, Julia hardly remembered him heading off to bed.

One night, Paul found her hunched over the kitchen table long after midnight. She had begun to make a list, a long, depressing list, of which ingredients they'd have to leave out of the cookbook recipes. When she finished, she'd break the news to Simca and Louisette.

"What's wrong?" Paul asked, shuffling into the kitchen.

JULIA

She looked up, having been so lost in her thoughts, she barely registered that he'd come in.

He bent to kiss her, but when she didn't even smile, he pulled a chair next to hers and grasped her hand.

"Julie? Has something happened? Did you receive bad news? Is it your family?"

She blinked, then wiped at her cheeks. "Oh, no, nothing like that." She sniffled, not even sure when she'd started crying. "I've done so much work already on testing the recipes, and now . . ." She dragged in a breath. "Now we have to change some recipes."

Paul's brows pinched together. "What do you mean?"

She explained some of her cooking mishaps, especially when trying out different types of flour.

Paul's expression cleared. "The flour makes that much of a difference?"

"Oh yes," Julia confirmed. "And now I've realized that we can't have anything in our cookbook that's not available in America."

"Well, that does make perfect sense," Paul said, scratching at his stubbled chin. "What's on your list so far?"

She turned her notebook so that he could read along with her.

"*Crème fraîche*," Paul read aloud. "You're right, that's not in America. And . . . shallots, chanterelles, and leeks . . . also not in America. At least not yet."

"You understand my dilemma now?"

"I do." He rubbed at his jaw again.

"What is it?" Julia asked, feeling wary all over again. She'd had a pit in her stomach for hours now . . .

"The butter," Paul said. "I remember your first meal in France—*sole meunière*. You were in raptures, and that's where you fell in love with French food."

"Yes," she murmured, her mind racing. "You told me the butter was from Normandy, and Normandy cream is unpasteurized and churned by hand." Julia dropped her head into her hands. "We'll have to redo almost every recipe. Start testing all over again."

Paul rubbed her shoulder. "I've never met a group of women who have been so determined and so talented at the same time. If you really want to bring French cooking to America, you'll find a way to adjust the recipes and still keep them authentic."

Julia lifted her head and gazed at her husband. "That's why it hasn't been done successfully yet." She straightened, squaring her shoulders. "We'll do it, and do it right."

"You will, my dearest Julie. If anyone can, it's you." He leaned close and kissed her.

She let him linger for a moment, then drew away, her mind back to business. "Since we're not sleeping anyway, help me with this list. I've just thought of Gruyère cheese. It won't be on America's shelves either."

"Which is too bad," he said. "American cooks use things like ketchup and margarine and Crisco."

Julia winced. "That's right. And what about the cuts of meat? That's one thing I've learned over here—the French butchers prepare different types of meat that aren't found in America. When I used to shop with Freddie, we never came across *lardons* for barding veal." She exhaled. "How could we expect to have recipes like chateaubriand, entrecôtes, kidneys, or tripe translate to American soil? It's impossible."

Paul nodded, his gaze somber. "Add tournedos and sweetbreads to your list too."

Julia scribbled down the names, hating to think of all the work this would take in adjusting the recipes. Would they still even be French recipes when all was said and done? She had to make this work—had to. Determination simmered inside her. If she did the legwork in these beginning stages, Americans—an entire country—would benefit. She had to keep her perspective on the end results and not get discouraged by the bumpy road to get there.

"I'm going to write to Freddie," she told her husband, "and request that she send me photos of meat cuts in butcher-shop cases. Everything I do now for the cookbook must focus on the fact of teaching *Americans* to cook French dishes."

The next months were filled day and night with Julia's testing recipes. She took a full day off when she received a letter from Dort that Dort was pregnant with her first child. Julia was happy for her, truly, but it just reminded her that she hadn't been able to have children—and that opportunity had probably passed her by for good. She had a good cry, with Paul telling her that she was perfect in every way and he wouldn't change anything about their life together. Then she wrote Dort a congratulatory note and was done with it. Mostly. She determined to celebrate every accomplishment and good news Dort shared with her.

That weekend, she and Paul took time off to visit sites and locations they'd dearly miss once their transfer came in. But Julia was back in the kitchen early Monday morning. She learned firsthand, over and over, to both keep things simple and not cut corners. When she made onion soup, her experiments produced either bland broth or a burned taste. Finally, she discovered that the onions needed to be caramelized through slow cooking in butter and oil, and only then was the robust flavor of the onion soup brought out.

Simca joined her most mornings, and they cooked side by side in the kitchen. They mostly complemented each other since they both approached the project with professionalism, but Simca was also not happy to have her family recipes altered. They had many vigorous discussions about what "Americanizing" actually meant.

Louisette joined them when she could, but her marriage was falling apart, and her emotional bandwidth was strung tight. She confessed more than once that cooking wasn't joyful when other parts of her life were in shambles.

By October, they had a well-oiled system in place. By day, Simca and Julia reworked recipes, and in the evenings, Julia typed up the newly revised version along with some handwritten notes in the margins. Finally, they completed the sauces chapter, except for one recipe that seemed to elude her. The white sauce, *beurre blanc Nantais*, which was commonly used on fish, never turned out well.

She kept thinking about the place where she'd had a perfect *beurre blanc Nantais*. "Paul, do you remember when we ate at the bistro Chez la Mère Michel?"

Paul paused in his nightly cleanup, which freed Julia to type up the day's recipe. "On the Right Bank? I remember it. We haven't been there for . . . a couple of years?"

"Three years," Julia said. "I still remember their fish sauce. Let's go tonight. I want to try it again and find out what I'm missing."

Paul didn't have to be asked twice. They were out the door, coats on, within minutes and walking to the bistro. They lingered over their most excellent meal, and when Julia spotted the owner, Mère Michel herself, she said, "I'm going to ask her and find out what her recipe is."

"I don't think she will give that up," Paul began.

But Julia was already on her feet, napkin and pen in hand. She introduced herself to the woman and explained the troubles she was having with *beurre blanc*. Before she knew it, Mère Michel invited her into the kitchen and instructed one of the cooks to demonstrate the white sauce. Julia jotted notes down on her napkin, then stuffed it into her purse.

"I don't believe it," Paul said as they walked back home. "You have their actual recipe?"

"I do," Julia said in triumph. "I'll have to alter it a little for the American audience, but now I have a place to start."

Paul slipped his arm about her waist. "Bravo, my dear. You have a way of hypnotizing people when you talk to them so they do whatever you want."

She laughed. "Is that why you married me?"

"If it was, I'm still hypnotized."

The *beurre blanc* sauce couldn't have been a more integral part of the sauces chapter, and in November, things shifted once again. Ives Washburn Publishing sent back the original manuscript that had some notes from Ripperger.

Louisette and Simca met Julia to show her the letter from the publisher.

Julia read, "The big job now rests on your shoulders, and you must be the absolute boss of what goes into the book and what stays out. Now that you, Mrs. Child, have taken over the helm, I am more confident than ever that a fine book can be made of this."

Julia looked up from the letter. "*I'm* the boss? When did that happen?"

Louisette gave Julia an innocent smile. "You are the boss, no? Look what you've done so far." She motioned toward the stacked recipes starting to indeed resemble a cookbook. "We don't even need to look at Ripperger's revisions."

Julia agreed with that.

"It seems they still want the book," Simca added with lilting confidence. "That's good news."

"Very good news," Julia said, although the conversation they'd had with Irma Rombauer about contracts and royalties and advances made Julia a little worried. "We've all put so much time into this book already, and we haven't even added up the costs of ingredients. Shouldn't we get an advance?"

"We should ask for one," Louisette said.

Julia's mind raced. She was out of her depth here. "I'm going to write to the publisher and explain our vision for the book. I'll send some sample pages as well."

Both Louisette and Simca agreed.

"We can tell them we'll deliver it next summer. In June?" Julia asked. "Can we all commit to that?"

"Of course," Simca said.

"I can do that too," Louisette added.

"In the meantime, I'm going to write to Paul's nephew, Paul Sheeline. He works for the law firm of Sullivan & Cromwell. Maybe he can help us with the contract?"

No one argued, and Julia realized she really was the boss for this project. Once her friends left, Julia sat down to write her letters—including one to Avis DeVoto, detailing the new updates. At the last minute, she included some pages from *French Home Cooking*, telling her to please be frank and brutal in her critique.

While Julia was waiting for replies to her letters on how to manage this publishing relationship, US Representative Fred Busbey visited one of Paul's art exhibits in Paris. The exhibit was comprised of fifty-six contemporary American artists whose work was on loan from the Museum of Modern Art. Busbey criticized the exhibit and called it Communist art. Which was ridiculous because some of the art was abstract, and that was banned in the Soviet Union. Regardless, this accusation caused a huge headache for Paul, and now the USIS was the target for all the Red-baiting going on in DC.

Not only that, but Paul was also saying that leaving Paris might be a good thing—at least a fresh start and a separation from Busbey's accusations. Julia hoped the whole thing would blow over soon.

When she received a reply from Avis, Julia felt overwhelmed with the positivity of the letter. Avis absolutely loved the pages and said the recipes and format were revolutionary.

"Look at what Avis says," Julia told Paul the moment he returned from work. She didn't miss the violet circles beneath his eyes—neither of them had been sleeping well.

Paul took the letter and scanned the words, his expression brightening. "She believes your cookbook will be a classic and sell forever." He laughed a genuine laugh, and Julia felt pleased to hear it. "This is incredible," he said, his fond gaze upon Julia. "Avis is outside of all this"—he waved a hand, indicating Roo de Loo and all of Paris—"yet her opinion is to be respected."

"I think so," Julia said. "At least I hope so." She couldn't help but grin.

"Wait . . ." Paul continued reading. "She wants you to submit to other publishers?" When he finished reading, he looked up, his brows furrowed.

"She says that Ives Washburn is small-time, and we need a bigger publisher," Julia hedged. "Is this just a best friend complimenting me?"

"It wouldn't hurt to try," Paul said. "But you also don't want to burn bridges."

"Right," she agreed. "Avis is partial to Houghton Mifflin because they publish her husband. She says that Dione Lucas, who is one of their leading editors, was the first female graduate of Le Cordon Bleu. What are the chances?"

"Small world indeed." Paul crossed into the living room and sat on the couch.

Julia settled next to him. "According to Avis's husband, Bernard, there's no such thing as a moral obligation to a publisher."

"Hmm." Paul reached for her hand. "Louisette is the one with the personal relationship with Ives Washburn, correct?"

Julia released a sigh. "Correct. Even if I wanted to submit to Houghton Mifflin, I'd have to convince Simca and Louisette as well."

"Cowriting *is* a bit complicated."

Julia leaned her head against his shoulder. "Yes, but I love it. I love my friends, and sometimes I marvel at how I got to this moment in the first place. Here I am, in discussions about publishing contracts for a cookbook when a few years ago, I couldn't even roast a chicken."

Paul wrapped his arms about her and pulled her close. "From the moment I met you, I knew you were special. I didn't know at the time how you'd become my whole world." He kissed the top of her head. "I think you should go for it. Pitch to the bigger publisher. I'll help you talk to Louisette and Simca. I'm sure they'll come around."

CHAPTER 27

Marseille, France
February 1953

"At 11:30 this morning, I had just come home from the markets, dishes unwashed, beds unmade, and Paul called up to say he was bringing six GIs home for lunch, members of the American Fencing team. So I made them a Soupe au Pistou, Larousse P. 871, with a few embellishments. I just thought it would be interesting if the most typical guys would like it. And they did, ate it all up and said it was a 'very wonderful soup,' and want me to give them the recipe. Interesting to see if and how these foreign methods appeal to the average American."

—LETTER FROM JULIA TO AVIS DeVOTO

Julia had known this day would eventually come. They'd been transferred to Marseille. Somehow, though, the past four years in Paris had sped by quicker than lightning during a thunderstorm. Paul's new position was the cultural affairs officer for southern France, and his office was in the American Consulate at 5, Place de Rome.

Everything was changing. Not only would Julia be working on the cookbook long distance, but she'd also miss all her Paris friends and have to rehome her cat once again. They couldn't have a pet in their sublet apartment at 28, Quai de Rive Neuve, which they were subleasing from the Swedish consul, who was on leave for six months. Julia finally found a new home for Minette with a family who owned the charcuterie on the rue de Bourgogne.

Julia and Paul's farewell dinner had been epic and had included their twelve closest friends. Curnonsky surprised them by showing up. Paul had brought his camera and taken pictures of Julia, Simca, and Louisette and plenty that had included Curnonsky.

JULIA

"You will get a break from the rich cream sauces of Paris, no?" Simca said, looping her arm through Julia's. "In Marseille, you'll be inundated with Provençal dishes with tomatoes, onions, garlic, pepper."

"I'll be reporting every day on my recipe testing," Julia said, squeezing her friend. "Besides, I'll be coming to Paris often."

"Yes," Simca said. "We can also rendezvous in Nice at our summer farmhouse. Now that we're officially under contract, we have more motivation than ever."

They'd signed with Houghton Mifflin, and the acquiring editor, Dorothy de Santillana, had been nothing but encouraging. They'd even received an advance of seven hundred fifty dollars. The cookbook finally had legs.

"Your farmhouse in Nice sounds perfect." It would all be fine and wonderful, Julia had to tell herself. Paul's orders had been marked as "temporary duty" since they still had to receive the transfer papers from the State Department. This meant they couldn't lease out their Paris apartment, and they couldn't sign a new lease in Marseille. They were, in essence, in limbo but were required to live in Marseille.

Julia certainly felt homesick, but there was also a lot to distract her and to learn. The only way she could describe the coastal city was a cacophony of movement and sound. The streets were crowded, the markets overflowing, the people always talking, laughing, and calling out to each other. The seaport was a melting pot of cultures and merchants and mariners. There was never a quiet moment, and Julia only had to step outside to be swept into another spectacular world. Despite her homesickness, she fell in love immediately.

And, of course, she threw herself into cooking and testing recipes, adding her mountains of kitchen gadgets to the very sparse kitchen. She grew to appreciate the sun-filled railroad flat on the fifth floor because just steps from her front door was the fish market, La Criée au Poissons.

"I need to know my fish," she told Paul one evening when he returned home after a long day. She'd prepared a watercress soup and crisp salad for their meal.

"You love fish, so what's to know other than that?" Paul teased.

Julia smiled and glanced out the tall window that overlooked the harbor and its neat rows of fishing boats. "Did you know there are more than two hundred recipes for fillet of sole in *Répertoire de la cuisine*?"

"I thought you were focusing on soups next," Paul said, taking another bite of his soup, as if for emphasis.

Julia pointed toward the seaport beyond their windows. "When in Rome..."

Paul chuckled. "All right, so what's your plan of action?"

"One of the hurdles is that many types of fish here don't exist in the States," she said. "So I'll need to find comparisons or substitutes. For instance, here we have *lotte*, which you'll find on every restaurant menu, but in the States, it's called monkfish—which is rarely served. And what about *rascasse*?" Julia sighed. "Maybe sculpin would work as a stand-in?"

Paul shrugged. "Possibly. When's your deadline with the new publisher?"

Julia laughed—a bit hysterically—then sobered. "I don't dare ask." She drew in a breath. "I *do* know I can't take Simca's or Louisette's word for things. I have to know for myself."

"That makes sense," he mused. "If you don't know the ins and outs, then the cookbook won't be transparent."

"Exactly." Julia moved to her feet and fetched a couple of cookbooks. "Look," she said, placing *The Art of Fish Cookery* by Milo Miloradovich and *The Gold Cookbook* by Louis Pullig De Gouy, on the table in front of Paul. "*The Gold Cookbook* contains a twenty-six-page index on French fish and the American equivalents."

"Ah, so the work has been done already?" Paul asked.

"Not exactly. If *I* don't understand it, then I can't be an authority on the matter, and I shouldn't be authoring a cookbook."

Paul tilted his head, scratching at his jaw. "I gather more is coming."

"I need to be the expert, Paul, and not rely on others' research or claims. So I'm about to become best friends with the deputy fish coordinator of the Department of Fisheries."

Paul's brows popped up. "There's such a thing?"

Julia grinned. "I've already sent him a letter."

He reached for his wine glass and winked. "Mr. Deputy Fish Coordinator certainly won't know what hit him."

"Let's hope he's up to the task of answering my questions." She flipped open one of the cookbooks. "I want to change American minds about fish. Few of them eat fresh local fish. Most, if they do eat fish, buy frozen cod or flounder. But here we are in Marseille, surrounded by delectable fish, which are made into masterpiece meals."

Julia hadn't needed to worry, because when the reply came from the deputy, it contained page after page of details. It was like walking straight into a gold mine with gold already lying at the surface. None of her questions had been overlooked, and she read with delight the details on freshwater and saltwater fish, the description of how firm or flimsy their flesh, and so much more.

This inspired her to write similar questions about meat and poultry to the Department of Agriculture. She didn't know if she was more excited each day to pick up her mail or to visit one of the fish markets, where she'd made several friends.

Over the next weeks, she typed up her newly tested recipes and sent them to her friends and relatives, who would also test the recipes and send back their notes. Paul often went to bed before she finished typing everything each night.

"Good night, my woodpecker," he said, bending to kiss the top of her head. "How many copies are you typing up tonight?"

Julia paused to answer him. She had seven pages of onion skin, interspersed with carbon paper, stuffed into the typewriter so that she didn't have to type a recipe more than once. "Let's see, Simca and Louisette . . . Dort, Freddie, and Rachel, and I'm sending them to Katy Gates in Pasadena as well."

"That's quite the muddle of guinea pigs you have," Paul said in a dry tone, his hands massaging her shoulders. "Are they all trustworthy to keep everything top secret?"

Julia laughed. She'd recently told Paul how everyone was instructed *not* to share anything about the recipes with anyone else. "They all understand secrecy. And each of my recipe testers is essential—each and every one. Now, stop distracting me. If I make an error, it's a beast to fix through all seven pages. I need about ten more minutes."

"Which means thirty," Paul said. "I'll be waiting up."

Julia smirked. "With your eyes closed."

With Paul out of the room, she continued to type, making sure she hit the keys hard enough to go through all the carbon copies. When she pulled out the finished pages, she handwrote "Top Secret" across the top and bottom of each page. It might be overkill, but she didn't want anything to leak.

This was her bouillabaisse recipe, at least one version of it. Throughout the entire week, she'd been researching the origin of bouillabaisse soup—which was in Marseille itself. She'd had more than one entertaining conversation with fishermen, each who claimed their recipe was the only authentic one. Julia knew this couldn't be the case since she'd personally witnessed it being made, and it was made differently each time. The recipe was never made the same way twice since it contained a combination of the leftovers from whatever the day's catch was mixed with the Provençal soup base of tomatoes, onions, garlic, olive oil, bay leaf, saffron, and thyme. Or sometimes, potatoes replaced the tomatoes, or some used pepper *rouille* instead of saffron.

Julia had chatted with fishwives, buying their catch of the day, and spoke to restaurant owners as well. No one used the same fish—most common was the *rascasse, conger,* and *grodin*. She also tried bouillabaisse with mussels, red mullet, and hake. There were no rules, although everyone claimed there were. Something Julia might have believed if she weren't actually walking through the fish market and asking questions.

Avis had already warned Julia that it was impossible to write a bouillabaisse recipe for the American cook, but Julia wanted to prove her wrong. Everyone needed bouillabaisse in their recipe arsenal.

She experimented with various methods of bouillabaisse, careful to pay attention to what was available in America and which substitution recommendations she could give. In the meantime, Simca wrote long, detailed letters about the recipes Julia was sending over. Any recipes that

Simca sent back, Julia would have to test inside and out, then send along the revision to her guinea pigs in the States.

Anytime Julia sent a new variation of French bread to the States, the recipes always failed. Julia hadn't had much success either, or there were too many other things that had to be tested. She finally told Paul she was axing French bread from the cookbook altogether—it would have to wait for a second volume. And right now, she had other issues to deal with. Like Louisette. She replied only occasionally, not much interested in testing and retesting recipes.

"Louisette must think this is another little book of fifty recipes," she complained to Paul one weekend as they took a stroll through a lively marketplace. Julia was introducing him to some of her new friends. "Simca and I don't always see eye-to-eye, but we are at least hashing things out. We're both equally committed, yet Louisette treats it more like a social project."

"Do you want her off the project?" Paul asked in all seriousness.

"Don't think I haven't considered it, but I know that Louisette is good for the networking of this book," Julia said. "She knows everyone influential in the cooking world, and she's the iconic Frenchwoman—whose image will sell copies."

Paul nodded. "Then keep her on, but also keep your expectations in check so you aren't frustrated with every communication with her. Or lack thereof."

"Yes, wise advice," Julia said, chewing on her lip.

"There's more?"

Julia paused in her step just before they reached a market stall selling fresh mussels. "I want this cookbook to be as professional as possible. That means not letting any pitfalls through. Simca and I cook quite differently. She improvises all the time, which is fine, but the cookbook needs to be more precise. I think I'm going to set up some rules for us to follow."

Paul's brows lifted at this. "Will Simca be put off by that?"

Julia shrugged. "If her feelings are bruised a little, she'll have to get over it. I'm the 'boss' over this project, so to speak, and we need some rules."

His smile appeared. "Like what?"

"This is no lighthearted matter," she said, but she was smiling too. "First, we should all be able to state our opinions without worry of offending the other person."

Paul nodded. "Very professional approach."

Julia continued, "Keep the book French."

"Very wise."

She nudged him. "Don't tease. Next, we must all follow the scientific method respecting our own exact findings. This, after we've studied the findings of each other and other authorities. From there, we work with exact measurements and exact temperatures. Once we have our established and agreed-upon method, that is what must hold up to rigorous testing."

"Excellent," Paul said. "I think I agree with Avis, my dear."

"How so? She has a lot of opinions."

Paul slipped his arm about Julia's shoulders and pulled her close. "This cookbook is going to be revolutionary."

Julia sighed and leaned into him. "If only it weren't taking so long. Maybe someday, I'll look back on all this testing and letter writing and debating with fishwives and know it was all worth it."

Paul rubbed her arm. "It will be worth it. In the meantime, we'll enjoy all the good food France has to offer. How about I treat you to dinner tonight? Get you off your feet and out of the kitchen."

"As always, let's play that by ear. I might become inspired today to tweak a recipe."

Paul glanced around them. "I think there's a good chance of that. I mean, you're just starting on the fish chapter, or are you still in the soup chapter?"

Julia pursed her lips. "There's some back-and-forth."

"At least, thank heavens, the sauces are done."

"For the most part," Julia hedged.

"How long is the sauces chapter?" he asked, even though he knew—because he'd actually counted one time. "Have you added?"

"You would know if I added," Julia said. "I'm committed to keeping it to only two hundred pages."

Paul stared at her, and she stared right back. Then he grinned. "I think two hundred pages is the perfect number."

"I don't know if you're teasing or serious, dearie, but you can never have too many sauce recipes."

Paul pulled her close and kissed her in the middle of a fish market in Marseille, but Julia could truthfully say that she didn't mind in the least.

The next months brought more of the same: Paul working long, fourteen-hour days and Julia working up to her elbows, quite literally, in cooking and testing and typing and shopping and asking questions. The first third of her advance from Houghton Mifflin arrived close to the time when Paul had to travel to Paris for a government conference. So Julia decided to take a few days off in celebration of not only receiving two hundred fifty dollars that she'd split with Simca and Louisette but also that she'd finished a chapter on eggs that she'd been writing on the side.

Avis DeVoto had responded that the egg chapter had swept her off her feet, adding that the growing cookbook was "Masterly. Calm, collected, completely basic, and as exciting as a novel to read."

It was on this high note that Julia and Paul returned to Paris for the conference. Julia felt like she was walking through a dreamland as she visited old haunts, saw her cat, Minette, and reunited with Simca and Louisette. They worked together for a couple of sessions in Louisette's kitchen, and it was as if no time had passed between them at all. Louisette threw a dinner party, which included Julia's former Le Cordon Bleu instructors Max Bugnard and Claude Thilmont.

"Julie," Paul said the moment he walked into their hotel room one of the evenings in Paris. "I've spoken to Charlie Moffly about taking a summer leave to the States next year."

Julia and Paul had talked about making a request to the USIS since it had been nearly three years since their last visit to the States, and they both wanted to see family. Julia especially wanted to visit her father, who was getting older. And she hadn't met Dort's children yet—Phila, who was a toddler, and Sam, a newborn. Oh, and she was dying to meet her best pen pal Avis DeVoto in person.

"You sound like something's wrong," Julia said, alerted by his urgent tone. "What's happened?"

Paul dragged a hand over his face and blew out a frustrated breath. "Moffly approved our leave to the States, but he also said we wouldn't be returning to Marseille after."

Julia's heart nearly stopped. Had Paul been *fired*?

"Apparently, the department policy is now that we can't serve longer than four years in a *country*," he continued. "By the time our summer leave starts, it will be nearly six years in France."

Julia could only stare at her husband. *Leave France?* No . . . That wasn't possible. She swallowed against the painful lump clogging her throat. "Did Moffly have any idea of where . . . ?" She couldn't finish her question.

"Germany." He paused. "Germany is most likely, but there's also the possibility of something in the Middle East."

Julia moved to the closest chair and practically collapsed onto it, her hand over her heart. "Germany? I don't think I could live where Hitler did." She closed her eyes for a moment. It hadn't even been ten years since the Nazis had surrendered.

Paul moved to her side and took her hand. "I'm not ready to move yet either, especially to Germany, yet I don't know if I'll have any say in the matter."

Julia squeezed his hand and looked up at him. "The very thought of being in the same place where all those concentration camps were and all those gas chambers and where all those Jews were killed . . . The heaviness is unfathomable."

Paul crouched before her and ran a thumb over her cheek. "I know. I feel the same way. But the war is over, and we all need to focus on rebuilding."

Julia knew he wasn't trying to placate her. She could see the real concern in his eyes. But she also knew that this was her husband's job—his career. And despite the number of times her father had offered to financially bail them out, all of which Paul had declined, she had to take pride in that her husband was determined to support them.

JULIA

"If we're given Germany, then we'll make the best of it," she said, trying to stay upbeat despite the overwhelming feeling of wanting to cry. "Maybe I'll fall in love with German food. Who knows?"

Paul cracked a smile. "I'm sure some German food will be wonderful, but it won't replace your love for French food."

"You're right." She leaned forward and embraced him. Come what may, they'd be together, and they'd manage. Somehow.

CHAPTER 28

Bad Godesberg, Germany
October 1954–April 1955

"Have been experimenting on Quenelles again, and have about gotten it down pat, using the electric blender and the egg beater. Had some quenelles in Lyon on the way up to Paris, just to see how they were, and I really and honestly did not think they were as good as mine.... They were more floury. Do I dare say that? Made them last Tuesday, and they didn't hold their shape enough for rolling, so I poached them in little ramekins and then un-molded them. Delicious and light."

—LETTER FROM JULIA TO AVIS DeVOTO

Julia did not fall in love with German food, but she did learn to appreciate it. They'd arrived in Bad Godesberg, Germany, on October 24, 1954, after only a month's worth of studying German. They'd been assigned military housing in the suburb of Plittersdorf. The housing was exactly how it sounded, stark, sterile, and formal. Apartment 5 at 3 Steubenring had none of the character or beauty of German architecture. Instead, it was part of a housing project with boxy white stucco buildings and brown-tiled roofs.

They'd hoped to immerse themselves in the charming small town of half-timbered houses, but instead, they were surrounded by Marshall Plan money that had built American-style pizza parlors, five-and-dime stores, and movie theaters. Julia determined to make the best of things. She took her walks along the western bank of the beautiful Rhine River, she signed up for German classes at the local university, and she dove deep into testing poultry recipes for the cookbook.

Paul's new assignment brought greater responsibility since he was the director of all the exhibits in the country, but he also had to wade through bureaucratic red-tape frustrations. Their home sat outside Bonn, which hadn't seen as much war damage as the rest of Germany. Yet the signs were all around them: damaged buildings, blown-out bridges, crumbling infrastructure. The Marshall Plan dollars had been hard at work, but there was still a long way to go in rebuilding Germany.

Julia had been apprehensive to interact with the German people, a people who had existed under Hitler less than a decade before, but she was surprised to find that she wasn't surrounded by Germans who revered Hitler. No, they reviled him.

She also enjoyed practicing her German at the markets when shopping and was met with friendly and helpful people. She took her English-German dictionary everywhere she went, referring to it constantly. In general, the Germans were happy to help with her translation, and it seemed that everyone was in rebuilding mode, improving their surroundings, and dusting off the past.

Most evenings, after completing her recipe notes and all their carbon copies, she dashed off letters to Avis and Dort. While in the States that summer, Julia and Paul had spent their first week in Washington, DC, then they'd headed to 8 Berkeley Street in Cambridge to meet Avis and Bernard DeVoto in person. The meeting had been surreal because Julia had felt like she knew the DeVotos intimately.

She even got along with Bernard, though Avis had warned her about her husband's eccentricities and strong opinions, which had earned him the nicknames of DeVoto the Magnificent and DeVoto the Impaler. Julia had happily discovered he was a westerner, too, originally from Utah. Julia and Avis couldn't get enough of each other's time, but they had eventually been forced to part ways. Julia and Paul had then reunited with John and Josephine. Then they'd headed out on the train to San Francisco, where they'd stayed with Dort and Ivan and had finally met their adorable children, Phila and Sam.

"You've got to see the supermarkets for yourself," Dort told Julia soon after they'd arrived. "So many changes and differences compared to France."

It was definitely a research trip, if nothing else.

As they strolled the bright linoleum aisles, Julia said, "You're right. So much has changed." She marveled at new kitchen gadgets, toothpaste with chlorophyll, the advertisements for television programs. Julia wrote down notes about the variations of butter and cream. She also checked out the meat thermometers.

"The chicken is different in California than back east," Julia commented one evening at dinner—something she'd prepared for everyone. "And I can't believe the frozen-food offerings. It seems that everything is prepackaged and frozen. Will a French cookbook stand a chance in a fast-paced world of convenience?"

"Nothing compares to fresh ingredients," Dort said. "Don't you dare give up."

"Oh, I'm not giving up," Julia said with a sigh. "The mountain to climb feels a little steeper though. Are you still keeping the recipes I'm sending you top secret?"

"Of course." Dort smiled. "Not that I know any other chefs, but if I did, they would never find out what my sister is doing from me."

It was so lovely to spend time with her sister and to delight in Dort's small children that Julia's heart felt heavy when it was time to leave for Pasadena. Dort sent them off with a warning. "Pop will never change his political viewpoints, so don't take them seriously."

Julia nodded. "I know. I hate how he treats Paul though—neither of us is aiding the Communist agenda."

Dort winced. They'd discussed one of Pop's previous letters, in which he'd made that accusation. Julia hadn't responded.

As she'd expected, the week they spent with Pop and Phila in Pasadena was like walking on eggshells. Pop had been so well-mannered during his Paris trip, but in his own home, apparently, he felt comfortable enough to engage in tirades about "fascists and Reds, and nasty foreigners, and intellectuals" . . . It became a relief to have their eight days in Pasadena come to an end. They headed back across the country and spent a blissful two weeks in Maine with Charlie and Freddie and their grown children. Julia celebrated her forty-second birthday there and ate all the lobster she could ever want.

Another highlight came during their final stop in Cambridge when Avis took Julia to meet the Houghton Mifflin editor, Dorothy de Santillana. From all accounts during their meeting, everyone was on the same page. Julia had finished the sauces, soups, and eggs chapters. She told Dorothy that she'd work on the poultry chapter next—Germany seemed like a good place to do that.

The final weeks of their leave had been spent back in Washington, DC, as they'd studied German and caught up with old friends, mostly from their OSS days. Gossip had been strident about McCarthy. Since his reelection in 1952, he'd been investigating government departments for Communist connections. His accusations had created a ripple effect among former OSS as they were scrutinized and brought in for interviews.

Frankly, Julia was grateful to be out of American politics for a while. And now, having lived in Germany for several weeks, she returned to her organized system to get through her recipes. She cooked a new recipe each day, and often, they'd have guests over to help them eat what she'd prepared. In January, she focused on chicken casserole, creating variation after variation. Finally, the agreement between Simca, Louisette, and Julia was that they'd include a chicken stuffed with mushrooms for the casserole offering. Then, in February, Julia focused on broiled chicken, landing on *poulet grillé à la diabolique*. She decided to create a table of American poultry names along with the French equivalent.

All of her cooking pen pals thought the poultry table was a brilliant idea.

"Germany has top-notch cooking equipment," Julia wrote to everyone. "I've bought mixers and grinders galore. You'd be impressed with the potato ricer I now own. Paul isn't surprised in the least that I've added to my kitchen equipment arsenal."

In the letters she received in reply, no one was surprised at her cooking equipment purchases.

"I don't know what to do about Louisette," Julia told Paul on a rare weekend where he didn't have to travel.

"Is something wrong?"

"It's the usual lack of participation, but the further we get into the cookbook, the more it's bothering me." Julia sat next to him on the porch in the cooling evening, where he'd just finished a cigarette, a book propped on his knee. "Simca and I know that we have about another year more of work to do. We're putting in forty hours a week, and Louisette is spending about six hours a week."

"Very lopsided," Paul murmured. "What are you thinking?"

"Well, I've drafted a letter to Louisette that I'll send to Simca for approval first." She handed over a typed-up letter. "I'm proposing that Simca and I be listed as coauthors and Louisette be listed as a consultant. The official title of the book would be *French Cooking in the American Kitchen* by Simone Beck and Julia Child, with Louisette Bertholle. We'd suggest that the royalty split be 45 percent for myself and Simca and 10 percent for Louisette."

Paul nodded but didn't say anything. He lit another cigarette. "Do you want one?"

"I'm fine." She paused. "Well, what do you think?"

"It's reasonable and fair," he said, "but it might backfire on you."

Julia sighed. "That's what I'm afraid of. I don't even know if Louisette wants to be part of our magnum opus—this cookbook is way beyond what any of us first envisioned."

"I can attest to that," Paul said with a half smile.

Julia closed her eyes for a moment.

"Maybe you should write to our nephew Paul and get his feedback."

She opened her eyes. "I'll do that." Their nephew Paul Sheeline had given her sound advice before. She was happy to have a plan of action.

She waited weeks for his reply, and when it finally came, she admitted she wasn't exactly surprised. The moment Paul came home from the office, Julia told him about the letter.

"Our nephew says we'll have to keep her listed as a coauthor since she's been part of the project from inception." Julia handed over the letter so he could see for himself.

"But he agrees on a lower royalty for Louisette," Paul read, then nodded. "That seems fair, for all parties."

JULIA

"He's suggesting 41 percent for me and Simca, and 18 percent for Louisette," Julia mused. "And for us to keep the royalty arrangements private. As far as the world will be concerned, we are all equal coauthors."

"I agree with that," Paul said. "It will keep questions and speculation out of the marketing side of things."

He wrapped his arms about her. "Just think, next year at this time, you'll have a completed cookbook on its way to press." He kissed the top of her head.

"That's what I'm counting on." Julia knew she had some time, though, before stirring everyone up about the contract terms. Another year, at least, but she wanted to prepare Louisette for the future. So after receiving approval from Simca, Julia sent her letter to Louisette, keeping them all named as coauthors but restructuring the royalty. Thankfully, Louisette agreed to the terms, and everything would be official once the final book was turned in.

Then, in April, everything changed. Paul was ordered back to Washington, DC, and at first, Julia rejoiced—thinking that maybe her husband was getting a promotion to head of the department. He was finally getting recognized for his tireless work.

While he was gone, Julia dashed off to Paris and spent time with Simca. She had started packing when she received a telegram from Paul that read, *Situation confused.*

Julia stood in her entryway for a long moment. What did Paul mean? Why had he been so cryptic? What was going on? Was there no promotion?

She paused in her packing and headed to the Deutsche Bundespost to send a telegram asking for more information.

Hours later, Paul replied. No one knew why he'd been called back. He'd been told to wait until he was contacted. His next telegram informed her, *The situation here like Kafka story. I believe I am to be in same situation as Leonard.*

This was not good news at all. If Paul was referring to Franz Kafka and Rennie Leonard, that meant *Paul* was being investigated. Rennie had been hauled before McCarthy's Un-American Activities Committee.

And now it seemed that the McCarthyism witch hunt had come to their front door. In France and in Germany, they'd felt several steps removed from the names that dominated the American newspaper headlines—those of teachers, intellectuals, liberals, writers, former OSS, and artists being questioned about Communism by the House Un-American Activities Committee.

It was all horrifying to read about, but it hadn't been personal . . . until now.

Julia's stomach bottomed out. She wanted more than anything to be at her husband's side to help him navigate the unknown. Not that she had any answers or solutions, but at least Paul wouldn't be pacing a hotel room alone, his thoughts growing more and more panicked.

Julia found herself pacing and waiting for news from him. Every communication grew more and more grave until he finally reported on the interview he'd had at the Office of Security, where he'd been interrogated for an entire day and evening by Special Agents Sullivan and Sanders. For hours, he had been asked question after question about what he knew about former OSS friends, including Jane Foster and a man he'd once given as a reference: Morris Llewelyn Cooks. They also questioned Paul about whether he was homosexual since they claimed there was a charge in the dossier. Paul had laughed and asked who had accused him. He hadn't been given an answer. More questions had been fired at him, and at the end of the day, they'd told him he was cleared. Simple as that.

Well, not simple, Julia thought when she heard the good news. She felt as if she'd lost a few years off her life. While waiting for Paul to make his travel plans to return to Germany, Julia wracked her brain to come up with why Paul had been put on anyone's radar. Yes, they'd known Jane Foster, but they'd never colluded with her politically. While living in Paris, they'd had the occasional dinner with Jane and her husband, George Zlatovsky, but they weren't all that particularly close. A few months ago, Julia and Paul had donated twenty-five dollars to a campaign against Senator McCarthy. Also . . . Julia had written an angry letter to a woman named Aloise B. Heath, who had accused five Smith College faculty members of harboring Communists. The accusation had been so

JULIA

ridiculous that Julia had not only written to Aloise about how unfair it had been but also that Julia was going to double her donation to Smith College.

Still . . . would that letter have been turned in and made it all the way to Washington, DC authorities?

When Paul returned to Germany, safe and sound, Julia felt overjoyed. It was the best day of her life, second only to her wedding day. They decided to firmly put the interrogation behind them, while Paul focused on his exhibits and Julia stayed busy with turkey and poultry recipes.

On a minivacation back to Paris, which was always a whirlwind, they ran into George, who'd married Jane Foster. He joined their table at the Café Deux Magots and told them that Jane had returned to San Francisco to visit her dying mother. While in San Francisco, Jane's passport had been confiscated by Ruth Shipley, head of the Passport Division of the US Department of State.

Paul groaned at the news. They both knew that Ruth Shipley had the reputation of refusing passports on unfounded accusations. She was like a dictator in her own kingdom and got away with it.

"Jane is going to need a good lawyer," Paul said.

"I'm going to write to her and tell her we consider her a friend," Julia said. "It's awful they're keeping her trapped." Even if it put Julia on the radar of the government, she refused to withhold her support as a friend. "I'll tell her to contact the American Civil Liberties Union. Someone has to be willing to stand up for her."

CHAPTER 29

Washington, DC
November 1956–January 1958

"Well, things have finally jelled, and Paul has accepted the post of Cultural Affairs Officer to Norway (Oslo). He will receive six months of language training, and we should be leaving some time in March. HOO-RAY. I think this is wonderful, and we are getting excited. And thank heaven, I really didn't like the idea of our drifting around, and Paul really feels a calling for government service and wants to do something useful and valid."

—LETTER FROM JULIA TO AVIS DeVOTO

When Paul was transferred back to the United States in November 1956, Julia felt elated. She'd grown to enjoy and appreciate many things about their years in Germany, but even though a move to the States would slow down the cookbook project even further, she was excited to be in America again. If they couldn't return to Paris, then living in America was the next best thing. She'd also gain a better understanding of what American cooks had at their disposal.

They spent the first weeks in the States making a wintry trek across the country, visiting family and friends from Pennsylvania to Boston to California and then back to Washington, DC. World politics was a topic of conversation with everyone they met. The Suez Crisis had been negotiated and was currently being resolved by the United Nations, with orders for Israeli, French, and British forces to withdraw from Egypt. The Korean War had been over for a few years, and now the newspapers were full of news about the Vietnam war that the US had entered the previous year. South Vietnam had elected a new president, Ngo Dinh Diem, and he was petitioning the US for support against the Communist north.

JULIA

During their traveling, Julia discovered that Swanson had taken over American cooking by offering frozen dinners and that people sat in front of their televisions while eating, or after eating. In addition, a chef named James Beard had published *The Complete Book of Outdoor Cookery*, and it seemed that flaming food cooked on a barbecue had become all the rage.

Julia quickly realized her cookbook was up against the quick-fix dinners, the prepackaged meals, and the shortcuts that American cooking had embraced. From frozen piecrusts to dehydrated onion soup, pancake mixes, instant coffee . . . the list was immense. And it all had a place, surely it did, but Julia wanted to appeal to those who loved cooking or who could be taught to love cooking. She herself was still a new cook, having taken it seriously only since her marriage. If she could turn her heart, then other Americans could as well.

Their home on Olive Street had been leased out for so long that it now required some renovation work. Or at least a facelift. Instead of immersing herself in cooking, Julia worked on the house for the first couple of months. She jumped into painting, replastering, and enlarging the kitchen as well as creating an office in the attic. Her favorite part of the renovation was purchasing a restaurant-grade range for the house.

Once their belongings arrived from Germany, Julia was ready to begin cooking again, filling their home with the aroma of French cooking. She wrote religiously to Simca, detailing the layout of the supermarkets and the kitchen items she was spoiling herself with. She bought a dishwasher and a sink with a food disposal. She found things like scouring powder for copper pots and sent some to Simca. Julia experimented with an electric skillet that had a thermostat and timer, then reported to Simca.

"You must come for a visit," Julia begged Simca in a letter. "You can meet so many of our friends here. It seems that Washington, DC is the gathering place for everyone we've ever known."

Simca eventually promised to come visit the following year, in early 1958. At that point, the cookbook had better be done, Julia determined, so they could meet with the publisher together.

Many weekends, Julia and Paul joined Charlie and Freddie at Coppernose in Pennsylvania. Julia and Freddie would cook together all day so Julia could continue her turkey-recipe testing. In addition, she spent a lot more time with Avis since Bernard had died in November 1955. Also, that previous summer in August 1955, Jane Foster had finally been granted a passport after the court battle *Zlatovski v Dulles* and was now in exile in Paris with her husband. Jane had written a long letter to Julia while Jane was still in Norway, detailing all the events. The ordeal had taken such a toll on Jane that she'd been in and out of psychiatric care.

It all felt surreal now, especially living back in the States, but Julia turned her attention to submitting recipes to ladies' magazines. Her publisher Houghton Mifflin thought it would help earn some name recognition, and Julia consulted Avis first thing.

"I think it's an excellent idea," Avis said. "You can get a sense for how your recipes might be received."

So Julia did. She submitted to *The Ladies' Home Journal* but was rejected because the recipes were too involved. She sent recipes to *Woman's Day* but never heard back. She interviewed with the *Washington Post*, which wrote an article about her kitchen but didn't mention Simca or publish any of their recipes.

Each time a new cookbook released, Julia bought it, scouring it for flaws or anything that might make her own whale of a project moot. She found flaws but never felt discouraged that she wasn't on the right track with her French cooking cookbook. When she learned that *Betty Crocker's Picture Cook Book* had sold over three million copies since its 1950 release, it only gave Julia confidence that Americans wanted to cook despite all the prepackaged meals on the market.

Yet she quickly realized that in order to fully Americanize the recipes for the fish and meat sections, she'd need more time. Like three or four years of more time. Every week, no, every day, she was hitting obstacles.

"American turkeys are oversized," she told Paul one evening after typing up her day's notes and walking into their bedroom, where he was reading in bed. "We have to cook them differently from French poultry."

Paul patted the space next to him, and she slipped under the covers. "How many of the recipes do you have to alter?"

Julia rested her head against his shoulder. "I don't dare count. But American veal isn't as tender, and it's hard to find fresh herbs, except for parsley. Americans also eat a lot of broccoli, something we didn't see a lot of in France."

"No," Paul murmured. He stifled a yawn. For the most part, his job was running smoothly, and they were both busy every minute of every day.

"Oh, and some of the recipes I'm retesting, ones that have all the same ingredients here aren't turning out like they did in France. I vented to Simca today in a long letter that I'm sure she'll love receiving."

Paul kissed the top of Julia's head, then shifted so that he was facing her. "You have enough chapters finished for an entire cookbook already, so maybe you should be thinking of a multivolume cookbook. Your publisher could put out volume one—on your soups, vegetables, sauces, and poultry, which will be finished within the year—while you keep working on fish and other meats."

Julia pushed up on her elbow. "That would be wonderful. Then I wouldn't have to pare anything down and choose between favorite recipes. Do you think Houghton Mifflin would go for it?"

"I don't know why not." Paul smoothed a bit of hair from her face, then dropped his hand to her shoulder. "Talk to your editor. This way, they can get your book out sooner than later—volume one, that is."

Julia leaned close and kissed him. "Did I tell you that I love you?"

"Not today." He grinned and kissed her back.

Julia was elated when Dorothy agreed that dividing their cookbook into multiple volumes would be an excellent idea, and they discussed a Christmas 1958 release date. Dorothy had already been cooking from some of the recipes and had fallen in love with the food. Julia rushed home to share the news with Paul, then write to Simca and Louisette to tell them that the first volume would be called *French Cooking, Vol. 1: Sauces and Poultry*. She knew this would complicate things with

Louisette because the more time went on, the less Louisette stayed involved. But they could work out contract details and royalty splits later.

Julia had the boost she needed to plow on ahead. Paul also became more involved, beyond pouring the wine and helping her clean up. They discussed testing and retesting methods, working out of her now thoroughly modern kitchen at their Olive Street house. Julia appreciated Paul's careful attention to detail, even though it added to the hours of fine-tuning the recipes. Simca was tasked with simplifying the recipes she sent over but keeping them authentically French.

When Simca finally came to visit in early 1958, they braved a snowstorm and spent eleven hours on a bus to reach Boston in order to deliver the manuscript to Houghton Mifflin on the appointed day of their meeting, February 24, 1958.

It was still snowing on the day of the meeting, but Julia and Simca had a lovely conversation with Dorothy. With a bit of trepidation, Julia handed over the heavy manuscript box. The poultry and sauces chapters together made up over 700 pages, and yes, it was large, but it was also thorough.

Dorothy was all smiles though—welcoming and encouraging. "I've tried the recipes you sent over in the sample pages. I've found them comprehensive and delicious."

All the women laughed. "Our job is done, then," Julia quipped.

Dorothy opened the box and thumbed through some of the pages. "I'm profoundly impressed," she said, looking up with a smile. "How about I introduce you around?"

For the next half hour, Julia and Simca were introduced to those in the office, then they parted ways with Dorothy.

"I'll run your manuscript through our standard evaluation, then be in touch," their editor said.

As Julia and Simca pulled on their warm coats and left the office, Julia felt deflated somehow. She should feel the opposite though—they'd just delivered years of work in what would be an outstanding contribution to French cuisine.

"They will fall in love with it," Simca said, linking her arm through Julia's. "How could they not? Everyone loves French food."

"You're right," Julia said, marveling at how her friend could read her mood so easily. "Dorothy was nothing but sweet and positive. We'll focus on that."

Julia's tentative enthusiasm was short-lived, though, because when the multivolume idea hit the budget-approval stage, she received a letter from Dorothy. Houghton Mifflin wanted only one book. Not multivolumes. Not an encyclopedia. General Manager Lovell Thompson had made the final call.

"We must state forthwith that this is not the book we have contracted for," Dorothy wrote.

Julia's pulse beat in her ears as she continued to read, "It has grown into something much more complex and difficult to handle than the original book." She scanned the editor's words that recommended that they revise the manuscript into a much smaller book, something that Americans would be more attracted to. Something that was compact, simplified, and more readable.

Was it all over, then? This cookbook plan of theirs? The years of cooking and testing and retesting, all for naught?

She had to deliver the bad news to Simca. Julia found Simca in the front room, reading a magazine. When she looked up, Julia sank onto the couch next to her and showed her the letter.

Simca was shocked, of course, then infuriated, mirroring Julia's feelings exactly. "We must reject their suggestion," Simca said, her expression dark. "We're not taking shortcuts and turning our work into canned soup and frozen-food additives." She visibly shuddered.

"We'll write to them," Julia said. "Tell them we reject their suggestions."

The women headed up to Julia's attic office, where Julia typed out a stern but brilliant rebuttal.

"The cook who interests us," she wrote, "is the one who has the time to devote to the more serious and creative aspects of cooking. She has to have a certain amount of sophistication and the conception that good cooking, especially good French cooking, is an art form requiring techniques and hard work. We, therefore, propose that our mutual contract for 'French Cooking for the American Kitchen' be cancelled, and we'll return the advance of $250 at once."

There. They'd send it in the morning.

Julia spent a sleepless night pacing her small office in the attic so that Paul could rest, although she suspected he wasn't sleeping much either.

By the time dawn cracked the March sky, she'd changed her mind. Bleary-eyed but clearheaded, she found Paul in the kitchen, brewing up coffee. Simca sat at the kitchen table, her hair wild, violet circles beneath her eyes. They both looked at Julia when she entered.

"We're going to have to start over," Julia said, her voice trembling, her throat scraped raw. "We'll condense to around 350 pages. Another publisher won't want our behemoth anyway, and we can't let all our hard work go to waste. What do you think, Simca?"

The woman rose to her feet and hugged Julia long and hard. When they drew apart, Simca smiled with tears in her eyes. "It will only take another year, yes?"

"Two," Julia and Paul both said at the same time. But they could do it. Cutting was necessary, especially for a cookbook sold to Americans who wanted easy solutions.

"We'll teach them how to prepare in advance, then reheat right before dinnertime," Julia said.

Paul grasped Julia's hand and kissed her cheek. "There's my wife. Always with a solution. Let's rip up that letter."

She wrapped her arms about him. It would all be fine, she determined. They'd eventually join the cookbookery world, and they'd do it with a new French twist.

The roller coaster of emotions settled into grim determination over the next days and weeks as Julia and Simca analyzed their manuscript from front to back. They'd have to be merciless in their cutting. Sections on how to sauté, how to caramelize, how to boil a potato . . . were only some of the parts they'd have to cut. A good chunk of the sauces recipes would have to go as well. Soup recipes that were pages long were nixed, including Oxtail soup, fennel soup, and tarragon cream soup.

They replaced *estouffade aux trois viands* with *boeuf bourguignon*, a less complicated recipe.

They both realized that it was nearly impossible to simplify the recipe for a true French roast chicken. The original recipe was five pages long because Julia was insistent that each step, from trussing to carving, had to be spelled out. And she couldn't leave out the basting and turning descriptions. So something else would have to be cut.

With each decision, it felt like a piece of her heart disintegrated.

But it was either this or no cookbook at all.

After Simca returned to France, Julia continued to test recipes, starting on the vegetable chapter. Her guinea pigs were friends and neighbors, whom Julia invited over frequently to test out the recipes. Paul was in charge, as always, of mixing and pouring drinks and cleanup. After Julia served a meal, they'd enter into a discussion of what worked and what didn't. Then Julia would type everything up.

She offered cooking classes in her kitchen, under the name that she and Simca had copyrighted: L'Ecole des Trois Gourmandes. She sent the recipes that she used to Simca, who was also teaching cooking classes in Paris to a group of US Air Force wives.

"This is delicious," Rosalind Rockwell told Julia one evening during a dinner Julia had prepared. "I can't wait until your cookbook is out."

"Don't hold your breath," Julia quipped. "It's still in the works but coming along very slowly."

Rosalind Rockwell and her husband, Stuart, who was the director of the Office of Near Eastern Affairs for the Department of State, were neighbors and frequent dinner guests. "The time will all be worth it, you'll see."

Julia didn't know where Rosalind got her confidence from. "I have fierce competition, it seems," Julia said on a sigh. "Americans are eating chicken cooked in canned mushroom soup, frozen fish sticks, canned vegetables with marshmallows melted on top, and, of course, barbecue everything."

"And now the dieting fads are taking over women's magazines," Rosalind commented. "We're all eating prepackaged meals, canned foods, and plenty of junk food—and our waistlines are expanding. Big surprise."

"So very true," Julia said. "We can have our butter, our desserts, our rich sauces—all in moderation though."

"I'll toast to that," Paul said, lifting his wine glass, with Stuart doing the same.

It was true that French food was rich, but Julia had been able to stay slender by eating fresh vegetables and fruit, keeping dessert portions small, and staying active. She didn't think she could ever give up butter though . . . Thus her long walks.

Over the Fourth of July weekend, they'd visited Avis in Cambridge and had talked about the possibility of moving there. Both Julia and Paul loved the community and its proximity to Boston and Maine. Julia's publisher would also be close, and she'd love to live near Avis. They'd even toured some neighborhoods but hadn't found any homes currently for sale.

"Paul, I need to do something other than cook in these four walls every day," Julia told her husband on a long summer weekend in August.

"What else do you enjoy besides cooking and eating?" Paul teased.

She nudged her foot against his as they lounged together on the couch, both of them reading different books. The day's mail sat between them, unopened.

"Maybe we need to take a vacation," she mused. "Can you request some time off?"

"I can." He reached for the pile of envelopes and handed over a couple addressed to her. One was from Simca and another from a name she didn't recognize—someone in Philadelphia.

She opened the envelope and read through the letter. "Oh, I've been asked to teach a cooking class in Philadelphia. Once a month, and they'd pay me."

Paul's brows lifted. "Very nice. Do you want to make that long drive each month?"

"It's four hours," Julia said. "The class sounds fun though. I can teach them how to make *oeufs pochés duxelles, sauce béarnaise* . . ."

Paul chuckled. "I think your answer is yes?"

Julia grinned. "And I can also teach *poulet sauté portugais, epinards au jus* . . ." She paused. "What is it?"

Paul had opened one of his letters, and his face had lost its color. He closed his eyes for a moment, then opened them and said, "We're getting transferred to Oslo, Norway."

CHAPTER 30

Oslo, Norway
March 1959–May 1960

"Dearest Simca and Avis: Black news on the cookbook front... The answer is NO, Neg, Non, Nein... too expensive to print, no prospects of a mass audience. Too bad. If it had been one of those quick books which tell few details, they probably would have taken it: 'COQ AU VIN. Take cut up broilers and brown them in butter with onions, bacon, and mushrooms. Cover with red wine and bake for 2 hours.' (Copy of letter enclosed.) Simca, I am most upset for your sake, as you have been in on this bloody thing for so many years and years. You just managed to hook yourself up with the wrong collaborator! Eh bien."

—LETTER FROM JULIA TO SIMCA AND AVIS

Paul put off their relocation to Norway as long as he could to give himself enough time to learn Norwegian. Julia was impressed with his dedication, and she figured she'd pick up the language much easier while living there, just as she had in France and Germany. The delay also gave Julia more time to get closer to finishing the cookbook. She and Simca had spent nearly seven years on the thing, and it was time to wrap it up. So Julia promised that the recipe testing wouldn't slow down one bit while she was in Norway. In fact, she'd ramp everything up.

Right before leaving for Norway, they bought a house in Cambridge that had suddenly come on the market. They'd had to make an offer on the spot since another buyer had been on their heels. Their offer had been accepted, and they'd rented 103 Irving Street back to the previous owner but had promised to do upgrades, which required a lot of long-distance paperwork and approvals.

JULIA

In Norway, Julia had no real complaints. They lived in a nice, white clapboard house in Ullern, with a gorgeous view of the fjord. They had a fun reunion with Fisher Howe, their old OSS friend, who was now deputy chief of mission in Oslo. He'd married Debby, a friend of Dort's from Bennington College. Debby introduced Julia to everything Norwegian—the shops, the markets, outdoor excursions, the embassy wives—who didn't seem to like to cook, and no one cooked French.

The main dishes in Norway were boiled or brined. There were few fresh vegetables and hardly any salad greens, but they served berries and potatoes with every meal. And the Norwegians were a skinny people.

"I haven't seen one overweight person in Oslo," Julia commented to Paul as she worked through the blistering heat of their kitchen one summer evening, testing a recipe. "How do they do it?"

Paul had been restless tonight, pacing the kitchen, helping but not really helping. Staring out the windows. He'd been spending hours studying Norwegian—again—because apparently, what he'd been taught in the States was Danish. Julia had had a good laugh when they'd first discovered it, but now it wasn't so funny.

They'd both taken a liking to the Norse language, though, although Paul continued to hit phrasing dead-ends with Norwegian.

"The Norwegians are nature loving," Paul said. "They're always biking or hiking or simply walking. I think it's their uncomplicated lifestyle."

"I think you're right," Julia mused. Today was their tenth wedding anniversary, but they'd stayed in for dinner instead of attempting a restaurant. She'd been determined to keep up her self-imposed cooking deadline, despite the stifling heat of cooking in the sun-filled kitchen.

She nodded toward the pegboard, where Paul had meticulously hung all her pans and pots and gadgets when they'd first moved into the house. He'd announced that she had seventy-four items on display.

"Can you hand me the small saucepan?" she asked.

Paul obliged and hovered next to her by the stove—it wasn't her favorite stove to slave over. But it had come with the house.

"What are you making?" Paul asked, dipping the tip of his finger into the heating mixture.

"*Riz en couronne*," she said. "A rice ring that I'm filling with reamed shellfish mixture with sautéed chicken livers with ham and mushrooms."

"Delicious," he murmured. "I'm glad we're eating at home. Your cooking far outweighs anything outside these walls."

Julia smiled gently. "This is it, Paul."

He met her gaze as she turned to face him. "This is what?" he asked.

"The final recipe I'm testing," she said. "For the cookbook. After I send my notes to Simca, and she replies, we're putting down our spatulas and tongs."

Paul gazed at her, unblinking.

"Once I type up any of Simca's revisions, I'm mailing the whole thing to Dorothy de Santillana. 750 pages worth."

"You're serious? This is the end?"

Julia laughed. "I've never been more serious."

Paul let out a whoop, then grabbed her and spun her around. When he released her, he leaned close and kissed her. "We need to celebrate. You didn't let us do much for your birthday, and today's our anniversary—and now this."

She couldn't stop grinning. "We'll think of something, but I want to share this moment with you, and you alone."

Paul kissed her again, not letting go until she finally had to tell him that if he didn't release her, dinner would be ruined. Which meant she'd have to redo the recipe. The rest of the evening was a blur since Paul kept offering toasts, calling her brilliant, and regaling the cookbook. "It's 750 pages of perfection. A primer on *cuisine bourgeoise* for serious American cooks."

And Julia had to believe him. Her elation continued into the next weeks after she'd mailed the manuscript to Houghton Mifflin and had written letters to every family member and close friends. She dove into Norwegian life, engaging in everything she'd put off to finish the cookbook. She and Debby Howe took up tennis, Julia joined a Norwegian class at the local university, and she started to garden.

Paul teased her about her new gardening obsession, but Julia didn't care. The cookbook was done, and she had to find something else to occupy her mind and hands. She was still cooking but not at a breakneck, obsessive speed.

When the editorial letter came from Dorothy, Julia was over the moon when she showed it to Paul the moment he walked through the door. "She loves it," Julia said, triumphantly holding up the letter.

He didn't even have to ask who she was speaking about.

"Listen to what Dorothy says," Julia said as they both settled onto the couch together. "'I am delighted with the book, and I'm truly bowled over at the intensity and detail. This is a work of the greatest integrity.'" Julia looked up. "She says that it's better than *Classic French Cuisine* by Joseph Donon, which was recently published."

"Of course yours is better." Paul kissed Julia. "Congratulations, my dear. You deserve this and more."

Julia pressed the letter to her chest. "I can't believe it's all truly happening. Here, read it for yourself."

Paul took the letter and read through the words, smiling the entire time. When he got to the end, he asked, "It hasn't passed budget yet?"

"Oh, that could take weeks more," Julia said. "Avis warned me about that. I guess Dorothy wanted to write in advance to give us the good news. I'm going to send a telegram to Simca and Louisette right away, even though they'll probably get their own letters."

"I'll come with you to the post office."

Over the next weeks, Julia vacillated between elation and a sense of surrealness. She didn't know the release date of the cookbook yet, but likely, this time next year, her cookbook would be available. She'd done it. They'd all done it. The cookbook had been years in the making, and she couldn't have done it without so much support—Paul, Avis, Freddie, Dort, Rachel, Simca, Louisette, all of her friends and instructors in Paris, and, of course, Houghton Mifflin.

When the next letter came from Houghton Mifflin, delivered in a diplomatic pouch, she waited until Paul was home before opening it. She wanted to find out together when the publishing date would be. Today was November 10, 1959, a day Julia planned to always remember with a smile. When Paul returned, he shared in her excitement, then made them celebratory drinks. They sat side by side at the kitchen table, and

Julia opened the envelope. The first thing she noticed was that the letter was longer than she'd expected. Perhaps there were some editorial notes included? And the letter wasn't from Dorothy but from the editor-in-chief, Paul Brooks.

So very official. She started to read aloud, her voice strong and joyful, but soon it faltered. The sentences blurred together, then jumped apart. Disjointed and frayed.

> *Your manuscript is a work of culinary science as much as of culinary art . . .*
>
> *However . . .*
>
> *This will be a very expensive book to produce . . .*
>
> *And the publisher's investment will be heavy . . .*
>
> *It is at this stage that my colleagues feel dubious . . .*
>
> *I suggest you try this book with some other publisher . . .*
>
> *Believe me, I know how much work has gone into this manuscript . . .*
>
> *I send you my best wishes for success elsewhere . . .*

Julia's eyes burned with tears. Was this a dream? A terrible nightmare? She looked up at Paul, and seeing his ashen face, she knew it wasn't any dream. She'd just been rejected. The cookbook had been *rejected*. Seven years of work. Two contracts. An advance. A complete revision taking two more years.

Tears fell fast and hard. Her ears buzzed. Her hands shook. She could hardly comprehend the words in the letter anymore. She felt Paul's arms come around her, she heard his whispered words that she could hardly understand. The letter didn't make sense. Nothing made sense. What had she done with her life? All the time spent? All the sacrifices? All the hope?

And now it was completely dashed to pieces.

The next several days felt heavy, and not much that Paul said could cheer her up. She and Simca sent telegrams back and forth, but it wasn't until Julia received a letter from Avis that Julia felt like she could hold up her head again. She was still afraid to hope, but Paul hoped for her.

JULIA

They pored over Avis's letter, who acknowledged what a blow it was for Houghton Mifflin to reject the manuscript.

"Avis says it's simply a business decision based on budget," Julia said. "I suppose the rejection is my own fault. I was aiming for 350 pages, but it turned out to be 750 pages. Don't smile, Paul."

He smiled anyway. "I think Avis is right. Send it to another publisher. Your 750-page creation is excellent. No need to dumb anything down."

"Well," Julia tapped the letter, "I suppose we'll see what Alfred Knopf publishing has to say. Although I hate to get my hopes up." Avis had begun working as a scout for Knopf and wrote that she'd taken the lead and asked Houghton Mifflin to send the manuscript to Bill Koshland.

"I sort of wish Avis would have consulted me first, but it's done now."

Paul shrugged and reached for her hand. "It was presumptuous of Avis, but Knopf will make their decision, then we can make our decision."

Julia puffed out a breath. "What are the chances though? I mean, is our cookbook too late for Americans? What if everyone is content with frozen dinners in front of their televisions?"

"Even if it is ten years too late for the general public, there's still value for a portion of them." He sorted through the pages of Avis's letter, scanning the words. "She says to keep the advance from Houghton Mifflin, so that's something."

Julia chewed on her lip. "I feel bad for Simca. She's put as much work into this as I have. Maybe she picked the wrong American collaborator."

"Nonsense," Paul said. "She wouldn't have gotten this far without you."

"Maybe, maybe not." One thing that Julia knew: She was tired of feeling down in the dregs. "Let's have a dinner party this weekend. We'll buy sea trout, leg of lamb, and potatoes. It will all be delicious."

"Are you sure, my dear?" he asked.

Was he really asking if was she up for it?

"Oh, and by the way, Debby and I are going to start cross-country skiing."

Paul chuckled, then pulled her close.

The next letters that came from Avis reported that Bill Koshland was cooking his way through her recipes. That would take forever, Julia knew. At least Avis's letters were upbeat and encouraging, but again, Julia knew fate would happen one way or the other.

In the meantime, she and Paul took a vacation for the Christmas holiday and spent time in England, France, and Italy, staying with old friends along the way. It was a much-needed pick-me-up and when they returned to Oslo, Julia started a cooking school. Her first students consisted of five Norwegians, one Hungarian, one Brit, and one American.

Another letter arrived from Avis, reporting that Bill Koshland had handed off the cookbook manuscript to Judith Jones, a junior editor who was credited with rescuing the manuscript of Anne Frank's *Diary of a Young Girl* from the slush pile when she'd worked for Doubleday. "Judith doesn't have power over acquisitions, but cooking is a passion for her, so we want her on board too. She loves French food and even lived in Paris for three years with her husband, who is a food writer and historian."

Now Julia had another thing to worry about—this so-called Judith Jones diving into the recipes. Would she be pleased? Enough to make a case for the manuscript at a staff meeting?

Avis's next letter only put Julia's nerves into knots. Apparently, there were office and family politics to deal with. Alfred Knopf had made it known that they already had plenty of cookbooks on their list, and the cookbook editor was Alfred's wife, Blanche. Avis had already brought other cookbook manuscripts to Knopf, including one by Elizabeth David and *Classic French Cuisine* by Joseph Donon. They'd also recently released a cookbook by Alfred's sister-in-law Mildred called *Cook, My Darling*.

Mildred's cookbook had sold several thousand copies, yet the Donon book had tanked, and Elizabeth David had a reputation for being difficult to work with. Thus, sending Julia's cookbook directly to Blanche would be a surefire way to get it rejected. Avis and Bill Koshland needed a more subservient approach. And that would be through Judith Jones and the newly hired editor Angus Cameron, who had had an illustrious

JULIA

career but had resigned from Bobbs-Merrill when he'd committed a political gadfly and been marked by McCarthy.

Julia handed over the newest letter to Paul. "Avis says that Cameron loves to cook, and he was an editor during the launch of *Joy of Cooking*, so he knows how to market."

"We have three people at Knopf cooking from your book already?" Paul asked.

"It looks that way."

He perused the letter, then said, "This is impressive. Avis says that Judith goes home for lunch and blanches the vegetables as outlined in your book, then finishes cooking at night."

"She does." Julia paused. "Read the last paragraph."

Paul did, his smile growing. "I really like Judith Jones," he declared. "She told Avis that your book is revolutionary and that it not only changes the language of cooking but makes the difference between ordinary cooking and cooking with finesse."

"I like Judith, too, but I don't know if my heart can take all this back-and-forth."

Paul set the letter down and pulled Julia into his arms. "You've done all the hard work already. You can feel peace about that. So now we wait."

Waiting was ever so hard.

The day that Avis called their phone in their Oslo home, Julia at first thought something terrible had happened. Avis always wrote letters. The only other time she had called was to tell them her husband had died.

"Are you sitting down?" Avis asked.

Julia couldn't read the mood of her friend long distance, and she waved Paul over. He sat next to her, possibly hearing some of the conversation but not all.

"Angus Cameron loves the book," Avis said, her voice tinny over the phone. "He told me it's remarkable and the best working French cookbook he's ever looked at."

Julia gasped. "That's a good sign, right?"

Avis laughed. "There's more, my dear friend. Blanche has been snippy about another cookbook being published that might overshadow her own authors. She also doesn't know why Judith is aspiring to this project when Blanche is the unofficial cookbook editor. Basically, Blanche has already complained to Bill Koshland."

Julia reached for Paul's hand.

"Bill, of course, knows that the pitch has to come from Angus—he has the most influence out of the three—and he's in your corner." Avis paused. "Angus waited to pitch the manuscript at their weekly editorial meeting when it was nearly lunchtime. So everyone was tired and wanted the break. Angus gave his presentation, lauding it as an astonishing achievement and saying nothing like this has been done before, etc., etc."

Julia's hand tightened on Paul's, and he squeezed back. She wanted to shout at Avis to get to the point. What was the outcome?

"Judith Jones added in her own accolades, and really, with two such heavy endorsements, Alfred had no choice but to agree."

"Agree?" Julia whispered.

"I believe the exact words were, 'Well, let's let Mrs. Jones have her chance,'" Avis said. "And then Blanche bolted out of the room, obviously not pleased that she'd been basically steamrollered."

Julia closed her eyes, hardly daring to believe. "So, the book was accepted? You must be very clear, Avis, because I can hardly hear you over my pounding heart."

"Yes, my dear friend," Avis crooned. "You have a deal. Judith will be sending everything over posthaste, but from what Bill told me, they are looking at an advance of fifteen hundred dollars, and the final version needs to be turned in by August 31."

Julia felt Paul's arm go around her. It was May—May 5, to be exact. They could do it though. She and Simca, and maybe Louisette would jump in too. Do the final testing and proofreading of everything.

"Thank you," Julia said, her voice a scratch. "Thank you so much."

"I told you we wouldn't give up."

JULIA

Julia could only nod and whisper, "Thank you," again because her throat was too tight to speak. After hanging up with Avis, Julia fell into Paul's arms.

"I can't believe it," she said over and over, and Paul just stroked her back, not seeming surprised at all.

CHAPTER 31

Oslo, Norway
July 1960–May 1961

"My loves: This about an hour after I talked to you on the telephone, I find I am somewhat limp and stunned, and not much to say except deep, deep pleasure and great gratitude to House of Knopf. Wow.... It was lovely just hearing your calm voices and I just wish we were all together so we could dance around the maypole, emitting loud cries of joy and relief."

—LETTER FROM AVIS TO JULIA AND PAUL

Julia didn't know if it was a combination of getting a cookbook deal, its royalties being completely unpredictable, and Paul's approaching sixty years old, but Paul opened the discussion about officially retiring from government service. They were coming up on two years in Oslo, and he'd already heard that his reassignment would be just around the corner. Julia was fully supportive of his retirement because neither of them wanted to chance being assigned to yet another country when she had a cookbook to promote.

How she'd promote it, she wasn't sure, but she knew she had to not only prove to her publisher that she could exceed their sales expectations, but she also needed to realize the fruits of nine years of work. That would require her to actually be in America. Maybe offering cooking demonstrations, doing interviews, and submitting articles to magazines? Starting another cooking school?

The contract with Knopf had been a bit sticky since they'd wanted to contract with only one author—Julia Child. So she'd had to work out her own terms with Simca and Louisette.

Unfortunately, Louisette was still expecting 18 percent of the royalties. But now, it was much too generous for someone who hadn't done any of the revising work or testing the past few years, so Julia sent a letter to Louisette, offering her 10 percent of the shared royalties. Which was still generous, in Julia's opinion.

The final contract stated that the cookbook would be released in fall 1961, soon after Julia's forty-ninth birthday. The fifteen-hundred-dollar advance would go against the shared royalties of 17 percent for the first 10,000 copies. Their royalties would jump to 20 percent on the next 10,000–20,000 sold, and then another jump to 23 percent thereafter. Julia had sent the contract to their nephew Paul Sheeline to review.

Meanwhile, Avis, Julia, and Simca all cooked their way through the cookbook one more time. Avis sent back her edits, including one that said the *boeuf bourguignon* recipe needed to be adjusted because the two-and-a-half pounds of meat that was supposed to serve six to eight, in fact, only served about four people. Edits like that, though, Julia was willing to make. She also found some grievous errors where a recipe calling for one-fourth cup should have been one-fourth teaspoon. Another catch was when she discovered that she'd listed the baking temperature of 530 degrees when it should have been 350 degrees.

Not only did she spend her days fine-tuning, but she also brainstormed with Paul on titles for the cookbook. Apparently, now that Knopf had officially contracted the cookbook, no one at the publishing house liked the title.

They needed something snappy, something that would appeal to a broad audience, and something that would sell books. She and Paul made endless lists, crossing out names and making more lists.

"What about *La Bonne Cuisine Française*?" Julia asked during one of their brainstorming sessions at the kitchen table.

"It's a bit . . . pretentious?" Paul said, and that was saying something from a lover of all things French. "How about *Love and French Cooking*?"

Julia wrote it on her list. "It's charming, but people might expect poetry on love."

He shrugged. "Would that be such a bad thing? I could whip something up."

"Be serious. I'm about to pull out my hair."

Paul's expression sobered but only a tad. "*French Magicians in the Kitchen?*"

This made Julia laugh. "We're hardly magicians. Cooking is science, not magic."

"You could have fooled me." He nudged her foot with his. "You've made cooking magic."

Julia refrained from rolling her eyes. "We're not putting *magic* in the title, but I'll add it to the list so that you feel like your ideas are valued."

"Then add *You, Too, Can Be a French Chef.*"

Julia's brows shot up. "I think that's worse than the magic one." She wrote it down anyway, if only to rule out coming up with it again.

They ended up with forty-five different titles, but none of them were standouts. They even challenged their friends at the US Embassy to come up with a title. Julia's favorite out of the lot was *La Bonne Cuisine Française*, but Knopf readily turned that down.

Judith Jones's letters included the suggestions of *The Master French Cookbook* and *How to Master French Cooking*. They were getting closer. Then, in a letter dated November 18, 1960, Judith said that they'd landed on a title, although they still needed to pass it by Alfred Knopf himself—which would take a bit of luck. But what did Julia and her gourmands think of: *Mastering the Art of French Cooking*.

Frankly, Julia loved it, but maybe it was because she'd exhausted all other ideas. And if everyone at Knopf agreed, she'd be happy. The next letter from Judith stated that the title had been approved but only barely. In fact, Alfred hadn't been impressed at all and had said that if a book with that title sold, he'd eat his hat.

Judith had said not to worry—Alfred rarely liked anyone's title ideas. And Julia was determined that the book would sell. She hadn't put so many years into the thing to have it flop. As the August 31 final-manuscript-submission deadline approached, Julia was stewing—quite literally—over Judith's request to add more hearty peasant dishes, like cassoulet and other meat dishes.

"I don't know what she's talking about," Julia vented to Paul. "I'm sending her a list of the recipes that are already in the book—all hearty peasant dishes."

Paul lifted his gaze from where he was sorting through recently developed photographs. "Right. You have braised lamb with beans, veal sauté, and beef daube all included. Why hasn't Judith said anything until now? Your deadline is in a matter of weeks."

Julia shrugged. "Maybe it's coming from one of the other editors—Judith said that four of them are cooking through the book." She rose from the table and paced the room. "I don't know who she thinks the 'peasants' are, but they're blue-collar and middle-class cooks like everyone else—with traditional French refinement." She stopped at the counter, where she had a copy of the manuscript, and leafed through the meats section.

"What are you thinking?" Paul asked after a long moment.

She turned to him. "I could add in a few to appease the editors, I suppose. Recipes that I took out when we did the big revision."

"Your cassoulet is excellent," Paul said.

She joined him at the table, now making a different list. The cassoulet Paul referred to was made of French baked beans with sausage and goose. They would have to leave out the goose since it was difficult to find in American supermarkets. She also wrote down *carbonnade à la flamande, pièce de boeuf,* and *paupiettes de boeuf.* "There, that should satisfy her. Now to write to Simca about it."

Simca's reply came back almost immediately, saying that a cassoulet wouldn't be a cassoulet without goose.

Julia wrote back that they had to provide options for American cooks—a point she'd belabored over and over. Simca was just as stubborn, though, pushing back to include the goose as mandatory.

"Simca won't back down, and we're at an *en passant*," Julia told Paul when he found her typing up a recipe revision of cassoulet. "Not surprising. I think we both want to throw the cookbook out the window. But we don't have time for continued debating, so we'll add our usual caveats to the instructions."

"Let me guess," Paul said. "Add goose if you want to cook authentically French, or use preserved goose in a variation of the recipe."

"Exactly." Julia continued to type, then pulled out the page from the typewriter. "There." She handed it to Paul. "Revision done and complete, forever and ever."

Paul read through the entire recipe aloud, and Julia nodded along. She'd been over it so many times, she practically had it memorized.

"Now I'm hungry, my dear." He bent to kiss the top of her head. "Let's get this mailed, and then we'll celebrate."

With the cookbook officially turned in and even more officially out of her hands, and the title finally agreed upon, there was nothing more to do but enjoy their final months in Oslo.

On December 19, Paul sent in his resignation letter. They had enough savings to retire on—modestly. Julia's inheritance continued to do well with the investments her brother had made, and Paul had saved every bit of their renters fees, first at their Olive Street house and now at 103 Irving Street.

"It's time we focus on *you,* Julie," Paul told her as they made their way to the post office, keeping to the snow-cleared sidewalks. "I've turned into an old man, and I've been moving every few years since 1932."

Julia looped her arm through his. "Well, if the cookbook doesn't sell, I can always teach cooking classes."

"We'll make our kitchen grand," Paul said with a smile. "It will be the envy of all of Cambridge."

"I expect nothing less," she teased.

When Paul's resignation was accepted, their departure date for the States was set for the following year in early June. Julia felt peace about moving on to another chapter in their lives, with or without the upcoming cookbook release. Paul continued to have stomach issues—which he'd suffered from occasionally as far back as Ceylon—and Julia knew that her own health had been neglected. Retirement for Paul meant that they could slow down a little and figure out some of their pesky physical issues.

The new year of 1961 began with John F. Kennedy's presidential inauguration and Julia's receiving a final galley deadline of May 18— which meant the book would go to press soon after. She hadn't sent either of her coauthors the galleys—had just written letters with final questions—because she thought if they saw the galleys, they'd want too many changes. And Julia wanted to be on speaking terms with them when the book launched. Her days and weeks were taken up with reviewing the copyedit of the manuscript, looking up minute details, and writing back and forth to Simca and Louisette.

Her coauthors didn't seem too invested in the final details, although Louisette requested that her name be changed on the cover of the book since she'd gone through a divorce. But the publisher said it was too late, the contracts had been signed, and the cover and galleys created.

"What about changing the word *cooking* in the title to *cuisine*?" Louisette had also suggested.

Julia couldn't even entertain making such a request to her publisher; besides *cuisine* was already used in so many other cookbook titles.

Then Avis suddenly decided that her friend Benjamin Fairbank should cook through the recipes, too, and he sent along some picky corrections, so Julia added those in. And one of the copyeditors discovered that there was inconsistent typography throughout the book. These were all great catches, but they also made Julia feel more worried that with so many eyes and hands on the book, new errors might be made.

And the index . . . oh, the index. Julia labored over checking and rechecking the index against the page numbers and adding in some lines she thought were missing. She knew the index would be crucial to the cookbook, but her eyes seemed to cross every time she sat down to go over the next section.

In another letter from Judith, Julia was told that any advance publicity they could rouse would be great for sales when the cookbook finally released. Julia wrote to Simca and Louisette immediately, and Simca was able to secure a series of articles that would include some of their recipes in *Cuisine et Vins de France*. Judith was pleased with that effort, and Julia scrabbled around and was offered an interview in a Norwegian women's magazine.

"What do we know about marketing?" Julia asked her husband when they were cleaning up dinner one evening.

"Nothing?" Paul said. "Oh, wait, I've been marketing exhibits for years."

Julia looped her arms about his neck. "It's time to direct some of your skills toward the cooking world."

"Are we talking about Oslo? Paris? Bonn?"

"New York, of course."

Paul grimaced. "We're going to have to start from the ground up, then. Who do we know in New York? More specifically, journalists who can crow about the amazing Julia Child?"

"We'll make a list of people we know, and hopefully, they'll know people too."

"Another list," Paul deadpanned. "And what is the *publisher* doing for marketing?"

"I'm not entirely sure yet." Julia waved a hand. "I'm sure they'll do something."

"Such a mystery," Paul teased. "We'd better get started on that list. We're going to need all the favors out there."

"Just think of the many people we've fed at our dinner table over the years," Julia said, releasing him and settling at the table to write a few names to start. "They'll all know someone, who will know someone else. And Avis will work through her network too. I'm happy to do private demonstration classes, but I don't want to do anything too public."

Paul watched her scrawl names for a few minutes, then he added several of his own.

"Oh, I forgot to tell you." Julia lifted her gaze. "Simca will be traveling to America for the launch of the book."

"Good news," Paul said. "The two of you will be excellent promoting together. An American who everyone can relate to and a Frenchwoman who everyone will find fascinating."

CHAPTER 32

*Cambridge, Massachusetts
June–October 1961*

"In many ways I hate to leave Oslo, as we are, after a bit over a year and a half, really beginning to get acquainted and feel at home. I really love it here. The city is just the right size, there are some nifty people about, and having free open spaces and beauty all around are all lovely. We have made quite a few good friends here among the Norwegians—not any, so to speak, among the American government types, but that is normal for us, it seems. And I can just feel more good friendships around the corner. Ah well, at least this will be the last time we shall spend 2 years making a life, and then have to leave it all again."

—LETTER FROM JULIA TO AVIS DeVOTO

Julia and Paul had returned to the States in June 1961, but they'd barely had time to sleep in their own bed—their *new* bed, that was, on 103 Irving Street, Cambridge, Massachusetts. They'd visited Charlie and Freddie in Lumberville, and they'd spent time with Avis while she'd been in Vermont.

In all their visits, the most talked about topic was the erection of a wall built in Berlin, meant to divide Soviet-occupied East Berlin from West Berlin. But even more concerning was the purpose behind the wall—to keep East Berliners from leaving. The wall had gone up overnight, and citizens of the city had awakened on August 13 to discover the barbed-wire barricade. Over the next weeks, it had been reinforced, and families had found themselves hopelessly divided.

Julia could only hope that the wall would be temporary while a better political solution could be worked out. And to think that she'd lived in Germany herself.

To make their move to the States feel more permanent and home-like, Paul insisted that they renovate their kitchen to Julia's standards and needs. So they hired an architect to discuss the renovation, deciding on details for a large square center island and extra deep counters.

Always at the back of her mind, morning and night, Julia was counting down the days until the cookbook's release on October 16. In the meantime, since their return to the States, she'd also consulted with a few doctors about some of her nagging health symptoms, and it was recommended that she have a hysterectomy. She wasn't pleased with the diagnosis, but she'd set a surgery date for the beginning of the year at Beth Israel Hospital, after the book launched.

While the clock ticked closer to the release date, they were finally taking a reprieve from traveling. Julia marked another day off on her calendar—today was September 28—and it was proving to be a productive one. Paul was bustling about, making measurements and plans for the wine cellar in the basement, and their hired carpenters were working on the kitchen renovation.

Julia felt antsy, but she didn't want to get in the way of the carpenters or Paul. There was still plenty of unpacking to do, she noted as she surveyed the stacked boxes that lined the hallway and crowded the living room. Some were from their storage out of Washington, DC, and some were from Oslo. With each box opened, it was like traveling back in time to previous memories. The nostalgia hit hard when she came across a box from their Paris years—photographs, Paul's paintings, a French poetry book by Charles Baudelaire, and small souvenirs. When the doorbell rang, it jolted her from her thoughts.

"Who's that?" she mused to her cat. Yes, Julia already had a cat.

The cat meowed but stayed in her sunspot near the living room window.

Julia opened the front door to the postman standing on the porch. "A delivery, Mrs. Child."

"Oh, thank you." She took the wrapped square package. "It's rather heavy."

JULIA

"Yes, ma'am. I hope you have a good day and stay out of the heat." The early autumn day was already warm and muggy.

Julia wished him a good day as well, then stepped back into the hallway. The return address read Alfred Knopf publishing. Her heart rate tripped. Could this be . . . ? She ran her hand over the heavy postal brown wrapping.

"Paul?" she called, then realized he wouldn't be able to hear her from downstairs with all the clamor in the kitchen. She headed to the top of the basement stairs, her mind feeling like it was floating somewhere in the sky. "Paul?"

He appeared a few moments later and took one look at the package she was holding against her chest. "Is that it?" he asked, as if he knew too.

"I think so."

Paul grinned as he headed up the steps. "Well, let's have a look."

Julia dragged in a breath. "All right." She walked into the living room, away from the construction noise, and found an empty space on the couch to sit down.

Paul shifted aside a couple of boxes and joined her.

The cat became curious and rubbed against Julia's leg before proceeding to preen herself.

Julia smoothed her hand once again over the wrapping, then she tugged at a corner. She meant to open it carefully, but in seconds, she was ripping the paper. She'd held the galleys in her hands many times, but this . . . this was different. The turquoise blue of the front cover jacket looked so bright and cheerful. The lettering on the cover alternated between black and red, and the publisher had included a colored illustration of a roast-and-vegetable dish.

"Oh, it's beautiful," she whispered.

"*Mastering the Art of French Cooking*," Paul read aloud. "The only cookbook that explains how to create authentic French dishes in American kitchens with American foods. By Julia Child, Louisette Bertholle, and Simone Beck. Drawings by Sidonie Coryn."

"Is this real?" Julia said with a half laugh. She turned the hefty book to look at the spine. "*Mastering the Art of French Cooking*. Child, Bertholle, Beck. Alfred A. Knopf." Then she turned to the back-cover jacket, and her eyes immediately filled with tears.

Against the dark peach of the back cover was a black-and-white photo that Paul had taken in France—of Julia with Louisette, Simca, and Chef Max Bugnard. She wiped at her eyes, her throat too tight to speak for a moment.

"Photograph by Paul Child," Paul read. "Authors left to right: Julia Child, Louisette Bertholle, and Simone Beck working with their maître, Chef Max Bugnard, over a final flavoring."

Julia leaned her head against Paul's shoulder, and he slipped an arm about her.

"It's so heavy," she said in a rasp.

"Well, it *is* over 700 pages," Paul said, a smile in his tone.

"I don't dare open it," Julia said. "I don't want to crack the spine."

"The book is made to be opened," Paul said with a chuckle. "It's made to be used every day."

Julia nodded and wiped at her cheeks. Then she opened the book, her heart drumming, both nervous and excited. Nervous that she might find an errant typo and excited to have the product of nine years of work finally a tangible thing. For a long while, she and Paul looked through the pages. The chapters were organized by recipe types—Chapter One: Soups, Chapter Two: Sauces, and so on. The French recipe names were translated into English in brackets, then the dish was explained, followed by the listing of ingredients and measurements in addition to the instructions.

The typeset of the book was innovative because Julia had insisted that there be two columns in each recipe to reduce page turning back and forth while following the recipe. The ingredients were listed in the left column, while the instructions were listed on the right-hand side, correlating when they were needed. The detailed line drawings also helped explain the intricate steps of creating French dishes.

"They waterproofed the cover," Paul said. "And I like how the book lays flat no matter which page it's open to."

"Simca and Louisette will love this, don't you think?" Julia asked.

"How could they not?" Paul knew full well the debates and disagreements that had happened over the years. "It's something to be proud of, even if there is more than one way to write a recipe."

Julia elbowed him. "Don't say that in this house again. It's blasphemous."

Paul laughed and wrapped both arms around her. "I think from here on out, I'll be forever known as Julia Child's husband. People will ask, *Who's Paul?*"

"That's not true." Julia leaned her forehead against his. "I wouldn't be here, sitting on this couch with my own cookbook in hand, if it hadn't been for meeting you."

"That's one way to simplify everything," he teased. "You would have found something else to be spectacular at."

The cat decided she wanted attention and leaped onto the couch next to them and head bumped Julia's arm with a meow. "All right. I think I have a cat to feed, and then I'm calling Avis and Dort. Today, the long-distance telephone charges will be worth it."

"You'd better call Judith too," Paul said.

"Of course."

The phone rang then, and Paul rose to answer it. "Yes, yes, she's here. Of course." He mouthed to Julia before handing over the receiver. "Speaking of the devil."

Julia answered and immediately thanked Judith for sending the book early.

"What do you think?" Judith asked.

"I can't even describe how beautiful it is, dearie," Julia said. "It took my breath away, quite literally. I don't know how I'm so lucky to have you as an editor and to have Knopf believe in the book and create such a wonderful product. It weighs a ton!"

"I'm happy you love the final product," Judith said. "I'm also calling with good news. I don't know how it will all turn out, but things are positive for now."

"What are you talking about?" Julia gave Paul a meaningful glance.

"Well, I was wracking my brain, trying to figure out whose hands we could get this cookbook into to give us some credentials," Judith said. "So I called up Craig Claiborne and told him about your remarkable book."

Julia's pulse skittered. Craig Claiborne was the esteemed food editor of *The New York Times*. He was considered reining authority on cookbooks.

"We met for lunch," Judith continued. "This was about a month ago, and I waited to tell you because I didn't know if anything would come of it. Anyway, we went to a French café near his office, and I talked to him about your book. He was gracious but didn't seem all that interested."

Julia felt like she was on a boat careening up and down huge waves. Did this story have a good outcome or not?

"I told him about how my husband and I love to cook together, grilling on our penthouse terrace. That caught his attention."

Julia frowned. Where was this all going?

"Claiborne said that if I'd invite him to one of my husband's grilled dinners and we let him write about us cooking together, he'd look at your book."

Julia was holding her breath. Had he looked at it? If not, *when* would he look at it?

"So, he came for dinner in August—it was blazing hot—and Evan grilled up lamb. We chatted and had a great time, and Claiborne wrote his article."

Julia remembered reading that article now. She'd even told Judith she enjoyed it . . . but, at the time, hadn't realized there'd been strings attached.

"To get to my point," Judith said with a laugh, "I heard from Claiborne. He's read your cookbook and says it will be a classic."

Julia's heart thudded, and she reached for Paul's hand. He'd heard enough of the conversation to know that this was good news.

"Do you think he'll write about it in the *Times*?" Julia asked, hardly daring to hope.

"I think he will," Judith said. "I don't know when, but I replied back to him with a thank-you and a reminder of the publication date."

JULIA

"Two weeks . . ." Julia sighed. "I guess we'll know soon enough."

"An article will be excellent but won't necessarily sell books," Judith said, a warning note in her voice.

Julia straightened at this. "Why not? I thought press would sell books—articles, interviews, and the like."

"It will all help toward the sum total, but the *Times* readership is upscale. We need to get you in front of the general population—readers—buyers."

"As you know, I have cooking demonstrations already set up," Julia said.

"And those will all be excellent," Judith said. "I'm working on a television spot with the *Today* show. You and Simone can do a cooking demonstration."

Julia blinked. She didn't watch a lot of television. In fact, they had yet to own one. But everyone knew what the *Today* show was. Her mind buzzed with questions and scenarios. If they got the spot, what would they cook? What would they wear? What would they say? "When will you find out?" Julia asked.

"Soon, I hope," Judith said. "I told them about Simone's arrival date and the book release date. So hopefully, it will be either launch day or soon after. Your host will be John Chancellor, who replaced Dave Garroway."

After hanging up with Judith, Julia turned to Paul. "Did you hear that? We might be on the *Today* show, and Claiborne might be writing an article about the book." She laughed. "We might be selling books after all."

"I heard it," Paul said, his smile growing. "You'll definitely be selling books."

On October 18, two days after the official and somewhat anticlimactic release of the book, *The New York Times* ran an article written by Claiborne, which was full of praise.

Julia couldn't read the article fast enough, looking for anything negative.

This is the most comprehensive, laudable, and monumental work . . .

It will probably remain as the definitive work for nonprofessionals . . .
For those who take fundamental delight in the pleasures of cuisine . . .
It is written in the simplest terms possible and without compromise or condescension . . .
The recipes are glorious . . .

Claiborne pointed out that although the cassoulet recipe was nearly six pages long, there wasn't a wasted syllable. She handed the article over to Paul, who read it aloud. By the time he finished, they were both wiping their eyes.

"His only complaint was that he doesn't like our use of the garlic press, and he noticed we didn't have any recipes for croissants or puff pastry." Relief jolted through Julia. "But he liked the book, truly liked it. I couldn't ask for a better review."

"He loved the book," Paul said, leaning close to kiss her. "Now, you should wake up Simca and tell her."

Simca had arrived and was staying with them, but she was dealing with jet lag. Later today, they'd be heading to New York and staying with Julia and Paul's niece Rachel Child, who had an apartment on the Upper West Side. There, in Rachel's kitchen, they'd practice for the *Today* show appearance.

After telling Simca the good news, they set to packing. They'd had plenty of debates over what to cook on the show, but since they wouldn't have a stove, only an electric burner, they'd settled on demonstrating an omelet.

"You'll have two minutes for everything," Paul told Simca as they set up the kitchen in Rachel's apartment.

"Two minutes?" Simca protested. "We can't cook anything in two minutes."

"That's why we're making an omelet," Julia reminded her friend. Of course Simca knew that, but it seemed that the more flustered she grew, the more stubborn she became. Her accent was much thicker, too, when she was upset.

"Ready for another round?" Paul asked, holding up his camera as if he were filming them.

Rachel took her place next to him, where they were sitting on garbage cans on the opposite side of the counter from Julia and Simca.

Julia smiled directly at Paul's camera—this wasn't their first run-through—and she was feeling more natural. But Simca was looking everywhere but the camera.

"Hello, I'm Julia Child, and I'm here with my coauthor . . ." She paused for Simca to speak.

Simca cleared her throat and gripped her hands together in front of her. "I am Simone Beck, and I am from Paris, France."

Julia understood her friend perfectly, but Paul raised a hand. "Again. I can't understand Simca."

Simca threw him a dark look, then said, "I'm Simone Beck, and I'm from Paris, France."

She practically spat out the words, and Julia decided to just move on, hoping Paul wouldn't keep stopping them. It was only irking Simca more.

Julia said, "We're the authors of the new cookbook called *Mastering the Art of French Cooking*." She paused again.

"We're demonstrating how to cook a French omelet," Simca said, rushing through the words so that not even Julia could decipher what she said.

"Speak more slowly and clearly," Paul interrupted.

Julia gave the faux camera a friendly smile. "First, turn on the burner and get the pan warming with a dab of butter, then we'll crack the eggs." She paused again, but Simca didn't say anything, although she picked up two eggs and cracked them at the same time on the edge of a metal bowl.

Well then. "We'll blend the eggs right in the pan as they are heating up," Julia said.

The afternoon continued on, with more practicing and Simca becoming quieter. Julia reminded her to stay calm and not to worry about the time—they'd get the omelet done.

The following morning, Julia wasn't sure if she'd slept more than a few hours, because they were on their way to the RCA building on West Forty-Ninth Street at the first sign of dawn.

As they headed up the elevator to Studio 3K, Paul said, "Think of yourself in your own kitchen. Look at Rachel and me in the audience and talk to us like we're in the kitchen together. Don't worry about all the other people."

Julia could do that, she knew it. She didn't really have any other choice at this point. But what about Simca? Her back was straighter than a flagpole, her shoulders stiff, and her hands clenched tight.

"Don't worry, Simca," she told her friend, resting her hand on Simca's shoulder. "I'll take the lead if you want. And you can fill in wherever you feel comfortable."

Simca nodded but still said nothing.

After meeting John Chancellor, they were quickly ushered into their places and set up for the demonstration. Julia spotted Paul in the audience, smiled at him, then surveyed the rest of the audience. Everyone looked friendly and welcoming. Interested.

"See, it will be all right," Julia told Simca.

But her friend looked like she'd swallowed lime juice.

As the cameras started rolling, Julia and Simca made their introduction, but when John Chancellor asked questions, Julia was the one to answer. Somehow, she was able to speak coherently—or at least she thought so since her stomach felt tight, her voice pitched too high, and her breathing seemed erratic. She didn't mind the audience or the cameras so much, but the thought of doing this live and not having any retakes made her hyperaware of the bright lights, the mute Simca by her side, and the pressure of making such a public debut with her cookbook. She wanted to make her publisher proud. She tried to focus her thoughts on the steps of cooking the omelet and to tell herself this wasn't that much different from other cooking classes she'd taught, save for the shortened time.

Everything was over much too quickly, but they'd made the omelet, and the audience had seemed receptive. They hurried off the set, where Paul and Rachel waited.

"You were perfect," Paul said, his whole face beaming. "If I didn't already have a copy of the cookbook at home, I'd be rushing to get one now."

JULIA

Julia hugged him. "I'm sure you're being nice. I don't remember a thing I said."

"You were a natural in front of the camera," Rachel added. "Like you've been doing it all your life."

Julia scoffed. "It was all a blur. I must have been on autopilot. Did it really happen? Should you pinch me?"

Rachel laughed. "No pinching necessary. It really happened, and you were wonderful."

CHAPTER 33

New York City
October–December 1961

"As a way to earn money and get a class going I gave cooking lessons at a friend's house for her friends. I would give them a great lunch, such as poached egg on mushroom and leek salad, a little pastry thing with béarnaise sauce, and chocolate cake. I did not have to worry about buying the food or getting the friends; I only charged $50 dollars; sometimes I would buy the food and give them the bill. They provided the wine. Then I would leave them with the dishes. I would leave with $200. I would not have made money in my own home. For all that work, you should make some money."

—JULIA CHILD, IN AN INTERVIEW WITH FOOD WRITER BARBARA SIMS-BELL

The day after the *Today* show appearance, Julia and Simca were scheduled to do a cooking demonstration at Bloomingdale's. Judith Jones had warned them that there might only be a few shoppers in attendance.

"What's the line for?" Julia asked as their taxi pulled up to the front of the building, its towering presence and multiple floors sending a thrill through Julia.

Everyone inside the car craned their necks to get a better view.

"I think . . . they're here for the cookbook," Paul said. "Look, a few of them are holding the book."

It was true, Julia realized. The line extended down the sidewalk, and several women held the 700-plus-page cookbook.

"Do you think they all read the *Times* article?" Simca asked.

"That or watched us on the *Today* show," Julia said.

"The show does have four million viewers," Paul said.

After the taxi stopped, Paul hopped out and opened their doors with a flourish. Julia and Simca stepped out into the crisp fall weather. Overhead, the sky was cloudless, and the sun seemed to be smiling down on them. Julia nodded toward the line of people, giving them a smile. The women stared back at her, curiosity in their gazes.

Paul grabbed the box of their equipment and groceries, and they all walked into the department store, with its black-and-white checkered floors. Inside, they were greeted and fussed over by the employees, who directed them where to set up.

Once they were ready, Bloomingdale's doors were officially opened, and the customers poured in. Those who didn't already have the cookbook bought one at the registers. Julia and Simca were outfitted with microphones, and they began their demonstration. Simca seemed more at ease with this type of audience since there were no rolling cameras, and she even answered several questions. Paul and Rachel sat in the back row, smiling the entire time.

The day was a whirlwind, and they spent hours signing the cookbook, even though the store employees said that they could leave because the allotted book-signing time had ended. But Julia decided that if these women, and a few men, had made the effort to come all this way to buy her book, she'd sign every last one of them, making sure she spoke to each person.

When Julia and Paul returned to their home in Cambridge at the end of the week, Judith had good news for them. "We're ordering another print run of 10,000 copies."

"Are we a best seller, then?" Julia asked, half joking.

"It has potential," Judith said. "We can't make any guarantees, but we're hoping to maintain steady sales. It doesn't hurt that our new US president loves French food. Did you know that he frequents Chambord and Lutèce as well as La Carvelle? He also has a French chef in the White House. This is all creating the perfect scenario since Americans are reviving their interest in French food. We thought it would take a year to sell out of the first print run, but it's moving quicker than we thought. And we're still waiting for more bookstore orders."

"Send us the updated list," Julia said. "We leave in a few days for our trek across the country."

It was a marketing plan that Julia and Simca had been working on for months. They'd contacted friends and family across the States, asking for a place to stay and requesting introductions to places where they could do a cooking demo and have it announced in the local paper. Paul would be the one in charge of equipment, set up, and clean up. He had retired just in time. So far, they'd scheduled stops in Washington, DC, Detroit, Chicago, San Francisco, and Los Angeles. They'd reach Pasadena by Thanksgiving, and they planned to share the holiday with her father and Phila.

Knopf had nothing in place that would reimburse them—that would all have to be made in the sales of books. So Julia and Simca were footing the travel expenses, and they hoped to earn out their royalty advance and start making a profit.

"Excellent," Judith said on the other end of the phone call. "You two are going above and beyond any of our other authors. Oh, by the way, James Beard wants to meet you, as well as some other food editors from the ladies' magazines. They might have ignored you over the years, but now they can't anymore. I also want you to visit with Dione Lucas—she'll be a big help in preparing you for all the cooking demonstrations you have planned."

Julia felt elation float through her. Dione Lucas ran a combined restaurant and cooking school called the Egg Basket, on Fifty-Ninth Street. She'd be an excellent resource. But Julia was most excited to meet the larger-than-life James Beard. He had multiple cookbooks published, wrote monthly articles for *Gourmet*, had done numerous television appearances, and had developed menus for some of New York's upscale restaurants. He was a culinary legend, but more importantly, Julia respected his cooking techniques.

The following week, Judith coordinated a meeting with James Beard at his townhouse on Tenth Street in Greenwich Village.

Julia was instantly charmed by James, who welcomed them to his home with warmth.

The man was both large in size and personality. "I've laid out a small spread," he told them. "Smithfield ham sliced so thinly you can breathe through it, and Italian mustard fruits that will make your eyes cross."

JULIA

Julia couldn't help but laugh.

"And if anyone wants a nibble of puree of spinach, help yourself." He offered them drinks as well, then said, "Now, tell me all about yourselves and your cookbook."

They spent a relaxed afternoon with James, and at the end of it all, he told them he'd introduce them to the culinary world of New York. "You've got to meet everyone now that you've become one of us. I'll introduce you to the food professionals, the top chefs, and the most influential food editors. A few of us will get together and host a launch party for your book. You say you'll be traveling to do cooking demonstrations for a couple of months?"

Julia could barely edge a word in. "Yes, we'll be back in December."

"It's settled, then," James said. "We'll hold the party mid-December."

Julia didn't know what to say, just that her mind was spinning with all that James told them. He either seemed impressed with their cookbook or just wanted to celebrate it; she wasn't sure which. Regardless, James seemed to know everyone in the culinary world, and Julia wouldn't mind the introductions. This was a new world for her, and any guidance would be welcome.

The first stop on their promotional tour was Gross Pointe, Michigan. Upon arrival, they discovered that the bookstores had sold out of their cookbook, and women showed up in droves to their cooking demonstrations.

Julia and Simca fell into a comfortable rhythm in their demonstrations. Julia did most of the talking, but everyone seemed to hang on Simca's words when she added in tidbits. As they signed books after their demonstrations, sometimes two or three hundred books in a sitting, Julia made it a point to visit with each person, albeit briefly. She would often ask the women, "What are you serving for dinner tonight, dearie?" Or sometimes, she'd ask them what their favorite dish was.

Once in a while, the women would ask for advice on a particular technique, and Julia had to come up with an answer on the spot.

"You are so talented," one woman gushed to Julia.

"My days are so routine," another woman said. "Doing the same chores day in and day out, but this cookbook makes me feel like I can be creative again."

"I didn't know I loved cooking until I tried the duck *à l'orange*," another woman said. "You should have seen my husband's expression. Now he wants to invite his boss over for dinner."

"My daughter wants to try the recipes with me," a woman told Julia. "She spent most of her teenage years hardly saying a word to me, and now we're in the kitchen every day together."

From city to city, they traveled, Julia and Simca focusing on their shared loves and ignoring their differences, Paul doing the brunt of the physical work. Most of the days were long and tiring but, oh, how rewarding.

"You absolutely shine when you're around all these people, my dear," Paul told her one evening when they were staying in the guest room of a friend's house. "You're earning one loyal fan at a time. They're not going to ever forget you, and they'll be scooping up your next cookbook like butterscotch candy."

"Hold on," Julia said, sitting on the corner of the bed to take off her shoes. "*Another* cookbook?"

"Have you forgotten? French bread? You need a book for that recipe." Paul's smile was teasing.

"I did want to do that," she said. "But every attempt I've made, I've failed."

Paul sat next to her on the bed, taking off his own shoes. "That's because you've always been caught up in volume 1."

Julia looked over at her husband and saw his clear gaze, his wry smile. "You think I should really write another cookbook? With Simone?"

"I think you should finish what you started—what you originally envisioned," he said. "I'll stay retired. Heaven knows that I'm busier on this promotional tour than I've ever been at any job. You have me working sunup to sundown."

"You are a very good assistant, dearie," Julia said. "Who knew that all your cultural attaché training would prepare you to manage the microphones, stage lights, tables, schedules, and scrubbing dirty bowls out?"

"Always had the makings of a stage manager, it seems." He leaned close to kiss her, and she looped her arms about his neck.

"Have I told you how much I appreciate you and love you?"

"Occasionally." He grinned. "Now, remember that when we're at your father's home and he's throwing out barbs left and right."

Pop was eighty-two now, and Julia knew the old man still hadn't changed his caustic viewpoint of life. "Maybe his recent illness has mellowed him out." She linked her hand with Paul's. They'd both been worried when they'd received the news about Pop contracting some sort of virus that had kept him bedridden for weeks. But now he was on the mend.

Paul squeezed her hand.

"Read to me," Julia said. "Unless you're too tired."

"I'll read to you."

They settled into bed, and Julia listened to Paul's mellow tone as he read a chapter of *The City in History* by Lewis Mumford.

The next days raced by as they attended one demonstration after another, cooking dishes like *soufflé de turbot*, *quiche a Roquefort*, and *Reine de Saba* cake. Their audience was growing, and at a theater in San Marino, California, three hundred fifty women attended.

Their Thanksgiving spent in Pasadena was full of the usual—walking on eggshells, and not ones that Julia had cracked herself. Her elderly father had fully recovered from his illness, and he didn't seem too interested in Paul's or Simca's stories about the promotional tour. A cookbook was a cookbook, in Pop's opinion. Phila was much more welcoming and positive. And it was wonderful to spend time with Dort and her little family. But overall, Julia was more than happy to return back to the East Coast and her cozy home and life she'd established with Paul.

James Beard made good on his word, and the culinary community welcomed Julia and Simca with open arms at a book launch party at the Egg Basket. Everyone was friendly, and when Julia told James about their on-the-road events, he seemed duly impressed.

"You're very likeable, Julia," he told her. "Have you ever thought about television?"

Julia had to laugh at that, remembering all the stress and work for a two-minute spot on the *Today* show. Imagine doing longer demonstrations on a regular basis in front of rolling cameras. Not that she minded the cameras so much, but there was really no flexibility or much room for error. She glanced over to where Simca was chatting with another group of people. "I think it would give my coauthor a heart attack."

James chuckled. "She's returning to France soon, right? It makes more sense for you to do the cooking show—you're American, and the show will be for American cooks. Maybe on your next cookbook you can adjust royalties."

Julia had never talked to James about her publishing contract, but she also had quickly learned that the publishing world was very, very small and gossip moved like a brushfire.

"Aren't there enough cooking shows on television?" she asked.

"There are plenty, but they're only getting more popular," James said. "And there's room for a French cook like yourself. My attempts have flopped. I'm not a warm and fuzzy personality—which is what's needed to connect to an audience."

"And I'm that type?"

James lifted his glass in a sort of salute. "You are. You're one of us, sure, but you're also one of them: a housewife, a woman of a certain age, a woman who learned to cook when she first married—these are all things that many people can relate to."

Julia tried not to bristle at James's pigeonholing her book into the housewife category. "My cookbook isn't geared toward housewives specifically."

"Oh, I know that." James dipped his chin. "We can't fool ourselves into thinking they aren't our bread and butter."

"You may be right," Julia said. "But I think you've put too much confidence in me."

CHAPTER 34

Cambridge, Massachusetts
February–April 1962

"Julia and Paul appeared with copper bowl, whip, apron, and a dozen eggs for her interview. 'It was my idea to bring on the whisk and bowl and hot plate. Educational television was just talking heads, and I did not know what we could talk about for that long, so I brought the eggs,' said Julia. The interview and demonstration were not taped, as usual, because of the expense of tape ($220 to $300) and the difficulty of storing it."

—JULIA CHILD

After Julia's recovery from her hysterectomy, she was notified that she'd been invited to appear on the television show *I've Been Reading* by the assistant producer, Miffy Goodhart, who apparently was a fan of her book. Julia would appear alone since Simca had returned to France. Professor Albert Duhamel of Boston College was the host of the show, interviewing authors about their books. Since there was no budget for appearance or travel fees, most of the authors were from the Boston area.

Julia accepted the invitation, after all she was an author living in the Boston area, but she didn't want to sit on a chair and answer interview questions. She wanted to do a cooking demonstration, so she called up the WGBH-TV phone number. A man answered, and after determining the man's name as Russ Morash, she said, "I'd like to put in a request for a hot plate for my appearance on Professor Duhamel's program."

The man didn't answer for a moment, and when Julia was about to repeat her request, he said, "You want . . . *what?*"

"A hot plate, dearie, so I can make an omelet. I'll bring all the ingredients."

Another long pause, then Russ Morash said, "From my experience, this is a first, but I'll pass it on to our assistant producer, Miffy Goodheart."

Julia wasn't fazed by the man's surprise. Certainly they'd never had a cooking demonstration on the show before, so she planned to bring everything else. Requesting a hot plate wasn't such a big deal, was it?

When she arrived on the set on February 11, 1962, with Paul at her side, she was ready. At least, she hoped. She and Paul had gone through the demonstration at least a dozen times. She'd agonized over what to wear and had finally settled on a white blouse, her red badge that said Gourmandes, and a pleated skirt. They entered the building and were greeted with a general haze of cigarette smoke.

Immediately, Miffy Goodhart eagerly greeted her. "I'm so pleased to meet you, Mrs. Child," Miffy gushed, looking up at her. "Everyone in Cambridge has been talking about your wonderful cookbook. I think your appearance will appeal to younger viewers, and it will be nice to offer something other than straight-laced literature, politics, and science. Lighten the mood around here, you know."

Julia hadn't followed the "mood" of the program, but she figured this appearance would help cookbook sales and maybe earn her some more speaking or demonstration events.

"I hope my request for a hot plate wasn't too demanding," she said.

"Oh, not at all." Miffy laughed. "It created a buzz, but in a good way. Everyone is looking forward to meeting you."

"Even the professor?" Julia teased.

"Especially the professor."

"I promise it will be fun, dearie," Julia told Miffy. "We'll teach the professor a thing or two. Just watch."

Miffy grinned, then took Julia on the rounds to meet Professor Al Duhamel and the cameraman. Other staff consisted of Cambridge housewives, who apparently volunteered as support staff.

"There's to be a cooking demonstration?" Julia was asked more than once. They wouldn't have time for any rehearsal, and she could see that the cameraman was a bit out of his element. Oh well, they'd all figure it out together.

Paul was already unloading the groceries onto the coffee table that was part of the set, nestled between two leather chairs. Next, Paul placed her long-handled omelet pan next to the hot-plate burner.

The cameraman was staring at Julia and, in fact, circled her, looking her up and down.

"Do you have a question?" Julia finally asked.

"How am I supposed to light you?"

Julia laughed. Obviously, the man hadn't dealt with TV guests who would be standing, let alone someone as tall as she. "I guess you've never worked with a T-Rex before?"

His lips quirked, consternation still in his eyes.

"How about we raise the burner?" She crossed to the coffee table and slid a few books that might have been props under the burner so it would bring it closer to the action. "Is this better?"

The cameraman peered into his camera, then raised his hand. "Much better."

Soon, Julia took a seat in the leather chair opposite Al Duhamel, who was already acting the conciliatory host, his smile friendly, his voice assured. The camera started rolling, and Julia told herself to focus on Al and not search for her husband in the small audience. She barely heard the professor's complimentary introduction to her cookbook, and then it was her turn to do the demonstration.

She stood from the chair and stepped behind the coffee table. "I only have a hot plate for this demonstration, so I'm going to make an omelet." She nodded to the cameraman, who'd inched closer. "Omelets are wonderful and quick to make, and you don't need a lot of equipment."

She turned on the burner and set the pan atop it. Then she cracked the eggs on the side of the copper bowl. Next, she blended them with a fork. She paused to add butter to the warming pan. "Now, you want to use real butter in your pan. It will create a delicious flavor when mixed with your eggs. The omelet should be thrilling in your mouth."

The butter began to sizzle in the pan.

"Once your eggs are beaten, you pour them into your omelet pan." She glanced at the camera. "Everyone needs an omelet pan, yes?" She picked up the bowl. "You need to be attentive because this will cook very fast—in about thirty seconds."

Julia poured the mixture into the pan, and the golden liquid began to bubble almost instantly. She grasped the long handle and began to jiggle the pan back and forth, moving the egg mixture around the pan as it cooked. "You might be wondering how I fell in love with French cooking and why I've spent years working on a cookbook with my coauthors. Once you taste French food, you'll understand."

She looked over at her host, who seemed to be staring at her in disbelief. He gave her a smile, though, and she smiled back. "This omelet will convert everyone because it's so delicious."

In a short time, just as she told the audience, the omelet was finished. "Now, we just slide it onto a plate." She realized too late that there was only one fork. "Try it, Professor. You take the first bite."

She forked up a section of the omelet and held it up.

Al stood, hesitated, then crossed to her, his expression dubious. He ate right off the fork, and Julia smiled, waiting for the moment she knew would come.

Al's face transformed as he chewed, morphing from skepticism to delight.

"There," Julia said in a triumphant tone. "The omelet is delicious, isn't it?"

Al's smile appeared. "It certainly is, Mrs. Child. Thank you for demonstrating an omelet for our viewers." He continued to say a few more things about the cookbook, but Julia was scanning for Paul's face beyond the bright lights. There. He sat beyond the halo of lights. His hands clasped together. Beaming.

"You were excellent," Paul said after they'd gathered their equipment, thanked everyone, and headed home.

"It was fun," Julia said, adrenaline still buzzing through her. "Truly fun. I didn't feel stressed at all once it started. I didn't have to worry

JULIA

about Simca being silent or the intimidation of the *Today* show. I could just be myself."

"And that's what made it so wonderful, my dear," Paul said. "You were your lovely self. Vivacious, witty, and charming."

Julia had to kiss him for that. "Well, it was a fun experiment, but I guess I should buckle down and begin writing the next cookbook since sales continue to be strong."

Paul nodded, but there was a gleam of confidence in his eye that Julia didn't quite understand until Russ Morash showed up on their doorstep two months later.

Julia invited the man in.

Miffy had called her to tell her that the television station had received a lot of positive feedback—phone calls and letters—after her appearance. And would she be willing to meet with Russ Morash?

Paul had immediately been excited, but Julia couldn't imagine why the man would come all the way to 103 Irving Street to meet her—since her appearance on the show was long over.

Julia ushered him into the house, and she and Paul brought him into the kitchen, where they had coffee waiting. Russ was in his late twenties, his dark hair cut short.

"You probably already have an inkling of what this is all about," Russ said, looking between the two. "Miffy has been ecstatic over the response we received after your appearance. We had multiple calls asking when you'd be back on the air."

Julia stared at Russ. She knew this—but hearing it from Russ, in person, felt like it carried more weight.

"I'll have to admit," Russ continued, "I'm no cook, and my wife, Marian, works—so we're content with franks-and-beans casseroles. Growing up, my mother had good intentions when cooking, but she cooked everything until it was unrecognizable and tasteless. The faster we ate the mystery food, the faster we could be excused from the table."

Julia tried not to wince, but she was pretty sure she failed.

"Long story short, Miffy has been petitioning me and our program manager, Bob Larsen. She's also called Dave Davis, who is the station manager, and Henry Morgenthau, who runs the whole operation." He paused, a wry smile on his face. "She's not taking *no* for an answer."

"No for *what* answer?" Julia asked, even though her drumming heart told her what might be happening—that Paul's predictions were coming true.

Russ spread his hands on the tabletop. "We want to offer a cooking show in our lineup, and we want you to be the cook. You have a gregarious personality, you have a compelling range in your voice, and you know your way around a recipe." Before she could answer, he continued, "We don't have a studio to accommodate a kitchen right now, and I don't know what kind of resources we can gather, but everyone who's watched your demonstration on *I've Been Reading* agrees—you're too talented and charismatic on television to *not* be on a cooking show."

Julia couldn't speak for a moment, and Paul reached over and squeezed her hand. She had no doubt what his answer was; she could practically feel the excitement reverberating from him.

"If you need time to think about it, we understand," Russ continued. "The station wants to put together three pilots and see how they do. If all goes well, then we'd plan out a full season of twenty-six shows."

Julia gasped; she couldn't help it. Her own television *series*? Paul's hold on her hand tightened. She was nearly fifty years old, and it was as if the opportunity of a lifetime had dropped into her lap. How could she turn this down? She knew there was a lot to work out, a lot to decide, a lot to prepare, but excitement hummed along her skin, making the hairs on her arms rise.

"I'd love to film the pilots," Julia said. "What's on the menu? Any preferences?"

"That's your department, Mrs. Child," Russ said.

"Oh, call me Julia, dearie."

Russ was still grinning when he said, "What about that omelet you made? Can you turn that into a thirty-minute show? We've heard about nothing except *omelet this* and *omelet that* for the past two months."

Julia threw a smile at Paul, then said, "Sure. I mean, there are different fillings that can be made, and if I cover those, plus explain the importance of the height of the flame and the type of pan and serving options, we could definitely fill up an entire show."

"Excellent," Russ said.

Julia's mind was racing full steam ahead. "How about in one of the pilots, we demonstrate a soufflé? It's the number-one question asked when I was on the road doing cooking demonstrations. Many people avoid the soufflé because they worry it will collapse."

"I think that sounds excellent too," Russ said.

Julia glanced at her husband. "And the third pilot show will be coq au vin, a true French classic."

That first meeting at their home with Russ Morash was one of many as they worked through the decisions of each stage in putting the show together. Russ told her that she'd have to practice speaking while cooking, and Paul took the lead on that. She and Paul spent hours in the kitchen as she practiced each recipe and kept up a running commentary. No two practices were alike, but Paul didn't complain, and the laughter was plenty.

The timing was critical, and during their rehearsals, they broke down each step. Some things had to be prepared in advance, or there wouldn't be a finished product at the end of thirty minutes. Paul became the master of the stopwatch, timing each step, then timing the entire performance.

"The camera needs to become your best friend," Russ had told Julia during one of their meetings. "On the other side of that camera is a person you need to make feel that you really care about them."

Meanwhile, Russ worked to find them a location and finally settled on a utility kitchen at the Boston Gas Company—a place where the company showed contractors how to operate a gas flame. The kitchen had a nice center island, with a cooktop cut into it, and ample cabinets. The only problem was that there was no running water. They'd have to find a workaround.

Then the debates began of what to call the cooking show. This reminded Julia of the headache of coming up with the title of the cookbook. So many people putting in their opinions made for a chaotic process. The title needed to be no more than three words and have the word *French* in it.

Paul and Julia brainstormed, laughing themselves silly over some of their ideas: *Gourmet Kitchen, Cuisine Magic, Table d'Hôte* . . . Finally, Russ Morash and his assistant, Ruth Lockwood, came up with *The French Chef.*

Julia wasn't French, of course, or a chef, but for the purposes of the show, she'd be cooking all things French. But everyone liked it, and it was straightforward, so Julia agreed.

CHAPTER 35

Boston, Massachusetts
May–June 1962

"We used 16 or 35 millimeter black-and-white film which ran continuously during the taping. There was no editing, no cutting in, and the only way to edit videotape was to literally cut the tape with a razor and tape it. We used two cameras, each the size of a coffee table, four only for the Boston Symphony, and when Julia moved from the stove to the refrigerator it was a very big deal that took careful planning."

—RUSS MORASH, WGBH-TV

Julia felt like she was writing her cookbook all over again with the amount of time she spent in her kitchen. This time, though, it was with Paul, and they were breaking down and staging the cooking demonstrations for the three shows she'd be doing for *The French Chef*.

Paul became the expert stage manager, and he oversaw everything from the arrangement of the ingredients to what Julia said and when to making sure they stayed within the allotted amount of time.

Russ Morash made several visits to their home with updates and advice. He told them that a group of women volunteers was decorating the set, putting up curtains, selecting kitchen items, coordinating napkins for each show, and more.

Each day, Julia checked in with Phila and Dort. Pop wasn't doing well and had gone through another bout of illness. The doctors were running tests because his weight loss was concerning. Finally, they determined that he had cancer, but he was told that he had a good five to six years left. His weight kept dropping, though, and Julia and Paul booked a trip to Pasadena.

Only hours after their arrival, her father took his last breath. In his final moments, he'd been surrounded by his children and grandchildren.

"I'm grateful it was a peaceful passing," Dort said in the quiet as the two sisters sat on the back terrace, like they had in their younger years. The house had settled down for the night, everyone else having retired to bed.

Despite her exhaustion, Julia couldn't sleep, and it seemed that neither could Dort.

"I wish I would have arrived sooner," Julia said. "He wasn't even talking when I finally made it."

Dort reached over and grasped Julia's hand. "He knew you were there."

Julia blinked against the stinging in her eyes. Finally, the tears were coming. "I hope so, unless it made him agitated since I married an intellectual."

"He was proud of you, you know," Dort said. "Both of you. He always talked about your adventures."

"You mean *complained*?" Julia said in a light tone, wiping at her eyes.

"That was his way." Dort shrugged. "He wasn't going to change in his eighties."

Julia released a breath, and they sat in silence for several minutes. "Maybe it was a blessing to go now and not drag on with the cancer. He didn't even look like himself after losing so much weight. Really, he was a shell of who he used to be."

Dort released her hand. "It's a strange thing to lose your last living parent. Makes me feel old too. As if life has passed by much too quickly, and it makes me wonder if I should have done anything differently."

Julia turned her head to gaze at her sister's profile. The older they grew, the more they resembled each other. "You took great care of Pop. When I was in Ceylon all that time and other times while I was living abroad."

"I mostly did it for Phila's sake," Dort said. "She's wonderful."

Julia wholeheartedly agreed.

JULIA

Her sister turned to look at her. Somehow, with a lot of twists and turns in their lives, they'd both found their own paths to happiness. And for that, Julia was grateful.

"What's this?" John asked, coming out onto the terrace, drink in hand. "I didn't know there was a family meeting going on."

"Oh, sit down," Julia said, waving at the nearby lounge chair. "We were plotting a way to cut you out of the will."

John settled on a chair. "It's good to see both of my sisters in one place, despite the circumstances. I don't remember the last time the three of us were together."

"That's because you're getting gray and old," Dort said. "Your memory is going."

"I'll never be as old as you two," he said.

Julia smirked. "I'm starting my second life. Haven't you heard, I'm a best-selling cookbook author now."

Both of her siblings groaned, then laughed.

"I think you just volunteered to cook us dinner tomorrow," Dort said.

Julia went silent at that. She thought of the few times she'd cooked in her childhood home—very few times. "It would be an honor. I'll make something that even Pop would love if he were here."

The next night, she cooked open-faced French omelets and garnished them with onions, peppers, tomatoes, and ham. As she served the meal, she told her siblings about how savory omelets were eaten for supper in France. Their conversation shifted from childhood memories to sharing stories about both their father and mother.

By the following morning, Julia finally felt ready to say goodbye to her siblings. With Paul stoically waiting with the luggage and hired car, she embraced each of them one last time.

When she and Paul arrived back in Cambridge, she felt more settled and at peace with Pop's death. He hadn't been the easiest father to communicate with, but he'd always watched out for her and offered generous help. He loved in his own way.

At home, Julia was greeted with flowers and cards from friends near and far.

Preparations for *The French Chef* started in a flurry. In the evenings, Julia wrote letters to her siblings, reminiscing about their childhood. She also kept Simca and Louisette updated on the progress of the show preparations. Avis dropped by regularly for visits, and they discussed every detail imaginable.

And finally, June 18 arrived—the day they'd film the first pilot. They would film the next two pilots on June 25. Today, for "The French Omelet," they'd film straight through, with no retakes or edits, so there was little room for error.

As Julia watched the final bustle of preparations taking place on the set and Russ Morash give his camera technicians their final instructions for their various angles and assigned shots, she tried to remember all the things that Paul had coached her on: not to breathe so fast or gasp. Not to close her eyes while she was talking or thinking of what needed to be said or done next.

Once the cameramen knew their instructions, Julia moved in and spread out her notes on the center island with the cooktop. The stage directions and dialog took up the right-hand side of the pages, and the camera shots were on the left side. Paul also had his own directions to help with the flow of the demonstration, such as removing the stack molds when she started buttering and removing the frying pan and its copper cover when she began the *pipérade*.

As Russ called for everyone to take their places, Paul gave Julia a quick kiss, then stepped to his spot.

They'd start with a closeup camera shot of the butter sizzling in the omelet pan. The camera would pan out, showing Julia mixing the eggs in a bowl, then pouring them into the pan. Within seconds, it would be cooked, and once she slid it onto a plate, she'd begin the full demonstration.

"Ready?" Russ asked.

"Ready," Julia echoed. She added a tablespoon's worth of butter into the warming pan.

"Let's shoot it," Russ called, and the cameras turned on.

Her heart rate soared, but she focused on beating the eggs, then pouring them into the pan.

"You're about to see a French omelet being made," she said as she began to shake the pan back and forth above the stovetop so the egg mixture would cook evenly. Then she dumped the omelet onto a plate. "You've just seen a French omelet made today on *The French Chef*."

She picked up the plate and set it on the other side of the cooktop, making room for the demonstration of the rest. She'd timed how much to allow for the theme music that Ruth Lockwood had come up with while Julia sliced more butter and added it to the heated frying pan. Then she picked up two eggs and cracked them against the edge of the mixing bowl at the same time. Reaching behind her, she dumped the shells into the waiting trash can.

"Welcome to *The French Chef*," she said, looking at the camera. "I'm Julia Child." She rotated the frying pan, moving the butter around. "Today, I'm going to show you how to make a real French omelet, and it's a wonderful dish to know about. It's not just for breakfast."

She took a deep breath, not too deep, though. "In France, they don't eat it for breakfast at all because they eat café au lait and croissants. In France, what you use an omelet for is lunch or supper. And there are all kinds of ways of making them: plain or with cheese . . . with ham. And I'm going to show you exactly how."

The thirty minutes sped by, and Julia barely had time to register that she was near the end. She'd explained the importance of having a frying pan just for omelets. She'd demonstrated chopping herbs for the herb omelet, showing how to hold the chopping knife, and how to make a cheese omelet, a chicken liver omelet, and a *pipérade* omelet.

"Next time, we're going to make a soufflé with a *béchamel* sauce."

She paused, her gaze moving beyond the camera for an instant to those in the audience. Her eyes found Paul's for half a second. His smile. His love. His support. It was all there. Wrapped into one being.

She felt her heart lift, and she looked directly into the camera and tried to imagine her viewers on the other side. She smiled then spoke the words she'd rehearsed over and over with her husband.

"That's all for today on *The French Chef*. This is Julia Child. *Bon appétit.*"

AFTERWORD

The pilots of *The French Chef* ran in August 1962, and Julia watched them at home on her new television. She wasn't overly impressed with her performance but felt determined to learn from them. Despite her self-criticism of how she looked too large on camera and how she appeared breathless, not to mention her habit of closing her eyes, the letters from the public poured in—delighted with her genuine personality.

With the pilots deemed successful, the production of *The French Chef* began in February 1963, recording at the breakneck speed of four shows each week. The debut day of the new television program was Monday, February 11, 1963, on Channel 2 at 8:00 p.m. (see this episode on YouTube: https://www.youtube.com/@JuliaChildonPBS). Julia cooked the "perfectly delicious dish" of *boeuf bourguignon* (*Dearie: The Remarkable Life of Julia Child* by Bob Spitz, 341). Julia might have been fifty years old, but her career was just beginning.

It didn't take long for Julia Child to become a household name, and by the fourth show, WGBH-TV was receiving hundreds of letters a day from viewers. Affiliates included "KQED in San Francisco, WQED in Pittsburgh, WPBT in South Florida, WHYY in Philadelphia . . ." were just a few to start (Spitz, 346).

The attention and acclaim overwhelmed Julia, especially when people stopped her in public to tell her how much they loved the show. This only made her more determined to prepare to the smallest detail and perfect each episode, with Paul as her right-hand assistant. Paul once said, "These evenings, when other folk are at the movies or the symphony or lectures, find Julie and me in our kitchen—me with a stopwatch in hand, and Julie at the stove—timing various sections of the next two shows" (Spitz, 347).

From the beginning of her television appearances, Julia refused to participate in commercialism of products on her show since it was

AFTERWORD

considered educational television. She didn't want to feel forced to endorse any products or services. If she liked a product, she used it, plain and simple.

On a return trip to France, Julia and Simca fell back into their close friendship, and Julia approached the topic of writing a second cookbook that would eventually become *Mastering the Art of French Cooking, Volume Two*. This would, of course, be authored by only Julia and Simca. Louisette's personal life had become very complicated, not only from her terrible divorce, in which her husband had incurred hefty debts and fled the country, but she was also dealing with arthritis in her hands, which made cooking difficult (see Spitz, 372).

Eventually, Julia proposed a buyout plan for Louisette. Julia was happy that Louisette was getting a royalty share in their book, but the contract also entitled Louisette and "her heirs the right to exploit and determine the future direction of the copyright, and that was *not* fine by Julia" (Spitz, 388–389). The agreed-upon buyout amount was $30,000, and in exchange, Louisette would relinquish all contract rights to the book (see 389). This amount came out of the advance that Julia received for *Mastering the Art of French Cooking, Volume Two*.

In planning out volume two, Julia reasoned that they'd eliminated so many excellent recipes when creating volume one that she and Simca already had a head start on a second volume. The new cookbook topped off at 555 pages, with seven sections, which included thirty-eight pages on modern equipment that hadn't been available when the first volume was published (*Appetite for Life: The Biography of Julia Child* by Noël Riley Fitch, 360). Knopf published this second volume, releasing it October 22, 1970, with the first print run of 100,000 copies.

One of the most requested recipes that Julia received from her readers and viewers was for French bread. She'd attempted to make it plenty of times, of course, but she'd never truly succeeded. She would deflect her readers, saying that even in France, the French made a trip each day to the neighborhood *boulangerie* to buy their baguettes. But when editor Judith Jones made the request to include a French bread recipe in *Mastering Two*, Julia could no longer brush it off. This led to a flurry of

AFTERWORD

experiments, first conducted by Paul since Julia was entrenched in writing, and the recipe couldn't be tested by Simca in France. It had to be a recipe that stood the test of American ingredients and American ovens.

Paul dove into what they called the "Great Bread Experiment" (Spitz, 382). His early attempts produced bread that was too hard and heavy and didn't hit any of the requirements of the flawless crust, the right crumb, the delicious flavor, and the perfect color. Eventually, Julia joined Paul in the experiments, and between them, they had eighteen different methods they continued to tweak. It wasn't until Julia and Simca arranged a tutorial session with Professor Raymond Clavel, a renowned authority on French bread, that Julia learned the secrets she'd so long been hunting for (see Spitz, 384). The final recipe? It was twenty pages long (see *Mastering the Art of French Cooking, Volume Two*, 54–74).

Throughout her television career, Julia received plenty of love and accolades as well as plenty of criticism. Cooking with wine on television was unheard of in the early 1960s, not to mention the audacity of a woman consuming alcohol on television. Over the years, and throughout many more cookbooks, Julia adapted and created recipes that would lend more to the health trends in America. Through it all, Julia stuck by her mantra of "moderation, moderation, moderation" (Spitz, 490) when she was scrutinized for the use of butter and other fats in her recipes. She called the naysayers against her French recipes "Nervous Nellies" (Spitz, 461), and she even adapted in later years by writing *The Way to Cook*, in which most of the main portions of the recipes were low calorie or fat-free (see Spitz, 461).

For many years, Julia carried a proverbial weight of a culinary nemesis. Madeleine Kamman had issues with Julia that included claims—in criticism of *The French Chef* show—that Julia was "neither French nor a chef"—which, of course, Julia agreed with (see Fitch, 352). But the title of the television program was already set. And despite Julia and Kamman's initial cordial friendship, Kamman took it upon herself to tell her students at her cooking school to destroy their copies of

AFTERWORD

Mastering the Art of French Cooking and to never watch *The French Chef* (see Fitch, 352).

Kamman also loved to spread untrue rumors by telling industry professionals that Julia was retiring (see Spitz, 403). Julia had no trouble correcting Kamman's misinformation and standing up for herself, but she was hurt that someone could be so vindictive. Julia got to the point where she refused to say the woman's name anymore (see Spitz, 404).

After writing their second cookbook together, Julia and Simca didn't coauthor again, but their friendship remained close. Julia and Paul spent most summers over the course of the next twenty-five years in France at La Pitchoune—a home they built on Simca's property. The arrangement was that the Childs would pay for the construction and maintenance, but once they stopped using the home, it would revert to Simca's family. The small house at La Pitchoune, completed in 1966, became a much needed refuge from Julia's increasingly busy schedule.

In her later years, when Julia was involved in the 1993–1994 television series *Cooking with Master Chefs*, it was decided that the second series would be filmed in her own kitchen at 103 Irving Street. This suited Julia well and saved her from traveling so much. It turned her house into a film studio, per se, where Julia welcomed and hosted America's chefs in her kitchen (watch the series here: https://www.youtube.com/@JuliaChildonPBS).

Paul's decline in health came on gradually, and in 1974, he endured a series of nosebleeds, adding to other symptoms that had plagued him for some time, including chest pain and a constant ache in his left arm. He continued to brush off every symptom until he ended up at the hospital in October 1974 (see Spitz, 408–09). It was discovered that he needed bypass surgery. The surgery seemed to be successful, but his recovery was agonizingly slow, and new, troubling symptoms appeared. Paul's speech had slurred, and he could no longer speak French. He had trouble moving and couldn't stand straight. It was eventually determined that he'd suffered several strokes during his surgery.

Paul's condition eventually improved, but he never made a full recovery. He could no longer serve as a support to Julia's writing and traveling

AFTERWORD

schedule, yet Julia insisted that Paul still accompany her in order to keep an eye on him, despite the challenges of his becoming increasingly forgetful and disoriented (see Fitch, 440–41). They were eventually able to resume their visits to La Pitchoune, but Paul had trouble reading and often asked Julia to read to him.

Unfortunately, while they were in France in July 1977, Freddie passed away from a heart attack (see Spitz, 417). She was seventy-three years old. In 1981, determined to slow down in life, Julia and Paul bought a home on Seaview Drive in Montecito Shores in Santa Barbara (see Fitch, 416). It was a huge blow to Paul when his twin brother, Charlie, died in 1983. They'd been brothers and best friends for eighty-one years (see Fitch, 430). Another blow came when Simca died in December 1991 at the age of eighty-seven. Her death came as a grievous shock to Julia—her best friend and coauthor had been as close as a sister, and now nothing would be the same.

Although it was with a heavy heart, Julia finally had Paul move into an assisted-living facility, Fairlawn Nursing Home, in Lexington, Massachusetts (see Spitz, 465). Paul's confusion had returned, and his incidents of wandering and forgetfulness had become unmanageable without professional help (see Spitz, 485). Despite Julia's grueling promotion schedule with another cookbook, she visited Paul every day that she was in Cambridge. Most of the time, he didn't recognize her, but "she would climb in bed next to him and rub his head lovingly, filling him in on everything" (Spitz 470). She'd also call him every night, and she'd go along with whatever topic he wanted to talk about. Sometimes, he'd switch to fluent French—it seemed his language skills had returned (see Spitz, 471). Paul died May 12, 1994, at the age of ninety-two (see Spitz, 494).

In 2001, at the age of eighty-nine, Julia permanently moved to California (see Spitz, 518). She agreed to donate her kitchen to the Smithsonian Institution's National Museum of American History: Kenneth E. Behring Center, located in Washington, DC, on the National Mall. She donated her house to Smith College and her papers and cookbook collection to the Schlesinger Library at Radcliffe (see Spitz, 519).

AFTERWORD

With Julia permanently relocated to California, she took on another cat—a kitten, this time, that she named Minou. Even though pets were not allowed in her Montecito complex, Julia insisted, "My cat's not going to bother anybody" (*Julia's Cats: Julia Child's Life in the Company of Cats* by Patricia Barey and Therese Burson, 133).

JULIA CHILD IN HER KITCHEN, 1978,
CAMBRIDGE, MASSACHUSETTS

LIST OF JULIA CHILD'S PUBLICATIONS

Reference: Julia Child Foundation

Mastering the Art of French Cooking (1961), with Simone Beck and Louisette Bertholle

The French Chef Cookbook (1968)

Mastering the Art of French Cooking, Volume Two (1970), with Simone Beck

From Julia Child's Kitchen (1975)

Julia Child & Company (1978)

Julia Child & More Company (1979)

The Way to Cook (1989)

Julia Child's Menu Cookbook (1991)

Cooking With Master Chefs (1993)

In Julia's Kitchen with Master Chefs (1995)

Baking with Julia (1996)

Julia's Delicious Little Dinners (1998)

Julia's Menus for Special Occasions (1998)

Julia's Breakfasts, Lunches & Suppers (1999)

Julia's Casual Dinners (1999)

Julia and Jacques Cooking at Home (1999), with Jacques Pépin

Julia's Kitchen Wisdom (2000)

SELECTED BIBLIOGRAPHY

Barey, Patricia, and Burson, Therese. *Julia's Cats: Julia Child's Life in the Company of Cats*. Abrams, 2012.

Child, Julia, and Prud'homme, Alex. *My Life in France*. Anchor Books, 2006.

Conant, Jennet. *A Covert Affair: When Julia and Paul Child Joined the OSS . . .* Simon & Schuster Paperbacks, 2011.

Fitch, Noël Riley. *Appetite for Life: The Biography of Julia Child*. Anchor Books, 2012.

McIntosh, Elizabeth. *Women of the OSS: Sisterhood of Spies*. G. K. Hall, 2000.

Papers of Julia Child, 1925–1993: https://hollisarchives.lib.harvard.edu/repositories/8/resources/9746.

Reardon, Joan. *As Always, Julia: The Letters of Julia Child and Avis DeVoto—Food, Friendship, and the Making of a Masterpiece*. William Morrow, 2010.

Spitz, Bob. *Dearie: The Remarkable Life of Julia Child*. Vintage Books, 2013.

NOTES

CHAPTER 1

Epigraph: *Appetite for Life: The Biography of Julia Child* by Noël Riley Fitch, 74.

Both of Julia's parents, John McWilliams Jr. and Julia Carolyn Weston (Caro), enjoyed an active lifestyle and belonged to multiple country clubs, participating in golf, tennis, swimming, and horseback riding (see Fitch, 17). Caro attended Smith College (class of 1900), and her athletic abilities were notable in basketball and track and field (see Fitch, 8; Prud'homme, 83). Caro was born into a family in which they believed they had the "Weston curse"—many died young from having high blood pressure, leading to Bright's disease or early strokes (Fitch, 9). She didn't marry until she was thirty-three, and she often told her daughters to see the world before they settled down (11).

CHAPTER 2

Epigraph: *Appetite for Life: The Biography of Julia Child* by Noël Riley Fitch, 66.

Even as an adult, Julia McWilliams had an allowance from her father, and she'd also inherited a sizeable sum from her mother, estimated by Phila Cousins to be "somewhere between $100,000 and $200,000" as well as other investments, such as IBM stock (Spitz, 87).

Although Julia mostly remembers her childhood kitchen run by a hired cook, her mother did cook occasionally, which included New England dishes like cod fish balls. When the cook had the day off on Thursday, Caro often made baking powder biscuits (see Fitch, 21). Noël Riley Fitch records the recipes as follows:

NOTES

CODFISH BALLS

One package of dried, salted cod
Cooked or leftover mashed potatoes
Two fresh eggs
Fat for deep frying
White sauce with two chopped hard-boiled eggs

BUTTERMILK HERB BAKING POWDER BISCUITS

3 cups all-purpose flour
2 teaspoons salt
4 teaspoons double-acting baking powder
1 teaspoon baking soda
4 ounces or 8 tablespoons chilled vegetable shortening
4 tablespoons fresh minced chives
4 tablespoons fresh minced parsley
2 eggs
1½ cups buttermilk

Mix the dry ingredients, then cut in the shortening. Add the herbs. Whip wet ingredients, then add to dry mixture. Turn onto floured board and knead. Pat flat to a ½ inch or 1 inch thickness, then use a glass to cut into rounds. Bake at 450° F for 10–15 minutes.

CHAPTER 3

Epigraph: "On This Day in 1942: 'The Battle of Los Angeles'" by Todd DePastino, see https://veteransbreakfastclub.org/on-this-day-in-1942-the-battle-of-los-angeles/.

On the evening of February 23, 1942, a 365-foot-long Japanese I-17 submarine traveled the Santa Barbara Channel and approached the Ellwood coast. Ellwood, California, was home to a large oil field and, at that time, didn't have much of a military presence, making it an attractive target for the Japanese Navy. At 7:15 p.m., Kozo Nishino, the sub commander, gave the order to fire at the Richfield fuel tank. The sub struck close to a storage facility, a tank, the Ellwood Pier, and other places like a pump house and catwalk. The damage might have been

NOTES

relatively mild, but public panic was triggered (see Spitz, 93, and https://goletahistory.com/attack-on-ellwood/).

CHAPTER 4

Epigraph: *Women of the OSS: Sisterhood of Spies* by Elizabeth P. McIntosh, 11.

Before World War II, US government intelligence gathering was relegated to departments within the navy, the army, and the State Department, yet there was no coordination between these efforts. The Federal Bureau of Investigation (FBI) was also involved in counterespionage. President Roosevelt knew there needed to be a central office that gathered and disseminated intelligence. On July 11, 1941, Roosevelt appointed General William "Wild Bill" Donovan to head up the Office of the Coordinator of Information (COI) (see: https://www.nationalww2museum.org/war/articles/wwii-secret-agents-the-oss).

The COI was not well established and organized enough to thwart Pearl Harbor's vulnerability to attack, and on June 13, 1942, Donovan proposed that the COI become the Office of Strategic Services (OSS). The reporting chain also switched from reporting to the White House to reporting to the Joint Chiefs of Staff. "Although there were several branches and departments, the main groups were 'Intelligence Services' and 'Strategic Services Operations.' The former was composed of Secret Intelligence (SI), X-2, and Research Analysis (R&A). SI officers were responsible for recruiting foreign agents, while X-2 was counterespionage, tasked with combating enemy spies overseas. R&A processed the intelligence received from SI" (see https://www.cia.gov/legacy/museum/exhibit/the-office-of-strategic-services-n-americas-first-intelligence-agency/).

CHAPTER 5

Epigraph: *Women of the OSS: Sisterhood of Spies* by Elizabeth P. McIntosh, 72.

After World War II, President Harry S. Truman dissolved the OSS along with other war agencies, and the branches of the OSS were merged into the Strategic Services Unit (SSU) (see https://www.cia.gov

NOTES

/legacy/cia-history/). Early in 1946, SSU created the Central Intelligence Group (CIG). The CIG performed independent research and analysis. This meant CIG could move beyond only coordinating intelligence to producing intelligence, but it was still hampered by the military branches and Department of State. So in 1947, President Truman signed the National Security Act to establish the Central Intelligence Agency (CIA). The CIA then served as an independent agency and was "charged . . . with coordinating the Nation's intelligence activities and, among other duties, collecting, evaluating, and disseminating intelligence affecting national security" (https://www.cia.gov/legacy/cia-history/).

CHAPTER 6

Epigraph: *Women of the OSS: Sisterhood of Spies* by Elizabeth P. McIntosh, 34.

Following the American War of Independence, the British sought to expand their international holdings. At the time, the island nation of Ceylon was divided between the Dutch and the King of Kandy. Ceylon was a key location for commerce, shipping, and travel for both the East India Company and the British Royal Navy. The British began a studious invasion, and by 1796, they'd taken control of all Dutch holdings in Ceylon.

In a series of wars against the Kingdom of Kandy, beginning in 1804 and lasting through 1818, the British wrested control from the people of Ceylon. It wasn't until 1948 that Ceylon was granted independence and became the Dominion of Ceylon, although it was still controlled by the British Commonwealth. And finally, in 1972, Ceylon became a republic and was named the Republic of Sri Lanka (see https://www.napoleon-series.org/military-information/battles-and-campaigns/the-british-conquest-of-ceylon-and-the-massacre-at-kandy-1803/).

CHAPTER 7

Epigraph: *Women of the OSS: Sisterhood of Spies* by Elizabeth P. McIntosh, 211.

Before joining the OSS, Betty MacDonald (Elizabeth McIntosh) was a war correspondent in the Pacific, hired to cover the Pearl

NOTES

Harbor bombing. In January 1943, she joined the Morale Operations Department, and it was in this capacity that she met Julia McWilliams (Child). Following the end of the war, Betty was employed by the Joint Chiefs of Staff to write the OSS China history, and her books, *Undercover Girl* and *Women of the OSS: Sisterhood of Spies*, were two of the results. Her research was comprised of over 120 interviews with men and women who served in the OSS and CIA as well as deep-diving into national archives, wartime albums, and translated archival documents. Betty married Colonel Richard Heppner, who'd been Julia's boss in 1946. Several years after Heppner's death, Betty married Frederick McIntosh, a former WWII fighter pilot (see McIntosh, ix–x). Interviews with Betty can still be accessed, such as this one on C-SPAN: https://www.c-span.org/video/?169597-4/women-office-strategic-services. Betty served in the CIA from 1958–1973.

CHAPTER 8

Epigraph: *Appetite for Life: The Biography of Julia Child* by Noël Riley Fitch, 95–96.

Various branches of the OSS included:

Research and Analysis (R&A): Collected and analyzed material for use in planning operations.

Secret Intelligence (SI): Collected covert information through agents strategically placed in the field.

Special Operations (SO): Planned and carried out undercover missions of guerrilla warfare, sabotage, and fifth-column activities.

Operational Group (OG): Paratroopers skilled in foreign-language and sabotage.

Maritime Unit (MU): Managed supplies for maritime sabotage.

Counterintelligence Branch (X-2): Monitored and controlled enemy intelligence operations. Worked with British intelligence in handling the information of the German enigma cipher machine.

Morale Operations (MO): Handled black propaganda, which included "persuasion, penetration and intimidation . . . disguising the truth, slanting stories, and developing rumors" (McIntosh, 13).

NOTES

CHAPTER 9

Epigraph: *Appetite for Life: The Biography of Julia Child* by Noël Riley Fitch, 93.

I only touched lightly on the topic of intimacy, but Julia did worry about her inexperience compared to Paul's since he'd been in a long-term living situation with Edith. Julia and Paul's shared love throughout their marriage ended up conquering any of these misgivings. But before she married, she did wrestle with her single-status and naivety, even though she brushed it off for the most part: "I am quite content to be the way I am—and feel superior to many a wedded mouse . . . I can do what I want! I had several [relationships] before meeting my husband, but we did not go all the way. . . . One did not in those days" (Fitch, 77).

CHAPTER 10

Epigraph: *Appetite for Life: The Biography of Julia Child* by Noël Riley Fitch, 100.

Patty (Phyllis) Norbury's fiancé was Lieutenant Roy Albert "Pete" Wentz Jr. He served as a captain in the US Air Force, Tenth Air Division, and after more than fifty missions as a navigator, he was shot down over Burma. Patty was certain he was alive, even though he was declared missing in action, so she volunteered for the OSS, intent on finding a way to gather information on his whereabouts. After the war, Wentz "was discovered in the Insein jail near Rangoon, starved and ill with dysentery" (McIntosh, 218). Patty and Wentz's reunion happened in Calcutta, and they later married once they reached the States, in Wilmington, Delaware. Wentz received these military honors for his service: Purple Heart, Distinguished Flying Cross, and Air Medal (see https://www.wikitree.com/wiki/Wentz-1152).

CHAPTER 11

Epigraph: *Appetite for Life: The Biography of Julia Child* by Noël Riley Fitch, 102–103.

The Battle of Leyte Gulf that took place October 23–26, 1944, was the largest naval engagement of WWII. The Allies wanted to retake the

NOTES

Philippines and block the Japanese military from natural resources of oil and rubber in Southeast Asia. The Japanese Navy suffered a huge loss of twenty-six warships and four aircraft carriers. The US lost seven warships and three aircraft carriers, some of them struck by kamikazes. The outcome of the battle gave the US command of the sea and air, but the casualties on both sides were immense: 16,043 American soldiers and 7,270 sailors were killed. Whereas the Japanese suffered 419,912 deaths or injuries (see https://www.britannica.com/event/Battle-of-Leyte-Gulf, and https://www.defense.gov/News/Feature-Stories/story/Article/1996596/wwii-battle-helped-secure-philippines-75-years-ago/).

CHAPTER 12

Epigraph: *Appetite for Life: The Biography of Julia Child* by Noël Riley Fitch, 110–111.

When the Japanese military took Burma, effectively cutting off access to the Burma Road, that stopped the Allied supply route to China, where 50,000 American soldiers and 200,000 Chinese soldiers needed matériel support.

The Allies flew over the Himalayas from India to places such as Yunnanyi and Kunming. The distance from Dinjan to Kunming was only 500 miles, but the route was one of the most treacherous in the world and was termed "flying the Hump." That was because the valley floor was only ninety feet above sea level, and planes taking off would climb 300 feet per minute until they reached peaks between 14,000 to 18,000 feet. The planes, with their heavy burdens, encountered extreme turbulence and weather problems of thunderstorms, monsoons, blizzards, dust storms, and freezing temperatures that clouded the planes in ice. Far below, the terrain was made up of thick jungles and swamps. A typical flight lasted about three hours, but turbulence slowed down the journey. By the end of the war, over 1,300 crewmembers who served in the CBI (China-Burma-India) had been lost in 500 crashes over the Hump (see https://www.nationalmuseum.af.mil/Visit/Museum-Exhibits/Fact-Sheets/Display/Article/3627010/ and https://www.airandspaceforces.com/article/0391hump/).

NOTES

CHAPTER 13

Epigraph: *Women of the OSS: Sisterhood of Spies* by Elizabeth P. McIntosh, 237.

The American Volunteer Group (AVG), also called the Flying Tigers, began their service in China, aiding in the war effort to defend China against the Japanese military. They served in the 14th Air Force, protecting the end of the Hump route. The AVG's base was in southwestern China, in the city of Kunming. There were no runways to land planes, so thousands of Chinese working class people volunteered to build the runways and airport. Without access to modern tools and machinery, the Chinese used picks and shovels.

The Flying Tigers's first combat mission was on December 20, 1941, when Japanese bombers attacked the Kunming airbase, in which nine of the ten Japanese bombers were shot down. Next, the Flying Tigers defended Rangoon in Burma, which was still a British colony. Although Japan eventually overpowered the AVG and Britain, when Rangoon fell in March 1942, the Flying Tigers made an impact by keeping supply lines open as long as possible (see https://www.npr.org/2021/12/19/1062091832/flying-tigers-americans-china-world-war-ii-history-japan and https://www.nationalmuseum.af.mil/Visit/Museum-Exhibits/Fact-Sheets/Display/Article/196654/).

One of the most important contributions the OSS made after the atomic bombings was their mercy mission squadron: "Mercy Mission teams parachuted into Japanese prison camps to prevent further harm to Allied POWs. The OSS contributed the bulk of the personnel, although several other organizations participated as well. This was done at great peril because many Japanese commands were not aware that the war was over. Eleven 'Mercy' teams from OSS China arranged for food, medical care, and the evacuation of POWs to Allied camps" (https://www.soc.mil/OSS/det-202.html).

CHAPTER 14

Epigraph: *Women of the OSS: Sisterhood of Spies* by Elizabeth P. McIntosh, 94.

NOTES

Eleanor (Ellie) Thiry worked for the OSS alongside Julia McWilliams (Child), traveling over on the same ship, the USS *Mariposa*, and serving in both Ceylon and Chongqing, China. While working in Chongqing, Ellie met Major F. Basil Summers, who was the assistant military attaché to the British Embassy in Chongqing. After the war, Ellie married Major Summers in London. In 1948, the couple moved to New York City (see https://www.findagrave.com/memorial/45209719/eleanor-helen-summers).

CHAPTER 15

Epigraph: Letter from Julia to Paul, https://iiif.lib.harvard.edu/manifests/view/drs:496235029$1i.

Letter from Julia to Paul: April 22, 1946, page 3 (see https://iiif.lib.harvard.edu/manifests/view/drs:496235029$3i).

NOTES

CHAPTER 16

Epigraph: *Appetite for Life: The Biography of Julia Child* by Noël Riley Fitch, 138.

Letter from Julia to Paul: May 7, 1946, page 1 (see https://iiif.lib.harvard.edu/manifests/view/drs:496235029$13i).

CHAPTER 17

Epigraph: *Appetite for Life: The Biography of Julia Child* by Noël Riley Fitch, 140.

One of the charming parts of Julia Child's cookbook is the way she introduces her recipes. She first learned how to prepare *coq au vin* with her sister-in-law Freddie. In *Mastering the Art of French Cooking*, Julia introduces the recipe as follows: "This popular dish may be called

NOTES

coq au Chambertin, coq au riesling, or *coq au* whatever wine you use for its cooking. It is made with either white or red wine, but red is more characteristic. In France it is usually accompanied only by parsley potatoes; buttered green peas could be included if you wish a green vegetable. Serve with it a young, full-bodied red Burgundy, Beaujolais, or Côtes du Rhône." For those cooking alcohol-free, cognac substitutions include pear, apricot, or peach juice, and red wine substitutions include alcohol-free red wine, beef broth, chicken broth, red wine vinegar (use ½ vinegar and ½ water), cranberry juice, or pomegranate juice. The full recipe can be found in *Mastering the Art of French Cooking*, 263–65, or online: https://www.eater.com/23065567/coq-au-vin-recipe-julia-child-mastering-the-art-of-french-cooking.

CHAPTER 18

Epigraph: *Appetite for Life: The Biography of Julia Child* by Noël Riley Fitch, 149.

Wedding Guest List for Julia and Paul Child:

John McWilliams Jr. and wife, Phila; Dorothy (Dort); John III and his wife, Jo; Patsy Morgan (Aunt Bessie's daughter); Charlie Child, wife, Freddie, and their children: Rachel, Erica, and Jon; Whitney and Lola Seymour; Richard Bissell and wife, Marie; Dick Bissell and wife, Ann Bushnell; Richard Myers with his daughter and son-in-law, Fanny and Hank Brennan; George Kubler and his wife, Elizabeth (Betty) Scofield Bushnell (Fitch, 144–45).

CHAPTER 19

Epigraph: *My Life in France* by Julia Child with Alex Prud'homme, 19.

In February 1948, the unoccupied house adjacent to Paul and Julia's home on Wisconsin Avenue in Georgetown caught fire. Soon, the fire leaped to Julia's home, and she and Paul were awakened by the smell of smoke at about four in the morning. The power and the phone didn't work, and they spent a few minutes tossing belongings out their bedroom window, including Julia's shoes that were hard to replace. They

NOTES

crawled through the smoke to the next room, unlocked the window and managed to jump to a lower roof, then to the ground. Julia rushed to the middle of the street and whistled for a taxi to stop. The damage was great, and they stayed at Charlie and Freddie's home for two months while repairs were being made. Their shell of a house was burglarized twice during that time (see Spitz, 167–68; Fitch, 146–47).

CHAPTER 20

Epigraph: *My Life in France* by Julia Child with Alex Prud'homme, 23.

One of the contentions in the McWilliams family was that Pop thought Paul was living off Julia's inheritance. She was careful with money, for the most part, in their early marriage years, but when living in Paris, she and Paul indulged in a lot of restaurant eating. She also became a cookery aficionado and used her inheritance funds for that. It was true that "Julia's inheritance gave the Childs freedom to enjoy a certain Parisian lifestyle" (Spitz, 207).

CHAPTER 21

Epigraph: *My Life in France* by Julia Child with Alex Prud'homme, 25.

Julia and Paul adopted a cat while living in Paris. Although Julia had always adored the creatures, Paul took a little more persuasion. But Minette quickly nestled her way into both of their hearts and even occasionally produced a mouse, earning her keep (see Barey and Burson, 15). Julia's affection for cats grew, and she took it upon herself to greet each cat she encountered, all of which she considered an immediate friend (23). Her affection for cats continued into her final years, after she retired to her Montecito Shores apartment, when she adopted a black-and-white kitten, Minou. Pets weren't allowed at the complex, but Julia skirted the rules by decreeing, "My cat's not going to bother anybody" (132–33).

CHAPTER 22

Epigraph: *My Life in France* by Julia Child with Alex Prud'homme, 62.

NOTES

In 1895, Le Cordon Bleu was established as a culinary arts school in Paris. Founded by the French journalist Marthe Distel, she used the school to promote her cooking magazine, *La Cuisinière Cordon Bleu*. The name Le Cordon Bleu derives from "blue ribbon" and originates from the Knights of the Holy Spirit established by King Henry III as far back as 1578. This French order of the knights (Chevaliers du Saint Esprit) wore blue-ribboned medals, and the knighting feasts were very grand affairs filled with excellent food. Thus, Cordon Bleu became synonymous with a brilliant chef. The reputation of the cooking school became world-renowned, and by 1914, there were four schools in Paris. In 1942, Dione Lucas opened a Le Cordon Bleu school in New York and became the first woman in the US to host a television cooking show (see https://www.cordonbleu.edu/our-timeline/en).

CHAPTER 23

Epigraph: *My Life in France* by Julia Child with Alex Prud'homme, 77.

Paul Child's inventory of Julia's kitchen was exhaustive: "Our poor little kitchen is bursting at the seams [with] pots, pans, vessels, sieves, measuring rods, scales, thermometers, mortars, timing-clocks, choppers, grinders, knives, openers, pestles, spoons, ladles, jars, skewers, forks, bottles, boxes, bags, weights, needles, graters, strings, rolling-pins, mullers, frying pans, double boilers, single boilers, marble slabs and fancy extrusion-dies, whips for sauces, long needles for larding roasts, a deep copper bowl for beating eggs, a *pèse-sirop*, a chinois, three little frying pans used only for crêpes, a copper sugar-boiler, stirring paddles made of Maplewood, tart-rings, and a whole gamut of flat long-handled copper pot lids . . . hanging from hooks, are pewter liter-measures, demi-liters, quart-de-liters, deciliters and demi-deciliters, innumerable scrapers, choppers, cutter-uppers, rockers, crushers, and enough knives for a pirate boarding-gang" (Spitz, 196–97).

CHAPTER 24

Epigraph: *My Life in France* by Julia Child with Alex Prud'homme, 78.

NOTES

Due to the 1951 Paris strike, led by the Confédération Générale du Travail (CGT), Julia Child reminisced, "As many streets still relied on gaslit lanterns, the dimming effect was reminiscent of a wartime blackout. Driving at night was hazardous, as pedestrians were invisible, bikes looked like fireflies, and other cars would dazzle you when they flashed on their headlights every few seconds. The few metros that did run were jammed to impossibility, and it took from two to four hours to make a metro trip that usually took forty minutes. Paul and I initiated the Blue Flash Bus Service, picking up and dropping off embassy staff all over Paris—at Port de Clichy, Gare de Lyon, Nation, and Commerce. We'd never seen such traffic. Half of it was made up of bicycles; the rest was army trucks being used as commuter buses, and any kind of vehicle that could be dragged out of scrap yards and root cellars and made to run on homemade fuel" (Prud'homme, 117).

CHAPTER 25

Epigraph: *My Life in France* by Julia Child with Alex Prud'homme, 119.

Julia Child first met Simone Beck Fischbacher (Simca) at the home of George Artamonoff. Simca told Julia about *Les Gourmettes* cooking club, which dined together every other Friday. Through Simca, Julia met Louisette Bertholle (see Fitch, 187–88). After attending some of the luncheons, Julia hosted *Les Gourmettes* at her own home, asking Chef Max Bugnard to cook for them. Julia hoped that her new friends would be so impressed with Bugnard that they'd also hire him out for catering jobs: "Chef Bugnard started us off with *tortues* of crab pounded together with shrimp and herbs and mayonnaise, served in pastry shells with toast on the side. Then came a fantastic *poularde Waterzooi*: chicken poached in white wine and white bouillon, on a bed of julienned carrots, leeks, and onions that had been pre-cooked in butter; slathered on top was a sauce made with egg yolks and cream. And for the grand finale, he served *crêpes Suzettes flambées*, which he presented with a theatrical, flaming flourish. Sitting back with satisfied smiles at the end of the meal, the delighted Gourmettes agreed that my dear old chef had done a fine job indeed" (Prud'homme, 114).

NOTES

CHAPTER 26

Epigraph: *My Life in France* by Julia Child with Alex Prud'homme, 147.

Simone Beck and Louisette Bertholle self-published their fifty-recipe cookbook, *What's Cuisine in France*. The small cookbook had been written in French and translated to English, with an introduction written by Curnonsky. It sold about 2,000 copies, and wanting a wider distribution, they expanded the cookbook, then resold the manuscript to Sumner Putnam of Ives Washburn, who bought it for $75.00 (see Fitch, 196). Helmut Ripperger edited the new edition and renamed it *What's Cooking in France*. The new book didn't sell well. By the time Simone and Louisette received the disappointing news, they were already well on their way to completing a massive 600-page book they called *French Cooking for All*. Their editor recommended that the two chefs collaborate with an American cook in order to adjust their French recipes to what an American would use (197). This became the push that led Simone and Louisette to their coauthoring proposal to Julia Child.

CHAPTER 27

Epigraph: *As Always, Julia: The Letters of Julia Child and Avis DeVoto* by Joan Reardon, 125.

Curnonsky, a pseudonym of Maurice Edmond Sailland, became a culinary icon in France. "Restaurants vied with one another to wine and dine him. Dining clubs found Curnonsky's presence essential if their banquets were to be a success. Writers of cookbooks felt that a preface by him meant the difference between success and failure," (https://www.theatlantic.com/magazine/archive/1958/06/curnonsky-prince-of-gastronomes/641307/). Simone Beck and Louisette Bertholle asked him to write an introduction to their first cookbook. Eventually, this also led to an introduction to Julia Child, and Julia was immediately charmed by the man. Curnonsky, dubbed the "Prince of Gastronomy," wrote or ghost-wrote dozens of books, including the twenty-eight-volume *La France Gastronomique,* cowritten with Marcel Rouff, which takes the readers on a culinary journey throughout regions of France. Their series

NOTES

became part of the Michelin Guide in 1926 (see https://bonjourparis.com/food-and-drink/the-grand-curnonsky/).

CHAPTER 28

Epigraph: *As Always, Julia: The Letters of Julia Child and Avis DeVoto* by Joan Reardon, 144.

While living in Germany from 1954–1955, Julia kept up her prolific correspondence with Avis DeVoto, confiding in her about the struggles of keeping Louisette as a coauthor: "This little business with Louisette is turning out to be something of a problem. My fault, as I don't see why we should have all the responsibility and do all the work, and she come along for the ride. And poor old Simca has been the work horse all these years. After having discussed it with Louisette in Paris, and having said I would send her a letter, I have now heard nothing from her at all, after our most carefully thought-out letter, batted back and forth between Simca and me. As she puts in probably less than 4 or 5 hours of work a week, and has produced just about nothing except a long chapter on game, mostly copied directly out of a book, I suggested that she consider herself Consultant, rather than Co-Author, and then she would have no twinges of conscience that S & I were putting in at least 40 hrs; and that we have a 10-45-45 split. . . . So I have written her another letter, asking her please to come across with her opinions, and saying that we were dopes not to have thought out this problem when we first began (we thought we were thinking of everything, of course). I also said that we should, when we had reached a decision, write up an agreement that would take care of the incapacity and/or demise of any or all of us, and have it legalized" (Reardon, 219).

CHAPTER 29

Epigraph: *As Always, Julia: The Letters of Julia Child and Avis DeVoto* by Joan Reardon, 318.

Jane Foster traveled to California in the fall of 1954 to visit her sick mother, but her passport was confiscated in San Francisco, with claims that she was an active Communist (see Conant, 263). She hired a lawyer and appealed multiple times to have her passport reinstated. After

NOTES

months of setbacks, she had a mental breakdown and spent several weeks in a psychiatric hospital. When she regained healing and strength, she fired her first lawyer and hired civil liberties attorney Leonard Boudin (270). Boudin immediately took the case and set out to prove that Jane's passport had been illegally confiscated by the State Department since there had been no evidence to support their charges. "It threw the Dept. of Justice lawyers into a tizzy" and in exchange for Boudin to withdraw his motion, they would issue Jane's passport within three days (272). On August 22, 1955, Jane Foster walked into the State Department and left an hour later with her passport (273).

CHAPTER 30

Epigraph: *As Always, Julia: The Letters of Julia Child and Avis DeVoto* by Joan Reardon, 331.

Avis DeVoto remembered the day that Julia and Simca made the trek during a fierce snowstorm to present their manuscript to Houghton Mifflin: "I waited up for them, and it was snowing fiercely. They went in to see Houghton Mifflin with this huge box of manuscript. [They] presented over seven hundred pages on poultry and sauces alone, which is when HM said they weren't about to publish an encyclopedia. Although Dorothy [de Santillana] was extremely anxious to publish the book, because she had cooked with a lot of the recipes and knew they worked, all the men said, 'Oh, Americans don't want to cook like that, they want something quick, made with a mix.' They were pushing a cookbook, a Texas cookbook, by Helen Corbett—there seemed to be marshmallows in everything, and that's where their advertising money was going. Houghton Mifflin has regretted it ever since" (Fitch, 241).

CHAPTER 31

Epigraph: *As Always, Julia: The Letters of Julia Child and Avis DeVoto* by Joan Reardon, 368.

In a letter to Avis DeVoto, dated September 11, 1960, Julia updated her on the continued negotiations with Louisette on the royalty split for the cookbook: "Thought you would enjoy that letter from Louisette. The last agreement we signed gave her 18%, which I think is crazy when

NOTES

she hasn't done one single sentence of work on either of the two huge manuscripts we have prepared single handed. I have written her another letter stating this fact, and asking her to consult her family and friends and come up with what she and they would consider fair and just under these circumstances. We are quite willing to offer her 10% to shut her up, then have no further collaboration, and retain exclusive right to 'Les 3 Gourmandes' as a trademark. Haven't heard from her yet. I just don't think she has any conception of what work is" (Reardon, 371). When all was said and done, Julia and Simone's royalty split was 41 percent each, with Louisette receiving 18 percent (see Fitch, 221).

CHAPTER 32

Epigraph: *As Always, Julia: The Letters of Julia Child and Avis DeVoto* by Joan Reardon, 376.

When James Beard passed away in 1985, Julia Child attended a tribute luncheon in his honor. Many culinary greats were there, including Julia's greatest nemesis, Madeline Damman. Julia was determined to be cordial and shook the woman's hand, much to everyone's surprise (see Spitz, 468). Word came at the luncheon that Oregon's Reed College, which had been gifted James Beard's home and belongings, planned to sell everything off. Julia immediately wanted to put a stop to it. James Beard was a "national treasure" (468), and Julia insisted that his property be a historical landmark, both in the culinary world and in New York City. She partnered with Peter Kump and created the James Beard Foundation in order to preserve her close friend's legacy (see 468–69). "On November 5, 1986, the James Beard Foundation officially opened the James Beard House 'to provide a center for the culinary arts and to continue to foster the interest James Beard inspired in all aspects of food, its preparation[,] presentation, and of course, enjoyment'" (see https://www.jamesbeard.org).

CHAPTER 33

Epigraph: *Appetite for Life: The Biography of Julia Child* by Noël Riley Fitch, 284.

Julia and Simone planned their own book tour, accompanied by Paul. After the launch in New York City, they traveled to Detroit, where Simone

NOTES

had a few connections from when she had done cooking demonstrations. By then, "Knopf had published a second edition with twenty corrections" (Fitch, 272), including updating the fact that the authors Beck and Bertholle hadn't graduated from Le Cordon Bleu. Avis had also helped with promotion by sending the book to key figures in the social and culinary world. This, combined with the book tour, enabled Julia to strengthen her culinary network (272). Julia and Simone's most popular demonstration was making their Reine de Daba chocolate cake (*Mastering the Art of French Cooking, Volume One*, 677–78).

CHAPTER 34

Epigraph: *Appetite for Life: The Biography of Julia Child* by Noël Riley Fitch, 277.

Julia's schedule when filming her cooking series was grueling and involved Paul every step of the way. She "spent the weekend planning and writing the program, spent Monday shopping with Paul, preparing the food and rehearsing" (Fitch, 288). Tuesdays were taken up with loading and unloading the food and equipment at the studio, where they'd tape the show. Since they taped the program live, Julia had to arrive at the studio with her recipes prepared in multiple stages. For example, "a raw goose, a partially cooked goose, a cooked goose, and a spare" (288).

The original payment that Julia received from the studio was $50 per episode, which included the cost of food. So the program truly was a labor of love and service for educational television. In 1966, Julia received a pay raise to $200 per episode, plus she could expense the groceries (see Fitch, 289). At the end of taping each show, the crew was invited to eat the meal that had been prepared. At first, some crew members were hesitant to try vegetables they'd never tasted before, but pretty soon, Julia had them all eating "asparagus, mushrooms, and chicken livers" (289).

CHAPTER 35

Epigraph: *Appetite for Life: The Biography of Julia Child* by Noël Riley Fitch, 278–79.

In the second cookbook *Mastering the Art of French Cooking, Volume Two*, Julia and Simone delicately explained that Louisette wasn't a part

NOTES

of creating or writing: "Now married to Henri de Nalèche, and living in the beautiful hunting country near Bourges, La Sologne, Louisette did not collaborate with us on Volume II. It was through her inspiration, however, that we three started both the first book and the school together" (*Mastering, Volume Two*, vii). Julia and Simone also paid tribute to Paul, who, "ready at a moment's notice, was there to make careful, detailed, perfect photographs of any step of any recipe at any time during the day or night" (xiii). The two chefs also acknowledged Sidonic Coryn and her 458 drawings used in the cookbook (xiii).

Louisette remained part owner of the title of the original cookbook, which meant that Louisette and her estate and heirs would have legal rights in the future direction of the copyright. Julia wanted there to be a clean break, so she bought out Louisette and came up with the figure of $25,000. Louisette countered with $45,000. With advice from her son-in-law, Louisette finally settled at $30,000, a sum which came from the advance of *Mastering Two* (see Spitz, 388–89).

DISCUSSION QUESTIONS

1. What surprised you most about Julia Child's life?
2. What are some of the differences between Julia's outlook on life and the traditional roles of womanhood and wifehood and those around her?
3. What were some of the challenges Julia had with her father's political views and opinions?
4. Have you ever been in a situation where you've tried to uphold family tradition, such as when Julia went to Smith College because that was where her mother attended?
5. Julia seemed to take international living in stride, despite not having a permanent home for many years. Would something like that interest you?
6. Julia had amazing support from her husband, from his encouraging her years of cooking experiments to her collecting kitchen gadgets to her starting a new career just as he retired. Do you have people in your life who support your ambitions?
7. Julia and Simone Beck (Simca) clashed a lot in personality and method, yet they seemed to remain friends as well as work as coauthors since they shared the same passion and goals. Do you relate to that sort of relationship?
8. What surprised you about Julia's efforts to find a publisher for her first cookbook?
9. What was there about Julia's personality, or cooking methods, that appealed to mass audiences and made her such an iconic figure?
10. Is there anything from Julia's later-in-life passion for cooking that inspires you to develop your own talents?

ACKNOWLEDGMENTS

Taking a deep dive into the life of Julia Child was fascinating. I thoroughly enjoyed the research process and continually ran into surprises. As with any long and well-lived life, Julia's path takes many turns. I spent a great deal of time searching out the original cookbooks by Julia Child in addition to those of her close acquaintance. I read every biography I could find written about her and *by* her and discovered she was a blessing in many people's lives. She knew how to be a friend, and she knew how to lift people. She demanded perfection in her recipes but was forgiving of human fallacy that surrounded her.

Throughout the writing process, I relied on many to ensure this story that covers twenty years of Julia's life was cohesive yet highlighted her significant journey. Special thanks to author and CIA retiree Traci Hunter Abramson, who read parts of the book for accuracy regarding the OSS and who graciously agreed to write the foreword. Thanks to Julie Wright, who fit in reading the manuscript amid her own deadlines in order to provide essential feedback. Many thanks as well to my agent, Ann Leslie Tuttle, who is always generous with her time and feedback. Thanks as well to Carol Callister for sharing her memories of living in Sri Lanka (Ceylon) so that I could add more authenticity to those chapters.

I'm deeply grateful for Shadow Mountain Publishing and their support of my work. The outstanding team includes Chris Schoebinger, Heidi Gordon Taylor, Lisa Mangum, Derk Koldewyn, Troy Butcher, Amy Parker, Haley Haskins, Callie Hansen, Tasha Bradford, Lehi Quiroz, and Brianna Cornell. Editor Samantha Millburn once again took on one of my books, and I'm ever grateful for her expert eye and especially her friendship.

ACKNOWLEDGMENTS

Gratitude extends to author friends who act as a daily sounding board: Jen Geigle Johnson, Rebecca Connolly, Mindy Holt, Taffy Lovell, Julie Daines, and Jennifer Moore. My family is the most important part of this earthly journey. Much love to my parents, Kent and Gayle Brown; my father-in-law, Lester Moore; my husband, Chris; and our children, Kaelin, Kara, Dana, son-in-law Christian, Rose, and grandson, Ezra.

ALSO BY HEATHER B. MOORE

Based on the true story of the free-spirited daughter of Queen Victoria.

Based on a true story. Inspired by real events. A riveting and emotionally gripping novel of an American soldier working as a spy in Soviet-occupied East Germany and a West German woman secretly helping her countrymen escape from behind the Berlin Wall.

Based on a true story, this gripping WWII novel captures the resilience, hope, and courage of a Dutch family who is separated during the war when the Japanese occupy the Dutch East Indies.

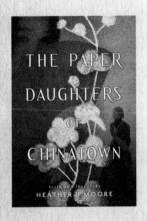

Based on true events, *The Paper Daughters of Chinatown* is a powerful story about a largely unknown chapter in history and the women who emerged as heroes.

Based on the true story of two friends who unite to help rescue immigrant women and girls in San Francisco's Chinatown in the late 1890s.

Based on the true story of Nancy Harkness Love, this novel captures the soaring tensions of WWII as aviator Nancy trailblazes a historic fight for equality in the skies.

Available wherever books are sold